# MONSTERS BORN AND MADE

# MONSTERS

# BORN

# AND

# MADE

## TANVI BERWAH

sourcebooks
fire

## Your hub for the hottest young adult books!

Visit us online and sign up for our
newsletter at FIREreads.com

 @sourcebooksfire

 sourcebooksfire

 firereads.tumblr.com

Published by Sourcebooks Fire, an imprint of Sourcebooks
P.O. Box 4410, Naperville, Illinois 60567-4410
(630) 961-3900
sourcebooks.com

Cataloging-in-Publication Data is on file with the Library of Congress.

Printed and bound in the United States of America.
LSC 10 9 8 7 6 5 4 3 2 1

*For Mini, who likes squids and crabs.*
*And for Papa, who took us to see the ocean for the first time.*

KAR ATISH

BONETOWN

SIRSA

SEA OF
SILVER

SOLLONIA

WRANGEL ISLAND

S

E      W

N

CHANDRABAD

GRIEVING ISLES

ISLANDS
OF OPHIR

KURU PROPER

MIRAGE

KURU MINOR

SEA
OF FLINT

HELLRUD

SOLLONIA

The Drone

Fisher Colony

The Sanctuary

Residence
& Markets

Welkon Crater

N

SEA OF SILVER

Thoroughfare

Guard
Station

Terrafort

The Cliffs

The Hidden Shore

Koral's Home
& Stables

Med Store

Opal Den

# ONE

**W**e hunt when the world sleeps. A risk that could kill us. A risk forced on us.

I try to awaken my brother, but he only murmurs sleepily, "Piss off."

"It's four already. Baba told us to be at the beach by now."

Emrik clutches his mattress like a crab stubbornly clinging to a rock. When I yank off his blanket, he snarls, "Get out of my room."

His shoe thuds against the door just as I shut it. I press my back against the stone wall, the chill grounding me.

Minutes later, Emrik appears. We're dressed alike: black pants, a fitted white shirt with collars up to our chins, and boots molded to our feet. Beneath, we're both wearing skaya-threaded watersuits. The Hunter siblings.

His fist tightens on the doorknob.

Being nervous before a hunt is good.

It means we're alert, not stupid.

"Koral," he says, voice hoarse. "Is anyone else up?" His hair is far past his shoulders, almost as long as mine. The single clip stuck through it shines in the anemic yellow glow of the light above the door. Before I say anything, Liria's asthmatic coughs echo in the silence.

The thought of our little sister choking on air isn't helpful as we climb the claustrophobic corkscrew staircase, leaving the safety of our underground house. But it's a good reminder of why the hunt needs to go perfectly, why we cannot let a maristag escape us tonight.

Because that's how we survive.

Capture maristags, breed them, train their offspring to tolerate land, and then sell them to the upper-caste Landers competing in the Glory Race. All at the risk of death.

Then, we dare to live. Until the next hunt.

The world outside is drenched in black ink, and the Ship of Fire constellation gleams red and yellow, taunting us. A sea wind blows in, carrying salt and storm, right as a bolt of lightning skewers the sky.

Emrik and I sprint toward the beach. It comprises the entire strip of gray sand on this side of the island. Despite the sea guzzling swaths of sand without warning, it's often stuffed with scavengers scraping at the metallic chips of zargunine on the low limestone arches that jut out of sea and sand.

Squinting for any scavengers, I end up having to sidestep a puddle of—"*Skaya?* Who's wasting skaya in high sun?" Do they not know how difficult extracting the jelly is and how much we need its protection against the hot sun? Though we're surrounded by water, our island is parched, and we roast with it.

Emrik frowns at the skaya puddle. The scar on his right eye, dripping like an angry tear, contorts. "Fewer people to bother with."

As we reach the U-shaped bend of the limestone cliff, thunder rumbles low. A monster waking up from sleep. The horizon, swallowed in darkness, doesn't exist yet.

Down the serrated edge, rocks shoot out of the volatile water like blue-gray fangs. My face grows numb from the bite of the storm. Rawness chafes my lungs with each breath. The rocky ground beneath me is slick with dead crawlies and lichen and the water slapping against it. I must tread carefully.

"You should stay out of the sea," Emrik says.

My temper flares. Years of hunting together, and he still doesn't trust me. "Why?"

"Look at the storm."

*As if you'd be any use alone.* I bite my tongue. No point fighting before going into the sea. "More reason for you to have backup."

"Stay out of the water, Koral. I'll need your help to drag the maristag out." His jaw is clenched, his face thinner—its contours razor-sharp. The black tattoo on the left side of his face twists, matching mine. He looks cruel in the dark. I suppose we both do.

Emrik is three years older, but we could pass for twins when we go hunting.

I don't spot a single maristag in the black waters—not ideal on the last day of hunting season. "Can you see any movement?"

Our family, stretching back generations, has kept detailed records of the maristags. They have never been seen outside the annual upwelling of the waters. Before the sun rises today, they *will* disappear and won't return for ten months.

Their biological clocks never fail.

Last hunt's maristags fell sick and died. Emrik *says* it wasn't his fault, that he had filtered the water like always, that the maristags brought the infection from the sea. Now we have only one female left. Without a male, we'll have no fawns to sell for the remaining year.

The Landmaster will act like it's not our fault, smile, and send us away with a subsidy payment lasting maybe a month. Meanwhile, a silent warning will circulate across the island: no loans to the Hunters, no jobs.

We'll starve. Like the year I turned eight.

And this time, Liria is too sick for us to make it an entire year.

"They're hiding from the storm," Emrik says, snapping me out of the horrible memories. "Two of us will cause a frenzy. Stay here."

"Fine, go die in there."

His glare is answer enough. He strips to his watersuit, arms himself with a zargunine quarterstaff, and, before I can take back my parting words, dives into the sea. Then he's a shadow, swimming so fast he could be mistaken for a maristag.

So fast he vanishes.

The sky is getting light, a terrible dawn approaching. Emrik is nowhere. Has the sea swallowed him?

*Don't be dead, Emrik, I'll murder you.*

Winds pick up, hissing through the water. There's nothing but the bruised curtain of sky, cut with the menacing red light of dawn, which stains the angry foam of the sea with the color of rotting flesh.

The world retreats, enveloped in an eerie silence.

Then—a fierce cry pierces the sea, and the rancid smell of sulfur saturates the air.

I remember the first time I saw a maristag.

We learned in school about the ten Islands of Ophir and the Panthalassan Ocean, which is the super ocean that engulfs everything else. Sea creatures that are terror made into flesh breathe beneath the black ocean. Fawkeses that release a strange tarry substance, which catches fire instantly when it touches air. Raptors with saw-like teeth will carve the land to let the sea flow through so they can hunt you down. Aquabats, screeching from one end of the world to the other.

And maristags, living nightmares that move as fast on land as they do in water. The lithesome creatures are bipedal. Their front limbs are shorter. Stronger. Clawed. Made to grab prey and to tear

4

muscles. Enormous antlers crown their heads. Their scales are luminescent and their blood green.

When maristags get angry, that's when the true horror of creation unravels.

I am five again. Kept away from the stables. That day, I remember seeing something bobbing beneath the smooth sea, water frothing around it. I stared, glued to where I stood, and the bioluminescent spots gleamed like metal in the sun and lifted. A head emerged. Sharp frillfin shot open around it, launching venomous barbs like harpoons.

One *almost* reached me.

I screamed.

That maristag vanished.

This maristag thrashes out of the water.

It's a stunning dash of green amid the cold, gray limestone. The blade-sharp frillfin along its neck have sprung open, shooting lethal barbs out. And clinging to its powerful body, bending its manefin, jerking away from the venomous blades, is Emrik—desperately digging his fingers into the scales of the maristag.

My hands are suddenly stone.

I expected to berate Emrik for stretching out the hunt until dawn.

Instead, he's wrestling with a damned maristag *in* the water.

The maristag is a glorious blur of bioluminescent green, slamming in and out of the angry black water. Between the frillfin and the antlers, Emrik has no control over the creature. One wrong snap, one treacherous slip, and it's all over for my brother.

My stupid brother.

I've seen corpses that suffered the wrath of a maristag.

I don't want him to become one.

"EMRIK!" I scream and wave. "HOLD ON!"

I leap into the freezing water.

A thousand cold needles stab at me, wrestling for control over my body, to tear it apart. The waves are crushing and dark. But I know these waters; I've grown up in them. I cut through the current, fast and smooth, forcing the water to part. Any second now, I'll reach him. I swim closer and closer, surfacing for one ragged breath.

The maristag jerks its neck. Venom, smelling like sulfuric acid, cuts the air again. Rear-curving fangs close around Emrik's arm.

My brother howls.

Coils of blood spiral into the water.

The quarterstaff slips out of Emrik's hold.

I gasp, saltwater smacking at the back of my throat. My jaw burns like it's made of metal.

The maristag is frenzied. I whirl back to the limestone. Gingerroots. I need gingerroots. Maristags are allergic to the prickly skin on the plant. Skaya vines slither over stone like fluorescent snakes, providing illumination, entangled with thick, tall grass swaying like ghosts. I frantically grab a fistful of gingerroots but their grip is too strong. I need something to cut it with.

My lungs sting and I'm forced to resurface. Lightning crashes far out in the ocean as a wave rolls toward the stones.

I brace myself.

The water still hits me like a block of iron.

The moment the wave breaks, I press my foot against the stone and pull at the bush of gingerroots. *It's not enough, it's not enough.* My fingers turn red, my grip slipping. *This isn't going to work, Emrik will die.* Blood on my hands. *Cut, already!*

The last thought escapes my mouth in a burst of air bubbles.

Pain lances my arms.

The bush snaps and I'm slammed back against the hammer-like crush of waves. I curl into myself, floating to the surface. With one deep breath, I dive back and swim into the bloodied water for my brother.

The maristag latches onto the gingerroots. It thrashes anxiously. A

6

loose layer of tissue that forms a second skin over its iridescent scales gleams an ethereal green, blood snaking away.

I'm hands away from my brother.

"The tailfin!" Emrik's cry slips into a gasp. "Don't let go!"

The maristag closes its frills, preparing to shoot the barbs again. Right at my face.

I wheeze, water gushing into my mouth. "Let go of it, Emrik! You're going to die!" I slam the gingerroots into the maristag's neck, at the delicate place where its frills emerge, and it tosses its head in a frenzy. A painful screech cleaves the water. I wrench Emrik's bleeding arm away from the maristag—hoping that *pop* sound I hear came from the animal and not from Emrik.

Behind us, the maristag shakes its second set of fins straight. The manefin fans off along its spine and vanishes midway. I'm frozen, waiting for an attack, but the maristag turns and stares across the sea.

There's not a second to lose. The waves are strong and Emrik is still bleeding. I hold him against me and swim.

We crawl to the shore, gasping for breath. My arms tremble under my weight, fingers twitching like something alive is choking inside. "Are you—"

"Why would you do that?" Emrik cuts me off, his shout cracking midway. Sand crusts every inch of him, coloring his brown skin gray.

I'm panting, panic creeping in me as my conscience understands something before I do. "Do what? Save you?"

"I told you to grab the maristag's tailfin! I was closer to the manefin!" Red lines his swollen eyes. "We could've got it!"

Our skaya must have washed off, but he's in a far worse shape. Blood leaks from his arm, soaking his torn watersuit and darkening the sand. He looks—green. His chest rises and falls, and without warning, he vomits. I jump back. He clasps my wrist tight like a shackle.

"You were supposed to work with me! You made me lose my grip on the maristag! Koral—that was the last of them!"

"No, it wasn't." I turn to the sea. The maristag, a magnificent green, is circling farther and farther from the coast. Its antlers rise and ebb as it gallops through the water.

Today was the last day of the hunt.

The maristags are gone.

# TWO

**W**hat are we going to do now?" Emrik wheezes.

There's a red diffusion of light before the sunrise splits the horizon. I turn to Emrik. He presses his palms against the stone, the maze of veins stark on the back of his hands.

"We have to go, Emrik," I whisper.

He curses. Tries to stand. Stumbles. Tries again. The red horizon disappears behind his dark hair. Is he going to yell at me? Scold me?

My brother's eyes are glazing.

He smells of sulfur. He smells of ruin.

*Are you okay?* I ask him in my head, still tongue-tied. The rock I'm standing on is teeth-sharp. It bites the sole of my shoe. But I can't move. All my bravado swam away with the maristag. I force my gaze to stay on Emrik. After every hunt, we hurt. We bleed. It's expected. You can't take on a full-grown maristag and escape unscathed.

But something is different in the way Emrik sways on his feet this time. His skin is cadaverous, his blood draining. "Koral—" His voice tapers. He looks confused. Then he brushes his fingers against his neck and holds up his palm. A tiny black thorn sits in the center, coated with blood.

I feel suddenly ill.

"We have to get you back," I say, grabbing his arm before he sways again and falls face-first into the craggy stones. Emrik doesn't argue. He understands the effects of maristag venom as well as I do. Delirium for a day, fever for the next, a coma for a week. Then it's over.

I place his arm around my shoulder and together, we stagger home. Emrik gets heavier, his head lolls toward me.

"Stay awake!" I shout over the dread pounding in my ears.

He bleeds.

I sink under my brother's weight. His blood dribbles down my torn shirt.

From the beach to the porch of the house, the world is marked with his blood. The day's burgeoning heat tingles along my hands even when I stumble into the shade with Emrik.

"Baba! Mama!"

The porch blurs and I fall to my knees. Mama arrives, then immediately rushes back in, shouting. Seconds later, my father is helping her.

Baba says harshly, "What did you do?"

I'm suddenly smaller than I've ever felt. "I—? Baba, he got stung."

Mama grabs Emrik's face, trying to wake him up. She's panicking, shouting for Baba to fix this.

Baba snaps, "Go quickly! Get an antidote for your brother before the store shuts down."

He doesn't give me money. I don't ask for any.

I only race into town.

～

10

The day rises and the air clogs with brine and fish, worsened by the high tide and still-brewing storm. I duck out of the thoroughfare and into the oldest part of the residential quarters. Communities burrowed in stone, carved into the rugged terrain make up the Renter neighborhoods on the island of Sollonia. Six thousand people live here, exposed to temperature that easily stays in the hundreds, making do with sand ink tattoos and skaya jelly as a sun shield. The Landers keep all the best heat repellents and sun blockers underground, even when they don't need them. And that's made the anti-Landers sentiment grow like algae inside every Renter's mind.

Cramped streets, darkened by awnings and sun blinds, blur past me like a runny water-painting. I'm forced to slow down once the crumbling structures start jetting out broken sewer pipes and cut rocks like elbows and knees. What am I going to say at the med store? We haven't cleared our debt. Last time we were here, the store owner turned us away. But Emrik could be dead in a week.

My pace picks up again. Distantly, I hear shouts.

A frightened face appears before me.

"Sorry," I blurt, tucking to the side to avoid collision. Four sickly people. A family. Huddled under a tattered brown shawl. They've probably never had a home. It's not uncommon in these parts. Houses flood, creatures invade. If we weren't sanctioned Hunters, this would have been our fate as well.

By the time I slam my hands down on the counter of the med store, I can't speak. Every breath is fire along the veins in my lungs. The store owner shakes his bald, tattooed head.

"What'd you do? Kill everything in the ocean today?"

"I need the antidote to maristag venom," I croak. The taste of salt water still stings my throat. "Now. Please. It's urgent. My brother..." I try to speak again, but I can only stare at him. My mind's not working right. I *know* it. My anxiety is rising, the cottony feeling pushing at the insides of my stomach, and I can't do anything about it.

"You have the silver?" he asks.

"Yes," I say before I can stop myself. A nervous spasm flits across my face. I hope he doesn't notice.

He grunts and vanishes behind a set of filthy curtains.

Cheap wax burns in a corner of the scalding store. The water clock drips seconds. My knuckles stand ridged. My bloody white sleeves are now streaked with grease from the counter.

The man finally steps out, heaving, and spills the medicine onto the counter in a shower of copper-colored packaging.

"Three silvers."

I swallow, my water-crinkled fingers curling against the warm counter. "I forgot. I actually don't have it right now. It slipped when I was coming here. I was running. It must have—"

"No silver, no medicine," he snaps. "You owe me too much already!"

"Please," I beg him. I know I sound frantic. Cornered. But I need the antidote today. There's no way around it. I have less than an hour now before Emrik's delirium gets out of control. He could hurt someone. He could hurt *himself*.

My pleading changes the man's entire demeanor. "Koral *Hunter*," he says with a sneer reserved for my family's name, a sub-caste of Renters. "Maybe your Lander friends can let you inside their med stores?"

Had it been Emrik in my place, he'd have leaped across the counter and beat the man at the dig. He did it once when we were here for Liria's meds.

I only say, "I'll pay double. Just let me have that antidote."

"You haven't paid an iron stone in two months and now you're going to pay double?"

"We have to pay for my sister's treatment every week! You know it! Everyone knows it," I shout. The sound reverberates in my head. My vision grays. If I don't get the medicine, my father will throw me out. But I don't care about that. It's Emrik. He'll wonder where I am. Why I'm not helping him.

"Selling out to Landers and not even getting paid for it?" someone calls from outside the store. "That's tragic."

Thorny vine tattoos begin at their foreheads and disappear down their necks. I can tell they are part of a street gang by the red bands around their arms—they collect bets for the Glory Race. Their leader grimaces, revealing pointed teeth in a twisted mouth.

These troublemakers try to provoke us every day of our lives, hating us for being Hunters. They think we sold out to the upper caste of Landers, when we really started out as mere guards for Renter fishermen in the earliest days of the settlement.

As if they don't go around fighting other Renters in the name of supporting the Glory Race charioteers they like best. And for what? Food? Money? Yeah, that's what we're doing, too. At least we don't *gamble* on the deaths of others. My blood burns. People *die* in the Drome. Trampled. Shredded. Pierced by the chariots. Ripped apart by the maristags.

The death you meet in the Drome is a violent one.

Of course, for most people it's the chance of a lifetime.

The death you meet in the Drome is a chosen one. It's immortality.

The point is blatant for Renters: The glory of this world is not for you.

You'd think solidarity with our own people would stop these street gangs from harassing others.

Mama says it's human nature to fight for dominance and thrive off the misery of others. I think it's just the cold touch of money.

After all, what do we really know about being human?

This is not where humanity first breathed.

This is where humanity came to die.

"A silver for your words," the leader of the group continues. "Tell us about the fastest maristags this year. Which ones should we bet for in the Glory Race?"

When I can only blink at him, half-terrified at the pharmacist's refusal and half-simmering at this intervention, another one of them adds, "The brother would tell us." The boy is heavily sunburned with a scarred face. He meets my eye, daring me to counter.

"Where is he?" the leader asks, silver gleaming in his grimy hands. "Oh—right, heard he's dead. Shame, eh? He always tipped us off. May the Water Horse watch over him, may he sail the ocean of stars—"

"SHUT UP! He's not dead!" I snap, frightened of the prayer for the dead. But my otherness immediately magnifies in front of these Renters. My speech is too much like a Lander, a dead giveaway of where I had the privilege of going to school.

I turn to the pharmacist. "He's not dead. Please."

"What's the deal, eh?" the troublemaker interrupts me. "If you stop hunting, no maristag. No maristag, no tournament, and if no tournament," he grins, "no glory to keep from Renters. Your brother won't be dead, either."

This time, I can't stop. "You're blaming us? You think we'd be allowed to do anything else? If not us, they'll find another family to do it. We're Renters like you, no matter what you want to believe."

The man glares. "Everyone's got choices."

"Landers forcing jobs on us is not a choice. You know what is?" The group stops grinning at my tone. I can see the crackle of anger in the leader, but I don't relent once I start. "Collecting bets and rooting for violence for nothing but *fun*."

It's not the group that responds. It's the one who holds more power over my life than I realized until this moment.

14

"Get out of my store." The pharmacist places his huge hands on the counter, obscuring the copper packets.

Too late, I say, *"Please—"*

"You think you're some kind of grounder?" he spits. "Talking down to us?"

"I didn't say anything to you!"

"That's what's different between us and you Hunters inside that house. Outside, we're all one. Now get out and don't come back."

The sea thrashing against the limestone cliff is loud, even here at the thoroughfare. People whizz past, children scurry up and down, and hawkers sell fuzzy firberries, pulpy opalfruits, and sizzling lobsters. Parallel rows of glistening fish lie on ice, all wearing the same expression of shock and weariness.

It's a cacophony. It's chaos.

It's Sollonia.

And I am at its center, surrounded by strangers, and beginning to draw attention. Sly whispers at first, then open stares and pointed fingers.

My head is spinning. I can't go home without that antidote. *Think.* Emrik is counting on me. What if I go to a Lander store? Pretend the Council of Ophir is allowing us free meds because they can't lose Emrik as a Hunter?

It could work.

It should.

And if it doesn't?

They'll imprison me.

Then they'll *have* to fix Emrik Hunter—

"Koral!"

Two hands grab my arm and yank. I go careening to the side and into a rock cut as an entrance to a marine food store. A moment later, a stretch of white-gray scales sweeps over me. It shadows the world for several seconds. By the time the capricorn thumps farther down the thoroughfare with its massive tail, people start shaking themselves out of wherever they'd taken refuge.

Sollonia has five capricorns—giant amphibians that are half-goat, half-fish. They're stationed at every corner of the island, and one always patrols the thoroughfare, *trying* to keep the ocean creatures where they belong. This one, handled by an equally burly armored guard with a staff so big it scrapes the street, towers over every building. A single nudge of one of its two powerful horns would send a human flying. Instead of hooves like the true mountain goats, it's got claws that can scratch and carve and dig through *anything*. The fins at the end of its body, which double as hind limbs, are strong as boulders and a hundred meters wide, so it travels on land just as well as in water.

I stand, pressed against the pillar at my side and leave a bloody handprint on it. The adrenaline is ebbing as a vice-like grip tightens around my arm. My instincts rise, ready to defend me.

"That could've knocked you to the next island! Is diving into the sea like it's a joke not enough of a death wish?" the voice says.

"Crane," I croak at my best friend. "I almost killed you."

"In your dreams." She pulls her scarf tighter across her face, the bones pushing against the fabric, and leaves only her eyes uncovered. "I hope Emrik isn't dead because—"

"No, he isn't! Who started this rumor?"

"Everyone at the Warehouse is gossiping. Thought I'd find you at the med store." She holds me at arm's length. "Who can blame them? Look at you." I do. My shirt is caked with slime and blood, the tangle of my hair half down, sticking to my cheek.

Crane holds out the strip of copper-colored medicine pack. "The moron was still singing about not giving you this. So I got it, of course."

My heart slams in my rib cage. "Three silvers, Crane. I can't take this," I say, clutching the meds tighter until the cellophane wrap becomes a second skin, until blood leeches from my hands.

"Yes, you can. I can afford for now. Father dearest sent his monthly love last evening."

"Wait, what were you doing at the Warehouse so early?"

Crane quirks a brow beneath her tight scarf. "Doesn't Emrik need the antidote right about now?"

I don't even say goodbye as I run home.

# THREE

The air in the hall quivers with the silence of a spying predator. I wish Emrik was here. But he's sleeping now, wrapped in gauze. The administration of the antidote was painstakingly slow, delirium taking effect as I returned. Baba chose to point out how much time I'd taken instead of being grateful that we had the antidote at all.

It feels like I have more bruises than skin, but we don't have painkillers. The ache jumps around my body, spiraling here, then there.

No one's talking.

I desperately wish I could skip this night and wake up once everything has fixed itself.

The tiny hall is bare, like the rest of the house, except for one of my blue pottery vases in the corner. The thorn-flowers it holds are withering. In a niche on the wall, a jar of water holds two small starfish, their luminescence ebbing and brightening with their gulps. It's the only light. None of the glass lamps Emrik makes are lit tonight. We're in mourning.

I chew on every bit of food like it's my last.

A feeling I remember from the year I turned eight.

The squelch of my chewing is too loud. I drag my steel spoon across the table to camouflage it.

Baba shoots me a sharp look.

I stop.

The silence resumes. It simmers.

Pain stings sharply across my palm. My hand slips. I grab for the spoon, only to snap the paper plate in half, spilling precious purple rice. The spoon drops unceremoniously to the floor.

"There was only one..." I start and falter. Mama's expression could be either pity or disappointment. "Even before I interfered, only one. Because of the storm."

The ache continues to throb in my fingers, blisters pinging, threatening to burst open.

"I didn't free it on purpose," I try to keep my voice steady. "It had its jaw around Emrik's shoulder. It was a big one. I couldn't—I didn't want to injure Emrik more than he already was," I finish feebly.

Mama watches the space between us. I can't tell what's on her mind. When I returned, Liria was coughing again, and Mama was too busy taking care of her, so I had to take care of Emrik.

"Leela," Baba says. "What did that pharmacist tell us last week?"

Mama's chest rises and falls. She tucks a strand of her brown hair back. Like always, it's parted in the middle, elongating her round face. Small circular tattoos follow her hairline and stop at her temples. She doesn't say anything. She doesn't have to. Emrik and I asked him for a one-month reprieve before he goes to the Renter magistrate. But the pharmacist wouldn't budge.

"He says he'll consider it," I lie. "Crane paying helped."

Liria coughs in her room.

The Landmaster knows Liria is too ill to hunt. A non-Hunter

name renders her ineligible for the annual medicines Emrik and I get at the start of hunting season. We can't complain. What we receive is more than most Renters.

I swallow the food in my mouth with difficulty.

"Yes, as if that's all we have left to do. Make ourselves low in front of those from Opal Den." Baba's gaze is cold, framed by his severe, thin face. I know what he sees: a reckless girl who's risked the entire family's well-being.

I should have controlled the maristag. I should have gotten it away from Emrik *and* filled the stables.

"Varman, she didn't—" Mama starts and is cut short by Baba, "Tell her what you told me this morning."

It's his tone, usually preceding him lashing out at Mama, which bubbles my fright into anger. If he thinks he can talk like that to Mama again, he's mistaken.

Then, my mother speaks.

"The medic said Liria's capacity to breathe in air is getting smaller. It's something that happens to people around Kar Atish. He's not sure why she's sick here, so far away."

Kar Atish is the city-island to our east, where zargunine and silver mining takes place. That's where the money and sun shields, especially for Landers, come from. People in Kar Atish have a glazed look in their eyes. No outsider wants to stay on that cinder-streets island for more than a few hours. At least, that's what people say.

"Her treatment has to change. It will cost us more."

Baba cuts in, "*Cost us more?* Two hundred and seventy silvers isn't *costing* us more, it's a death sentence for us all!"

I look from my father to my mother, trying to imagine how we'll keep Liria safe if we have no maristags to sell this year.

I wait for a denial.

They don't offer me one.

With sickness pooling inside me, I ask, "What will we do?"

"You," my father says, "are going to sign up for the marriage draft and get us that bonus so we can clear off this debt first thing."

Two years ago, I was feeding a maristag and he slammed his antlers against me. I struck the ground like a rock hurled against a cliff and for several moments, colors bleeding into one another, I couldn't move, couldn't think. There was only a vague understanding that something terrible had happened.

That's what I feel like now.

My mother leans toward me, pressing a hand to my arm.

I manage one word. "No."

Baba says, "I wasn't asking you."

"When have you ever asked what we want?" I yell and stand. The table turns, spilling whatever remained of dinner across the floor.

"Koral!" Mama cries.

"So you'll do what you want even if it means your sister dies?" Baba says. "If we can't pay for something as simple as damned painkillers? That man will be here in a week for his money. We have nothing left! If he drags us to the Magistrate, if we lose the stables, we'll be on the streets."

It's a punch in the gut. This house may be bare and without even a direct water pipeline that isn't meant to serve the stables, but it keeps us safe. From the harsh sun and the cruel ocean. From the creatures that would kill us before we draw a breath. "That's not what I'm saying."

Baba's eyes harden, his voice drops even lower. "If you don't do this, that's exactly what you're saying."

"And what did you do?" Hot, angry tears pour down my face, but my hands are shaking too bad to wipe them. "What are you doing while Emrik and I risk our lives over and over again in the sea? What have you ever done, Baba?"

He raises his hand, and my mother stands between us. "Varman, don't! She's a child! She doesn't know what she's saying."

I can't imagine the amount of courage that must have taken. My mother is a broken woman. Baba blames her for everything: when we don't have enough food, when Liria coughs so much we fear it's the last time, when a maristag goes wild. Everything. She tries to deflect and deny, but we know. We see her, head bowed, shoulders slumped, agreeing to everything my father demands, never once raising her voice.

Yet here she is, standing up against the man who destroyed her, to protect me. It's probably that detail, my mother's face opposing him, which pulls my father together.

There's blood in his eyes, a vein pumping in his forehead.

I want him gone.

He must read it on my face because he throws it back at me, "Go to your room! Now!"

If I did go to my room, I'd probably break something. So I go to Liria's instead.

She's dressed in one of my old shirts and a patchwork skirt Mama stitched for her. I sit at the edge of her mattress, my old one. My fatigued muscles scream with the relief of finally sitting down and staying put.

"How's your hair still like that?" Liria pouts. Her large eyes, framed by her short bangs, are wide. She hasn't gotten her tattoos yet. "Didn't you half-die?"

"The one who did the dying was our very brave brother."

Liria giggles, not really knowing how close to the truth that is. But she turns to her side, trying to hold in a cough.

"I made a new painting," she says in a soft voice to hide the hoarseness. "Crane got me new paints yesterday."

"Is it in there?" I reach for the small secondhand table where she keeps her paintings. Emrik and I salvaged it from the black market. On top of it is one of the blue pots I make, studded with shells Liria loves. Baba was ready to throw the table in the ocean when he realized where we got it from, but for Liria's convenience, he let it stay.

For Renters, the safety of our house is a dream even though it's a dugout of four matchbox-sized rooms and walls with bone-like edges. It is also a threat from the Council of Ophir, who govern all the ten islands, wrapped in a reminder of the work we do. Of our fragile place in the grand scheme of things.

Baba loves pretending our bare luxury doesn't come at the price of our family being forced to hunt forever. So do our fellow Renters who see us as traitors. Having the Hunter name has always meant being alone in this world.

Liria curls up next to me, one arm around my waist, and rests her head on my shoulder.

She used to do this as a toddler—before she fell sick. Emrik and I would sneak her outside at night. At the beach, we would talk and run and laugh, watch the red-yellow stars of the Ship of Fire glimmering like pinpoints of candles in the sky. Night is when the island of Sollonia is prone to the whims of amphibians like maristags, so there are restrictions, but night is also when we can breathe and let the air kiss our skins with abandon.

I thumb through the drawings. "You drew the Sanctuary?"

Outside the official city boundary, at the end of a sandbar, sits the relic of Ophir's past: the Empyrean Sanctuary. A gleaming black behemoth, the Sanctuary is one of the Wonders of the World. It rests on the exact spot it crashed a thousand years ago, carrying the voyagers, our Empyrean Elders. The spherical structure that was pieced together from the shattered remains of the ship by historians and laborers is now partly a museum. Whatever method made the original ship work went to rest with the wisdom of the Empyrean Elders.

I'm struck by how odd the concept of chance is. What if the Sanctuary had crashed elsewhere? Right into the ocean? In the middle of hungry raptors?

Would I even exist?

The thought is sobering.

I smile at Liria. "It's lovely."

"You're the only one who gets it!" she exclaims, sitting up straighter, delight bright in her eyes. "Emrik thought it was a weird cloud."

We giggle together at our brother's remarkable observation.

The next drawing is a sketch of the Drome. Or Liria's interpretation of the stadium because she's never actually been to a Glory Race.

"You think I'll get to see it this time?"

She was only three, very fragile and sick, four years ago when the last tournament had taken place.

"I hope so." The Glory Race is the island's single biggest event. So much goes into it, with the celebrations, the parades, the parties. Besides the betting and the killing, of course. Ten Landers risk their lives charioteering with ruthless maristags that hold their lives between their jaws. And one of those Landers becomes a Champion with more gold than they'd ever need in one lifetime.

That kind of victory can change a family's fortunes for generations.

What would it be like to live in a mansion underground? To want for nothing?

To not fight in the ocean?

"What about Renters?" Liria asks, immediately bringing me back aboveground.

I shrug. "We watch the race." Renters not racing is one of those unsaid rules you don't question, let alone cross. I remember seeing a crinkly historical manifesto on the Glory Race at the Warehouse once, nowhere did it say Renters can't participate. But only Landers do.

"Too bad. You're so good at taking care of maristags. You'd win if you participated," she says with the earnestness of a child who's been kept from the sun her whole life.

I sigh and turn to the next drawing. My heart lurches to my mouth.

"That's not finished," Liria squeaks and stretches her arm out for the sketch.

I pull it out of her reach. "What's this?"

It's a self-sketch, I can tell from the bangs on the girl. She's floating under the ocean. Her eyes are closed.

Liria looks back at me with large eyes. "What happens when you die?"

"I don't know."

"Do you think I'll die?"

"What? No. Children don't die. Old people do."

"But I'm sick."

"Well, you can get sick, sure. But you won't die until you're a hundred years old. Haven't I told you about Bitterbloom? She's a hundred years old." Where did she get this in her head? My chest caves in with each breath.

Liria shrugs. The pressure behind my eyes builds.

"Okay," she says. Then adds with absolute nonchalance, "Did you know you can mix pigments to make a new color?"

"No!" I put on my surprised face. "Really?"

"Yes, you can make all the colors if you have three primary colors." As she talks, I study her limp hands, her hollow cheeks, her slow breaths.

Mama arrives then. Whenever she enters a place, you can immediately sense her. She's—*warm*. Not warm like the grainy air that

25

scrapes at your skin outside. Warm like a bonfire beside the sea on cold nights.

She gives Liria sleeping meds, despite the whines for "just a few more minutes."

As we tuck Liria into bed, Mama beckons me outside.

In the silent hallway, she stands in front of a mirror and brushes her hair. The top of her head reaches only my chin. Just a few years ago, I used to skip behind her, collecting shells at the beach, barely reaching her waist.

We look alike in the way most mothers and daughters do. But Mama's full lips, big eyes, and softly rounded face make her look winsome. You see her and you think of home and safety. I'm more like a confused secondhand copy trying too hard.

I wonder what she wants to talk about. Did I forget to wash the utensils again? But no—we filtered some water yesterday. There won't be any tonight. We have to conserve water for our last maristag. Although what possible use we have for her now escapes me. There's no male maristag for her to breed with. And she's a strange specimen anyway. No Lander wants her for Glory Race. They think she's jinxed.

"Don't talk to your father like that again," Mama says.

Shocked, I'm about to retort but the hollowness in her voice stops me. Her weariness weighs me down. She pats my hair, stark black compared to her and Liria's bronze. "You are doing so much already. Both you and Emrik."

Her gaze holds mine.

"Landers see us taming maristags and anything that looks like power in a Renter's hand burns their blood. But it's our own people whose fears and frustrations you must be careful of. The margin of the margins is a dangerous place to be, never forget that."

I used to think my parents were exaggerating people's perception of us. But once I started at school, it was clear as sea crystals. We have no place out there. Only here, with each other.

"Do you remember what you used to dream about the most?"

Even with the dark pressing at me from every direction, I murmur, "Flying."

My tone coaxes a smile out of my mother, too. "You will not give your father any chance to take his anger out on you again. Understand? And promise me, today, you will not stop dreaming of flight."

She can talk in circles all she wants, but my father's demand drills into my head. I saw today what the lack of money will do to us. If Crane hadn't arrived in time... "How will we pay for Liria's continued treatment, Mama? How will we get out of this debt?"

"I will not have one daughter destroy herself for another." She's moved to determined anger. I've never seen her like this before. Extended family and friends told me Mama used to laugh and speak her mind so strongly that everyone got annoyed, and Baba looked at her like she was his world and fell in love.

It sounds like the mythic tales about the Empyrean Elders now.

In my memories, she's always let my father get away with everything. He thinks we don't know. But bruises on your mother's body are hard to miss when you embrace her, and she gasps in pain.

Suddenly, I get it. What my mother's been doing all these years.

I keep my mouth shut.

It's exactly my mother's quiet suffering that makes my decision. I will never enter the Council's marriage draft, but I will not simply waste away like Baba, either.

Despite my father's best efforts, I never *did* learn to give up.

# FOUR

I leave home before Emrik wakes up. He might be physically weaker, but he's likely better enough that if he knew I was going to the Warehouse's black market, he'd go feral. Officially it's an abandoned warehouse. So, of course, Renter traders can store goods for a short time and quarrel among themselves in there without disturbing anyone. But as with all things left alone by the Landers, it's little more than an illegal trading hub and criminal den. And a haven for rebels.

So I *have* to make sure Emrik doesn't follow me.

I slip into the tarp-covered network of the Renter neighborhoods. Strewn with streams of water and layers of dead beetles, a chalky alley leads farther into a neighborhood where parents instruct their kids not to go. The natural black walls are painted with crass graffiti, fading symbols of the renegade group Freedom's Ark, and tar leftover from the graphene-filter factories.

But I can't avoid Opal Den, as Landers call it. Crane lives here, or rather, her Lander father left her here when she was born, and her Renter mother died in childbirth. According to him, a father's job is to pay a monthly stipend in exchange for her agreeing to never look for him.

The street goes from a worn, crusty path to a collection of stones stuck haphazardly over drains. Awful pungent odors pervade the air. Houses here are bare caves, without even the slatted shutters of other neighborhoods.

One of Crane's neighbors tries to hail me. "Have you seen my son? He went to the store at the corner."

It hits me like a blow. It always does.

Her son is a Renter who simply vanished one day. Likely thrown in the ocean by Lander forces for whatever he did. Spoke a word against the Council. Was informed against. Or made a scapegoat. And we're not supposed to talk about it. Not unless we want to be next.

Death is a game played by the Hunters. But we always come back from the brink. I've never lost anyone I love. Never known what it is to look at a void and try to remember what existed before.

"Sorry, Remide," I tell the old woman for the hundredth time. "I haven't."

"He'll be back soon..." She retreats under the tin-sheet board propped up as a door.

I should say something. Comfort her. If this happened to us, and Mama was left alone, I'd want someone to show her mercy.

But then I catch sight of a poster stuck on Crane's door.

It's a Freedom's Ark invitation with one phrase stamped in bold: No gods, no Landers. Trust Crane to be popular, even among rebels. I tear the poster down before knocking on the door.

Crane answers with a pinched expression. Her hair is piled on top of her head, making her sharp-edged brows seem more angular than usual. A tattoo in the shape of 'C' covers most of the right side of her face. She's probably just gotten out of bed, yet she already has stones glittering in her ears.

Yawning, she says, "What do you want in the dead of night?"

I push past her.

The room's cramped walls are the toothed black stone of the island. It's bare, save for a flat stone we fished out of the sea that Crane uses as a table. Right now, there's a clay bowl on it, filled to the brim with syrupy oranges. I pick up a slice gilded with gooey syrup. They *are* a luxury.

"The Lander Father's server said he was in a good mood. Even offered extra tix for the Drome if I want."

"Glory Race really livens up everyone, doesn't it? Even this no-name Lander Father," I say.

"Next we hear, your father will actually do his job and not blame Aunty Leela for his misplaced brain."

Grim as the entire thing is, I laugh. "Speaking of which, I'm going to the Warehouse. We need money."

There's nothing you won't find at the Warehouse's black market. Loans, especially. Even med stocks—you can always smuggle stuff aboard the ferry to Chandrabad Island where the University's Medic Center has spawned an entire world of contraband drugs.

To get there, I must go through the Terrafort without raising suspicion, and I need Crane to cover for me.

Shadows I don't recognize fall across Crane's face. "*You* don't have to do anything."

"That pharmacist said he'd call his debt in a week. I don't think the Lander left you so much silver that you can clear our debt *and* take care of yourself."

"One of these days, Varman will do things himself. Or Emrik will make better choices. Won't happen if you keep cleaning up their mess."

I'm stung. It's not like I have a benefactor who, for all his terrible life choices, makes sure I'm fed without having to work a day in my life, or pay off pharmacists.

"It doesn't matter whose fault it is," I snap. "It only means Mama and Liria will suffer."

"If you keep living your life for everyone but yourself, you'll never get off this island."

The syrupy sweetness of the orange turns to sand in my mouth. I came here for Crane's help, not for a lecture.

Is it so easy to leave a world that's all water and ten pieces of land for thousands of miles in every direction? There are only two escapes: get married like Baba said, or run.

With what's happening to Mama, I'll jump in a raptor-infested ocean before marrying. And running? Ha. Not even a real choice.

I'd be hunted.

And *say*, I managed to escape—how would I ever live without Mama and Liria? Mama, whose entire life revolves around us, who has stayed with my dread of a father for us. And Liria, the baby of our family, who reminds us every day we're still human and capable of love.

What would Emrik do without me? Look what happened yesterday.

"Koral," comes the high-pitched voice of Agata, Crane's guardian. She stands at the door, head and face wrapped in a scarf even inside. She must notice the tense air between Crane and me, so she tries to change the topic. "You're going to the Glory Race registration later, child?"

"That's why I'm here, Agata," I lie with a smile. The registration is the last thing on my mind, but I'll say whatever it takes to get Crane out. I turn to her. "You'd better come. Or I'll go alone." Let her say no now. Let's see what Agata will make of her refusing. Probably that we're fighting, which would only make Agata worry that Crane was spending time with the rebels instead. And nobody wants that.

Her frown tells me what I need to know before Crane even opens her mouth.

"Fine, I'll come."

The island of Sollonia narrows in the middle, to the southwest from our house. There, the western side of the island is a sheer cliff that rises in an isolated peak. Inside exists the hollow that was turned into the home of the Landers, the Terrafort.

The Terrafort's entrance is set halfway in the ground, amid two large towers, topped with sirens, to keep an eye on the ocean. Its switchblade door, made entirely of zargunine and enforced twice, is up like an awning. If, one day, the Panthalassan Ocean came collecting its debt from humanity for persisting on the land still, the door would withstand its force, protecting everything inside.

The door gives way to the entrance plaza, which vaults high. There's nowhere on the island outside where you don't sense the peak staring down at you, though 90 percent of the Terrafort is subterranean; level after level carved into the ground, harboring the entire population of Landers on Sollonia.

Renter services and tradesmen bring their work underground.

As always, the Terrafort makes me feel small. I can no longer see the sky, however brutal it is without the skaya. Only the western side offers a glimpse of the outside world—a panoramic window with thick, protective glass meant to let light in at dusk. Where the Renter spaces are hard, simple, and precise—the Lander ones feel softer, more human.

The plaza is bustling in anticipation of Glory Race registration. There are tourists and Race hopefuls from other islands, and everywhere you glance, the favorite charioteer of this year's Glory Race smirks at you from glossy banners.

Dorian Akayan, son of an illustrious Lander, a descendant of one of the island's founders.

Dressed in a crimson-and-silver jacket, he sports the look of drowning in his own conceit, as if he salvaged this world and the rest of us are guests here.

For the longest time, I didn't want to believe it of him, but I guess once a Lander, always a Lander.

I'm too busy glaring at the nearest banner when I get caught in the jostle of the Landers. I cannot avoid seeing how different those who live and die underground are from us. No matter the color of their skin, they *shine*, with bones that are either too sharp or too smooth, a testament of having no lesions from sun exposure; no ridges of bones broken and rejoined together *wrong*; no wounded eyes stitched haphazardly; and no tattoos. Instead, they have strong perfumes loaded over vibrant tunics and dresses, flowing hair and silk ribbons, and beaded jewelry. The sea of faces walks tall. Of course it does; no monstrous creature creeps up and swallows families whole inside the Terrafort. Nothing swoops down and flies away with someone clasped in its claws. The throng cackles. Not caring if they're blocking someone's path. Renters snap out of their way even if dragging cartloads of goods.

This is how we keep the peace.

Nobody wants a repeat of the first wars. Right now, Liria's meds cost too much, but none of us would be alive to fall sick if our society returned to what it was—an exhausted people struggling with starvation, isolation, and on the verge of ending humanity's story on this island before it even began.

The plaza is an island of its own. Streets unfurl in every direction, lined with shops and inns. The squeaking of the cartwheels in the city below thunder under our feet, almost camouflaging the hiss of the steam turbines at the back of the plaza. Clashing smells of marine food shops and bakeries suffuse the wispy air.

Outside, Renters and Landers are in such close proximity only during the Glory Race. Which is why the guards—in their metal masks with wide visors and black uniforms—meld with shadows in every alley. Several tunnels lead out of the plaza and into the underground. At the mouth of these, cramped apartments rise where Renter tradesmen live.

"Stop gawking," Crane says. She hooks her arm in mine and, refusing to apologize for bumping into Landers, drags me across the plaza.

Beside the window-wall, a silver street sign shimmers with ornamental lamps over the Agora Square. Workshops, mechanics, secondhand shops, and grocery stores line the terrace at the back, surrounded by tall colonnades. A year ago, when things *seemed* less dire, Crane and I pooled our personal savings to buy a small space. We got an easy deal because the previous owner, a Lander lady, died by suicide and no one wanted it.

The setup is precarious; Crane sells our wares—blue pottery and glass lamps—at the workshop. I take over only on bazaar days with Emrik when school is off for Lander kids and we have an easier crowd to swindle, pretending we're helping my friend out. It doesn't yield more than fifteen irons every month or so. But Emrik and I have nothing else to do with the things we make. Even if it's ultimately a waste of time and money... It's a good distraction, and it keeps us from having to be jammed inside with Baba.

Crane opens the shutter as I answer random queries from fellow craftsmen and workers about the Glory Race like I'm the one organizing it. To be fair, having read some of the archived now-illegal documents at the Warehouse *and* being from a Hunter family, I do know more about the tournament than any of them.

"Are you sure?" Crane says again. "You haven't been there in a while, Koral. Things are different now."

"Things are never good at the Warehouse, especially not for Hunters."

"Yes, but," she looks away, "you're more and more recognizable. And you don't make a habit of keeping your cool when it comes to the rebels."

"I deal with maristags. I think I know how to handle unfriendly situations."

Once I have witnesses to my presence at the Agora plaza, Crane takes over the shop.

I slip out the back door and step onto a terrace. It takes several minutes to hook my fingers around the barely-there crack at the end. I pull the hidden door and step into the Warehouse.

Cardboard boxes, gnarled seagrass, and dried vines tumble over the space. A couple of people sit in a corner, murmuring. My footsteps are loud in the emptiness, and they look up, alert. I raise my hands in surrender. "Nyn bazaar," I say *black market* in local Renter dialect.

They gesture for me to carry on and go back to the conversation.

Empty glass bottles and cans litter the floor. Scraps of chariots and masts and shining metal are shoved up against the walls in case a Lander guard stumbles upon the entrance. But behind the dusty curtain fluttering in one corner and through a short alley, Sollonia's black market thrives right inside the domain of Landers.

This is where the Freedom's Ark rebels survive. I didn't care, not until Crane began listening to them, and I had to come drag her out. The rebels didn't like me interfering in their business. After that, Emrik and my visits down here have been especially rare.

Thick smoke wafts in the air and hushed voices take form in the darkness. The sense of being watched trickles down my spine.

I keep my gaze straight. No turning. No looking. Everyone knows everyone here. So it's best to keep your head down and not cause trouble. Once you get blacklisted at the Warehouse, say goodbye to your money, your reputation, and any help you came for. And if you're someone who lives on daily transactions, pack up and jump in the ocean. Even the sun doesn't hurt as much as a hungry stomach does.

Blocks of zargunine line one side. The sea-metal revolutionized life—traces melded with construction materials create a shield against the sun. Landers don't need it when safe inside, but Renters pay whatever they can—even for the illegally mined and scraped stuff—some pay metal, perhaps food, maybe a kidney.

There are other things out of our reach here. Jars of refined skaya, seasilk clothes, and silver jewelry. Chili peppers, vegetables, lentils—plant food smuggled out of the Lander traders' green-houses. I'm not starving, not yet anyway, but the sight makes saliva flood my mouth. The plants that grow out on the island are useless scrubs at best, and poisonous thorns at worst.

Then, I see it: in a corner, a Freedom's Ark meeting is taking place.

Freedom's Ark started as a subsection of the group of traders who petitioned the Council for space in the Grand Bazaar. From there it evolved into a political movement, but without a central leader it scattered into various factions. Some called for social reform, some called for blood. Ultimately it dwindled to what it is now: disgruntled stone throwers and disillusioned speech givers. Restless, defiant, and unable to truly challenge the status quo. But even then, when they get too bold and try to take a stand publicly, the Lander crackdown is furious, and it falls not just on people still calling themselves Arkers, but on every Renter.

I watch them, keenly tuned to the man standing on an elevation.

They're wearing matching masks and silver armbands fashioned as chain-links. A collective identity I haven't noticed before.

This isn't surviving. This is thriving.

Is this what Crane meant?

I look around. Lot of good that does. But even in the dark, nobody seems upset about this blatant display.

"Koral," calls Bitterbloom. "What are you doing here?"

It's not her real name, but she loves eating the bitter seagrass. Though, as a dealer of zargunine through back channels, she's far more dangerous than the name she answers to. She probably doesn't even remember her given name; rumor is, she's over a hundred years old.

"Where did they all come from?" I point at Freedom's Ark. "And what fairytale are they spinning now? More nonsense about finding underwater cities if Landers won't give us land?"

"If Landers can dig through land to live under it, why can't Atlantis exist?" she says, using the name the rebels spray-painted on the limestone arches when they were peddling the idea five years ago.

"We left gods in the old world. We should've left fairytales, too."

"So caustic," Bitterbloom smiles patronizingly. "They're trying only to survive, you know."

"No, *I* am trying to survive. They're trying to cause trouble. Organizing like this. We don't have the resources to rebuild our lives again after fanciful rebellions."

"Your Lander school taught you that?" She waves a hand. Her fingers are blackened, the color seeping upward along her deep brown arms, melding with her tattoos. It's an occupational hazard and stands out in contrast to the crown of her big, white hair.

I swallow. "They're not wrong."

Bitterbloom laughs a dismissal. "What are *you* still here for?"

"I need—"

"You're not aware?" Her wrinkles turn more pronounced as she squints at me.

"Of what?" I ask, grinning at her. "How have you been, Bitter? Here." I hold out a box of bitterblooms toward her. "You love them, I know."

Bitterbloom's expression momentarily softens.

"I need a loan. Urgently."

"Thought as much." She puts the box down and yanks me to the back of her crammed shop.

"What are you doing?" My hand finds the pocketknife I carry, especially in the Warehouse.

"Put that away before you hurt yourself, child." Bitterbloom huffs and pulls a stool. She sits, her joints cracking loudly. "You are in enough trouble already." Her tone stops me short. "You argued with Arkers?"

"Who?"

"The street gang that takes bets on the northern side of the thoroughfare? Those boys are members of the Freedom's Ark."

"I don't know what you're talking about." But then, I do.

*Everyone's got choices.*

Bitterbloom shakes her head, recognizing my comprehension.

"It wasn't exactly an argument. Some talk on the street is hardly something to corner me for, Bitter." Despite my nonchalance, I can't control the pounding of my heart.

Freedom's Ark whoops and shouts in the distance.

Bitterbloom takes a moment to respond, a moment in which the air in the small room sharpens into a loud keening in my ear, blocking the commotion outside.

"They came after they were done above," Bitter says quietly. "Spoke all sorts of lies." I don't ask how she knows what they said were lies, but I doubt it matters. I doubt anything matters; it is what I've begun to understand deep in my bones.

Bitterbloom's next words still cut like a knife.

"You are not to receive any trade from the Warehouse. You are blacklisted."

# FIVE

I stumble back home, still dazed from the verbal blade Bitterbloom thrust into my gut so kindly, hands shaking at my sides. Crane offered to come back with me, but I didn't want to subject her to what's coming now.

The mood in the dark hall wasn't festive to begin with, but whatever my mother reads on my face makes her tighten her grip around the brush she's holding.

"You're pale," Mama says. "Eat something."

Emrik sinks against the wall, cradling his slung arm against his chest. His hair is an untied tangle of dried vines.

I try to pick my words, but there's no way out now.

Baba enters the hall, dressed in a Lander-like suit, as if he's going somewhere—which is not possible. Four years ago, he said I was old enough to hunt and that was it. He hasn't worked a day since, except for presenting the trained maristags to the Landmaster.

He spots me. "Are you done dragging this out, finally?"

Has he heard what happened? For the second time in two days, it's my fault we'll likely starve this year. At least those of us who survive.

Dismay drapes over each of them, and pain is gushing inside my chest.

We're not getting help from the Warehouse. The Landmaster's one-month subsidy will clear our debt for now but create another at the Council office. And then, nothing. On Sollonia, you work and contribute, and if you don't, you get no resources. It'll be our second debt. The chances of the Council stripping us of our name and bringing in new Hunters is higher than ever. Each door is shutting with the bangs of a drum against my skull.

In a corner is my mother's voice, urging me to fly.

Then I'm saying something without thinking, but it's our last option. The only one I can grasp.

"I'm participating in the Glory Race. I'm going to win and bring us gold."

Baba is the only one whose face exhibits no shock; he just pinches the bridge of his nose. Liria gasps, her hands cupping her mouth, and starts coughing. It takes Mama a few minutes to calm her.

"How would you even get in? Do not do anything stupid." Baba's brows pull down, like I've sprouted fins for hair. "And racing with maristags," he scoffs. "One nearly killed Emrik."

"The maristag that *didn't* kill Emrik because I saved him?"

"Come on, Baba—" Emrik starts but is cut short by Mama. "Emrik, be quiet." Then she says to me, "What your father means is, don't be reckless. Renters have never been charioteers."

"She'll die if she's in the Drome," Baba says. "That's no place for her. Those monstrous creatures and those...those *Landers*. You think gamblers will risk a Renter upset in the Drome? No, she will drag us down like—" He heaves and falls quiet.

A tense, sickening second passes before he walks out.

Mama's face becomes the oldest story in the world: she's too tired to argue. She turns to Liria. "Come, sitara, time for your meds."

41

Liria glances back at me at the threshold of the room, eyes filled with awe and fear.

Then it's Emrik and me.

"Do I tell you what a bad idea this is," Emrik says, "or do you know?"

"You have a better idea?"

"Uh, yeah, be serious."

"I'm pretty serious."

"No Renter has ever dared to cross this line. You cannot, either."

"I don't care! We have to take care of this. That's how it works!"

"Yes, *we*! *You* don't have to risk your *life*. There must be something else we can do." The scar under his eye seems to shift, a snake riving a stream in two.

I stare at him, unblinking like Baba would if he were here. "Like what? Starve until we die? Did you forget what happened last time?"

Emrik flinches. The flash in his eyes is unmissable. He can't forget what happened eight years ago any more than I can.

Two maristags went mad in captivity.

And when the ocean's stags go mad, no power in the world can control them.

The bigger one, a beast of green-brown, slammed his antlers on his stall door, hard, and the reinforced wood shattered like glass. Frothing at the mouth, with curved incisors that would eventually kill our stable master, he tore at the other door, releasing the second maristag. They fought and lashed and smashed the stable.

They killed the smaller maristags—including their own offspring—and several handlers.

Baba and Emrik were critically wounded. I had broken bones in my legs where the courtyard's fences trapped me, barbed wire spiking me. There was blood everywhere, so much that for months, I hallucinated its smell. The maristags stormed through Sollonia,

42

crushing anyone foolish enough not to take them seriously. They returned to the sea, leaving bodies and blood in their wake, our meager luck trailing behind them.

The treatments, along with fixing the stable and the house, devoured our savings.

For months, we survived on algae and water. You could see the bones on my wrists jutting through skin that turned the color of sour cream. We were in no shape to hunt and offset the loss.

Emrik glares at me. "You're digging graves to make your case now. They won't ever let a Renter in, even if they don't fill up the slots." There's a sting to his words and I'm taken aback. Emrik and I argue constantly, that's not new. This sharpness is.

And it makes the panic in me volatile. My voice rises before I understand what's happening, "If you don't want to help, then don't. Let me do what I want."

Before we start brawling like we did as children, I storm out of the room, a loud ringing in my ears.

I hurtle up the stairs, two steps at a time, the sensation that I'm about to fall whirling inside me.

At the landing, the sudden light overwhelms me, and I trip, flailing for the balustrade.

From here, I can see the edge of the cliff. *Lander boys laughing at me, while I hid underground, bleeding, panic boiling.* My breaths come in hard as I try to shake off the memory. Without Baba's or Emrik's deterrence, the impact of my announcement hits me like a crashing wave.

Why did I say that? I can't participate in Glory Race.

Emrik is right; I can't get in.

Even the thought of trying to enter the tournament as a Renter feels mortifying.

"You don't care about anyone, do you?" Emrik catches up, but doesn't step out onto the porch, half of him blending with the shadows. Probably forgot to put on skaya again. "If there's anyone in this house who should race, it should be me."

He's serious. Amazing.

He genuinely believes he should race instead of me, even though Renters aren't allowed in and despite having a broken arm and a crooked nose that's purpled the half of his face that isn't scarred and tattooed.

"Get inside before a maristag gets you, Emrik."

He yells after me, "You don't care what they'll do to us, do you?"

"Perhaps you can save yourself for once," I call back without turning, tightening my fists to keep my fingers from shaking. Emrik and I were always a target for Lander boys at school and Renter radicals outside. We don't fit neatly in either community, and this will only make things worse.

But I can't stop. Not now.

Emrik or Liria. If I *am* forced to choose a member of my family, it will always be Liria.

The ocean roars to my right. Below the limestone edges, the water is white with froth. Confirmation that the maristags are gone. Sure the aquabats and gorgons and raptors still wait for human prey, but they keep to the water's margins. Usually. Tourists will arrive from all over Ophir tonight, overflowing the inns and hotels.

The Glory Race is more than a tournament after all these years, it's a revered Lander tradition.

And I'm planning to disrupt that tradition.

But I can't give Baba and Emrik the satisfaction of watching me back down.

The bronze board above the gate announces the stable owners:

HUNTERS OF SOLLONIA

Hunters of Sollonia. As if there are any other Hunters. But we're neither allowed to charge beyond a certain sum nor have the luxury to be assured that this profession won't be ripped out of our hands if the Council so chooses. Only our family is legally allowed to hunt and named the Hunters, but there are stables on other islands working for the Council. They don't hunt, but they do raise the adolescent maristags that the Council sends to them from our stable when we reach capacity. And what if they're told to start hunting as well? We can never be too comfortable.

I tread down the empty stalls. This used to be a secluded place. But Baba and Mama, with permission from the Landmaster, revolutionized the sale. For a fee, you can visit and ride the maristags before purchase. When the Landmaster came to inaugurate the new system, she grinned while ruffling my hair and said, "It's for the state, of course. The maristags are such an important part of our tradition, aren't they?"

Now, once more, the stables are too still, too cold. Usually handlers would be running up and down, holding quarterstaff, ready to pull back the maristags who love nothing more than fighting to declare dominance.

A maristag is an extremely defensive creature. Training them requires years, starting with providing them with ample food so they know, at least, they will not starve. They're also moody, intolerant of too much touch, and prefer their own company. You train a maristag when it lets you. It's why the Glory Race takes place only once every four years.

The echo of my footsteps is haunting. I miss the maristags.

They are beautiful, even if their sudden brutality comes with no warning. Before you can even draw breath, their claws sink in you, and before you can turn to see what's coming, they bury their fangs in your throat. That's the strange nature of this world; the viciousness creeps up on you. What the ocean can't do to itself, it unloads onto us, the encroachers. Perhaps that's what happened to Emrik, the way he refuses to see we're hurtling toward our doom. He's grown careless enough to think we'll make it out just *because*.

I can't let that happen to me.

The stables are scrubbed clean. They smell wrong. Sharpness of bleach and chemicals coats the doors. Something coppery.

Brom Warden, a slick-haired Lander boy I know from school, was our last patron. He bought three maristags, unsure of which one he really wanted. We spent a whole week with him awkwardly walking around the stables, muttering to himself and asking me the same questions over and over again before giving up. I wonder what it's like to be spoilt for choice. And I wish he hadn't bought them all; the remaining two male maristags dying wouldn't have left us in such a dire place.

A soft sniffing sound breaks the quiet. Tapping on the stone floor. Then silence again. I shiver.

I tiptoe to the back of the stables. In the stall at the end is the last maristag. She's carved with brutal efficiency, her profile diamond sharp, even the venom frillfin around her, mercifully closed for now, has geometric precision. Her antlers are only two tines, though as majestic as any other maristag's. But put next to the others, you can see the difference: she's a deep, sooty gold like metal shimmering beneath the dark ocean, with only the teal edges of her scales assuring you she *has* any. She was born in captivity, so unlike the sea-born maristags, there's no second tissue layer, but also unlike the land-borns, her birth color never receded behind green as she grew up.

She hadn't sold even when someone needed a last-minute purchase.

Everyone can see she's strong, but this difference stymies them. Even a tiny doubt breeds fear. *She's unlucky*, they say.

A clawed forearm rests against the bars on the door. She's staring at the back gate, at the sliver of sky. It's not simply a look, but a fixation.

The ocean slams against limestone outside. Even if I *do* risk taking her, she's never been out. I can't win the Glory Race with a chariot pulled by an uncertain animal. She could lose her temper. I'd be crushed before the first race started.

My hopes dash before they'd even taken shape.

In the distance, a conch shell echoes across Sollonia. Midday.

The 150th Glory Race Registration officially begins in one hour.

I start to leave as the maristag grunts. In the emptiness, the world cracks open and swallows the entire ocean. She's all there is. She nudges the bars on the stall door keeping her in. Her golden coat gleams with storm-like iridescence, but it's her eyes that lock me in place. Elongated and almond-shaped, the milky membrane concealing the large pupils makes them look empty—ghostly. A free-falling abyss. *Hunger.* Her fangs click together. Sharp enough to rend the world.

She waits.

The abyss starts to terrify me.

And a thousand oceans whisper in my ear: *yes.*

I am the one who raises the foals in this stable and I'd already learned, as a kid, to recognize the strength of a maristag. I've always known how much to push one during a race, which one to bet on, and which of the charioteers would find themselves thrown off their chariot before the final race could start.

I approach her.

I draw her out of the stables. The staff fastened to my belt at my back feels conspicuous. She's strong as any animal we've ever sold and stands tall for me—eighteen hands. But she's still shorter than most maristags.

She's used to me, of course. I raised her myself. I've fed her with my own hands. It's not the same as having trained her for the chariot race, but a fed maristag is more negotiable than one constantly hunted.

It strikes me that we never named her. The maristags were always leaving anyway.

"Hi," I murmur. "Do you have a name?"

The maristag steps back, not alarmingly, but to study me again. I hold my hand out for her tentatively, trying not to break my gaze. On land, maristags breathe through capillaries all over their bodies, and are never short of breath, which means *should* one lose its control and turn violent—you're dead.

The sea calls to them, their blood still green.

And the maristag suddenly senses it, brine clinging to air. She bares her fangs, a growl low in her throat.

I take a step back, but keep talking to her, coaxing her toward my voice. She does trust me, if she didn't, she'd have stabbed me through with her antlers already.

"Helios?" I almost laugh. If I took a maristag named Helios to registration, they'd fine me for interrupting the tournament with an ill-timed joke. "No," I tell her. "Not sun. We're not the sun, are we?"

She raises her head. Such a dark gold, a low brightness that's not the danger of the blazing sun, but a new, rising beauty. The specks of gold-green hidden beneath the black rocks of her scales look like glimmers of hope.

"Stormgold," I say. "Your name is Stormgold of Sollonia."

"She's so pretty."

I gasp.

Framed in darkness by the stable gates, my little sister looks at me with her head tilted, as if her wandering over here is the most natural thing.

I freeze. If Stormgold loses control at this interruption—*no*.

"Liria, don't," I whisper, frantic. "Stop right there."

She pauses, hovering at threshold, uncertain.

I make sure I don't make any sudden movements, and head slowly to my sister. Only when we're back inside the stable, at a considerably safer distance, do I loosen my breath.

Liria looks at me, her eyes dimming. "Are you really going to race?"

"It'd be rude not to, now that I have a maristag."

"What's rude is leaving me alone with our brother." She pouts and bunches up her skirt in her hands. I can't help but laugh. Having Liria in the stables is a sight as odd as the Terrafort being aboveground. "How did Mama even let you out?"

"She didn't."

I stare at my sister.

"Liria!"

"You're being stupid! Emrik has always been stupid! Why can't I be stupid, too?" She starts coughing so hard I forget everything and fall on my knees.

"Are you okay?"

I gather her in my arms, and she clutches at me, wheezing. There's no fighting her. No arguing. I tell her, "If you're worried about me, don't be. I'm strong and if there's a charioteer on this island, it's me."

"I know." Liria pulls back, her face splotchy. "Promise me you won't let the maristag hurt you?"

"I promise. We'll be fine."

She hugs me softly. She smells of her meds. Meds she needs to stay alive. I hold my shudder and tighten my grip around her, focusing on the other smell: seaweed oil that Mama puts in our hair. The smell of home.

I take her to the house through the back door and put her to bed. "You'll win, Koral," my sister says as she closes her eyes. "I know it."

At least one sibling still believes in me.

Blinking back tears, I return to the stables.

I might have backed out before, but not now. Not after Liria's faith.

I test Stormgold on the beach, behind the stables, away from the direct sight of the house. No point in aggravating Baba. We walk, though I sense the maristag itches to run, all the way to the ocean if it were up to her. After her proving that she isn't going to cause me trouble, I mount the maristag.

The ground plunges from behind the antlers. The black ocean thrashes wildly at the edge of the world beside me. My mind clutches tight to the sensation of the scales that dig against my tendons. The brutal wind cuts like sharp threads around my eyes until I'm blinking furiously.

Stormgold fidgets with the hunger of her nature. The spike on her spine in front of me pushes against my midriff. I adjust my seat and urge her to canter. It's a leap of faith based on nothing but a gamble that she trusts me.

And she does.

Stormgold breaks into a lightning rush, like a snake streaking from a predator in deep water. For a wondrous, enchanted moment, I'm in the sky—wings wide, cruising through the air, and the leap of faith has transformed into an expanding hope lit up with the light of a thousand suns. I *can* do this. I *can* win.

Just as swiftly, I snap back to the ground. "Enough," I whisper, leaning away from her antlers. "We're going to be late."

# SIX

The white sun burns, tinting the thoroughfare. But the excitement of the Glory Race burns brighter. Shouts and laughter rip the air with the wild fangs of sea beasts.

Banners hang from buildings—hiding the ruins of the island for now—faces of past Champions sneer at everyone, as if to say, *down there is where you belong, looking up to us.* Today is a grand, full-day festival that bleeds into night.

If it weren't for the gorgons and aquabats threatening to climb up the land, maybe we could have lived during the nights, safe from the heat. But the invisible harm of the sun is far more tolerable than claws tearing flesh.

I tighten my hold on Stormgold's copper-wire lead, a special type of tether that goes around the maristag's body, keeping its frillfin secure. Here, in a crowd, it's especially necessary. Stormgold's getting antsy. Fangs bared, eyes focused.

A holler at my back immediately transforms into fists and kicks. No surprise the tournament fans are already fighting. Unlike the street gangs, which collect bets, there are those who are unpredictably violent. Some rivalries go back thirty years when, upset with a rival charioteer leading, some fans hurled metal cans onto the track and concussed him.

The crowd around the brawl grows and withers, synchronized with the scale of blows. The worse the fight, the more entertaining it is.

A kid runs past me with an inflatable maristag tied to a string and immediately stumbles, yelping when he realizes an actual maristag is next to him. His friends hurtle after him, splatters of color all over them, shouting for everyone to come see the fight, then shouting for everyone to come see the maristag. It isn't my first time having fingers pointed at me. It won't be the last. One of the kids throws a fistful of green powder in the air, and I dodge the cloud, placing a protective hand around Stormgold's muzzle. She snuffles indignantly but walks tall beside me like she's done this her entire life.

Perhaps she's tired of staying locked in the stables.

Not that *that* will matter if she loses control.

Squeezing past the narrow, tarry alleyways of Crane's neighborhood is a task. People stare. Stormgold balks. Even in the shadows of cramped stone buildings, where she has to turn her head sideways to keep her antlers from grazing the walls, she glimmers like silky ink. We get to Crane's back door, which opens into a small yard. Crane is in the kitchen, making a loud messy attempt at celebratory cooking.

She opens the door, dressed in a green-collared shirt and floor-length, pleated skirt. She looks like a Lander woman—except for the streak of paste across her cheek.

"Am I so excited for the Glory Race that I'm hallucinating an entire maristag beside you?"

"I'm going to leave her in the yard, so Baba doesn't get any ideas about letting her go to spite me. And then, I'm going to register for the Glory Race."

Her lips press in a thin line. She says flatly, "Well then, we need to figure out how to actually get you in."

The Drome has four entrances. One for the Landmaster, one for the charioteers, one for the audience, and one leading to an arcade that opens straight onto the tracks. The arcade is where the would-be charioteers assemble before registration.

From hundreds of hopefuls, twenty names are shortlisted a week before, in an anonymized selection. Anyone wanting to withdraw is allowed to and replaced with someone else. From those twenty, ten finalists are selected at random. Unless you're a legacy contender like Dorian Akayan, with a confirmed spot, your entry in the race depends on the official announcement this morning.

There have been attempts at swindling spots, of course, but not many—none successful, anyway—and none from Renters. Plus, the shame of the subversion isn't worth it for Landers. Unless you're crowned Champion, you'd end up shunned from society, always the person who tried to "act like a Renter."

I already am a shunned Renter.

Four Helix Stratis guards—an armed security force for Glory Race—in their blue-maroon uniforms stand at the entrance.

One of the guards notices me. My face is half-hidden behind the scarf of the servers' uniform Crane got me. "Where are you coming from? Everyone else is already inside."

Suddenly I can't speak.

Everyday people make choices that they think have no impact on their lives. But if you look right instead of left, you don't know who you'll meet and who you'll miss. If you take a route away from the thoroughfare, you avoid the capricorn, but it's possible you get swept up in the pincers of an aquabat. Choices can mark a turn in fate that we might never get back.

I have a choice in this moment. I can back out, things will continue as they should, and I won't have to face death in the Drome.

I'll head home and watch the inevitable disintegration of my family. But *that* is not going to happen.

"A contender's father wanted confirmation on the maristag he's taking for the tournament if he's chosen. They have an unruly wrangle."

The guard takes an immediate step back as the others behind him frown in unison, hands going to their stunguns, as if a wrangle of maristags is about to charge at them.

"That one," I say for emphasis, pointing at the first contender I see: Brom Warden in a corner, sulking.

The guards glance at the Lander inside, then back at me. If they decide to call him here to check, that's it. No matter what I say, no matter how I plead, I'll be imprisoned for trying to dupe a Lander. I can't run from here now.

Then, the one in the front nods. "Fine, go in quick."

I hold in my surprise and hurry past them.

The arcade is brimming: frustrated handlers pace, medics murmur to themselves while shaking their heads, and Renter servers—some of them obviously gamblers—snake through the crowd, keeping their ears peeled for tips in favor of or against a charioteer.

Beyond, I can hear people swarming the Drome, regardless of ongoing inspection of fixtures and seating arrangement.

Everything is bellowing out of control, as always.

It's almost a trance, the wild thrum of excitement concealing a jittery underlying current, moving in waves throughout the space.

Just out of my line of sight, I can *feel* at least one of the Helix Stratis tracking my movements. I hurry toward the servers' station at the back. Most of the Renters on duty move through the hall, making sure the Landers are comfortable and everything's running perfectly. Two servers stand back for now, until the announcement begins—or two *would* if the server whom Crane locked in her house were here. Instead, I take her place.

Across from me, at the top of the room, is an ornamental box, guarded by two more Helix Stratis. It is filled with twenty entries, but in a few minutes, ten of them will be randomly removed in front of everyone.

After, the box is sent ahead, and the Landmaster presides over a small ceremony. One by one the names are called, and the charioteers revealed. No one knows how it happened, but over time, a curse has seemingly gripped the tenth name announced. Out of six centuries worth of Glory Race only three charioteers who were picked last have won.

Someone whoops, loud enough even in the commotion of all the charioteers yelling and celebrating, and the Renter servers hurry around for last minute checks.

"Seven minutes before registration starts," the Renter server next to me says. "Are you ready?"

"Seriously?" I whisper. "My hands are shaking."

"Pull yourself together," Crane, disguised under the scarf same as me, orders. "You can't drop the box with your shaking hands."

"Thanks, that's very helpful."

But she's right. I force-stop my emotions from taking over my body. Try to maintain the pace of my breathing. My entire plan hinges on Crane and me delivering the box without hitches, replacing one of the cards inside with my name. We can't let anyone think we're not up to the mark and change the deliverers.

The thing about Landers, though, is that they assume themselves invincible. Put a scarf on Renters' faces and we're more a mass than individuals to them.

I start speaking, telling Crane I'm okay—except her eyes deaden. What did I do wrong? Is someone walking toward us?

She says, voice matching the darkness that's swept over her, "Not everyone's him I suppose. Wish we could specifically take *his* name out."

Oh, no. Is he here already? No, please no—

Dorian Akayan strides inside the double doors. He's dressed in pristine black pants and a shirt with polished cuff links, a suave picture. Everything on his person is chosen for its austerity and intimidation. If marble was carved with the sharpest of blades, he would be the result.

I hope he trips.

I wish I could be in his place.

I want to know, even now, why he was simply gone.

As if he hears my thoughts, he looks right at me. His flaming hair falls in waves around his face. Two years later, he still hasn't learned to push his hair back. I hold myself still, betraying no reaction, and he turns back. Of course he doesn't recognize me like this. But a strange disappointment still flares in my chest.

I wonder if his pride still stings to forever know his charioteering is due to my keeping his secrets; I'm aware of the crack in his facade.

Crane continues to mutter something foul about the assumed Champion. If I hadn't stopped her back then, she would've found him and dragged him down the thoroughfare.

"You know, I would very much like if we *didn't* focus on him," I say.

Crane huffs but shuts up, thankfully.

The water clock dings. And it's time to start removing ten entries from the pile. The servers and handlers weaving through the arcade back up against the walls and instantly, the energy changes. Now everything's business.

First, Dorian steps up, stands separately. He's legacy—already in. A loud cheer rises from everyone assembled, including the Helix Stratis guards. A chant of his name picks up. Even the Renter servers join in. Dorian is the favorite of the entire world apparently.

Crane and I exchange glances.

And soon, the ten random entries are out of the box, leaving ten names in, one marked in gold for Dorian. Crane and I make our way up. Throughout, I feel like someone is watching me. As if Dorian knows who I am beneath the scarf. I glance at him and—

Ugh. He *is* watching me. Tracking me.

He doesn't know—he *can't*.

It's such a simple, silly thing. Picking up a box. I'm not hurting anyone. Yet the entire arcade converges on me. Like everyone saw the exact moment I lifted it. The Helix Stratis is moving toward me. Any minute now—

*Stop.*

I inhale and exhale through my mouth. No one is cornering me. The guards are still where they were.

Slowly I unclench my fingers and adjust them on the handle, counting each breath like Mama taught me.

Crane raises a brow. *Are you okay?*

I nod imperceptibly.

We carry the box outside from a side door, into the Drome. The ceremony takes place at the circular end of the Drome, exactly one hundred steps from the arcade entrance where the Landmaster, her three state helpers, and a Representative from the Race Committee sit at a long table on a temporary podium. It is ready now, and once the box is placed, they'll be joining us mortals in the sun.

Crane takes a step up, moves at an angle from me. It hides me from the workers still on track.

The podium is upon us in mere seconds it seems.

I have no time to hesitate. As we put the box on the table, the envelope curled beneath my sleeve, carrying my name, grazes my skin as I pull it out. Swept up in the celebration, no one notices when one of the entries inside switches with mine.

# SEVEN

The Drome is the grandest building on any of the ten islands. An oblong structure with one end a flat square attached to the Landmaster's Tower and the other a soft circle, it's made entirely of shimmery white marble, each block smoothed to precision, glinting in daylight. The builders must be people gifted with the ability to see the future—how else can you begin something so colossal without knowing its end?

Huge slopes, doubling as seating, go around the racecourse. The upper area where you can watch the entire race without interruptions is reserved for Landers. The lower seating is separated in smaller spaces lest the fans should start fighting. Not like that stops anyone.

The ticket Crane's father sent her was for the topmost end of the lower area.

So much for generosity.

The arcade is emptied of the servers and the box of entries, but the Landers continue to rumble, preparing to walk out of here and present themselves as the charioteers of the 150th Glory Race.

This time, without the server uniform, my presence here has

shaken the scales. I can hear incredulity running through the Landers. Glares and whispers and frowns and confusion. At least no one's laughing. Yet.

Amid the noise and the nervous giggles—a silence uneasily pushes at the walls of my mind. The pretense with which I've carried myself is beginning to falter.

I wish Crane could've stayed.

Now I'm barred with no escape. My name is on one of those entries, even if I back out. Will the Landers abide by their usual show of decorum if they see a Renter name instead of one of their own?

Calls from loudspeakers erupt outside, telling people to clear the racecourse that is laid around a divider called the Spine. The jostle causes what sounds like a small-scale riot, which is pretty daring given that the Landmaster must already be here.

"You're the Hunter?" someone asks.

It's one of the hopefuls.

*Why's he talking to me? Does he know? But how could he? If he had his doubts, he'd have said something before. Right?*

"Yes," I say carefully, resisting the urge to check if the Helix Stratis are still guarding the door.

"I'm Judas Pereira," the boy says. "It's my first time in Sollonia. If time permits, I'd love to see your stables." He has warm eyes and floppy brown hair, his face strangely unassuming for a Lander.

Behind him, a Lander girl is frowning at us. I know her from school. Arlene Bashir. Even with the frown, she has the most striking face I've ever seen: garnet-black eyes, lips my grandmother would call 'like petals,' and arched eyebrows.

"Sure," I stammer.

Before Judas says anything else, the front doors are pulled from outside. Daylight floods the arcade, dampening the lamps and nearly robbing me of vision.

As my eyes adjust to the brightness, my blood begins to pound against my skull.

Even from here I can see the tracks littered with streamers, glitter, and powders—incriminating proof of festivities that have gone on all day. Fifteen minutes ago, my focus was so rapt on the box that I missed everything else.

I've attended registration from the other side with Crane. We'd sit here, munching on opalfruits and candied firberries. One by one the Landers would strut out and make a show of entering the Glory Race.

The first one called is Arlene Bashir. Her name rings out from a loudspeaker placed right over the doors. She strides to a round of scattered applause both here and outside.

I exhale and try to stop shaking.

Then the second Lander steps out. Dressed in all black, as if to defy his name: Isidore Grae.

Third.

Fourth.

"Fifth—" Two Lander boys, in anticipation, take involuntary steps up—and stop. No one calls out either of their names. No one calls *any* name.

I've faced death on land and in sea. I've lost control and made mistakes that might have cost my life. Maristags have hurtled at me with serrated teeth and pointed antlers. But I'm still here. My nerves are my steel. The fear that I have, the anxiety that coils in my mind, is my armor. I should trust in that.

"What if they messed something—" a Lander calls, but her doubts are drowned by the loudspeaker.

"Koral of Sollonia."

Dorian glances my way. Surprise flickers across his face, softening the marble. A reaction so strong, so sudden, after years of pretending we're strangers, it makes blood rush to my cheeks.

Judas stares at me, shocked, but his eyebrows furrow even deeper when another Lander somewhere in the hall shouts, "*What?*" his voice dying midway.

*I'm sorry*, I want to say. *For you people, this is just a game of gold and glory. But for me, it's life or death. My sister's life.*

The Landers don't move as I twist my way around them. Their lips are gummed together. I'm moving amid statues. Every step I take is a disaster waiting to happen—one of the statues might gain life and grab my collar—the Helix Stratis might shoot me in the head.

My heart leaps in my chest.

Breathe in.

Breathe out.

Arlene and the other three charioteers stand rigid beneath the podium, glaring at me with open hatred. Too soon, I take my place at the end of the queue. Hands locked behind me. Chin up, gazing straight at the podium.

Landmaster Aiala Minos surveys me. If my unexpected presence troubles her, she doesn't show it. Her quiet poise is crafted of ice. A pale gray cloth embroidered in silver covers the top of her head. Beneath, crystal-white hair shines and frames a thin face, which resembles translucent paper stretched over blue veins. She's dressed in a traditional sari trimmed with silver and gold so pale it may as well be white. Her staff, topped with a stark red jewel, lies in front of the table.

For a minute nothing happens.

Then the Landmaster waves a hand, and the Race Representative continues calling the names.

As luck would have it, the sixth name is Dorian Akayan.

He steps up beside me. I glance at him involuntarily, closing my fingers over the pulse in the other hand as if that would hide it. He's looking right at me. His eyes are bright hazel in the posters, but right now, they're dark.

I look away quickly.

I can't tell what he's thinking. My insides curl into rotting seagrass.

Dorian has been preparing for this forever.

*I* have helped him prepare to win.

How will I *ever* beat him?

One after the other, all the charioteers line up. As the last ones—Saran Minagi and Judas Pereira—step up, the Representative puts the stacks down on the table. He looks straight at me.

I steel myself for what I know is coming.

"What's this?" one of the Lander state helper calls. "What's your purpose here, Koral Hunter?"

They always say my name with my profession attached, to remind me Renters must be identified by how we've been grouped. By our jobs and the island we are bound to. We don't get distinct family names. That's Lander prerogative. Their names don't need to justify their existence. Ours do.

The Renter state helper removes his glasses and says, "Is this some kind of Hunter business?" He squints at me. "Where's the other one, then? Your brother? Why are you here alone?"

The Landmaster is staring at me with an unblinking gaze.

Somewhere far, the ocean has quieted. A conspicuous silence floods the length of the Drome. No shoes scraping, no children laughing, no men arguing. No one breathing.

"I am here alone, Councilor, for the Glory Race. As I understand, there are no teams in the tournament for my brother to join me."

One of the charioteers swears in amazement at my audacity.

The Landmaster is still serenely watching me, but confusion breaks out among the four men. They huddle together, shooting me glares as if to make sure I don't get complacent.

I feel exposed. If I move, I know I'd sink into the ground beneath me.

Nobody says anything for a while. The wind picks up, singing cruelly. I want to leave. To simply disappear. I've never felt so out of my depth. They're staring at me like I'm the first maristag to step out of the ocean, like I'm heralding the violence of this world.

"You're a Renter," the Lander state helper says, blinking rapidly at me. Almost a question.

"I am."

There's a ruffling at the table, murmurs and frowns. "This is unprecedented," the Renter state helper adds. His voice is uncertain, but it's a strange kind of uncertainty. He's not sure if he wants to be uncertain.

"Yes," adds the other Lander helper. "The Quadrennial Glory Race is a historical tradition. You went to our school, didn't you?" he addresses me directly. "And you're an expert Hunter. That's what you're meant to do. It's an honor in itself. Why do you ask for more?"

The Renter state helper's white, scarred face turns a frosty shade of red. The words must hit too close: Even being on the Council doesn't change our true place in the world. He glances back at me— not with warmth, but definitely not with the acrid annoyance of before. "You know how to ride?"

"I raise maristags by my own hand," I say. "If there's anyone on this island who can race one, it's me." I immediately regret my tone, but someone chuckles. It sends ants crawling in my blood.

"The true spirit of the Glory Race is the will to fight," the Landmaster says.

Somehow, her taking my side makes me shrivel.

"Rules are rules," she continues. "Representative, what do the rules say about registration?"

The Race Rep straightens on being addressed. He must not usually be involved in the proceedings. Everyone over the age of seven who has had any primary education knows the rules of the Glory Race by heart. "Registration will remain open until ten entry cards find their way back to the Race Committee, or the last ray of sun on the day, whichever comes earlier."

"Indeed."

The rules are rusty, but they exist, and for the first time, they are in my favor.

"A three-race tournament spread over a few days. Ten charioteers. Age limit sixteen to twenty," I recite. They look at me, surprised I'm speaking over them. I press on, "Nowhere does it say non-Landers *can't* participate. The first Glory Race didn't even have written rules."

The first Glory Race, after all, was never meant to be glorious.

Voyagers from the Sanctuary—our Empyrean Elders—established civilization here so long ago that the past is a fragmented myth, the truth of it lost to the sea.

But we know that the Empyrean Elders were giants of their time. They fled from their corrupted home territory and arrived on our islands with hope for a better future. They saw great wars for the control of resources, but also established the best gift for our choking world: advanced medicine. And after that came years of a world renaissance in which one group of descendants consolidated the knowledge. They became Landers, calling first rights on the safety of the caves in the lone mountain that later became the Terrafort.

They carved places to live underground, discovered ways to thrive, built more sea ships even though travel over water is dangerous. It was a time of artists and architects and engineers—legends of a golden age that has never returned since.

They also assigned roles to everyone else: the Renters.

A Landmaster was appointed for each of the ten livable islands, to keep the peace. The prisoners of wars and criminals of society were thrown into a fight with maristags, as a reminder of the brutality of this world and what happens when you can't match its power. One prisoner survived. He tamed a maristag and rode it—his long, silvering hair flying behind him. The First Champion, he was called later. His courage earned him a pardon.

And in his honor the Glory Race was started.

After that first punitive race, taming a maristag meant taming this world.

Only the last parts of this story get told, scrubbed clean of ideas like wars and fighting. But it's not easy to hide the truth from Hunters who are descended from the First Champion, who was a gifted maristag whisperer and who ended up being forced to guard fishermen and hunt maristags.

The Landers know how to twist even victories into defeats.

The Renter helper puts his glasses back on. They slide down his nose, and he pushes them back up with a frown. "The public will not support her. It could be dangerous."

"The rules are clear," drawls the Landmaster. "Presumably, the public is not who decides the rules that drive the tournament."

"Of course not, Landmaster Minos," the Representative mumbles in my favor.

"Then let the girl be," the Landmaster says. "Her name was announced. What is the point of drawing this out more than necessary?"

And like that, I'm officially a charioteer in the Glory Race.

# EIGHT

don't wait a second after the officials descend the podium. I bolt. The way Arlene and Saran and a couple others were glaring at me, I don't think what just happened amuses them the way it does Landmaster Minos.

I've almost crossed the arcade and am headed for the safety of the outside when hurried footsteps make me half-turn. Before I can see anything, I'm shoved against the gate of the arcade. A sharp pain bursts in my back. There are no Helix Stratis guards anymore. Not that they'd be much help.

"How dare you?" Brom Warden shouts. His eyes are wide, the corners of his mouth trembling. "You took my place! My father will never forgive me!"

I almost laugh at the sense of his own value. "How did I take *your* place? The names are chosen at random."

Across the arcade, I see silhouettes gather. Breaths drawn. Not for fear of what might happen, but for the sheer entertainment of this.

But the others' presence brings Brom back to himself. A second is

all it takes for me to shove him back. "Don't think yourself so important, you circus clown."

I don't look back as I stride into the closed alley leading from the
arcade to the street outside. Before I can exit, I hear Brom's baffling,
personal rage: "You'll regret this."

Crane and I sneak inside my house. Best not to cross paths with Baba
until the Opening Ceremony tonight. Then he'll, of course, be mor-
tified and probably disown me. But at least he won't be able to stop
me from participating in the tournament.

In the darkness of my room, I hurriedly pull my clothes out from
my shelf—a long niche cut into the wall. I have to extend my hand
to grab the farthest clothes.

I cannot wear my regular clothes to the Opening Ceremony.
Landers dress in their fineries—even the spectators—let alone the
actual charioteers. I don't think I have anything that matches even
half of their grandiose clothes.

"You can borrow one of my better dresses," Crane whispers. "We
have to get a chariot, too."

"We have to get a *what?*"

I drop the leather shoes I'm holding. They thud against the cold
floor.

Emrik is standing at the door, a candle in hand. His arm is in a
sling and his scar looks raw, almost new, in the warm light.

"What an unexpected surprise, running into you here," Crane says.

Emrik glares at her. "I don't see how, seeing as you're inside *my*
house."

Crane raises her hands in a gesture of surrender and as Emrik is
turning away from her, sticks out her tongue at him. He ignores her
and surveys the clothes spread everywhere on the ground. "Koral,"

my brother says, trying to hold in the wince, "did you really enter the Glory Race?"

What's the point in denying it? His anger seems to have deflated in my absence. And even if he *was* still angry, the deed is done.

"I'm not going to withdraw now," I tell him.

He glances behind him, as if to call someone. Baba, probably. Instead, Liria coughs, the closed tunnels of the house carrying the sound to us.

Crane's shoulders drop.

"What about a maristag?" Emrik asks.

"I took her. The gold one."

"You've got to be kidding me, Koral," Emrik says. "That maristag is unruly. You're going to be killed."

"She's *not* unruly," I say. "She was sick of being locked in."

"Where is she now?"

"Crane's yard. There's plenty of space and no one will bother her. She's had no training, she needs free air. And she's far more docile than you think."

Emrik makes an incredulous noise. For a moment, my brother and I just stand there, watching one another. If I were him, maybe I'd think I've gone mad, too. Letting a maristag out. Calling it docile. Entering the Glory Race. But I know what I'm doing. My instincts have saved me countless times in the ocean, why should I not trust them on land?

"If you want to help," Crane says, intervening, "now would be a great time."

"Help? Why?" he says, dangerously close to the same annoyed tone he carried when I left the house.

"So when I make a fatal mistake, you get to say 'I told you so,'" I snark at him.

"It's going to happen and it's entirely avoidable!" Then, cringing, he shuts the door softly behind him. The three of us stand in the tomb-like room, the flicker of the candle the only light.

Emrik frowns. "And what is this? Are we going to a funeral?" He gestures around at the mess, his hands dark with years of scars. Of course he'd try to make a joke. If I were to walk in dressed as a Renter, it wouldn't be like at school, where the teasing and the attacks were confined to corners. This time, everyone will see. My brother looks at me strangely, as if he knows this isn't about clothes. I'm not ready for that kind of scrutiny.

"Please do this, Emrik," I say. "Help me."

He exhales. "Where will we find a chariot in so short a time?"

Crane says, "Do you know what Bitterbloom has?"

"What? We're not taking it." Emrik and I say simultaneously.

We look at each other.

He says, "Probably get someone in on the grand plan if you want them to help."

"The First Champion's chariot," Crane barrels on. "Can you imagine the shock on those Landers' faces when Koral is on that silver chariot?"

"That chariot has been missing for a decade," I hiss. "And you think I'm going to take that out to a race where everyone's already churning the sea that I'm even participating?" Arlene and Saran's glare burns at the back of my mind.

Crane seems put off by that. Emrik says to her, "That's the most foolish thing I've ever heard, even from you."

"Then where are we going to get a chariot?" Crane asks.

My brother is still frowning, the line between his brows as permanent as the funny little bald patch behind his head, which he hides by clipping his long hair. He's torn, I can see that. Still somewhat angry, but he won't abandon me now. He's thinking. His eyes have grown narrow, as do mine. As much as we might argue, we're very much

70

alike. It's probably why Emrik hates, and is still upset about, my having gotten the idea to enter the tournament first. He's compensating by trying to call me a fool now when he *wishes* he'd be the one racing.

Then, Emrik says, "I'll arrange for the chariot."

With that, my brother steps out and the gust from the door snuffs out the candle, a trail of smoke snaking in the sudden darkness.

The Opening Ceremony takes place in the Drome. This time, we converge at the Charioteer Hall, on the ground floor of the Landmaster's Tower. The thumping music outside makes its muffled way through. Unlike the arcade, this place is bare but large enough to accommodate all charioteers and their maristags. The ten posts that lead straight onto the tracks are across the hall. For now, the starting gates are closed.

I've attended three Opening Ceremonies in my life. The focus of this whole glitzy event is the music and fireworks. The charioteers are out for barely a few minutes, but we are introduced with an element that comes back in one of the races. Last time, the charioteers dragged behind them a trail of tar to make elaborate designs, and in the first race, they were racing against not just one another but fawkeses setting the tracks on fire.

Landers, and their lack of self-preservation, can be lethal.

The Drome's handlers have readied all ten maristags, fitted them with standard-issue copper leads and placed them at the gates. The shining green scales of the other maristags glimmer, mixed with various reds, blues, and purples. None have the curious color of Stormgold, with dark gold encased in the silky teal edges of her scales. She glimmers like a jewel in front of the door marked fifth. Behind her, the copper chariot that Emrik found looks painted with soupy mud. The effect gets even worse when I see Dorian's maristag standing beside her, attached to a gilded chariot—a huge, iridescent silver-green maristag I recognize immediately, though he was taken from the stables five years ago.

It was a year before the last Glory Race. Memories of having starved were too fresh, and I was desperate to sell every single maristag. We needed to—that was the year we got caught in the vicious cycle of never-ending debt.

Guilt and grief consumed Mama. Liria's condition had begun to worsen. She was so small, her hands even tinier than a regular baby's, and her eyes two huge gray pearls. When she smiled, it was like the glimmer of a new star. I didn't want anything to hurt her even then, before I understood her illness.

We scraped by for two years, and I didn't know what we'd do if we suffered another empty year, so Emrik and I did our best to pretend that our stables were unrivaled. One of us was always at the stables—giving no Lander a chance to turn their backs. We learned to manipulate and charm, letting Lander kids take rides on the most volatile of maristags, crossing fingers nothing went wrong.

That day, Lander boys were racing recklessly on the beach. But they'd paid and we still had six maristags to sell.

I kept an eye on the brats from the back gate, chewing the same mint for hours, and hoped one of them actually purchased a maristag. Constant money was good, but a sale boosted our credit in the Landmaster's record office.

The front gate banged open, and a Lander blazed into the stables, trailed by a boy. The man was blood-dark in the face as he started shrieking. I shifted in the shadows instinctively the second I recognized him. Solomon Akayan. The way the boy behind him bowed his head and hunched his shoulders, I knew it must be his son, Dorian. There had been a small festival going on near our house. They seemed to have come from there.

"You embarrassed me!" Solomon shouted. He stood large above his son, his shadow sweeping over the entire stable like a giant's. His brown hair, slicked back, was crackling with anger. "Is this what you do with your time? Mix with scum? Is this how you will win the Glory Race?"

Dorian was only two years older than me. He was curled into himself. Protecting his body, expecting physical violence. Fear welled in me for the Lander boy.

"This world is nothing but our name!" Solomon grabbed Dorian's collar. My stomach hurt. "Will you ever give them a chance to raise questions about our family?"

Dorian answered mechanically, "No, Father."

"If I ever find you playing that thing in these wretched gatherings instead of preparing for the tournament," he dragged Dorian closer, "I will throw a real party in your honor."

The drop in his tone forced me to stay in the shadows, hoping I never had to talk to that man in my life.

"A party where everyone will be present. You will play for them. And there will be poison. And there will be an accident."

"Yes, Father."

"Do not come back until you can tell me you will win the Glory Race!"

Solomon stormed off. I was still holding my breath, unsure of what to do. Back then, the thought of my father threatening me was incomprehensible.

Dorian fell to all fours.

He cried.

I wanted to help him so much.

His entire body trembled like a feverish fawn as he sobbed. He took out a musical instrument from his jacket and slammed it against the door of an empty stall. He stayed there for several minutes, still crying.

Then, he got up and opened the door of a stall and coaxed out a young, intelligent-eyed maristag. His coat was a darker gray then, with the silver-green tinge of his scales shining through, gleaming bright against his shocking white antlers. Most people are frightened of maristags tearing at them, slashing them—and they should be. Even when born on land, maristags inherit an acute hatred for humans from their ocean parents.

A wild maristag can be trained, but the chances of it killing you are much, much higher, which is why part of our job is to release the wild ones back and train ones bred in captivity to not go berserk at the sight of humans. Dorian, obviously, had been taught enough.

It took me a minute to understand what was happening. An illustrious Lander heir, who was frightened of his father, wanted to get back in his good graces. He was going to an extreme length to do so by stealing a maristag. Probably to teach himself riding in secret and surprise his father.

I made my way into the stable, ready to start yelling.

Dorian immediately pulled himself together and locked his hands behind his back. He pretended to be admiring the maristag.

Up close, I noticed the ashy remnants of tears under his puffed eyes.

Instead of taking the silver maristag back inside the stall, I held out the reins. "It's the strongest maristag in this batch. When you're ready for it, you'll win the race. And then maybe things will be better..."

Dorian must have understood that I'd seen everything. If that shamed him, I couldn't tell, but he took the lead. The maristag followed him calmly. It was fascinating. At the gates, Dorian looked back. I thought he'd say something, but he closed his eyes, inhaled deeply, and left.

But he came back. Again and again.

Until the day he didn't.

It was my foolish, *childish* fault to let him take that maristag without recompense. I don't know what I was thinking—I didn't want to see him cry, so frightened and alone.

And that moment of sympathy cost me everything. It is costing me now.

Because now, I'm readying to race against him, but this is what he's been building toward since he broke his violin.

I have to win. It's the only shot I have at saving Liria, at saving my family. Even if that destroys him.

I force my jelly legs to move. In the din of the hall, my steps make no sound against the stone as I cut through the predator-like crowd spread out everywhere. Around me, leather jackets and tulle dresses studded with glass beads and stones and silver chains abound. Even the Landers' clothes are loud, clinking and clattering. I recognize Judas's floppy brown hair. He's dressed somewhat neutrally, a black frock coat with floral silks over leather pants. No cantankerous noises from his clothes. But ocean knows how much that one coat cost.

The Landers are truly delighted to be here, they were meant to be here. Like Dorian Akayan, they've trained for this.

Arlene blocks my path. Her brown skin is highlighted blue and gold like a glittering dance ball. Her clothes hidden beneath dangling silver sequins. She gives me a once-over.

Crane ultimately told me to dress in the way I found most comfortable: like I'm readying for a hunt. Black pants, white shirt. She added two fake gold accessories, to match my maristag—a belt and corsages around both wrists.

"You can't hide who you are," Arlene says, her voice abrasive.

I swallow hard. It takes me an eternity to answer her. "And

what's that? A Renter about to expose the mediocrity of Lander charioteers?" Without waiting for an answer, I stride away.

"Hi," I whisper, tentatively reaching for Stormgold. She snaps her jaw and lashes her tailfin. I stop dead. But then she leans sideways and dips her antlers away from me. This was sport, not a threat. I know to be cautious around maristags, but will I ever drop my guard enough to look at her the way she's looking at me?

With trust in her eyes.

I freeze.

What am I doing? She isn't trained, she doesn't know what to expect on the tracks.

Pulling a chariot is nothing for any green-blooded maristag. Stormgold can be a terror if she wants, but risking her out in front of the monstrous stags who've been training for years?

They tower over her.

As if she reads my mind, Stormgold lifts her head and snorts. The curved reddish fangs inside her gaping maw are bared for a second.

Thorns prick at my spine. I tighten my hold on Stormgold's lead. She tosses her head and closes her mouth. My heart takes a whole minute to slow down. One glance around, and I know she's not the only one who's antsy.

*It's safer than in the sea.*

The celebrations outside are loud, drums going strong, but the nervous energy crackling beneath the charioteers' forced laughter and conversation is louder. They are aware of my presence but ignore me. That alone says more than words.

I don't blame Judas Pereira for ignoring me. He cuts my path, starts to apologize, then sees who I am and frowns.

Only at school have I felt this misplaced. Like a set of gleaming antlers, but on the head of fish. At least there, I was given instructions and told what to do and where not to go. How do I control this unsettling crawling of tiny insects in my veins? What happens if I do or say or touch the wrong thing here?

The dread of failure looms in my mind but I push it away. I can't face my father again unless I've won, and I can't *afford* to not win.

I wonder what's going on at home, if Baba has calmed down.

Emrik is already in the stands. There was no point for him to go home after bringing me the chariot. But that means he can't help Mama bring Liria here. I hope Crane does.

The thought of my family solidifies the ground beneath my feet.

And it's at that moment Dorian strides in.

He's dressed in a white shirt and black pants.

But he's a king. His version of the same clothes that I wear is a rich ceremonial outfit: the pleats of his shirt embroidered in what looks like actual silver. His boots are shinier than a full moon on a clear night.

He doesn't greet anyone and heads straight to his chariot. His hair is woven around a crown of silver leaves—his family's insignia. Akayans are drowning in enough metal to buy the entire island if they chose.

Everyone's climbing onto their chariots. If the race was tonight, there's no question about it: I'd die. I'm used to the maristags; I have strength, but I'll need every waking moment of the next two days to prepare my body for the chariot.

As I climb, the chariot wobbles under me and, not for the first time, I recognize what a foolhardy thing this is. I squeeze my eyes shut. Remember why I'm here. If I win—I'll take Liria and Mama out from under Baba's control. Liria will receive the medical attention she needs.

The handlers check the straps on every chariot before stepping out of the way.

What's the introduction going to be this time? I can only

77

thank the ocean we haven't been set on fire. I do *not* want to race fawkeses.

The massive gates swing open, and in addition to the music and conch shell signal of commencement blasting in, a great roar of water rushes into the stone hall.

# NINE

There's a waterfall in front of each post.

Stormgold bucks, tossing her head so violently that I cringe and pull back. A maristag shrieks, another follows. *No, no, no.* I tighten the lead, pull Stormgold ever so slightly so as to not give her another shock. She snorts and shudders.

Dorian's maristag is stomping. So close, if he loses control, he'll take down Stormgold and me too. But Dorian, unperturbed, levels the maristag with the lead and makes him focus on his voice. Immediately, the maristag turns grim and focused. Where did Dorian learn all this? There's surety to his every movement—the lean toward his maristag, the twitch of his mouth as he murmurs soothingly.

It's a deeply intimate moment.

*Why am I staring?* I turn away from him.

Fortunately, the unpleasant surprise of the water fades. The maristags are rejuvenated by the scent of wet sand that suffuses the hall.

Beyond the waterfalls, the music of the ceremony and the

crowds gradually fall silent. The Landmaster must have stepped out in her balcony box high above the Drome. I can imagine her, serene and tall, shining like sparkling waves of silver water and everyone on the stands turned to her like the Ship of Fire constellation chasing after the moon. Whatever else she is, Landmaster Minos has an authority that seems to emanate from the very essence of the waters.

"People of Ophir, today we celebrate the power of the Heirs of Empyrean!"

An explosion of fireworks reverberates, distorted colors shimmering beyond the rushing waterfall. The crowd erupts—whoops and cheers thud against the ground.

"For centuries, the Glory Race has brought us all together in peace and prosperity, to celebrate our lives and the bonds we have forged on our islands. For one winner, this is a chance to bring glory to humanity and prove our resilience in the face of extraordinary odds!"

Another round of flowerpot sparklers and cheers follow. The drums outside beat louder. Passing through the water, it all takes on a surreal quality, like I'm in a half-awake dream.

"The rules of the Glory Race are simple. The three race events are a display of skill and prowess. Each event will see the charioteer who crosses the finish line last eliminated.

"As is tradition, the Opening Ceremony will give to you a taste of what is to come. Each charioteer, upon being called, will cross through the waterfalls you can now see at each of the posts. How many of you know that maristags can react strongly to a change in the elements? Not many, I wager." The Landmaster laughs. It's a soft laugh, but it pulls at my teeth like fishhooks. Ignorance of creatures we share this world with only seems funny to Landers. "When each charioteer brings out their maristag, they will show us how in control they are of the beast. You see these balloons lining the roof? When the maristag crosses the water and reacts by shooting out barbs in defense, the charioteers will have a split second's time to aim those barbs right at the balloons."

I stare at the waterfall, for a moment hoping the words that passed through the water were garbled to the point that I misheard them. But when everyone else merely grabs their leads stronger, I blurt, "Is she serious? We have to burst balloons with maristag barbs?"

From the far end, Arlene answers, "You're still here? Thought you'd have stolen something and run home by now."

There's a smattering of laughter.

Icy pricks stab at the sides of my body, memories of school flaring in my mind. "I hope *you're* still here when I steal the Champion's crown."

This time, the silence is heavy with something that's decidedly not laughter.

To my right, Dorian's head tilts slightly in my direction. At first, I brace for his laughter to join the others. He's long proven he's just like the others. But when I look up, he's staring at my maristag.

Without my noticing, my hands have clenched up the lead. Pulling Stormgold back so her jaw strains, ready to attack an invisible force. I relax my hold.

From outside, we hear the Landmaster, "And now, presenting the ten charioteers of the 150th Glory Race. First, Arlene Bashir."

The bar in front of Arlene swings up. Music blasts through the gap and Arlene pulls at the reins of her maristag. She hurtles forward through the waterfall. Her maristag shrieks before being swallowed by the rush.

The delighted roars of the crowd wave through the Drome.

One after the other, the bars lift, and the charioteers leave their posts. My worn chariot wobbles beneath my feet. What if it shatters against the force of the water? What if Stormgold gets loose? They'll have her shot.

Drums boom inside my mouth, my head, my blood, and my bones. They echo in my soul. Rising and rising.

I don't know what to do.

Then the bar before me gives way, and my sense of dread swells a thousand times stronger than it's ever been in the open ocean. Stormgold pulls the chariot, and then breaks into a run. Cold sprays of water sting my face. I blink and brace myself for impact.

The water rushes at us, devastatingly fast and strong. It blocks out every other sound. The chariot vibrates. I shout, afraid. There's a great roar. Stormgold cries. I slam against the stinging water as it drenches me.

For an infinite moment, I'm suspended in that screaming water; the maristag, the Drome, the spectators are all one, while I'm the *other*, alone.

Before I can gasp and steady my hands, Stormgold's frillfin slams open. The chariot is still intact. Overhead lights flood the Drome with a brilliant, honey-tipped glow. I can't see the crowds. But there—right above me, giant black and white balloons tied with silver strings block the entire roof. I pull, tipping Stormgold's head back a few degrees.

The poison barbs launch.

And every single one of them pierces the balloons on either side of us.

They burst in a shower of golden confetti. Screams and applause ring in my ears.

A swirl of fireworks shoots across the Drome's cover and explodes in every color possible. Every few stands, spiraling, colorful powder bombs follow suit, and banners wave behind the crowds.

And still the music pulls and pushes, the world rebirthed in this moment.

I direct Stormgold toward the other charioteers.

One after the other, the remaining charioteers rush out of the posts to an explosion of water and confetti and fireworks. My heart hammers against my ribs. The charioteers glimmer alongside the golden shower, burning bright. I look down, and see how misplaced I am in front of the world, dressed in old clothes I've had for years. Drenched as they are now, the difference is even more obvious: all the charioteers are dressed in fabrics that repel water. My clothes stick to my skin.

Were the others informed of this display?

Was I the only one walking into the Drome ignorant?

Heavy pressure pushes at my ribs. So this is how the Landers think they'll show me my place. Too bad the ocean is my home. Water doesn't frighten me, and the clothes I'm wearing won't matter if the crown of the Champion is on my head.

I force the doubts back and remind myself to beam for the spectators.

So it's a whiplash to find Dorian staring at me, his jaw tightened. Then, he speaks to me for the first time in two years, "You shouldn't be here."

Rage roars in my veins. After everything, a drop of hope still remained. That there was an explanation about why he left. But here he is. Arrogant and every bit the Lander he was born to be. I don't falter—cameras are still trained on our faces, broadcasting every detail across the Islands of Ophir. "But I am."

His voice is the touch of a venomous serpent. "I'm going to win, Koral, even if I die doing it."

I know he will do anything to win.

I hold up my chin, ignoring the cold shiver running down my spine. If he thinks he can intimidate me, he's wrong.

Water drips down my face. I'm colder than a chip of ice. But I toss him a dazzling smile. "I'd love to see you try."

# TEN

I nside the Charioteer Hall, laughter bubbles bright, excitement and nerves clamoring in ribbons of colors. I watch it all unfold from the shadowed sides. Uninvited.

No matter. I'm not here to join their parties.

As soon as the Opening Ceremony closes, the doors are pulled open from the outside.

The rest of the charioteers have a straight way out, an underground tunnel that connects to the Terrafort. I wait for Emrik, so he can help me detach the chariot. Leaving with Stormgold still dragging the chariot is pointless. The crowds jostle too much. Not worth the risk of setting off Stormgold accidentally, especially not on a night when the sea is thrashing against stone. I wouldn't be surprised if at least one siren across the island blares a warning—or when they find the bodies in the morning, after the beasts have finished devouring.

The euphoria of the Opening Ceremony is wearing off, leaving me bone tired. The entire island seems to be drowning in chaos. Fireworks still going off. A faint chorus rising. Perhaps it's my muddled brain, pulled down by the ache in my limbs, but I can't figure out what the raucous chant says.

The second Emrik enters the Charioteer Hall is when Dorian is on his way out. They come face to face. My brother watches him coolly, then moves first.

His expression softens when he sees me, but he throws tense glances around, the fist of his slung arm clutched tight against his chest.

"It's happening," he says. Another cautious look around. The Hall is empty save a few handlers wrapping things up. At our backs, the waterfalls continue to roar, masking most sounds. "People thought your name on the list was a rumor. A joke. Now they know it isn't."

"And?"

"The Landers are running amok outside," Emrik says. "They're starting a riot at the Drome's gate."

"What for?"

"For *you*," Emrik says. "Because you were in the Drome tonight. And what you did right now—"

"What did I do?"

Emrik's eyebrows furrow. The bright light of the Drome, filtered through the water, reflects on his face. It almost looks like we're under the ocean.

"You were the only one who got all six darts to pierce the balloons. Not even Dorian got all six."

I startle. Not even Dorian? I must have misheard Emrik.

"Shut your mouth." He scowls. "You look like a fish."

"You look like a clown."

"And you look like a—"

"Shut up, Emrik. We have more important things to deal with. Like *riots*." I glance toward the gates. "How will we get home? And

what about Mama and Liria?" I know better than to hope Baba
came at all.

"Crane found us shortly after your display. She knew it was
bound to happen, so she moved quickly to get them out. We'll take
the back alleys home."

The ground beneath us rumbles.

"You take the chariot. I can't have Stormgold freak out in an alley
and break it before the Glory Race even begins."

"You're still going to continue?" he says, shocked. "Was I somehow unclear when I said *riots*? We have to go home and hide until all
this blows over."

"If you think anyone can squash me under their boots like a snail,"
I say coldly, "you're wrong."

My brother sighs and begins detaching the chariot.

Emrik wheels the chariot into an alley, and I bring Stormgold at a
distance, the dark shielding us for the moment.

I pick off golden confetti from my cheek. The Opening Ceremony
feels light-years away.

We can see it now. Immediately outside the Drome, a furor has
broken out. Screams and the rush of people. Flares light up the
night. I think of the fireworks and sparklers, bright and joyous,
across the Drome. But I know this is not the light of fireworks. It's
the flash of an angry mob carrying fire. My grip on Stormgold is
strong, probably *too* strong, and it's her directing me rather than the
other way around.

"No fried shrimp or salted scales today," I murmur. Emrik makes
a face.

Usually after public events, we would hang around the rows of
snack shops on the thoroughfare. That's where most of the crowd

collects. Under normal circumstances, it's the safest place at night, and two capricorns ensure it stays that way.

Now, we slink into the back alleys through Renter neighborhoods.

"That pull at the last moment that drove Stormgold's barbs sideways—it was really great," Emrik says.

My grin cuts itself off as the reality hits me.

The jeers and the awful sound of the mob begin ebbing in this part of town as we cross several empty streets, feeling safer, until Emrik stops at the start of another corner. At the other side, a rowdy crowd streams past. I press back, as gently as I can to not startle the maristag. We backtrack quietly and keep moving until there's at least half the island between us and the Drome. Even from here, the top of the stadium rises majestic, lit with thousands of brilliant points of light. I wonder if one can spot it from the next island. Tonight, I think they can.

As the pathways begin giving way to the rocks of the island, the ratty drag of the chariot rumbles over the noise. It's too inviting.

"Emrik—"

"I'm not leaving you."

Stormgold clicks her fangs sharply at his voice, knocking at the stone walls of the alley with her head.

"Stop it," I whisper, fear commanding steel into my voice. "I know it's not ideal, but it's better than being burned alive." A shiver runs through me as the words leave me and I look at my brother. How bad is this riot? In my living memory, I can't recall Landers ever stepping out of ground to *protest*.

It must be worse than it sounds, half-smothered by the roar of the ocean pummeling the island from all sides tonight. The chilly night is deep and dark, the awful haze of protests the only light.

An uncertain wind susurrates through the bone-like alleys. All around, the great rush of voices, panicked and demanding. What if our house is surrounded? Would they demand my surrender?

It's just a tournament.

Stormgold squeals suddenly, her frillfin struggling to open against the lead around her neck. I immediately step back. In the dark, against the hellish stone walls, she looks like a shadow come to life.

Emrik grabs my hand. His is cold.

To my right, a hiss fills the air, streaking closer and closer. The squat houses are ink black, solid and frozen. I hope they're empty inside. Because a cloud of smoke is rising high. A spurt of orange leaps into the air, then the fire is sizzling through the alley we left behind.

Maybe I started a war.

"Come on." I pull the lead, but Stormgold balks. Her frillfin still pushes against the lead, the muscles beneath her manefin rippling. She's adamant, not moving forward, and we're left struggling in the night as the fire gets closer.

"We have to go now," Emrik says. "Get her under control."

But she plants her legs and lashes her tailfin. The fire is red in her eyes.

"You continue ahead. I'll bring her. Don't argue," I say, as he opens his mouth to protest. "Neither of us will get home if we keep stopping like this."

Emrik swears and drags the chariot over the uneven ground. He turns the corner and disappears. I can hear the chariot as I try to pull Stormgold forward.

I wonder who else can hear it, and who might come looking for it. The noise of a chariot is pretty recognizable. Isn't it? Right now, people would know who might be moving secretly in the dark.

If Emrik gets hurt because of me, again—I can't even think the thought through.

There's a clap of thunder. A shriek. A thud against the wall and a stone hitting flesh.

A crowd is screaming. Chanting.

*No Glory to Renters. No Glory to Renters. No Glory to Renters.*

Fury bubbles in me. The fire dances at the corner of my vision. I stand in front of Stormgold. "Move!"

This time, she listens.

We hurry down an intersection of streets without incident, even with Stormgold huffing, and then slip into an alley similar to the ones at Opal Den. Cracked ground. Exposed plumbing that suffuses the stench of sewer lines through the air. I try not to retch. Reptiles cling to every shadow beneath the odd windows that are taped tight but still spill a ray of candlelight.

I turn a corner.

The way is blocked by three Lander boys. They have Emrik.

*The maristag. Emrik's blood spilling into the water, his skin turning gray with venom.*

My body isn't enough for the ferocious mix of fear and fury burning in me. I strike hard at the closest Lander, sending him to the ground. A horrible warmth emerges along my knuckles. There's a familiar squeal behind me, but I ignore it for the moment. To my right, another sound cuts. A second's distraction. Someone grabs my arms. My shout drowns behind Emrik's "No!" and a short blast nearby.

At first, I think it's a gunshot, and the world tunnels to nothing, raw fear climbing up my throat. Then pain explodes in my shoulder. A punch so hard it nearly dislocates my arm. I curse and buckle down, limbs shaking with pain, with the *effort* of balancing my body. My palms hit the ground. Someone's fingers—and *nails*—dig into my skin. Then, before I can push myself up, I'm dragged across the jagged rocks, and another assailant is struggling with Emrik.

My brother and I lock eyes. Simultaneously, we wrench ourselves forward. The sudden, unexpected burst of strength catches the Lander boys by surprise. I press down my shoulder and stumble up, the muscles in my legs twisting brutally as I try to balance against the wall. *I've fought maristags, these are only humans.* I forget the pain, and I push it down as I steel myself up.

Emrik and I are shoulder to shoulder, facing the three Lander boys.

We're alone here. I'm not at my best, and Emrik is hurt. That's the only reason we were *almost* bested.

Emrik's cast is turning red. I swear. "You're bleeding."

"Far better than what will happen to you," one of the boys rasps.

I hate the way these boys look at me. Not only because of what one of them has said. But because they *truly* believe it. This boy thinks he's invincible and I'm weak. That's my supposed place in the world. Isn't that why I must beg for medicine for my sister? Isn't that why I must risk my life and my brother's in the waters every year?

So we can have a home. So we can eat.

But this dark, in this moment, is the world as I've known it.

I step in front of my brother, ignoring him when he tries to grasp my arm and pull me back. This time, the squeal cuts the air sharper. Closer.

"What's that?" Emrik is the one who asks. Makes sense. He's the one who will have recognized the sound.

A growl behind the Lander boys, in the direction I arrived from.

"Koral," Emrik sounds fearful now. "Where's your maristag?"

The Lander boys go silent at his tone. One of them takes a step back and trips over the contraption I'd pulled open before joining the fray.

I grin. "You were saying?"

91

It's at that moment Stormgold, unrestrained by a lead, jumps at them from behind.

Then there's nothing but screams.

I manage to grab the lead before Stormgold actually kills someone. But I know those three will never forget this night, no matter how far they run.

Shrieking as they do.

The night is far from over. Despite my adrenaline-induced ignorance of what could have happened if I wasn't able to restrain Stormgold on time, I'm glad I did *something*.

Emrik winces as the maristag glares in his direction, sniffing at the air. She can smell the blood on him. He says, "Do you know who they were?"

"No. And I don't care." Why should I? Would knowing them have made a difference? They could've killed us if the maristag hadn't scared them off. On an ordinary night, one scream from a Lander, and my brother and I would have been shot on sight, Hunters or not. Forgive me, Emrik, for not caring.

"It's one thing to enter the Glory Race." By now the sounds of the riots are cooler so his voice echoes in the empty alley. "You know I'm with you if you insist on doing this. But almost killing Lander boys?"

"I *didn't*!" The fear of what I've done and what might happen if those boys complain, isn't *completely* lost on me. But I don't need this from my brother.

The maristag grunts.

Slower, I repeat, "I didn't." I tell him what I've been telling myself from the moment I entered the tournament. "None of this is going to matter when I'm wearing the crown of Champion."

But I don't think my brother believes me.

The ocean reaches the thoroughfare in its fury tonight, and perhaps that's the only reason the Landers haven't wormed their way toward my home. But three streets are blazing behind us. Houses gone only because I entered the Glory Race.

Deep down, I'm terrified. How much worse will things get?

# ELEVEN

**M**y body is frozen stiff when Emrik bangs on my door. "The sun's been up for hours!"

I pull my arms over my ears but that doesn't stop the racket.

"Get up, Koral," he calls with another kick to the door.

He must be enjoying himself so much. When was the last time I needed to be woken up instead of the other way round?

I push myself up on my hands. My muscles tremble. I hiss as I slam back onto the mattress. It's years old, hard as stone, and nearly breaks my jaw. I press my palm against my face, lined with the sheet's creases, and flakes of gold come off.

By the time I open the door, Emrik is ready to smash it down.

But it's Liria who jumps at me and sends us both careening.

"You were so good! Stormgold was shining! I saw it all! Crane gave me a seat at the top! I saw everything! You know there was a giant balloon maristag? So many people were dressed up! Did you see the silver fireworks?" she's yelling, out of breath, so close to coughing.

Over her shoulder, I look at Emrik. He's wearing his hair down today. Probably to hide the bruises coloring the non-tattooed side of his face. He gestures toward our sister and shakes his head. Liria has no idea what went wrong at the Opening Ceremony, then.

"The Landmaster cut some deal overnight," he says quietly. "From what I understand, she's spinning this as her plan all along. One Renter addition to the tournament. Of course, that has Arkers roiling like the sea because," he scoffs, *why a Hunter? Why not one of us?*"

I make an incredulous noise. "Cowards."

Emrik rolls his eyes.

As long as the Landmaster has control of the situation, however that serves her, I'm not worried. The Glory Race is an expensive event, she won't let a bunch of angry, entitled Landers *or* Renters ruin it.

I let my shoulders sag and ask Liria, "Did you take your meds?"

She nods enthusiastically. Her face is flushed, so different from how she usually appears. Her joy is real, so real it makes my heart too big for its cage of bones. If it were up to me, I'd freeze time in this moment.

Emrik tries to pull Liria off me. "Let her stand," he half-laughs.

But I push him away and hug Liria, aches be damned. It's so good to hear her this excited. I've missed my baby sister's laughter and her infectious happiness the most. Just as I kiss her cheek, and she finally squirms against my grip, Baba's voice rings in the hall.

Emrik scoops Liria up in his arms effortlessly and even as she reaches to pluck more golden confetti out of my hair, he says, "Baba wants to talk."

Already tired of the coming conversation, I pull on a jacket and head down.

The only light in the hall is the one creeping from the top of the staircase. The day is warm. Can't say the same for my father's expression.

"You will end this idiocy now," he says.

"Will you throw me out, Baba?" Make it easier for people like those Lander boys last night to get me. But he doesn't see how hard it is to exist as us, does he? For him, these stone walls are his entire world. How long could he have kept these stone walls if Emrik and I hadn't been able to hunt for him?

"When did you turn into...this?" he says.

My father and I stare at each other from across the room. The darkness isn't complete, but it might as well be. This abyss between us will never have enough light.

"Did you hear how Liria was laughing just now?" I ask him, blinking rapidly, unable to control the stinging in my eyes. "Don't you miss it?"

His face doesn't change. If there's any feelings in his eyes, I miss it in the dark. "You will not take down this family with your foolhardiness."

*Do you even listen to yourself?*

"I'm already in the tournament. The Landmaster herself allowed me in."

"Like I said," my father continues as if he doesn't even hear me, "you will not take this family down."

"Fine. I'll go. I'll leave this house," I say hotly.

"And where will you go?"

"Anywhere is better than here."

I whirl on my feet and stomp out of the hall. On the stairs, Emrik is waiting for me. He says nothing. He doesn't have to.

Baba's voice echoes behind us, "At least then we might be spared."

When we came home last night, Emrik warned me to expect Baba's reaction. He even said I shouldn't go inside but stay in the stables until things calmed down. But I didn't listen. I thought the riots would change Baba's mind, make him give a damn. He only waited until Mama and Liria were back and went to sleep.

I push against the wall, settling on the low bench in the stables. At the far end of the empty rows, Stormgold is beside her stall. I left the copper lead around her frillfin but took the second half of it off. She's content for now, minding her own business, free to roam inside the stables. Neither Emrik nor I thought it fit to lock her up again. As an intuitive whisperer, I work primarily with younger maristags—to have an older one trusting me, it's odd. This strange trust that she has for me exists only because I took her out.

"You can't stay in the stables permanently," Emrik says. "For one, it stinks."

"It's only for about a week," I say quietly.

Emrik sits next to me. "Don't count on—"

"I don't want to hear it, Emrik. I'm tired. All I want is to practice. As much as I can." Desperation seeps into my voice. "I need you to actually believe in me, not say you do. If you're not going to help me, keep your words."

Silence falls between us. The stone bench digs into my thighs, worsening the iron weight of the ache in my legs. I breathe in. The ocean is simmering in the air, last night's tide still a ghost roaming the island.

"Why the Glory Race?"

"What do you mean? We need the money."

"We could become smugglers for Bitterbloom. Not at the Warehouse after the blacklisting but she always needs people on other islands. Crossing the waters won't be a big deal for us. But instead, you entered the Race. Why?"

"It's…" I frown. "I don't know. It's legal and public so we won't run into more problems when we get the gold, I guess."

"That's not it. Let me know when you figure it out." Emrik leans forward, his hair spilling down his shoulders and concealing his slung arm. "Come on, you've wasted enough time. Go practice."

~

Charioteers in the Glory Race have access to the Drome where an underground arena has simulators for preparations. But to get there, I'd have to cross the entire island. The back alleys won't be much help in the sun. Nor do I think I want to travel so close to streets that burned because of me.

Instead I head down the cliffs. The strip of gray sand that hugs the shores is hidden beneath the outcroppings, and good thing, too. Landers from all over Ophir have arrived in Sollonia; they probably don't care about riots or protests so long as they're not affected. For them, the island is drowning in celebration, aglow with lights and decorations even during the day. Landers trampling the peace of our shores is part of the Glory Race. They always arrive like this: sudden and in droves, a mass of blurred faces. Drinking and yelling and pushing one another out of way. Like a nest of raptors released on schools of fish.

The sun hangs burnished today, the cliffs etching shadows on the shore. Still, I shiver against the cold breeze. But the same breeze blocks the sounds of the island, where I know people are speaking against me, conspiring to somehow get me out of the tournament. The fires of last night have been put out only physically.

I'm powerless unless I have enough gold to shut them all up.

Stormgold grows nervous. She senses my feelings. Maybe all maristags do, but we don't understand them enough. After all, when have I ever spent this much time with a grown maristag? Baba never allowed us to form any attachments.

*Monsters don't make good pets*, he always said.

I stop under an outcropping, the water crawling at the shore. Stormgold lashes her tailfin and snorts at the ocean. My hand trembles as I reach for her lead. Couldn't someone make a practical version of the contraption that works during the actual race as well?

Perhaps the danger *is* the point.

I swallow and gently pull the joint around Stormgold's neck. The lead splashes in the water beneath our feet.

Stormgold tosses her head, half-hopping backward, until the yoke of the chariot pins her in place. She squeals, annoyed, but shuffles back. Good. Using a staff to make her listen feels counterintuitive. I climb aboard, the base of the chariot rattling dangerously. The reins curl around my palms as I pull myself straight.

One sharp tug.

Stormgold stays where she is. Unlike the Charioteer Hall, there are no other maristags here. No one in front of whom she must prove herself superior. She stays.

"How lazy you are," I chide.

Except a foot splashed in water, and a lashing of her tailfin, I get no response. I step down from the chariot. Stormgold's maw hangs open. She sniffs the air. Smoke. Not the kind from last evening, but seafood being roasted.

"You can have as much food as you want once we get through this."

Stormgold growls. Maristags suffer no fools.

But I must make her listen. If only Emrik were here. Maybe we could've figured something out together. I get on the chariot again, tugging on the reins and pleading.

It goes on for what feels like an hour.

I'm about to give up when there's a rattle in the ocean.

"What the—"

Stormgold tears forward.

Toward the ocean.

My world becomes wind and water, the elements assaulting my senses. Salt fills my mouth. She's so fast—

Just as the thought crosses my mind, pain clinches at my fingers and I'm flying.

I crash against the ground, reins tangled around my hands. The reins catch Stormgold and she spins backward, hurtling out of the water. The chariot rounds with the force of a stone flung across the ocean. It slams against my legs.

Pain rattles my bones so hard my voice vanishes, only a startled, shocked gasp leaves me.

Stormgold takes that as an invitation to attack and explodes into a frenzied scream. She's a living, angry thing. Her mouth red as blood, a fierce tongue sliding between sharp incisors.

Terror freezes my bones. I can't move. Even as she screams in my face.

I'm on the ground, hands digging into the sand. The maristag looms high above me. Her ghostly eyes are even paler, nostrils huffing with wildness. One lunge and she'll have my head in her mouth, teeth rending my neck clean. Then she'd be on her way into the water, while Emrik will probably find the rest of my body here. She watches me with serpentine milky eyes. I don't move. I will myself to stay as still as the cliffs behind me.

Her frillfin flare.

Stormgold lunges. One giant tine driving at my face—I dash from underneath her, the rush of water along the shore pulling me down like gravity.

How do you control a delirious maristag?

I've done it a thousand times at the stables.

Why don't I remember it now?

My thoughts are all over the place, but I can't keep running forever. She's not going to tire. Her hindlegs stamp onto the ground, and I'm sprayed with water and sand, saltiness flicking in my eyes and mouth.

Raptor-like calculation gleams in her white eyes.

My father always says, *a mad stag is a blind stag.*

What does that mean? I *know* the meaning behind those words, but—why can't I remember it?

The muscles in my arms shake.

A blind maristag's senses are dulled. It's only working on feral instinct. Like the maristag that attacked Emrik.

Emrik was screaming at me to grab the maristag's tailfin, easier for me while he had access to its manefin. The body part that helps them navigate.

I run toward Stormgold. Panic rises in my blood. *Please let this work.* Stormgold gets bigger and bigger and then she's about to tear into me but before she has the chance to, I slide underneath her, wet sand giving way beneath me, and grab the reins.

They snag around Stormgold's antlers, and she jerks to a stop. Blood pumps in my arms. I tug. But she leaps forward, and I slam onto the ground. My skull rings, blurring my vision. Immediately, Stormgold retreats—at the same fiery speed, and I only have time to curl into myself to narrowly avoid being trampled.

A dance of death.

Stormgold tosses her head. She'll kill me the second she's free. I hold on to the reins for dear life. She struggles and drags me behind and I'm screaming. How do I get out of this? There's no time! Pain crushes my head.

And then, a short keening whistle cuts the air from somewhere nearby. Stormgold comes to a sudden stop, ears perked up. She looks around and steps back from me. As if the past few seconds never happened.

I stand, legs shaking; hot, angry, *painful* tears spill down my face.

If I can't even control my maristag, what *can* I do? Maybe the Landers were right. The tournament is their space, and they will never allow me to simply *be*. I'm always going to be the one to curl into myself to avoid others, to step out of their way, even if they're the ones blocking my path.

Or chasing me down a cliff.

It will always be me stopping myself at every turn.

"You thought it was child's play?" A voice that is more familiar than it should be. I gasp and catch myself. His silhouette against the sky looks down at me.

Dorian Akayan. How long has he been here? Did he see me cry?

I whirl, the rage at his sheer audacity fueling me. Stormgold now acts calm. Like she never once bared her teeth.

"You were going to get a maristag and win the tournament as if maristags are tiny merilfish?"

"Who are you trying to convince?" I say, even though I don't want to engage with him. The corners of my eyes are still stinging. "Because I know how easy it is for some people to get a maristag and call it a day."

Dorian jogs down the cliff. He moves with an assured step. Like a scavenger. Once, we were both up there, climbing down, holding onto each other protectively. I swallow hard. *Nostalgia* for him is the last thing I want.

And what does *he* want? Why does he think he can just come up to me? This place isn't visible from the beach. It looks like it's completely underwater. That's the whole reason I wanted to practice here.

*Some practice*, I think bitterly.

By the time Dorian arrives below, I've put the lead back around Stormgold. She snorts and huffs but doesn't make any sudden moves.

His collars are upturned against the cold ocean breeze, sharpening the angles of his face. A simple band holds back his rust-red hair. That's a surprise. In the shadows of the cliff, his hair looks even darker. He stops in front of me. Too close. Like someone familiar. Or like someone used to people moving for him.

"A different wind affects a chariot as much as the weight it carries," says Dorian.

What kind of a person speaks with such comfortable serenity while trying to humiliate someone?

My gaze flicks to the string around his fingers. A whistle of sort dangles from it. He notices me looking. "Funny how you're the one who hunts maristags while I'm the one who knows how to control them."

That keening sound. Stormgold had immediately backed off. It was because of this whistle. Dorian's eyes glitter with challenge. He wants me to ask him for it, so he gets a chance to return the favor.

"Tricks of a booted minstrel are hardly going to help against the full force of nature."

If there was any hint of our former amity in his eyes, it's now gone completely. It occurs to me, forcefully, that Dorian Akayan is a Lander.

"You have no business in the Glory Race," he says darkly. "Centuries worth of Lander blood has polished the tracks of the Drome. What has a Renter to give? Sweat and tears. You think hunting maristags means you can control them? You can't even control *one*. If I hadn't stopped it, you'd be dead. That's what Renters are in this world. Here one second and gone the next. Forgotten. The Glory Race burns with life. It means fighting and winning. For us. You think you can win against that? Against me?"

I snarl, "Yes. I know I can."

He isn't expecting that. His eyes lose their hard glitter. But he recovers quickly. "My every word is a command for Rhyton. Can you say the same for your maristag?"

I burst out, "Rhyton was mine before he was ever yours!"

The strangled silence that follows between us, as we heave with our frustrations, is giving way to everything—*everything* I don't want to remember. Everything I buried so deep within.

This is where it started, this hidden strip of sand that no one else knew about.

Once a week, Dorian came to me with the silver maristag, Rhyton, and I helped him train next to these waters. Back then, his face was softer and his eyes brighter. Hair just as red. He told me later he didn't know what he was doing, only pretending. He'd needed my help far more than he let on.

The first time when he returned, quiet as a phantom and almost scaring me to death, he said, "Rhyton likes it out here better."

The surprise of his voice made me pull my staff out. I almost knocked him down. My staff against his chin, his hands raised in startled surrender, and me, breathing hard.

"Rhyton should know how dangerous this place can be," I said.

Dorian shrugged. "Not any more than he's used to."

I pulled back my staff and extended my hand. "Koral."

"I know," he said, shaking my hand. "Dorian."

He had loved learning about maristags and training. Emrik used to get bored too quickly, but Dorian found them fascinating. He was *almost* as intuitive as me. Rhyton liked Dorian. Which wasn't very hard, I found out.

That was my mistake, but I hadn't known it then.

In that small space, locked on each side by the cliffs and the waters, we were Dorian and Koral. Not a Lander and a Renter. We were two kids who liked maristags and the sea and not our fathers.

And like a fool, I thought this golden boy cared about me.

Being with Dorian was like being in the middle of a storm, surrounded by a chaos that didn't touch us until he walked backward, without explanation, taking the calm with him and leaving me the inexplicable, sudden wild winds.

"You think I wouldn't have recognized you because you wore a scarf?" he says, eyes blazing. "Everyone thinks you got in because of the Landmaster. I could find the server whose place you took. I could make them talk. What do you think will happen then?"

"To think I imagined you as a halfway decent person," I say. "But don't worry, *your* secret is safe. No one will know you're a thief. I won't fall to your level."

Behind him, the ocean roars with a sudden wave rushing toward us. He doesn't seem perturbed. "Do you know how long I've worked for this?" he says softly, pointedly. "How good I am?"

"So why are you scared of me?"

In a voice so cold it freezes my blood, he says, "You have no idea what you've gotten yourself into."

# TWELVE

The day passes in a snatched blur. I bring Stormgold back to the stables as the sun begins dipping and the horizon reddens. She's quiet once more. Tentatively I managed to reattach the chariot, even though it took hours for me to find balance atop it. Step forward with one foot on the rim. Give it my strength. Distribute my weight. Beating Dorian is the energy fuel I didn't know I needed.

Every remembrance of his composure sends a hot pulse of hatred through me.

But as much as I can balance myself on a still chariot, it's not easy to stay upright when it's moving as fast as Stormgold pulls it. Especially not with the added reminder that maristags can lose control at any moment. A few minutes in and my fingers begin slipping, numbed. Nothing like the Opening Ceremony night.

The stables are a strange place. Built aboveground, fanlight windows spread out everywhere, not even shielded with black tapes. It's one of a kind. The stretched, bloody fingers of the setting sun reach its corners.

The space still smells of sharp chlorine, which clears my mind.

I drag a plank from the stables and balance it on a rock outside. It keeps seesawing in the wind. I push it toward the right, just a bit, and it stabilizes. Okay, I can do this. I know riding; I've grown up swimming, I know my body. It's one step to make sure I can handle movement beneath my feet. If I get this right, I'll have a better chance at balancing atop a moving chariot. Breathing through my mouth, I place one foot on the plank. Then the other.

The plank gives way. I gasp. Flail. The world turns and I slam against the ground. A thousand stone bells ring in my head. For a moment, I forget I can get up. The sky above me looks drenched in stale blood. It darkens rapidly.

Tears sting my eyes.

I push myself off the ground, nails scuffing against the stone. No one's around to point and laugh. It doesn't matter how many times I fall today as long as I don't tomorrow on the track.

This is why I have to practice.

I stand on the plank again. It sways. It stays. I hold out my arms on either side, feeling the wind part around me as it spirals through the back gate of the stables. It teases me, almost making me fall again, but I hold strong.

When we were children, Emrik and I used to train. Building strength and endurance. Standing on one leg for hours on end. Holding our breaths underwater. And learning to tolerate pain. Sometimes that tolerance worries me. What if my body bears its aches to such a degree that I wouldn't even realize I'm bleeding out?

Have I made a mistake?

Dorian's cold voice takes the shape of a claw in my head.

*You have no idea what you've gotten yourself into.*

I inhale, gasp, cough. And I fall.

A face looms over me. "Don't think that's what you were going for," Crane says.

She holds out a hand and I grip it. She pulls me to my feet in one swinging motion, as she has done often. I check for Stormgold, but the maristag is leaning against the door of her stall. Halfway inside, probably never letting herself be locked in again.

I look back. Crane's carrying a box of fried shrimp. "Where's Emrik?" I ask.

"Oh, he's helping Agata with some…" She scrunches her face. "You know what? I don't really know. I just didn't want to go to the Terrafort, so I told him to go. I'll owe him one."

"And he was willing to go to the Terrafort?"

Crane brushes me off. "How's practice coming along?" She waggles her eyebrows toward the plank. "Anything I can do to help?"

Crane tightens her grip on the plank, kneeling in front of me, and nods.

I take a deep breath, dip my head closer to my body, and focus on my movements. My foot lifts in the air. Touches the center of the plank, without ever moving it. I feel the board beneath my sole, the sand particles stuck on my skin grazing against the smooth wood.

One step at a time.

I used to have far more patience.

That's where I need to go.

I extend one hand.

Crane clutches it. "Love the idea of the race, by the way. Who wouldn't want their lives completely in the hands of an animal that could chew their head off in less than a second?"

I ignore her and lift my other hand to her and my foot to the plank at the same time, with a swiftness that hunting maristags demands. The plank wobbles but Crane's support gives me enough leeway. The wobbling stops.

Crane lets go.

And I stay like that.

I close my eyes.

*One…two…three…twenty…fifty-six…hundred and twenty…*

"Focus on my voice," Crane says.

She's to my right. There's nothing but the dark red behind my shut eyelids. But in my mind, I can see her. Her voice is a thread that holds me straight. She keeps talking. In the distance, Stormgold grunts impatiently. Crane doesn't falter. Instead, she starts asking me questions.

"Did you see the rebels when you were at Bitterbloom's?"

"Yes," I say. The word emerges from deep within me in a straight line. It doesn't distract my balance. "Wish they'd stop being foolish."

"Not everyone can enter the Glory Race to change their fortunes," Crane says. "All they want is to be treated like they matter."

"Who is everyone? The Renters who would enjoy me or Emrik or Liria dying because the Landers forced us into being Hunters?" The rage, too, is contained. Almost. I tremble.

*Breathe.*

"Not all of them. The old factions have had their time. Their ideas about outcasts and social rank are what led to the Renters being subdued in the first place. The Landers never fell prey to that stuff. The younger factions move with care, learning and being fair most of all. I've seen them talk at the Warehouse."

"If they had their way," I say calmly, "the Landers would crush them all. Or did you miss the part about how the old wars ended? And not only them, every Renter will pay the price. You, me, Emrik, and Liria."

She makes a disgruntled noise but mercifully quietens.

I stand like that for half an hour.

By the time I step off the plank, the muscles in my legs are stiff.

I go up again. And again. Until the pain recedes behind the sound of rushing blood in my ears. I know my body a little better than I did this morning.

"Koral!" Crane calls from behind me, slightly to the left. I've barely turned. A stone comes flying at me. I catch it and—she throws another. I catch that, too. *And* I keep my balance on the plank.

Crane grins and gives me two thumbs up.

After a few more rounds, my stomach rumbles. No point pushing myself so hard today that it all goes to waste tomorrow when I collapse on tracks.

Crane brings food over. For the next few minutes, we sit and eat quietly. The sea breeze is cold, clashing with the heat of the island. In the distance, the usual chaos of the Glory Race days is a comfort. I let myself feel the pain in my limbs, think about the way Stormgold turned on me. It wasn't spontaneous. Something in the water had spooked her.

The thought is relieving, at least it means Stormgold hadn't *intended* to pierce me through. But it is so easy to set off a maristag.

I'm racing with my life tomorrow.

And I am by no means an expert charioteer.

Crane insists we do thumb fights, and I humor her, despite feeling like a two-year-old. As we do, she asks about the Opening Ceremony. I notice, of course, how determined she is to not bring up the riots. She continues to ask about every nook and cranny of the Drome, mainly to distract me.

That's when it hits me.

She still has something to say.

I don't push her. If I do, she'll lock herself in a box and never come out. It's a game we play, I have learned to wait, until that part of her that never learned to trust anyone retreats.

She didn't tell me her father was a Lander until we were friends for three years. Mama knew before me. She was the one who told me patience was the best gift I could offer Crane. But I'm not patient, I only pretend. A game, I tell myself. Even if she's my only friend. She continues to fiddle with the ring on her finger—it's orange-red. I can't tell what stone it is. She's always had a penchant for digging out the strangest, most beautiful seastones.

She throws her hair over her shoulder and that's when I spot the gleam on her arm.

It belongs to a chain-link band.

"What—Crane..." I stare at her in horror. "What did you do?"

She notices what I've seen and pulls back her hand. "What we should have done years ago."

"No. *No.*" I dragged her back from the Warehouse. I tore the Freedom's Ark poster off her door. How did they get to her? "The rebels are dangerous—the Landers will get you—their guards—so much could go wrong—why would you?"

"Oh, but when you enter Glory Race, that's sensible?"

"That's not—" But words vanish in my mouth, and I can only stare at her. So this is why she's been defending those rogues. The rage that had barely begun to rise dissipates. Instead, I feel my heart break.

"It's because of your Lander father, isn't it?"

"Don't try to read me, Koral. I don't ever want to know who he is or even care," Crane says. "But I'm sure he'd love hearing my name when the Freedom's Ark brings the Landers down."

Then she leans back and smiles wickedly.

I pace around the empty stables, much to Stormgold's chagrin, who's trying very hard to catch some rest.

How can Crane not see that Freedom's Ark only causes trouble for all of us? That's what they did when we were children. Clashed with the guards yelling *No gods, no Landers* and got shot and brought our lives screeching to a halt by getting us curfewed.

Maybe she's not actually a part of it. Like last time, she could be hanging around the Warehouse. No wonder she'd been to the Warehouse without me these past few weeks. I squeeze my eyes shut. I see no red this time, only infinite black, like no light has ever existed. I wonder if that's what it's like deep inside the Terrafort.

It's in the black silence that I hear the creaking of the main gate of the stables.

There's no wind right now. The moon is sharp, it's a cloudless night, and at the other side of the Terrafort, the Glory Race tourists are still feasting and dancing. Stormgold is in the central yard of the stables, having refused to enter *any* stall again.

Every inch of this structure is stamped in my brain.

I can hear them move in the shadows, trying to hide their presence. Who could it be? Dorian? He knew where I was practicing. *He*'s familiar with the stables, too.

Running is pointless. This close to the back gate there's only one way out: toward the beach or down the cliff. I could shout. Though my voice would drown in the island's celebration and the high tide.

I make my way out anyway. When I turn, I see silhouettes in the gateway—three of them. At first, I think it's the boys who cornered Emrik and me last night, but they wouldn't have recovered so soon. Pretty sure one of them was bitten.

They rush at me, and I take off. *Can't have one normal day*. My heart races faster than I do. I dodge my pursuers, but on ground, I'm not fast enough.

Two sets of hands grip my arms from behind. Shackle-shaped pain bursts through my limbs. Adrenaline jumps in my veins and I'm half-flying, arms caught, kicking at the air. I gasp, struggling against the grip.

The ocean is seemingly endless below us, the great waters waving rhythmically. The dark abyss sends panic through me.

And panic makes my common sense vanish. I bite down on one of my captor's hands and right as his grip loosens, I start attacking my assailant wildly—recklessly. *Why couldn't Stormgold have lost control now?* A *whoosh* from the other side makes me jump. A fist comes at me. I block it with a cross of my hands. The impact jars me.

"Not so quick now."

"Brom?" I gasp. Without waiting, I kick at him. He cries and staggers. But the other two lunge for me. Bruises already form down their faces and they seem to be in pain. There's a small burst of satisfaction in me. I scramble for my pocketknife. They grab my hands. *Damn it!*

"Don't. Be. Stupid. Brom."

"You're the one who acted out of line."

"So you're going to—what? Kill me? What will that—"

The other two tighten their hold on me. Pain cuts at my arms, and I cry out. They drag me back from Brom. I kick in the air again, fighting, shouting.

*Do not stop struggling. Do not let them take you to another location. Do not be quiet.*

"Your circus hiring new clowns? I mean you had to have hired them, you don't have any frien—"

"SHUT UP."

"Is this how you're excusing your bad luck? Shifting the blame on me?" I squirm, trying to make myself smaller, digging my nails in the arms barring me.

"Bitch." One of my captors jerks my arm. *Good, if only I can make them loosen their grip.*

I look up just in time—something slams against my face. A hand holding a piece of fabric drenched with some liquid. Smelling of heavy sweetness.

The lights of the island split in multiple colors, my vision fading in and out. I grow weightless, floating. I try to kick away, get up. But feel only the sensation of fingers tighten around my arms.

"Let me go." My voice barely leaves the thickness of my tongue.

"She's still not out," Brom snaps. Too loud. A hammer against my skull. "Told you the dose should be higher."

"Be quiet, Warden," one of the others says. "What do we do *now?*"

"Lock her in anyway."

The world is suddenly both light and heavy. I'm lifted in air and shoved against a hard surface, the pain leaking into my consciousness. I strain to open my eyes. A blurry silhouette leans close, a ghost stepping through a sheer curtain. "Nobody wants you there anyway. They won't miss you."

Then comes a thud against my temple.

Darkness.

# THIRTEEN

*I'm falling, falling...*
   *Dreaming...*
   I jerk awake, eyes wide, gasping for breath. Darkness greets me. An absolute stillness that coats every inch of the world. My breaths are hard, dry stabs in my lungs. I wheeze, trying to pull myself together. Distantly, I register sensation. A throbbing in my shoulders, at my temple, down my spine. I'm lying at an angle. Severe pain cuts sharply at the back of my neck, like if I lifted my head my vertebrae would crack under the weight.

   I press my hands to my sides and try to get up.

   I can't.

   The panic continues to build, leaving me disoriented. There's no sound except the gasps I make. My fingers search for purchase in the dark. Where am I?

   A rush waves over me, a sort of whistling. But not of wind.

   *No.*

   They *couldn't* have thrown me in the water.

   Locked inside a box.

An involuntary cry escapes me.

I'm running out of air. How long until I'm choking and dying?

Maybe I haven't woken up.

Maybe Emrik hasn't gone out hunting yet.

But I know I'm not dreaming.

*I will kill Brom Warden. I will kill all three of them.*

Fresh tears spring in my eyes, slipping into my mouth. I kick at the box. I slam a fist against it.

A new pain flares along the heel of my hand.

I swear. I'm not dying here.

*Pull yourself together, damn the ocean.*

*Okay, okay.*

*Breathe.*

I'm still breathing. My heart is racing, but it's still beating. That's good. I'm still alive. That counts for something.

*Slow your breaths.*

I press my hands to either side of the box and crouch. Look up. I have no sense of direction. I go still and wait. What are my options? Break open the door? I quickly run a hand down my sides. The knife is still in my pocket.

Suddenly, the box sways.

The tide.

There's a sickening crunch. I stare in horror as the side buckles. If it breaks suddenly, the water will crush me.

I have to be deliberate.

The knife in my hand is too small.

I swear some more.

Will someone know? Emrik would have come looking for me in the morning. But how many hours have passed since then?

Maybe the Glory Race is over.

The thought wisps away the courage from my lungs. My knees hit the floor and like quicksand, I feel a sense of life sinking away from me. Like the last time I found myself cowering in darkness, trying to protect myself from Landers, exactly like that. I put my arms around myself. Make myself smaller. Let out a sad, defeated cry. Tears continue to spill down my cheeks, salt coating my tongue.

The air grows tight, the weight of generations of Hunters smothering me. They were in my place, living with monsters, but now they're gone.

I'm going to die in here, aren't I?

Numbness begins building. I try to pull my thoughts together. To not let panic take over. I need my brain sharp.

*They're not here. You're okay. You'll be okay.*

"I will kill Brom Warden," I whisper wetly.

The box groans. Something taps at the side of it. A noise like rumbling pebbles. The kind that's loud enough for human ears even in water.

How far could they have taken me? In the dark, they'd have wanted to get rid of me quickly. Down the cliffs, maybe? Right where I was practicing earlier in the day. The tide was fast and strong. That's where Stormgold lost control and turned on me. But not on her own. Something was in the water.

I remember the rattle at the shore, right before Stormgold went wild.

And that's when I realize: there's a raptor in these waters.

If it's rattling against the box, it's interested. It will cut through.

But maybe that's what I need.

There's a chance the raptor will overpower me, but what else can I do? Wait and die?

Or fight and die.

My choice is clear. I press the button on the knife. The blade springs out.

I stare at the knife for a moment. This could go *so* badly.

The point of the knife pierces my skin. I curse at the sting of pain. But it's gone just as quickly. I feel warmth bead up. Resisting the urge to press the cut to my lips I hold up my finger to the top of the box.

*Please let it be enough.*

The box groans again. Nothing else. Not even another tap.

The thin, small trail of blood dries.

My breaths grow shallow. A sharp pain starts building at the center of my forehead. I see nothing, but I know my vision is dying.

How long until I've used up the air?

Is this how Liria feels all the time?

Something slams against the box.

It shudders. Slips. I brace myself.

The rattling grows, and comes closer, closer. I can't stand, I don't know how else to protect myself. Before I can think, before my reflexes kick in, a sharp white fang sinks through the steel wall half-an-arm away from my eye. Then another.

Water gushes inside, the sour, organic smell fusing with the air. And then there's nothing but water and the rattling of a raptor in front of my face. Teeth pierce the box in the shape of a circle. A chunk of the wall flies out. Metal crunches, the box shatters, and water explodes in face. My lungs burn. Then there's no air and I'm gasping water.

The raptor charges at me, mouth wide open. And out of sheer luck, the box flips backward, and I slip out onto the floor of the sea, struggling against the overpowering water.

The raptor is above me. A reptilian, octagonal body with four little strong feet and a long mouth with a snout. Tusks curl around the snout, sharp as new blades, with nails long enough to stab me through and rip my spine out.

I plunge the knife into the membrane of its soft underbelly. Black blood spurts out of the wound, smearing one side of my face. The raptor yanks itself away. I waste no time in pushing myself up. Toward light. Toward air. The rush of water forces me down. But I can't stop. I need air.

I break through the surface of the sea with a massive crash. My chest expands. My breaths are loud, and I'm crying. Because of the terror. Because I can *hear* myself gasp.

The reek of the raptor's blood clings to me, sulfuric and sharp. But the shore is close. *I was right.* I half-swim, half-lurch on the ground beneath me, panting and scraping my way up to the sand.

Every inch of my body screams as I slam against the rocks, clawing at the solidity, desperate for dry land. The rattle cuts the air again, and I press into the cliff, tears obscuring my vision. But the tide is receding. For a few moments, I'm safe.

I collapse to the ground, my trembling hands giving way, and spit out black blood and water.

Staggering back to the stables draws more energy than I should have expended. The sun's heat needles in my exposed skin, red dots pricking up on my arms like insect bites.

Yellow tape cordons off the area on the beach. Helix Stratis stand guard. For me? Can't be. As the stables come into view, Crane and I see each other at the same time.

She shouts and runs to me. With one arm slung around her, I drag myself to the back gate.

"Stormgold?"

"Emrik got her and your chariot," she says quickly. "I said I'd find you and get you there. It starts in about an hour. Are you going to—I mean, you don't have to—"

"I will," I snarl, the taste of salt and blood still in my throat.

Crane takes off her scarf and wraps it around me. I double over and sink to the ground. Breathing through my mouth, I press my palms to the ground and rest on my knees. My gaze is still focused on the ridged rocks. I try to stabilize my vision and rest my mind so I can think straight again.

Water drips from my hair, trailing down the tiny peaks of the stone in a pattern of three.

"Where were you? What did he do to you?"

"Tried to kill me by locking me in a box and throwing me into the sea." I can feel a spark of anger now that the fear is dissipating. The anger is growing, simmering. "Thought that's all it takes for his humiliation to vanish."

"Wait," Crane says. "Who are you talking about?"

"Brom Warden."

There's a beat of silence. Outside, the throng continues to celebrate. "What's going on?"

"The thoroughfare is being shut. It's related to the event. Not sure what though." Crane adds, "Koral. It wasn't Warden."

I look at her sharply.

She frowns at my expression. "Well, it wasn't him alone, then. Solomon Akayan made him do it."

"How do you know?"

"I went to the Drome a while ago. Thought you might have turned up there. He seemed very...sure you weren't going to turn up."

Those two rats with him must have been Akayan's hired thugs.

Crane continues to speak, elaborating on exactly what Solomon said. I don't hear anything. Solomon Akayan tried to kill me. And of course Brom Warden, who thinks somehow I stole *his* spot, was eager to help. These people are so easy to manipulate, drenched in their own excessive pride.

Even though I was prepared for retaliation, rage bubbles red in me, scalding and violent. Before I can hold myself back, I start screaming.

My throat burns raw, and my ears go numb and pain explodes in my head anew.

But I scream.

I scream with sixteen years' worth of keeping quiet.

I scream until I can't anymore.

Breathing heavily, I let the shudder pass.

I push myself off the ground. Every bit of pain has receded behind the anger. "First Emrik, then me." Crane closes her eyes with understanding as I add, "Keep Liria safe until I return."

Changing into dry clothes, fixing my appearance, none of it matters. Not when I choose to walk with my head held high. I scrub skaya over my exposed skin and keep Crane's scarf.

Then I charge toward the Drome.

I don't want to be late for the 150th Glory Race.

"What the hell is wrong with you?" Emrik demands as I stride toward him. He's next to the chariot, staring at me, his jaw dropped.

"I'm fine," I say. Which is undercut by the need to spit salt water out of my mouth. I brush my mouth with the back of my hand, leaving beads of sand crusting my lips, then having to wipe them *again*. "What did I miss? Anything I should know?"

"No," he answers reluctantly. "They told me it's on the charioteers to be on time. If you miss it, you're eliminated automatically."

Half of the charioteers have already mounted their chariots, positioned in front of each gate. The same gates as on the night of Opening Ceremony. We'll ride out from under the Landmaster's box and then the track curves before the race begins.

Other charioteers, still fussing around, glance my way. Judas pales in shock at the way I appear. Arlene looks mutinous like she can't believe I have the audacity to walk in here. But it's Dorian whose eyes I don't look away from. Let him see the lengths to which I will go to survive, no matter what he and his father and any of their minions do. I push back the hair seeping out from under my scarf, not breaking eye contact. The hatred in him could stare down the burning sun. The silver crown on his head tips backward as he turns away and marches to his maristag.

*Do your best, Dorian Akayan.*

Excitement thickens the air—the hurried shouts of the handlers, the taps of zargunine staffs against the ground, footsteps pounding everywhere. Cutting tension bisects the entire hall.

Stormgold looks well rested and doesn't struggle against the lead. The chariot is tied in place as well. "Thanks for getting her ready."

Emrik grabs my chin, shifting my face up and down. "Are you even thinking straight?"

I nod. I know better than to tell him how woozy I feel. But it will go away in a few minutes. It has to.

"Who did this?"

I refrain from glancing at Dorian. I know he's listening.

"What's this?" Emrik closes a hand on my collar. His fingers come away black with blood. He clutches his other hand, the one that's in a sling. "Koral," his voice drops with true fear. "*Where were you?*"

"Wherever I was, I'm here now."

He grabs my hand. "Get out of here. This isn't worth it. We'll figure out something else."

"It's not that bad," I whisper fiercely.

Emrik tries to pull me along at the same time as the speaker atop the gates bursts with the Landmaster's voice. I look down the row of chariots. Their golden gleams flash in my eyes, and my vision immediately darkens. I curse and blink rapidly.

Everything is wrong, loud and silent at once, moving fast and slow at the same time. The world is upside down and my head is spinning.

A handler hurries over, asking Emrik to clear away.

"Come on, Emrik," I say, still feeling a vague distance from everything around me. "We both know I'm not backing out now."

Emrik curses, then pulls out a med bottle. "Take this. It's a rehydration solution for Liria."

"It's for *kids*."

"Anything helps," he growls. A sudden pain drums behind my brows. I raise my hand to press it but reach for the bottle instead. One swig, and my vision clears. However temporarily.

"Don't you dare die." Emrik crushes me in a bone-breaking hug and steps out of the way.

I close my eyes and take a deep breath. *Stay awake.*

A shadow falls on me.

"Emrik, seriously, I'm okay—"

But it's Judas Pereira. He kneels, which is how I know I've sunk to my knees next to my chariot. And how utterly tired I am.

"I'm guessing if you were to enter the Glory Race today, you wouldn't be as successful."

I scoff. And wince at the ripple of hurt at the back of my head.

Judas stands and extends a hand. Emrik and all the other charioteer companions have already been escorted out. It's only us. Scattered about, preparing to race. And Judas Pereira is here, offering help.

I want to get up on my own. But I take his hand.

"Seriously though, are you all right?" he asks, pulling me up.

"I've seen better days."

"I hope so." He speaks so earnestly that it's easy to forget he's a Lander. As before, the calm of his face unnerves me. I remember he wanted to see the stables. When has a Lander genuinely been interested in the stables, or in talking to us?

"What island are you from?" I ask.

"Chandrabad."

An academic. That explains his abnormal friendliness. Those in Chandrabad are too busy poring over their leather-bound books to care about the differences between Landers and Renters. "What was your area of study?"

"The ocean."

"You and everyone."

"Which is why it comes as no surprise that I'm here. Too bad I'm not going to win, thanks to the curse of being last."

"*That* isn't my fault, I switched somebody else's card. This is pure chance," I point out. Then immediately want to cut my tongue off.

A handler directs us to mount up. That's when I notice Dorian watching me. Us. He looks away. But not fast enough.

Judas nods to the handler and waves my apology off. "I was joking. I don't actually believe in a curse." He grins wickedly. "But you did play the hand of chance, and now I have a challenge. Nothing is a better motivator for an academic."

As Judas goes back to his maristag, I wish a challenge was my only motivator.

I climb in, my stomach in twisted knots, and check my belts and straps and numerous guards. Slow energy swirls along my hands.

The hall turns dark, gaps of light beneath the doors leading into the Drome the only illumination. Nervous energy thrums in my pulse. A strange mix of *hope, fear, hope, fear* curdles the air I breathe.

Stormgold's ears twitch, a gleam running down her antlers.

The Landmaster briefly describes the history of the first Champion. A sanitized, made-up, non-rebellious version of it. Then she finally gets to the main point: today's inaugural race event.

"For our first race, charioteers will compete for the top spot by capturing one of the nine flags placed at the end of the thoroughfare. In a first-of-its-kind event, they will leave the Drome and their race will be considered complete only when they return home to the finish line."

Some of the charioteers immediately break out in confusion. At least they weren't informed of *this*, and I was left ignorant. Not Dorian, however. He sees me looking.

"Try to fight people way out of your league again? Wouldn't be the first time."

I say, "One wrong touch and your maristag will canter away screaming."

"We both know you won't hurt a maristag, though."

It hits me where he intended. I've let him know that I still think about us. Still wonder if he *ever* cared or just wanted my Hunter expertise under the guise of friendship. Clearly he wastes no time on unimportant things. *Stupid.* "Don't be presumptuous."

Dorian smirks. "Well, don't trip on the tracks."

I push my breath against my chest, feeling it harden, resisting the urge to get off the chariot and scream. He's crueler than I ever thought possible.

"People of Ophir," the Landmaster's voice interrupts us, "welcome to the 150th Glory Race!"

Roars stamp the stone of the island.

Crane will stay with Liria, and Mama won't leave their side. I haven't seen Liria and Mama since I almost drowned. The yearning to see them, to hug them, is fierce. I wonder about Baba—has he come to see my first race? He must know everything I'm doing is for Liria, for them, so that none of us will have to beg again.

For a second, a minute, vast silence fills the world and I'm under the ocean again, locked in a box. I can't breathe.

The corners of my vision go black. Dorian's breathing is shallow beside me. Even now, I'm perceptive to the smallest changes in the way he exists.

*What is happening to me? I was sure I had moved past Dorian long ago.*

*Not now, please, I have a race to win.*

The countdown starts, and the crowd chants. Every inch of my body is alight with—fear? Anticipation? All I know is that hot blood is pumping through my limbs. Before I have a moment to adjust my grip on the reins with my jelly hands, conch shells blare across the island.

The bars rumble open slowly.

And the 150th Glory Race begins.

# FOURTEEN

anic seizes me. My vision explodes with a thousand stars. Dust clouds swarm the tracks. Flashing light and incomprehensible screams and the thunder of my heartbeat. The dust needles the back of my throat. My sides slam into the chariot, my ribs pushing forward painfully as if to break free. I pull at the reins and find my footing.

The world is ash. Wind rushes through my hair as I soar.

Shadows emerge on either side of me, large and looming.

Directly beneath the fire lamps, the gold on the chariots is striking. Stormgold and I are so far behind.

And that's good.

As we near the arcade gates to get out of the Drome and onto the racing circuit, the maristags are snapping at one another. I check Stormgold, easing her farther back from the warring maristags.

I dip my chin, concentrating on keeping my feet firmly *inside* my rumbling chariot. The darkness of the arcade converges. All charioteers have streaked out. One is behind me. On my tail. I tug Stormgold straight, away from fighting with the other maristag, and pull her attention to the front.

Several chariots tremble as the maristags pass over the bump outside the arcade.

My chariot leaps over the bump. For a moment, I'm in the air, my hair lashing at my face. The chariot slams to the ground, sending a jolt through me, and I *barely* avoiding getting knocked out.

Stormgold rushes forward, escaping the narrow exit of the arcade, and then we're zooming out of the Drome and onto the street.

The spectators roar back in the Drome, their voices carried on the wind. I'm under open skies. The ocean to my right, the city to my left. Beyond the taped borders, crowds throng, cheering the charioteers on. How many people *are* here? Has all of Ophir descended on Sollonia this year?

There are Renters in the crowd. Wearing scarves and jackets and headcovers over tattooed faces—a distinctly Renter crowd among the blur of Landers. Fist-pumping and cheering as I pass.

Far ahead, the top of the Terrafort looms over us. The sun is high, casting a golden-white glow on the peak.

The others start falling in my line of sight. Judas and one of the other charioteers, Saran Minagi, race within a wire. Saran's spiked wheels glisten dangerously. Arlene, Isidore Grae, and another charioteer are a few paces behind them. The huge antlers on Arlene's maristag sway dangerously toward the other beasts. There's a space between two of the charioteers. Too narrow. Too much of an invitation to death.

Behind me, I hear the others pulling up. Wind snaps at my ankles, lashing like whips. The ocean roars all around us, filling the air with salt.

Stormgold's frillfin flare, and she screams. In response, another maristag howls far ahead. A scuffle breaks out amid two chariots running too close. As they split and a path clears for me, I see him.

Far ahead, leading us all: Dorian.

My priority is staying alive. But if I keep pulling back, I'll never catch up with the others. I release the reins.

Stormgold bursts forward. I can feel her powerful muscles thumping against the ground. Her jaw drops in a roar. We hurtle around the skirmishes of other maristags. Saran's chariot nears mine. The ocean is loud in my ears and the dark of death looms in my eyes. Saran glances at me over his shoulder. The next instant, he races ahead, and Isidore slows to match my speed.

As if Saran ordered him to take over.

But Stormgold regains her stride, antlers held high. My eyes begin watering. It's dangerous to wipe my face. We're so close to a skirmish between three of the others, one of them Arlene. Their chariots clang and someone shouts.

If I'm hit—*no*.

"Steady, Stormgold!"

Arlene splits from the thoroughfare and takes a left. I watch her chariot vanish behind a corner as I hurtle by. Of course—there's no rule that mandates staying on the thoroughfare, we're only meant to grab a flag and return to the finish line.

I know a shortcut around the Terrafort. I whirl to the left, too, into a steep terrain of crumbling gray pillars. The chariot slips, wobbles, but bangs right in place. It's so old that I fear it might shatter, leaving me splattered on the ground.

Stormgold races ahead, even as the black and gray surroundings narrow to the point I'm scared they'll squash me to a pulp. But just as soon, the network of alleys gives way to a rocky square. A small, empty fountain at its center. Children in dirty clothes, adults loitering.

These people don't care what's going on in that Drome.

"GET AWAY!" I yell as people jump out of Stormgold's path, screaming. The windows on the stone houses on either side of the street are thrown open. Carts screech to a halt.

I turn the corner and my chariot slams in a rugged wall. A shower of golden sparks erupts from the clash between the chariot and the ancient black stone of the island. My hands burn. I swerve, cutting the contact. The street narrows again, going two separate ways. Three groups of people stand at the mouths, a cart jammed across the way, staring at Stormgold in frozen horror.

We're going to crash. We're going to kill someone. Or *I'll* be the one battered against a wall.

It's too late to stop Stormgold.

I pull at the reins.

Stormgold leaps in the air.

And as if time stops in the moment, I'm flying, suspended in infinity. The force of Stormgold's fins blast open the copper-wire lead around her neck and she surges over the shocked crowd.

When we land, the impact jars my bones. Despite the years of hunting, despite practicing balancing.

The twists and turns of the coiled neighborhood end abruptly, and we're on a broad street, the terrain smoothed into submission. In the distance, I hear the roars of the other maristags again.

The street veers right and suddenly we're charging through a pile of broken crates. I spit out dust as the turn throws us right back onto the thoroughfare. We're far past my house and nearing the edge of the island. Right as we break through, Arlene charges at me.

"Get the hell out of my way!" she screams. I lean backward, trying to go straight instead of breaking the yellow-tape border and jumping off toward the beach. Arlene's chariot slams into mine.

A giant staff smashes against the loosening contraption on Stormgold. I duck in time. Arlene has a damned weapon. Is that even legal? She snatches her reins in one hand and attacks me again. This time, I grab at it and *yank*.

With a shout of surprise, Arlene loses her grip and falls into her chariot. For a wild moment I think she fell *off* it. But she rises, protected by her straps.

The weight of the staff slows me. Arlene races ahead. We're at the edge of the island. Nine poles stand hundreds of meters from us, at the very end of the cliffs, waving with the Glory Race flags.

There are only four left.

I can hear another chariot behind me, closing the gap. Something inside me tells me to be afraid of what Arlene might do if she reaches the flags first. Take them all off? Leaving me with no flag to take?

I don't care if it's just paranoia. I pull at the reins, only slightly so Stormgold doesn't skew off the path, and jump. My feet land on the rim of the chariot. I flail, but I stay standing. Blue skies are above me, the ocean roiling on all sides—the thundering rumbles traveling from the soles of my feet to the bones in my skull. I hold the quarterstaff like a spear.

I lean back and gather tension at my waist, aiming at Arlene.

And I *throw*.

The staff flies in the air in a perfect arc, the metal shining brilliantly as it catches the light of the sun. It goes right through the gap between Arlene's carriage and her maristag, angling against the shaft of the chariot. She crashes into it. The maristag screams. They go tumbling to the side.

I snatch one of the flags and turn my chariot around, dashing through the thoroughfare, back to the Drome. To the finish line.

As the charioteers surge toward the gates at the same time, a maristag tumbles and pulls its entire chariot down.

Screams wring out from the scene.

I fly by the fallen rider—Ozcivit Sasha. His black shock of hair peeks out from beneath the broken chariot—*sparking* chariot.

There's nothing I can do for him. The skies close behind me, and I sweep back into the Drome. Stormgold swings us toward the left of the tracks divided by the Spine. Colors flash in and out of the corner of my eye. Dorian.

He's catching up but I'm still ahead by several inches.

I'm going to win the first race of the Glory Race. I'm closer to winning the entire thing. Closer to providing safety for Mama and Liria.

The thought urges me on—

Something slams into my chariot.

Dorian's chariot rams against mine. And sparks fly from the wheels.

My hands shoot out, scrambling for grip, fingers crushed around the flag. The raised side of the chariot catches in my hands. I writhe with pain, but drag myself up, wind cutting my dangling feet. Had I been one second later, the maristag behind us would have trampled me.

"What are you doing?" I scream, terror in my voice. "You'll kill me!"

Dorian lifts his gaze from the wheels of my chariot, and we lock eyes.

"Afraid of the Glory Race yet?" he shouts, and swerves at the last moment to avoid slamming into me. He cuts Stormgold off and races ahead.

Stormgold skids.

And suddenly I'm facing the wrong way. The chariot groans under the pressure. Sand gets in my eyes. I try to rub them, but it's futile. My eyes burn, the grains points of knives against the membrane. The stands are roaring, I hear the thumps of feet against the stone, the slaps of palms against the balustrades. I tighten my grip to the point that the circulation in my arms slows to an echo, pulse booming in my ears, desperately trying to pull Stormgold back the right way.

She's so close to the divider Spine, her antlers strike it. One wrong move, my chariot will catch fire.

Then the *scree* of wheels against the Spine rends the air.

Warmth flares to my left, sparks stinging the back of my hand. Instinct makes me want to snatch back my hands, but I hold on.

One after the other, the chariots bolt past me.

I open enough distance so as not to burn against the Spine—the image of Ozcivit Sasha's chariot sparking still in my mind—and I let Stormgold go.

With a huge spurt of speed, Stormgold pushes herself against gravity. My splintering chariot hurtles, wheels loud, sparks flying everywhere.

Wind screeches in my ears. Blood pumps fast through my heart.

I urge Stormgold on.

One after another, the chariots cross the finish line. The first spot is gone, so is the second, and onward. Dorian's silver headband glints as he brings his chariot to a stop and faces the tracks.

The last thought that echoes in my head is: *I hate you*.

I wrap the flag securely around my fingers and at my signal, Stormgold bounds ahead, skirting around the chariot in front of us.

The laser of the finish line turns from red to green for the fifth time.

And finally, as if someone turned the volume all the way up, I hear the cheers and screams of the Drome.

# FIFTEEN

ifth is better than eliminated. Fifth is better than dead. There are still two races left, I try to tell myself.

But I'm trembling. It should have been me at the top, the first one to cross that line. I wanted to prove that I'm here to win. Not for simply playing a game of chance and blood.

But it's Dorian Akayan for whom the crowd cheers. It's for him that the silver and gold fireworks trail the edges of the skies.

Back in the Charioteer Hall, I catch sight of Dorian. He looks away coolly as if he doesn't even recognize me, as if he didn't attempt to derail me. I can't stop myself. I push my way through the handlers wrestling with the maristags, trying to get the leads back in order, and limp my way up.

I don't know what I'm going to say to him.

But he tried to kill me. Twice. I need to say *something*.

Dorian strides down the row of corridors at the back of the Hall. The first one leads to the tunnel connecting the Drome to the Terrafort, the next is lined with small rooms used for stocking emergency supplies for the maristags, another is fitted with linoleum-floored medical stalls. The smell of dried seagrass and chemicals pervading the area is so strong that I stop in my tracks, which is when I hear raised voices. In the chaos of the post-race wrap-up, nobody else notices. The maristags are still too loud, the handlers trying desperately to calm them, and the medical staff is patching up the charioteers who have already arrived.

"What do you mean you don't know how?" I recognize Solomon Akayan's voice.

Why's he back here? And if he had to talk to his son after the race, why are they hiding?

"I'm not the only charioteer on the tracks, Father," Dorian says. "It's a professional race." His words are low but firm.

There's a loud thud. I peek in.

Solomon has Dorian slammed against the wall. He grips his son's arm and presses him back, practically breathing on Dorian. "You let that girl distract you, didn't you? Do you think me blind, boy?"

"Please, Father," Dorian snaps. "I did exactly what you said. Her maristag pulled them off. That's neither in my control nor my fault. Should I have chased them or finished my race?"

Stormgold hadn't pulled us off. It was Dorian who veered his chariot away at the last moment.

But Solomon shakes his head, seemingly mollified. "I trusted the Landmaster for too long. I will not stand by as she brings us all to ruin."

"But she said—"

"Those are long odds with the way this girl raced today. Fifth! While a Lander boy got his face burned off."

*Ozcivit.*

"Fifth is nothing to worry about. She can finish second and it wouldn't matter. Only one Champion, Father. That's going to be me. We know that." After an uncomfortable silence, Dorian adds,

"Father, the Landmaster was very clear. She wields too much power. Don't defy her. We cannot take her head-on yet."

Solomon shoves away Dorian's arm. "Who is this girl? Made of dust and nothing!" He huffs, then turns to face his son again. In a softer, deadlier voice, he says, "You have always weakened yourself by wanting to see the good, even in those who will rip us apart. But never forget that we cannot share this world. Not unless we wish to die. For you, and your children after. For our family.

"If that girl wins Glory Race, everything we built will be for nothing."

Maybe it's a good thing the Lander Father did not bring up Crane. I wouldn't want to lose my best friend to a man like this.

"She can't win anything, Father. Can you imagine talking so big in front of everyone and having *this* to show for it? A barely there passing? She'd be too humiliated to even come out for the First Celebration, let alone the next race."

"Have you talked to her?"

"No, Father."

Solomon growls with frustration. "That Warden boy turned out to be useless. His audacity at demanding we help him get reinstated as if he were chosen at all—only to do nothing on his end."

"I told you to keep him away," Dorian says. "I can take care of this problem alone. I don't need anyone else to do my work for me. Not even Arlene. She's not in control of herself and is going to get herself *and* us in trouble."

"*Your* misplaced priorities are going to get us in trouble. Do not let Arlene interfere with your mind, either."

"I wasn't planning on it," Dorian says dryly. "She barely finished the race dragging her broken chariot."

Relief trickles through me that Arlene is alive but also annoyance that she finished the race at all.

"Useless girl. At this rate, the Bashirs *will* have to sell their house and move into those miserable apartments. That'll be fine, won't it? Roshan Bashir's family—living in a market!" His voice drops, sounding dangerous. "I'm counting on you to see this through, boy. The Landmaster may have forgotten who we are, but I have not. I will not be disappointed again."

"Yes, Father."

They turn to leave. I scuttle back and hide around the corner. What would the Akayans do if they caught me eavesdropping?

The footsteps fade out amid the chaos of the hall.

I exhale, slumping to the floor.

Solomon's relationship with Dorian hasn't changed.

After everything, I should be glad to see Dorian cornered. I should savor the opportunity to see him at the mercy of someone else again. Especially now that I have no misconceptions about who he is. But, as I dwell on what just happened, I see him cringe as if by muscle memory. I remember the days when he had eyes swollen with tears. I recognize the need to make yourself smaller to not set off someone. I understand the need to act first so that no one can catch you off-guard.

And understanding someone is dangerous.

It makes you wonder. It makes you hesitate.

I have always known one thing: Dorian isn't racing for glory.

He's been forced into this for the same reason I have.

Our fathers.

Which means he'll fight for this all the same.

The sun dips down, and the horizon is darker, yet the glare Baba gives me when I push my way into the house is a moonless night. But he won't stop me. He can hear the fireworks across the thoroughfare. Only miles from here, I pulled off the flag and took it back.

For tonight, a Hunter is celebrated.

For tonight, the hostilities are gone.

I head straight for Liria.

Her lips turn blue sometimes when she sleeps. Then, a few moments later she wakes up choking and wheezing, back arched as if she's growing out spikes.

For now, because of the regular medicine doses she's been getting, she sleeps peacefully. But it will run out in ten days. It's seven days until the last race.

When I look at Liria, I think *fragile*.

That's not how a child should grow up. That's not how my sister should live. I want her to have nights of jumping up and down in the sand, running chalk on the walls of old alleys, colored food mushed against her mouth with laughter that never ends—like my childhood. Emrik and I also grew up in a constrained world, but we had our health and some control over our bodies. This is why my winning matters more to me, and always will.

I crouch next to my sister, brushing a thumb across her cheek. Her eyes flutter open. She stares at me, as if still dreaming. Maybe I shouldn't have, but she's cute as a hatching flonner with its huge eyes and fuzzy ears, flopping on the beach and returning to the ocean to make its way through life.

"Did you win?" she murmurs.

"Not yet. But it was one hell of a race."

"Crane didn't let me go. I'll never talk to her again."

"The race wasn't in the Drome anyway."

Liria's little eyebrows pull down. "It wasn't?"

"No."

We listen to the sound of drums pounding at the beach as she pushes herself up on one elbow. Her hair sticks down the side of her face. She reaches out. "Are you hurt?"

I am. But it's not the hurt my sister can see that bothers me.

Above us, I hear footsteps on the porch amid the celebration's rhythm of musical instruments made of stones, strings, and water.

"It happens during the race. Don't worry yourself." I kiss her forehead and tell her to go back to sleep.

If I, too, don't sleep now, I'll drop dead. How long has it been? Discounting the time I spent drugged in a box, of course. But I know what I heard. Someone's here. So I make for the hall, where I grab the first shawl I can find and climb up the stairs, each step heavy with exhaustion.

The brightness of outside is always a shock. Never once have I managed to step onto the porch without stumbling. The Terrafort in the distance glitters with lanterns in the pattern of a sea wave adorning its steep sides, a twin to the lights of the Drome.

My parents stand under the awning, my brother outside the arch.

The pharmacist is here, asking for his money by the looks of it. He didn't come alone; I recognize the two behind him from the group loitering outside his shop when I'd gone to get the maristag venom antidote.

Judging by his companions, the pharmacist is clearly part of the Freedom's Ark. I almost understand his insistence on his money, as the rebels have no other way of surviving except scraping sand. But the rebels are also Renters, who all cheered for me during the race.

The pharmacist notices me. "Ah, here comes the Champion of Champions."

Emrik turns and says, "They're here for the debt. Go back inside."

He does a great job of hiding the tremor in his voice. I only catch it at the very end.

"Look at this," the pharmacist says, half-laughing, "now they want to hide the girl who flies with Landers."

"Leave her out of this," Baba says. He places a hand on my shoulder.

The pressure nearly sends me to my knees. I'm trembling, suddenly realizing the pain gnawing at my body bit by bit. I slip out of his grasp.

The man wants his money now and Baba is shoving me away, but they're not making any sense. "It'll be seven days," I remind them, stepping forward even as Emrik tries to pull me back, "and you'll have your silver repaid in gold."

"How?"

"The Champion is awarded gold," I say, bewildered for a moment.

One of the men behind him snorts right as Baba snaps, "Shut up, Koral. Leela, take her inside."

*Shut up?* I blink rapidly. Baba is humiliating me, as always, in front of outsiders. And not just anyone, people who have taken *joy* in our plight. Heat burns in my eyes, in my throat. If they see my family shutting me up, how will they *ever* feel assured I'll get the money? How can I do what's needed if no one takes me seriously?

Fireworks continue to sparkle in the night.

"Didn't you come fifth today? The curse of the placement is afoot." The pharmacist sneers. His companion adds, "Keep coming fifth and all you'll get is a medal made of maristag dung."

Dorian thought I'd be too embarrassed to show my face anywhere. Is that what *everyone* thinks, Landers and Renters alike? Is that what I *should* feel?

In the distance, I hear laughter.

Cruel, caustic laughter.

Can they hear us? Is my embarrassment a show to be enjoyed?

Tightness moves in my chest like stones. "When I win, I'll pay you back double. How's that for one more week?"

The pharmacist begins to look like he might consider it, but the man behind him prods him in his back. Any doubt vanishes off his face. "I don't care about a week. I need the money tonight, or I'll make sure you don't get a single drop of med ever again."

"Why tonight?" I challenge.

"The re—"

"The money. Tonight." The man behind him interrupts. Above the swirls of black tattoos, he has a scraggly beard, because half of his face is burned. Burned faces are common among Renters. But this one makes me think of Ozcivit.

"I don't have it tonight," I say. "What will you do?"

"Take every single thing in this hole until the cost is recovered," the man growls.

"You can't," Baba stammers.

Even through the swirl of anger, at him and everyone else, I hear the fear in my father's voice. The shame. It's one thing for us to fight inside our four walls, underground, where no one else hears us. Another for someone else to make my father look afraid in front of the world. Suddenly all my animosity vanishes, and I *hate* that all I want is to never see my Baba's eyes lowered again. He's the head of our family, no matter what. I try not to flinch from the thought, try to ignore the tense hotness grazing my stomach like wire that *wants* me to not interfere. Because *why* is he the head when he does nothing but abuse and humiliate us? But no one *ever* can talk to *him* like this. Because if they can make him take a step back, what about the rest of us? That's why I'm taking his side. That's why I *must*.

The men stride past us, but Mama bars the way. "You can't go in."

"Now you'll stop us, Leela Hunter?" scoffs the man with the beard. "You should go in and hide. That's what you do best."

They push forward, but Baba gets there first. I didn't even see him move. I freeze on the punishing stone pushing its way through the sand. The wind is wild and battering, turning each breath a pin of fire. They're fighting, arguing, and shouting, shoving at Baba and cursing at Mama, and I'm suddenly overcome with a desperate need to not see this, to disappear, to breathe.

141

Emrik lunges and sends the pharmacist to the ground. I hear his cold voice through the fog in my mind, "There's no need for you to take one step more. I have the money."

Baba, Mama, and I stare at him with astonishment.

"Wait here," he says and disappears inside. My gaze drops to the ground. The boards of the porch are still stained with Emrik's blood. Reminding me how we earn the right to live on this island.

Emrik returns, his face grim. He pushes past me and holds out an unlidded box. Silver coins gleam inside.

"That's sixty silver, fifty for you and ten to pay off the guard tonight." Emrik speaks coldly and quietly. If I were younger, if Liria was here, we'd probably both step back from this version of our brother.

The men behind the pharmacist exchange frowns, while he says, "You owe me three hundred, plus the overdraw of twelve last week."

"What's more important? Your Ark meeting tonight or wasting your time by trying to hawk everything inside our house?"

"How do you know about the meet—"

Emrik cuts him off, "Go back to your darkness and leave us to ours. You'll have the rest of your money when Koral wins. And so help me, if you stay here for one more minute, I'll throw you in the ocean."

# SIXTEEN

For the first time, it's Mama who asks, voice steeled, "Where did you get that much money?"

"What does it matter?" Emrik says roughly.

"Sixty silver coins?" I clutch the balustrade of the porch. The wind claws and shrills, and I'm *trying* not to look like I'm crying. "Did you rob the Landmaster?"

"It's done—"

"No, it's not," interrupts Mama. "Have you any idea what will happen if someone comes asking and we cannot explain where we got the money? Varman, will you—Varman?"

I look up at the change in tone.

Baba's staring at Emrik, hands crossed. His face is carefully devoid of expression, but he's thinking. Calculating. And coming to a conclusion. "Against what?"

"That she'd stay in the race."

"Sixty for that?" Baba glances at me. "Everyone thinks the same, I suppose. Can't blame them."

Their meaning is not lost on me. Emrik made a bet on me at the

Warehouse. He won all that silver because dozens of people didn't believe I'd stay in the tournament after the first race.

But that's not what makes my blood storm.

"Are you out of your mind?" I yell. "You went to the Warehouse? Now?" The storm pounds in my skull. "With all those rebels acting up again? What if someone saw you? How did you even manage it, we're blacklisted!"

"They're off our backs for now," he says.

"What's done is done," Baba adds.

"The rebels are dangerous," Mama says, taking my side. She locks eyes with Baba. "Worse than entering the Glory Race. Do I need to remind *you*?"

Baba only says, "That danger is what is allowing me to step back inside my own house tonight."

"Emrik, you won't do it again. Never beg in front of another Arker again," Mama says, a finality in her tone. She follows Baba. I want to stop her; I know there's an argument brewing, but what's the point of it anymore? We'll get the winning gold and leave here in a week.

Baba's goodwill isn't what I care about at this moment.

"You fool," I groan. "What were you *thinking*? The danger, Emrik. You've always stayed out of there. Why now? And what's this meeting? Why do you know these things?"

Silence.

"What if a rebel marks you for breaking the blacklisting and decides you're the next Renter who should pay for their upkeep? Have you ever seen what happens to those who say no to the rebels?" Broken homes, broken businesses, broken bones. The rebels see no kinship with Renters who deny them. Especially not with traitors like the Hunters.

"The rebels won't bother me," Emrik says, defeated. Even the wind slows sadly around him. "It was Crane who sent me there."

The bruises on my body are a violent shade of purple this morning. Everything hurts. But not enough to keep me from preparing. And I will do it every waking minute. I'm already going to miss precious hours tonight to attend the post-race gathering: the First Celebration. But I have to go.

Tonight is mine. No one will take it away from me.

Stormgold rushes along the shore. My grip tightens. The raptor could still be here, licking its blood, waiting for a mistake on my part. I don't want to test the myth that their teeth can cut through the island's black stone.

Still, the reins are the most I'm willing to go to make her listen. No whips or staffs. Not that I need it for now. One night in the stables again made Stormgold restless. She rushes forward, pulling the chariot, with her maw open as if to swallow the wind and the world. We cut through the sand, zigzagging to evade the water and keeping as dry as possible and lurching over and under rock arches. I feel her body become used to the obstacles and mine to the moving chariot. The lack of physical reprimands, which I always tell Landers at sale time not to use and which they ignore, helps. Stormgold *enjoys* running with the wind.

We do five full rounds of the beach, one edge to the other, then head back to the shore down the cliff.

The chariot rumbles treacherously, having taken the worst hits during the first race. Emrik and I reinforced it with leather this morning. Nothing else could be done now. I can neither get zargunine from the Warehouse to fix it, nor a new chariot. After Emrik gave the coins to the pharmacist, we are not going *near* the Warehouse again, or even to that side of the thoroughfare.

It would be like stepping inside a capricorn's mouth. Maybe the giant creature would be too lazy to shut its jaws; maybe it would crush my skull on contact.

We dive under a passageway to the beach above, and I notice someone.

It's Crane.

The wind rises, bringing the ocean up and obscuring her shouted words. Stormgold squeals, her short arms suddenly tensing. She lashes her tailfin sharply and we bank.

"Pull yourself together!" I roar.

Because I don't want to see Crane. I don't know what I might say to her for putting my brother in such danger.

So, instead of one more round, we do ten.

It's two hours later, when even Stormgold starts screeching as I pull the reins, that I stop. The island is celebrating. Rows of stalls line the side of the beaches closest to the Terrafort, where a capricorn is always patrolling in case the seas spit out a raptor or two. But of course, that means tourists throng to the stalls, with ribbons and sparklers and the scent of spiced fish everywhere.

My stomach growls. And then I spot Crane again. She's descending the cliff, precariously jumping here, then there. It takes physical effort to not shout directions at her.

Why did she have to wait all this time? Couldn't she have given up and gone home?

She straightens on the ground and frowns at me. I suppose I look less like someone who completed her first Glory Race event and more like a corpse that's washed up in the sewers of a poor Renter neighborhood.

"Koral," she says. "What happened? I went to the house, and they said you've been here since before dawn? Fifth doesn't mean anything. None of the ranks matter in the first two races. They're just elimination rounds."

"It matters enough for people to have no faith that I might win."

146

Something flashes in her eyes. "What people? Landers who don't want you in that Drome to begin with?"

"You don't understand," I say. How hard is this? "I don't care about Landers, and I don't care about overthrowing them, either. Whatever it is you think you're doing, hiding in that Warehouse—I can't believe you let my brother in there. You said he was helping Agata. You lied to me."

"So did he," she says sharply. "But suddenly everything's my fault and he's *your* brother and I'm nothing to either of you?"

I bite my tongue before I tell her my brother is my blood. What's wrong with me? Crane's my best friend. We've grown up together, bandaging each other's wounds, crying to each other about everything, and most of all, believing in each other. How can I think these things?

She continues, "Bitterbloom promised to help the family if even one bet favoring you came through. She can get the terms reworded to get us extra money later. You know she can."

"And will Bitterbloom be able to stave off the likes of those who don't like to lose money to a Hunter? Has she ever interfered in what happens aboveground? Bitterbloom's words here are worthless."

Crane looks away. She knows I'm not wrong. If someone loses money, they always lust for broken bones. "Everyone makes bets," she says.

"Not everyone is a Hunter."

"Emrik isn't in danger," she snaps. "I'm getting really tired of this. My word should be more than enough."

It would've been, a week ago. But it isn't now. Something's changed in Crane. She's...different. She's up to her eyes in this rebel business. Hiding things from me. From *me*.

She steps forward, brushing her hair off her forehead. No matter how tight she always pulls her scarf, her hair is always slipping out.

"You can get upset about this, but do you know my reasons?"

When I say nothing, she adds, "You entered the Glory Race to get money for Liria, didn't you? The Glory Race isn't over for another week, and the pharmacist was *not* going to wait." She says it with such conviction that I'm reminded of Emrik insisting it was in their best interest to take the money last night. "Emrik's money sent him away. Isn't that one less burden on your shoulders?"

"Why was he not going to wait?"

"Things are changing at the Warehouse. Freedom's Ark isn't hiding anymore," she says. "We're going to strike soon. I can't tell you anything more unless you join us."

"You made Emrik enter a bet so he could collect money and then give it to that man...a rebel. That's what you did," I whisper as it all falls in my head like puzzle pieces. "This was about the rebels getting the money they needed for...for whatever it is you're doing."

I take a step back.

"And so what if I did see a potential to deal with both the problems at once?"

I open my mouth to counter, but Crane cuts me off again.

"I'd like if you stood with us, but I'm not forcing you to join."

"They assaulted my parents! You weren't there!"

Her eyes narrow. "What?"

"It wasn't the Landers who did it." I'm so angry I'm crying. "They're too self-absorbed to bother us. One word from the Landmaster and everyone went back underground. And who cares what the Akayans are doing? Solomon's always been like this, as if you don't know that!" Crane takes a step back. "But even he hasn't humiliated us like your rebels did. You keep me and my family away from this."

Crane steps back, too. "Come on, Koral, I didn't know."

"Of course you didn't! That's what I'm trying to say: Freedom's Ark are no one's friends."

Crane purses her lips. "The lights of that Drome have gotten in your head. Get out of the race. The rebels will lay off for a while, and we can get the money with bets like we would have before. I'll do it in my name, and you can clear all your debts."

I stare at Crane. It was her who helped me get in. And now she wants me to back out? As if that isn't what everyone's waiting for across the island. From those rebels humiliating me to Akayan wanting me *dead* for transgressing against Landers.

"None of you think I can do this, do you?" I shout. "No, I'm going to win this time. And after I win, I'll be repaying everyone whose money Emrik got in that bet."

Crane stiffens. She stares at me like I'm talking of taking down a capricorn bare-handed. Like I'm a danger to myself and everyone around me. She doesn't understand what being a Hunter means, that we have to stay loyal to the Landmaster if we don't want her to bring her wrath down on us. But Crane's concern is not us. She's too tangled with the rebels.

"That is a way to make sure the rebels see it as an act of rejecting them and their cause very specifically," she says carefully.

"That is exactly what I'm doing. In a week, we'll have all the money we need. We need nothing from the Freedom's Ark. Not even their pity."

Someone from the Landmaster's office is waiting on our porch. I recognize the blue uniform and the gold sigil of the Glory Race. An inverted triangle with two-tined antlers on either side. My heart is pounding, remnants of the conversation with Crane swarming in my mind, and I have so much to say to her still, but I pull myself together, *focus*, and head toward the officer.

"Koral of Sollonia, I'm here on behalf of Landmaster Minos. She sends you her congratulations on your performance in the first race and a gift from her office for the party tonight."

Party. Because of *course* that's what First Celebration is. On Sollonia's streets, every Glory Race day is a celebration. Powder bombs and balloons and music. People dance and carry on plays and cheers throughout the night. Street gangs threaten one another and get into fights on every corner.

But this isn't that kind of party.

First Celebration takes place at the Landmaster's Mansion in the Terrafort. It was never supposed to be for me or mine. Just like the next Glory Race events: the Sanctuary Pilgrimage and the Crowning Ceremony.

I take the wrapped gift—it's a dress. The Landmaster probably doesn't want me to ruin the look of her party if I turn up in my regular clothes again.

"Please be reminded that the Charioteer Greetings start exactly two hours after sunset," the officer says.

I nod and say flatly, "Please convey my thanks to the Landmaster."

Inside, I stand in the shadows off the slanting daylight. I can hear Mama in the kitchen. I sag against the wall, clutching the translucent wrap to myself. It reminds me of the med pack that Crane bought for Emrik.

I hadn't meant to draw a line between myself and Crane. I stormed away from her as she called my name, to keep myself from getting even more upset, and now I'm here, with a fancy dress in my hands, which only makes me think of how between the two us, it's always Crane who has any sense of clothes or style.

*Go to her, fix this before it worsens.*

But is she thinking the same, or still putting her rebellion first?

I shake my head.

In the kitchen, Mama looks from me to the dress, and says, "You're not eating with us tonight, then?"

"Apparently the Landmaster wants me there."

Mama presses the heels of her hands to her brow. "Show me what Minos sees fit for you."

In the ashen light of my room's single starfish, we lift away the wrap and the dress falls out in feathers. Iridescent feathers belonging to birds that can't fly.

"She's kidding," I say. "How many birds were killed for this?"

"Take it up with the Landmaster tonight," Mama says humorlessly.

A flicker of recognition, the play of blankness to cage in feelings.

I've avoided asking after her and Baba since last night. As if acknowledging what happened out loud would make the experience somehow worse. But her face is so stark, so drawn, that I can't help myself. "Mama...are you okay?"

"Your father and I have seen worse."

"That doesn't mean you can't feel bad—"

"Don't," she says quietly. "You don't need to think of it. Come, let's find something you can actually wear to the First Celebration."

I hesitate, not knowing how to approach this. My anxiety begins churning again, as if fingers were grabbing for my shoulders in the dark, tugging me back like ghosts of the past. The thought of fighting with Crane, who wants more than anything for me to cut ties with Baba. And Baba...a heavy stone settles on my chest. The way I wanted to defend him even when he was telling me to shut up in front of outsiders...

Does Mama truly want me drop it, or does she want me to keep pushing until she tells me what happened between her and Baba? *What Baba did to her...* What changed my parents to this—a loveless, lifeless relationship knotted together only by the promise of safety from the heat in these stone walls?

Mama brings out a bundle of colors from her room and unfurls it. I reach out and my hands land on the softest, silkiest fabric. A form-fitting bodice joins a floor-length skirt. One shoulder is embroidered with flowers and leaves, which joins the gilded belt at the waist, where the green of the top bleeds into the blue of the flowing skirt. The entire dress plays tricks of light, shimmering like water one second, and then floating green like seagrass.

"Where did you get this?" I ask, my voice hushed.

"It was part of my bridal trousseau. I wore this only once." She sounds distant, detached, but she smiles, "You'll look lovely in it."

Some sense of self-preservation makes me wonder, nervous, if I should defy the Landmaster. But my heart has already latched onto Mama's dress. The blend of green-blue. It's a dress made for *me*. It reminds me of the maristags, of the sea.

And no matter where I go, the sea will always be my home.

# SEVENTEEN

The Landmaster's Mansion sits ten whole levels below the Grand Bazaar in the Terrafort. My heart pounds the entire way down in the elevator, every second dreading that this will be it, *this will be it*. The elevator will drop, crushing the pulleys, destroying the counterweight, and I'll be lost underground forever. But after ten long minutes, the grumbling of the machine stops.

I step out into a hallway lit so brightly that it feels like the seaside. Noises of a crowd echo across the space.

In the center of the hallway, a door is carved in stone, easily twenty feet high. I tilt my head back to take it all in, until a server at the door says, "Please," and gestures me inside. They don't ask for my invitation. They know who I am. I'm ushered through the entrance hall, with its polished geometric-patterned marble floor and huge pillars that hold up the massive domed ceiling. A large chandelier hangs from it, each socket shimmering with many-colored candles. The walls aren't black stone, jabbing at you if you walk too close, but tiled and insulated.

Tall lamp holders form a path along a short hallway, which leads into another hall. The usher says, "The State Ballroom. Charioteer Greetings are set to start in ten minutes."

I nod.

The walls of the Ballroom vault higher than the main entrance hall. Its many pillars and alcoves glitter with gold and thick satiny curtains. I've never seen so many pillars outside the Agora terrace. From the domed ceiling, instead of a chandelier, the maristag sigil of the Glory Race hangs, its antlers glimmering as light hits it from every corner. Beneath the dome and at the very center of the room is a pond filled with clear, glittering water that reflects the sigil.

The Ballroom is brimming with illustrious Landers, chatting and laughing and drinking. It feels like a dream, a hallucination. How can any of this be real?

My stomach clenches.

*Only a few minutes. That's all.*

Once they know I'm here, that I will not hide, I can leave. Nothing is keeping me here, trapped in this unreal, upside down world. But how long will it be until I find all the other charioteers? Maybe even Solomon Akayan. Just the look on his face would be worth all this trouble.

But then, a group nearby notices me. They are a strange blend of colors, decked in brash neon dresses and jewelry and gilded with body paint. All of them are scrutinizing me. It's clear I don't belong; even the way I walk is different—I feel clumsy.

I steel myself.

*This is the ocean, and you're a Hunter. You swim with monsters; these people cannot scare you.*

The charioteers begin gathering next to the pond, bathed in the splendid golden reflection of the sigil above. They're dressed in crisp coats and shimmering dresses and bladed grins, all deeply engaged in their conversations, and I watch them as if through a glass wall, an unbreakable barrier I'll never cross. Their laughter echoes across the hall.

Dorian, by virtue of his radiant copper hair, stands out from everyone else. For once, he's not wearing that annoying silver-leaf crown. He nods at whatever Isidore just said, sipping his drink. His gaze drifts slightly and finds me. Something changes on his face. His laughter fades, leaving an annihilating expression in its place.

*Look at me*, I think, *I'm here and I'm not scared of you.*

He does not take his eyes off me as I move toward the group. And I finally begin to feel his gaze like a touch. Unnerved, I keep myself from looking at him again. Before I betray myself.

The server accompanying me asks the others to line up as well.

"We've been waiting forever for you," says Arlene.

I can't help but gape at her. She's wearing a black tuxedo with a skirt, the jacket slashed at the sides and ruffled at the shoulders. The whole set, embroidered with crystal paisleys, shimmers from top to bottom. It's a jolt; my grandmother loved paisley; she always wore that pattern. But more than that, Arlene doesn't seem like she's ever met an accident in her entire life, let alone one nearly as fatal as tumbling from a chariot alongside a maristag *yesterday*.

It must be some kind of body paint, it *has* to be.

"Didn't think you were coming," Arlene continues, obviously enjoying putting me on the spot. "Clearly you didn't want to be here, either." She glances at my face, the black scales of my tattoo on one side, but clean of silver or gold paint. Even my hair, which I usually wear down, is tied back high on my head without embellishments. Mama said it looked good with the one-shouldered dress.

Dorian shifts so smoothly I don't even notice he's stepped away from the group. In place of the crown, he wears a silver insignia as a pin on his breast pocket, attached to three chains going over his shoulder. He takes his place beside me, still looking at me strangely.

Only when the line straightens and we turn away from one another do I realize there's a lack of hardness on his face; instead, there's curiosity. It makes him look like the Dorian I knew.

I expected the first person to greet us would be the Landmaster, but it's the Race Sponsors, starting with Solomon Akayan. He shakes hands with Arlene, then Isidore, and my heart pounds so loud in my ears the noise of the party recedes behind. The moment he reaches me, I resist being sick all over him.

"Congratulations on making it through the first race." He glances once at Dorian, then returns his gaze to me. "Must have been scary. But to come fifth is—"

"—not enough." I smile. "And I'm not planning to stay fifth in the final race."

He catches my trembling hand in a crushing grip. "Indeed, we hope to see great things from you in the next one."

He immediately moves to his son.

Only when he steps away, do I breathe, my chest rising and falling like I've run a hundred miles.

The official greetings are over and regular Landers start crowding around us. I don't start any conversations, yet I'm always surrounded by someone. No conversation is ever complete without the mention of Akayan. The Landers worship him. This world around him is gilded; it gleams, no wonder he wants to keep it so desperately. No wonder he doesn't want to share even an inch with those outside the depth of the Terrafort.

I swipe the back of my neck. As much as I wanted to come here at first, a sense of doom grips me like giant hands, waxy fingers slipping over my shoulders and my waist, trying to pull me and bury me underground.

At the back of the hall, stained, reinforced glass separates us from the actual Panthalassan Ocean. For once, it's not an artificial setup;

the dark, flowing water is on the other side. Below the glass, a chorus sings the Ballad of Rhyton, a hymn for the First Champion's mari-stag, and musicians play along. The tune is unfamiliar.

Even our songs are different.

One entire side of the banquet hall is backed up with more types of food than I have ever seen. Waterfalls of liquors and juices, Terraforts made of fruits, flatbreads, and curries, and cakes iced black and blue like the planet with ten chocolate islands, huge towers of candies embellished with sugar powder, and webs of spun sugar draped delicately over them.

I can taste the sweetness of Mama's treats from before Liria was born. She used to love experimenting with different cuisines.

Ocean food reserves a whole block. Eels, crabs, oysters, clams. Someone asks if I've ever tasted a salted lotus flower. My family is literally forced to make our living out of the ocean. Who *else* would know about ocean-based food if not us?

A Lander woman, decked head-to-toe in silver body paint, laughs—with me or at me, I can't tell—and places a palm against my bare arm. Her palm's studded with tiny beads.

I force myself not to flinch.

Crane would've tripped this woman and not even blinked.

"How did you get your eyebrows like that?" she trills. "I wish mine cooperated so well!"

Of course, lucky me the current trend in eyebrows favors thick ones. But that's what most Renter features are to Landers: a trend. Here today, gone tomorrow. Soon, thin eyebrows will be back in fashion, and we'll be uncouth again.

But I stay quiet. It's one thing to argue and yell for the Glory Race, completely another to raise questions outside the Drome.

"I bet they stay like that even after a race. How do you do it?"

I force an answer for her, "They're naturally like that."

Her eyes turn huge, silver foundation crinkling incriminatingly around the corners, as if what I said was the single most absurd thing she's ever heard. "Of course, Renter styles have always been different. You know, the tattoos and the scarves. Are they always in fashion?"

If by fashion she means every little thing we do to survive, sure they're always in *fashion*. But if prejudice could truly be fought with facts, why would it even exist for these well-educated Landers?

"You do stay out in the sun a lot." She runs a hand glittering with fish scales along my arm again, pointing out how she's never spent a day in the sun in her life.

*Stop touching me!*

"That's true."

She goes on and on about her perfect life, where she can afford to stay in the shade and protect herself while Renters, denied of not merely shade but of medical services, die gruesome deaths under the sun. Cancers and disorders and what not.

I can't stand this woman.

"Excuse me, may I borrow Koral for a minute?"

The woman reels away, heading for Arlene next, and I turn, grateful to—"Judas?"

"You looked like you could use some help," he says, an amused look in his eyes. "Care to dance?"

"I—I don't know how to," I say truthfully. The Lander dance, the *waltz* if I remember right, is incredibly strange. How is this a *dance* at all? Where's the rhythmic storytelling, the expressions?

Judas laughs shortly. "Just follow my lead."

He gestures for me to take his hand, and I go along. His other hand comes around my waist and mine on his shoulder.

"See?" he says. "Not so bad."

I find my feet keeping up, my instincts sharp as they are, but I don't know if I like this. "Compared to that woman? It's heaven."

We move around in our place and catch sight of the woman cooing over Arlene and Saran, both of whom look pained but continue entertaining her. Even from the distance she appears surprisingly horrible.

Judas says, "Who doesn't want the feeling of someone gluing themselves to you very, very slowly?"

"I'd personally love to see her around the maristags."

"*I* would love to see the maristags," Judas says.

"Right, you wanted to visit," I smile. "Maybe after the second race?"

Judas begins nodding when I catch someone saying Brom's name. We're at the edge of the dance floor, and a group stands close, talking among themselves.

"The Warden boy? He really has had bad luck this year."

"Yes, first his whole tantrum for getting kicked out of the tournament," a bad attempt at whispering, "now this."

I tense under Judas's hands. Are they not even going to *pretend* to be tactful?

"What do you expect when you bother Dorian Akayan? That one has always been strange, too."

Someone hushes them immediately.

I force myself to keep silent, hands clenched on Judas's shoulders. Polite as he is, he acts like he hasn't heard a thing.

Suddenly I wish I'd worn the dress the Landmaster had sent me. It had no trains, no softness. It was a better shield.

Judas is speaking, but my mind races far away. Near the cliffs. I haven't seen Brom since that day—what happened to him? And *what* did Dorian do?

Over Judas's shoulder, I scan the Ballroom, wondering if I'll see Dorian again. The hall's energy is getting wilder. Seems like the entire population of Landers is stuffed in here. Around us couples dance, the music swaying, and lights shimmering.

And still, it doesn't take too long.

Dorian is leaning against a pillar in the corner, only a few feet away.

Staring at me. Dancing with Judas.

A gaze full of darkness. My inattentive smile at whatever Judas was saying fades. Dorian doesn't bother looking away even when I've caught him. He follows our every movement. There's something so savage, so visceral in his gaze that under the heat of the lights, I shiver.

I wonder what he might do if there weren't so many witnesses. There's almost an unnatural silence around him now, given how everyone wanted a bite of his attention before. It's so easy for him to carve his space, hold it, demand it.

"Judas," I say, "excuse me a minute, will you?"

"—and when the second round—I, of course." Judas stops himself in the middle of his sentence with a surprised look. He lets go of me and steps back. With a quick apology, I make my way toward Dorian.

"What did you do to Brom?" I ask. In the chaos of the Ballroom, no one else notices. And still, instead of answering, Dorian empties his glass in a pot of prickly-leaf plant and slips sideways into what I now see is a door.

*Stop*, warns the voice in my head. I shut it up with one touch of the knife tied beneath my belt and follow Dorian. The dark hallway swallows me up. A lone lantern, flickering sadly, hangs halfway down. This place is downright miserable.

Dorian turns, frowning, like he didn't expect me to follow. "What do you care?"

"I need to know." I need to know why I've been deprived of my revenge. If Brom thinks I'll forget what he tried to do to me, he's mistaken. I will never let him get away with his conceit-driven pride. Once everything settled, once Liria's treatments started, it was going to be the first thing I did after becoming Champion.

Hunt down Brom Warden.

"I have to say I didn't think you'd have the nerve to come down here."

"Just answer me."

"I didn't realize you cared *this much* about Warden?" Dorian raises a brow in challenge, but in the half-light, a smirk plays at his mouth, as if I'm supposed to laugh this off. Like he did something for my benefit. Like he didn't threaten me less than three days ago. Like he didn't try to derail me *yesterday*.

"Whatever I did, I doubt the rat didn't deserve it," he adds. "Rest assured he's not going to clown around in public for a long time."

"Why?" I don't grasp that the blade of my knife has sprung open at first, only when it kisses the skin on Dorian's neck. The flicker of the lantern diffuses on the blade. "Because I lived? Because he failed to keep me locked in that box?"

Dorian's eyes change. Anger shines in them.

"Make me bleed," he says in a deceptively soft voice, "and you'll never make it out the door alive."

Clearly, neither of us are the children we were the day I handed him the reins of the silver maristag.

"Locking me in a box and dumping me in the sea didn't stop me. You think I'd let a bunch of drunk Landers hold me back?" My gaze flicks to the knife.

Dorian stays quiet for a few moments, the pulse in his neck beating against the blade in my hand. I can hear my heart drumming in the thick silence between us, and I don't dare move. Our bodies are slid so close together that they could fit like a puzzle. A forgotten reaction almost makes my hand lose its grip on the knife, settle my fingers on his shoulder instead. I don't know what will happen if I breathe deeper.

"Tell me what he did," Dorian murmurs.

"Why? So you know exactly what he did *wrong*? So you and your father won't make the same mistake again?"

"I warned you to keep away from this tournament, didn't I?" he says. Like he doesn't even care that he could die with one twitch of my fingers. "You just had to come in front of my father again, didn't you?" He stops speaking. Only stares at me. Somehow, when he speaks next, his voice is even colder. "It's not safe for you, Koral."

"Not safe—?" I can hardly keep the incredulity from my voice. "Of course, it isn't. You're the one who's been trying to kill me. I'm not safe from *you*."

"Yes," he says. "But the other contenders are here to make friends with you, no? Tell me, is Judas Pereira good at dancing?"

"*What are you talking about?*"

He's so close I can see the shadows beneath his eyes. The hazel of them darkens to black mirrors. I see my reflection. If he leans a touch forward, the heat from my skin will burn him. Blood rushes to my head so fast I tighten my hold on the knife, pulling myself back inside my body.

"So, what's the next great plan?" I ask, if only to deflect the old, unwanted feelings pirouetting in my stomach. "How will you try and kill me tomorrow?"

"There are so many things I'd like to do to you," he breathes. "One day, I might."

# EIGHTEEN

I ease my way back into the Ballroom, as quietly as I can, hoping no one's noticed my absence. It's different than sneaking into my own home. There, darkness is a cover. Here, the cantankerous noise and the oceanic size of the structure helps keep me off everyone's radar.

Or not.

I stop dead.

Landmaster Minos is watching me from across the hall. How long has she kept an eye on the door? Did she see Dorian leaving as well? Oh, no. What does she think of that? I should have waited.

She rounds the pond and comes to a stop before me, her red-topped staff tapping the floor.

She starts to speak, then pauses. "I am not sure what honorific you prefer."

I bow customarily. "Koral is fine, thank you."

"All right. So, Koral, is the First Celebration to your liking?"

"It's breathtaking."

"The Charioteer Greetings have been done with, I assume?"

"Yes, Landmaster."

"What an interesting bunch of charioteers, don't you think?"

"Yes, Landmaster."

Strange for her to be here. If nothing else, I learned from party gossip she's not one to mingle with people. Her eyes are rimmed a delicate white, sharpening the crystal blue inside. It is the only color on her person, which is odd, given the brash gold and silver shimmering in every corner of the Ballroom, dappled with the dark reflection of the ocean. Even her sari is a blend of white and sheer silver, with shimmery edges.

We observe the party together. How can people talk so much? Then again, the Landmaster's silence is making the food in my stomach turn. What does she want?

"You see this architecture? It's a blend of ancient civilizations. Our Empyrean Elders are said to have belonged to all kinds of realities. Everything here from these pillars to the gilded tiles and the ornamentation around the facades comes from them merging their art together during the world renaissance."

"Oh." I sweep my gaze to the pillars and arches and walls again, a sudden kinship to the stone of the grand building warming in me. Everything that the Empyrean Elders went through is the reason my world exists.

Solomon Akayan suddenly crosses our line of vision and heads straight for Dorian. Father and son get into a heated argument. *Serves Dorian right*, I think. But the Landmaster's eyes are also narrowed toward the Akayans. I reluctantly glance again. Dorian looks smaller in front of his father, nothing like the brute who came to threaten me at the cliffs. As if he's three different people. This, the one I knew, and the one who races.

Solomon snatches Dorian's glass and tosses it. The glass splashes in the pond, sending the crowd scrambling.

*Dorian is not the one embarrassing you now.*

My blood heats and I look away. I didn't come here to witness another Akayan family drama.

Landmaster Minos, too, doesn't like it.

"In the Council of Ophir," she says softly, "leaders are not hereditary. It is a good system. Keeps a check on ambition and keeps our governance in the hands of those who can bear the weight of the responsibility. Not those who think they can. That's true for everything."

I wonder why Renters cannot join the Council, save the scrap of being a state helper. I wonder why the Hunters are hereditary, why my family is forced to exist as not simply people, but our profession.

The Landmaster continues making small talk, pointing out the people and what they do. The man across from us with a big white turban and large feathered eyebrows discovered a mine out in Kar Atish. Someone else's family made a fortune harnessing the sun's power for energy. Another woman is an architect specializing in Renaissance designs.

"I remember when you were nine, Koral," she says. "The first time you accompanied your father for the final sale of the year."

Years that sell out every maristag are rare. The memory comes back to me immediately. The Race Council bought the last ones for the Lander Training Center as backups—desperate to not have another year like the one before. But stronger is the recollection that I tripped on my feet and landed in front of the Landmaster.

I gasp. She remembers?

"You asked what I do," she says, and if my ears aren't deceiving me, fondly. "And once your father explained, you expressed your wish to take my place one day."

"I'm sorry, Landmaster, I—"

"No need." She waves a hand, then narrows her eyes slightly. "It is good to see your ambitions have not drowned as you've grown."

Ambitions? She sees my racing as ambitious? All I want is money for my sister's meds. If it hadn't been for the Arkers, I would've borrowed some at the Warehouse. I didn't want to race. I'd still give it all up in a heartbeat if there was another way to make sure we'll never beg for meds again.

"You chose different attire."

"Only because," I say carefully, "the chosen dress didn't fit me well."

"Pity." There's a dread of a silence between us, before the Landmaster asks, "Are you familiar with the tale of Icarus?"

"I'm afraid not."

"It is a good story. I often think of it, Koral. First spoken in the glory days succeeding the Great Landing, I believe."

I politely wait for her to sip her wine.

"Forgive me for not having the talent of a storyteller," she says. "Here goes: In the first red dawn of Ophir, a red-haired Icarus was born. A master craftsman, a master hunter, and a master liar. People came to him with their problems, for he knew the answer to everything. But he underestimated our new world. When the desire came upon him, he searched for aquabats, whose wingspan matched his body, but did not remember they are creatures of the seas *and* the skies. He flew to the sun, even as his father begged him not to, and the aquabats came for him. With torn wings, he plunged into the ocean. As Icarus had risen, so he had fallen."

A chill skitters down my spine.

"Remember Icarus, Koral."

Save the occasional rumbling of the elevators, the world lies silent outside the Landmaster's Mansion. Like ruins. All the lights are turned out, only the inside of the doors casts a dull haze the color

166

of yellowing flesh. Without the lights, I can *almost* picture this as a cave—untouched, uninhabited.

The guards have moved inside, leaning against the pillars, joking, and drinking their wine. I stand in front of the door, breathing the cold, sharp air of the underground, ready to go home. The Landmaster's Office is only on the first level. This is the first time, ever, that I've been so deep underground.

Buried, but *safe*.

I'll come back here. Bring Mama and Liria, too.

I turn to leave as I hear it.

Music. Drifting down the hallway.

Emrik sings, Liria paints. The artist gene of my family skipped me. It's a miracle if I can tell a violin from a sitar. But I do adore listening to music. It pulls at me, soothes me. On the nights my parents were busy helping Liria survive one more hour, and I was burrowed alone in my room, music was my sole companion.

The melody right now is soft, an entire world of melancholy. It fills the air and the stone, real and tangible, emanating from down the craggy hallway. Notes, like strings, wrap around my wrist and tug. I reach the dead end, and the space veers slightly to the right. The rocks in the corner are hewn into almost a flight of stairs. That's where the lone figure sits, hidden in absolute darkness, playing a song.

Dorian.

I should go back.

But I freeze.

Stray glitter gleams in his hair like pinpoints of stars. His eyes are closed. The sleeves of his shirt are rolled up to his elbows and the muscles on his arm grow taut as the music heightens. I don't want to break his concentration.

Will he open his eyes?

What will he do when he sees me watching him?

I should go.

But the absurdity of how vulnerable he looks has me rooted to the spot. Nothing like the darkness boring into me, warning me to stay away. He looks like he doesn't belong in the gilded Lander world, but rather in this quiet, dark place of his own.

He's forever going to be the arrogant, spiteful son of Solomon Akayan, if he doesn't cut ties with his father. From that false world.

Or maybe I'm seeing what I want to see. He's probably just drunk. Not once did I spot him at the party tonight without a drink in hand. At least not until his father snatched that last one away.

I force myself to take a step back. It's a startled, unbalanced step that disturbs him.

His eyes open but his hands don't stop. For the longest moment, he stares ahead, a frown between his brows, continuing to play. As if he's lost in thought and doesn't truly see me. I am a ghost to him.

Then, perhaps when I don't disappear, his hands pause. I feel something clamp on my heart, the absence of that music, but I don't react. He gets up. Comes down the flight of steps. Walks closer.

"You're still real," he murmurs.

He didn't realize it was me.

What did he think? A hallucination? A dream? What might a Lander, forever safe and in possession of everything he could possibly want, still find to dream of?

Years ago, I asked him once, and he said *nothing, I dream of nothing*.

But perhaps this is what he dreams of. Playing music.

*True freedom is worth more than gold, Dorian Akayan.*

Once again, I hold a secret that belongs to him in my hands. And once again, despite his wickedness, I want to keep it safe for him. I won't betray Dorian. For the sake of what we had. Especially not when I can see that Solomon Akayan is doing to him what Baba has been doing to me.

There's something else I can do to show him that he can't destroy me to save himself.

Wear the crown of Champion.

The hour of midnight on Ophir is special; the creatures born in this world own the night. Some say it's the hour of the Water Horse, a leviathan spirit in the Panthalassan Ocean, so huge that its head and its tail are always on the opposite ends of the world.

At midnight, the Water Horse gets restless. All bad things are afoot at this dark hour.

So, as I'm trudging down the streets and I see the bright glow where my house should be, my walk breaks into a run, until I'm sprinting, out of breath. A tangible force of hot wind knocks me down.

A crowd gathers outside the fence of my house, faces bright blue, reflecting the horrific flames, a familiar voice screaming.

*It's a nightmare, a bad dream, it's not real.*

I cannot make myself walk through the crowd. Toward my house.

The strange blue-gray fire has hold of the wooden balustrade on the porch. Smoke bellows through the door, spilling in circles from the twisted staircase. The fire grows and grows, guzzling the porch. A monster of fire, lighting the whole sky up.

"Mama! Emrik!"

"Stop the girl!" someone shouts to my right.

An arm comes around me. "Your parents are there!"

Startled, I look. And curse out of relief. There they are, holding onto one another, watching our refuge go up in flames. Baba's face is frozen solid, the fire casting cruel shadows across him. Mama has her hands pressed to her mouth, tears shining in the light. An angry welt across her arm, burned through the cloth, sneers at me.

I run to my parents. My feet tangle in the long train of my dress. I fall down in front of them.

Baba blinks, bewildered, as if shaken out of a trance. Mama reaches for me.

"Emrik," I breathe, tears streaming from my eyes, smoke in my lungs. "Where are Emrik and Liria?"

Mama grabs me to her chest and her cries break free from the cover of her hands, "Get my children out of there, Varman!"

I hold my mother in my arms as she collapses. *No, no, no.* My siblings can't be—they're not—

I scream. A sharp pain cuts at the center of my forehead, passing through my skull. There are no firefighters. The ocean is right there! So much water. But none for us.

Powerlessness courses through me, the alien feeling tangling through my veins. What can I do to fix this? There must be something. I can go in—get them out. I know the house better than anyone. How many times have I snuck in late?

The thought barely finishes when I get up and move.

"Don't be stupid," Baba shouts. He pulls me back so hard my arm nearly gives out. "I couldn't stop Emrik," Baba's voice cracks, "I'm not letting you get yourself killed, too!"

I try to counter, try to make sense of my world crashing down around me, but the smoke makes it impossible to speak. It slinks everywhere, curling around our limbs like serpents. At any second, they will lunge and strike our jugular. The heaviness in my lungs drags me down.

The crowd starts pulling back as the fire roars even higher. It turns with the wind, toward the stables.

"Stormgold," I cry. "Where's my maristag?"

That's when Emrik emerges from the mass of gray, his face dark with soot, an unconscious Liria in his arms.

"What happened?" Smoke gushes inside my mouth, the burn of it down my throat. All around us, chaos erupts anew as Mama and Baba draw Liria to them. She's not waking up.

Someone calls for help, someone else mentions burn meds, and the thought of even more meds makes me want to tear my hair out.

Emrik grabs my arms and makes me look at him. "I hope your party was worth this."

# NINETEEN

Our shop in the Agora has no window, not even space to move side by side, but it's our haven right now. Baba, torn between telling us off for keeping this secret from him and glad that we have this box-sized shelter for Liria, grips the edge of the shutter. On one side, Emrik sits, holding an oxygen mask. His eyes are red and focused on Liria.

In the pale light of the Terrafort that's streaming through the door, she's waxen as smooth marble. The medic shines a light in her eyes. He shifts, uncomfortable in the tight space, and bangs his knee against the wall.

Baba apologizes.

Liria has an oxygen mask strapped to her face, too. Unlike Emrik, her face is so small, it pretty much vanishes behind the mask. The medic taps her knees with a tiny hammer. There's no response.

Liria can't be dying. She's a survivor, a fighter. They told us she wouldn't live past her first year. But she did. And every year since. She draws and laughs and sings and cries. She has so much life to live. It's impossible for her to—

"Wake up, Liria," I cry into my hands.

Maybe it was finally too much for her to take. The constant fights between my parents, between Baba and me. The darkness of the stone walls. The never-ending strings of tension cutting across our house. And then the wildness of the fire. Perhaps she thought I abandoned her. Emrik found her already unconscious. Did she lose her senses while thinking we left her there to suffocate? To die? That we gave up on her? That I broke my promises?

Suddenly I'm a child, clinging to my mother's dress. *Fix this please.* I beg my parents, rage howling.

"Any word on what happened?" the medic asks, checking Liria's pulse.

No one answers. No one *has* any answers.

"She's in a coma," the medic says. "At the hospital, we could've put her through tests. But out here..." He shrugs apologetically, avoiding my parents' eyes.

Out here, we're on our own. No access to the treatments reserved for Landers in their fancy underground Hospital.

"Aren't *you* a doctor?" I shout. "Do something!"

Baba turns at that, to tell me to shut up probably, but his face contorts in confusion as he looks over my shoulder. "May I help you?"

I turn.

It's Judas Pereira, standing next to the pillar, watching us. He's still dressed in his party clothes and his face shines with silver streaks.

"I—" The charioteer looks from me to my parents. Then glances at where my sister lies. He's so misplaced here it's absurd.

"What are you doing here?" I say. Then mouth: *go away.*

"You know him?" Baba asks.

Judas straightens at the tone.

"I know him from—from..." I don't think now is the best time to say where I know him from. I step away from the shop. Behind him groups are still gathered around pillars, other keepers are sitting in their shops. It's the middle of the night. Yet, without shame, they are here. Waiting for news about the Hunters, waiting for gossip.

"What do you think you're doing?" I say angrily.

Judas seems to realize what a terrible idea it is for a Lander to roam here at this time of the night. Especially one who might be recognizable. Already I can hear whispers, comparing memories and notes, trying to put together where they've seen that familiar floppy brown hair.

"We heard what happened," he says, glancing at the shop. "I told you I wanted to see the stables. So then, I—someone said you were at the Agora, so I wanted—I thought—Koral, I'm so sorry."

My fingers tighten around my zargunine staff for support. Good thing Crane and I kept extra staffs stashed here.

"Is your maristag okay?"

"Yes," I say heavily. I left Stormgold tied on the beach. What else am I supposed to do? Where can I take a maristag at this hour?

"And your family?"

I hate that the immediate answer to that isn't a clear yes. Cold wind cuts at my arms. I rub my hands against my skin, trying to warm up.

"My sister isn't waking. She was inside when it happened. She's already been sick with some kind of persistent cough and then all that smoke." I look behind me. Baba and Mama are watching Liria like children gazing at sweets they can't afford inside a glass box. They look helpless and sad.

But Emrik is watching me with narrowed eyes.

"Is that her doctor?" Judas asks.

"Yes."

He bites his lip. Hesitating. "Do you...mind if I talk to him?"

Confused, I shake my head. He's an ocean student, what's he going to do about a smoke-induced coma?

The medic and Judas talk for several bewildering seconds at the end of which Judas takes a step back. "But what about zargunine?"

"What do you mean?" Mama intervenes, looking at Judas.

"On this island, the air smells of metal," Judas says. "All of you use it so much. It's detrimental to human health. It's slow poisoning."

The sudden tension in the air catches Judas off-guard. He looks from my parents and brother to me. "You don't know? Is this not common knowledge?"

"We've always used zargunine," says Mama.

But have we? I stare at my staff. It's only Renters who use it. Landers don't, not for anything that isn't a weapon. The places inside the Terrafort have no need for zargunine screens.

Judas narrows his eyes. "What was the fire like?"

"Blue," I say immediately. "Gray-ish blue."

"Yes, that's zargunine fire."

Emrik and I exchange glances. It doesn't take the Landmaster's justice to figure out who started the fire. Renters, of course. And who has access to spare zargunine kept at the Warehouse? The rebels.

When he takes the oxygen mask off, I see the damage on Emrik's face. All the way here, I was so focused on Liria, that I didn't notice how hurt Emrik was. One side of his face is burned and bandaged, half of his tattoos singed off. His face is ghastly white, like Landers who don't see the sun for weeks on end, spider-veined in red.

Judas is gone, still stunned at Sollonia's rampant use of zargunine and because nobody has died yet, the little excitement we provide the other shopkeepers is also deflating. Mama sits with Liria, and Baba...who knows where Baba is? Maybe he'll mine us some hope, like he did when he found this medic years ago, but I've stopped relying on my father.

Emrik and I pace down the edge of the terrace, away from the crowds. The second we're clear, he says, "How long until the patrol comes around and asks us to vacate the premises?"

"We're going to be fine."

Emrik makes a noise halfway between a laugh and sob. "Liria is dying as we *speak*."

I hold back my tremble. "She's not. I will win this tournament, and we will put her in that damned Hospital in four days. She'll hold on for four days. She has to."

"I was in there, Koral, in that fire. It consumed everything. It was going to burn our sister alive. We'd have found nothing but ash!"

"That's why I'm going to make sure we never suffer like this again! That *Liria* never suffers!" My heart pounds in my throat. The image of Liria burning refuses to leave my mind.

Emrik snaps, his voice rising to match mine, "You think you're going to win a stupid tournament, and it's going to magically change everything? That the Landers will suddenly accept us as one of them?"

The barb hits with too much force. "It wasn't the Landers who burned our house down. It was those cowards down there," I roar, pointing toward the Warehouse. Suddenly I don't care who listens. "Why are you taking their side? I'm your sister! You're supposed to care about me! Be my support! How can I do any of this alone? You're no better than Baba!" I'm crying hard now, tears and snot running cold down my cheeks and neck. I've ruined my mother's dress.

Emrik pulls no punches. "What do you think the rebels were mad about? You attending these fancy parties!"

"It's only me they have a problem with! As if Lander charioteers don't do it every time!"

"Because you declared yourself as one of them! You've chosen a side, and we're going to get destroyed because of it!"

Over his shoulder, I see someone moving toward us. It's Crane, hurrying over. She looks harried, her scarf wrapped in a mess around her face, no fake jewelry on her fingers. Her eyes are dark, like she's holding the seas inside her. She doesn't resemble the Crane I know.

I haven't seen her since we fought. Since she made her choice.

"Keep it down," she whispers angrily, breaking in between Emrik and me. "I could hear you both halfway down the Agora. Emrik, damn it, you should be resting." Her hand cups her mouth as she takes in Emrik's wounds.

Emrik ignores her.

"How's Liria?" she asks. Then, noticing that Emrik and I haven't backed down, she adds, "Stop this nonsense. Nothing matters but Liria."

Emrik scoffs. "Tell her that."

"Shut up, Emrik," Crane says.

"No, Emrik," I say. "Tell *her* what we know. Tell her *who* caused the fire that nearly killed you and Liria. Tell her what her friends did to people she considers *family*."

Crane's eyes change. In the dark, I see her look at me as if she hasn't seen me in years. There's a wildness, a shame. She knows what Emrik might say. She sees it on my face.

But it isn't only Crane staring at me. It's Emrik.

I don't know what they think they're doing.

So I do something that doesn't make sense, either. I smile. I wear my smile in defiance for what I'm about to do. And, as Emrik yells for me to stop, I storm away from the Agora and toward the open night.

# TWENTY

At the mouth of the Terrafort, two sirens rise high in the shape of curved fangs. In the sea, a windlass lies idly, a monster in the dark of night, stars in the sky lining its head like bioluminescent thorns on a sea creature. This is the hour when Emrik and I would normally hunt maristags.

So let it be the hour when I hunt rebels, too.

A squeal cuts the air. But the sirens stay unlit, silent. One horn for a lone predator on the thoroughfare, two for more, three for a swarm attacking. So, no attack, just a creature somewhere at the edge of the water testing the land. Nothing new in that.

Guilt sharpens the cold skittering down my spine. I hope Stormgold is okay. She's a maristag, after all. It's not like she can't take care of herself.

I wind my way down from the Terrafort toward the older quarters. Crane's with Emrik. She won't be able to intervene this time.

A cold sea gale whirls over the island. The pathways of the farther neighborhoods are winding and narrow, making it difficult to get *anywhere* in time. So I head down backstreet after backstreet, leaping over low yard fences and crumbling stone. Only when I reach the street leading into the Renter medicine shop and the other disguised shelters, do I stop.

They're here; at the other end of the street, still lounging around the shops. The essential stores on this street are always open, shifts divided between family members. I knew I'd find at least *some* of these lower-level rebels here. The ones who sleep through the day, avoiding the sun, and living for the nights. The ones who act on orders in the dark when it's easy to hide.

Some are enough to send the message to all.

I straighten. The sharp alcoholic odor of freshly mined zargunine drifts in the air. I'm used to my staff, so I know it's not from my own weapon. Maybe I'm imagining it, but maybe this smell will never leave me. I will always see my house burning with blue fire.

It is so dark here that the group of rebels could be spirits risen from the ground, melded with the night, inhuman. Bone-deep hatred seethes in me.

The line of shops and curtained houses is on one side. But the other side is nothing but black stone, jagged and dangerous. The odds aren't in my favor, but I can sneak up on them. They're all drunk. It doesn't matter if these specific people were involved in the burning of my house, they must have known. Don't they always pride themselves in *knowing* everybody's business and *laughing*?

*You can do this*, I tell myself. *Hurt them. Like they've hurt you.*

I press myself to the grisly wall, behind a large block of stone jutting out of the ground. Across from me, a group of street urchins watch me suspiciously. They're dressed in tatters, scraping at a niche in the wall. Perhaps an extra layer of cloth is stuck inside, perhaps a discarded bite of food. But after one look at my face and my staff, the kids hiss with panic and flee. The pattering of bare feet on stone is loud in the night.

The disturbance rouses the group.

"Who's there?" one of them calls lazily. A moment's silence, and they resume their banter. Good. I lift my leg, ready to move, when a voice whispers behind me, "What are you doing?"

I spin back into the shadows, staff held across me to strike, and scan the darkness.

A person lifts the hood of their cloak. Red hair.

In the dark I'm seeing things.

Dorian Akayan stands a hand's length away, arms crossed and frowning. He isn't even truly frowning, but the way he looks at me—as if he has any reason, *any* right to disapprove. Where did Dorian even come from? *Here.* In a Renter backstreet?

"What are *you* doing?"

"Really hoping not to get killed." He glances over my shoulder. "They're more than you think from here. They'll kill you."

"There are no Landers here," I snarl, hands tightening around my staff. "I doubt your threats are going to work, so be very careful of what you're saying. Or I *will* make you bleed." He has a staff as well, tucked at his waist. But I have my knife, too. My hands reach for it and meet air.

"Looking for this?" He holds my knife, closed, in his palm. So assured of himself. How can he be this nonchalant, exposed on a Renter backstreet, so far from the Terrafort?

I gape at the knife in his hand.

"Apparently you're not the only magician who makes things disappear from inside envelopes," he says. A quirk of his brow. A challenge.

"Apparently you're not drunk anymore." I snatch the knife from him, hating the familiarity of his hands. "How did you find me? Are you *stalking* me?" Was the party only hours ago? The sound of music and conversation, the taste of warm food, the confidence of never walking in sooty backstreets again. It feels like a dream. My entire world is capsized in the space of a few hours. And yet I'm still dressed as I was earlier, so I know it was real.

"No, actually. I thought to myself, do I know anyone reckless enough to take on a whole group of rebels by themselves. There weren't many options." Then he adds, "We're getting out of here, before you start something you can't finish."

"This has nothing to do with you."

I turn around. But my hands are shaking, the ocean loud in my ears, and then the night rushes back. With it, the realization that I wanted to *kill* someone. Not *one* person. Several. I don't even know if any of them were involved in the burning of my house; I just wanted to send a message and not seem powerless. And those children, I frightened them. I was their monster in the dark.

What was I thinking?

That's the thing—I wasn't thinking at all.

I left Emrik and Crane because I was sick of looking at their disappointed faces.

As if wanting a better life is a crime.

"If you don't come with me right now," Dorian says, "I'll shout and alert them all."

Damn him. I've already made up my mind to return, but I doubt he'll take my word for it. He seems just chaotic enough to actually start shouting.

So I grit my teeth and follow him, my eyes focused on the ground, pretending I'm walking my own way out. But the second we push through the network of backstreets and onto the thoroughfare, Dorian says, "Have you thought about the fact that you have anger issues?"

I jerk to a stop.

Undaunted, he continues, "All this hunting and fighting, maybe your mind is so warped, it thinks that violence is the only answer?"

181

Those words—*anger, violence, warped mind*—given life, by a Lander. The weapons their sophisticated society uses to discard us. Me. As if anger is why I'm *small*.

"Of course, I'm angry. But it isn't rage that makes me angry." My words are broken. Shards of what I want to say. Burned like my house. "I am—I am—I am *in pain*." My breath catches in my throat, but I have to say what I want to say. I don't even know what I truly need to say. But how dare he? How *could* he? He knows what I've lived through, and still he wants to pin it on me. "I was born in anger; I live with it. It's everywhere. It's in the way people look at us. It's in the way we *exist*. It's the way we *burn*. What do you know of how angry I am, Dorian Akayan?"

"I know that you are even angrier than you think you are," he speaks clearly, carefully. "I know that every hope you've ever had is surrounded by this anger, and you worry, always, that your anger will overpower you. That your anger will consume that hope." His face is deliberately blank, like he's speaking off a screen, or something he *knows* so deeply that it feels like he's practiced it countless times. "I also know that if you don't control this anger, pain, or whatever else it is, it will destroy you."

"Do you?" I say, teeth gritted, to not let my words turn into tears. "Do you know how to control your own misery? Isn't that *your* rage? Since you were a child?"

I know I'm not being fair, saying this now when we both have had a silent agreement to pretend *we* never happened, but it's true, isn't it? Dorian's need to win, his frustration at me refusing to back down and damage his chances, his anger. All of it stems from being treated less like a boy and more a machine to show off.

Dorian is frowning at me. Probably unsure of what to say.

*See how it feels to have your thoughts stolen from you uninvited, Dorian Akayan.*

But a rustling and fall of footsteps behind us sends us both pressing into the wall. Voices come toward us.

"It's the Arkers, if they catch us…" Dorian glances down the path, then at me. He closes the gap between us so fast that I can only gasp.

"What are you—"

"Be quiet. There's no other way they wouldn't want to know why we're out so late."

Understanding floods me. Dorian erases the last remaining sliver of space between us, his body pressed against mine. My incredulous laugh at his audacity is cut short by the heat barraging through my core. His hand slips around my waist with the same ease from two years ago. Assured, like it belongs there. He holds up his other arm, shielding my face, drawing his own closer.

His hair falls on his forehead. As if my body remembers how it must react, my hands reach and push his hair back. Like I always did. And his face turns into my palm, as if on its own. We both freeze, realizing what we're doing. A maristag sensing a trap. His throat moves up and down, so slowly. I stay still.

He's grown taller in the past two years. But so have I. Somehow, we fit together now even easier than before. My chin reaching just enough to fit against the crook where his neck meets his shoulder.

My heart flaps desperately in its cage.

This should not be happening.

"Trust you to dig problems for yourself out of the ground," he says. The husk of his voice shivers against my throat.

"I can deal with my problems fine on my own."

"Not this one, my star," he says.

I grow still under his hands, not at him doubting me, but at what he calls me. That term of endearment—my star, sitara—that only those closest may use, for people they would die for. That Mama uses for Liria.

That I taught Dorian.

He looks away for a fraction of a second, his jaw tight. But he doesn't take it back.

The voices grow nearer, disrupting the stunned silence between us. Dorian adds, "Close your eyes." Then, without warning, he dips his lips toward my ear. I don't think he meant to make contact, only pretend. But the brush of the small touch is enough. The sensitive skin directly beneath my ear ignites, sending a crackle of fire racing across my skin.

The Arkers turn the corner, busy in their conversation.

"Its security unit has fifty guards at every time." I don't recognize who it is by name, but I've heard the grazing tone before.

"With a bunch of Landers inside," says another, "they'll be careful of how they carry out the checks if someone raises an alarm and oh, what is this? Get a room, boy." The men laugh, and my rage rises. I clutch my hands on the front of Dorian's shirt. He tightens his grip in reminder and turns slightly, hiding me out of view, and pretends to have a laugh along the rebels.

"Will do, uncle," he says bashfully.

"Kids these days," one of the men grumbles.

They continue their way, and we stay pinned against one another, not daring to move. But the rest of their receding conversation makes it obvious: Freedom's Ark is planning to break inside a Lander dominion.

As they vanish down the street, the silence feels magnified. Dorian drags his hands away, slowly, his skin against mine, as if trying not to disturb something wild and unpredictable. I look back at him through my lashes. He's barely an inch away from my face. He's breathing hard. His eyes are shining and, despite everything, I'm terrified of what his hearing the rebels might mean for all Renters.

"Where do you think they're aiming for?" I say, trying to gauge him.

"If it happens soon, probably another Glory Race event."

"The Crowning Ceremony? They couldn't possibly be so daring."

"You seem surprised," he says flatly. "Or worried that I might connect you to things—hanging out as you do, a bit too close to the rebels."

"I have never been involved in any rebel activity," I say. "You know that." Please, *please*, don't let him report this to his father. To the Landmaster.

"No, I don't think a lot of Renters are involved at all."

I frown.

"If *that* many people were involved, we would have found out where this black market was."

I say nothing.

He smiles grimly. "You have no idea how many times Landmaster Minos has almost gone bald trying to find the hideout."

For a desperate, treacherous moment, I wonder what's the worst that would happen if I revealed the location. If I brought everything to an end. They burned my house. They may have killed my sister. And they hate us. They hate *me*. If I'm the one who leads the Landmaster to Freedom's Ark, perhaps she'll remember that. Perhaps I'll have her gratitude, and with it—help for my family, health for my sister.

The moment passes quickly.

I know what will happen if the Warehouse is exposed. Freedom's Ark and its traitors will probably escape unscathed. The few that are caught will either die or be thrown into the sea. But countless people who want nothing to do with the rebels would lose their one source of income, their lifeline. Innocent Renters don't deserve that—a lifetime of anger born of pain and misery.

A slight smudge of light spreads in the night sky. Dawn is coming and with it, a new day. And the second race.

Silence stands between Dorian and me. I look at him, again

misjudging the distance between us, for an infinite moment. I wish we weren't standing this close, where I can still feel his warm breath on my skin. Where, if I moved slightly, I'd touch his skin. I thought seeing him again would be easy, I thought I was prepared, but neither that day at registration, nor today was *easy*. My feelings are never one thing when it comes to him; never what I want them to be.

It's a dangerous thing, to not know your own self.

"I'm sorry about your house," he says.

"What are you sorry for? You tried to *kill* me."

"It was in the middle of a race. Things got out of hand. If I really wanted to kill you, I had an opportunity. In fact, I have one right now."

Unbelievable. I extract myself from the shadow's embrace. The air is fresh, clean. Too clean, suddenly. In the far distance, I can see my house. What's left of the burned husk. Behind it, the stables are collapsed, except for the very back of the structure. The fire was almost put out by the time it whooshed across the stables, but it still left enough damage for no animal to ever find rest in there again.

Dorian comes up behind me. "Regardless, I don't wish bad things on people who don't get in my way. Like your family."

"Judas said it was zargunine fire," I murmur, my gaze locked onto the smoke still diffusing in the air.

"Judas Pereira?"

I look back at Dorian's tone and raise my brow in challenge. "Yes, he came to see me."

Dorian smirks. "Of course, he did. Can't keep out of your business, can he?"

"You sound jealous," I say, only with the intention to annoy him.

Something flattens in Dorian's expression. His voice drops to a merciless whisper, "And if I am?"

A rushing fills my ears, drowning the sound of the ocean. Fury building like never before. I stalk up to him, stab a finger in his chest. "Don't you *dare*. You selfish, arrogant jerk—you enjoy hurting me so much, don't you?"

He starts walking away, leaving me simmering. I wonder if I know the answer to my own question. My feelings have long been burned, the only remnants were of curiosity, to know why he left. His, perhaps, were never even real. That's why he finds it so easy to make light of things.

*Love* was never a word spoken between us. I thought, like a fool, it was something we both felt. It must amuse him now.

Movement has picked up on the thoroughfare as well. Early morning fishermen, haggard half-awake shop owners heading to their establishments, and street urchins returning to their corners. In the distance, the sea splashes backward from the island.

I turn to go home. And stop with a sudden sense of nausea when I see the remnants of the place that was my home again. *Safety and hearth*. That's what we lost—that's what I cost my family. The one thing that protected us from the world outside.

If I don't win the Glory Race now, if I don't defeat Dorian Akayan, I wouldn't just be the Renter girl who reached too high and was shown her place—I'll be the cautionary tale of one who brought her family to complete ruin.

I trudge the other way, toward the Terrafort. Once more, there are stares and whispers following me down the street. After being shaken out of a maelstrom of emotions, I try to make myself feel something. But there is only a dull ache in my head.

Dorian is a few steps away. He has his hood on again. No one will ever recognize him. He knows how to blend in with the crowds of Sollonia.

The alley he found me in is one of the worst-kept spaces, miserable to its core, and he was so misplaced there. And yet, at ease.

Moving through the network of backstreets with the same familiarity. He didn't once stop when he was guiding me out.

The crowd is getting thicker, the screeches of the sea creatures getting louder. They're going to have a hard time fishing *anything* today. Probably better to go to the other side. Behind the Drome, maybe. But that area is often patrolled by Helix Stratis guards as well as the security for the Sanctuary. They never leave Renter workers in peace. As if so many guards don't depend on help by those same workers when sea creatures attack.

As soon as I think that, a groan erupts from the Terrafort. Dorian stops and I fall in step beside him. The zargunine door at the entrance is plunging heavily.

My breath catches. "What the—"

Dorian and I break into a sprint, trying to get through the door before it locks us out. Damn it! My family is in there without identification for the shop; if the officers are on a patrol today—I hope Crane stuck around.

Even as Dorian and I push, gasping for breath, we know it's futile. My hands slam against the hard metal. Pain shoots along my arms, ending in a spasm along my shoulders.

The door does not budge. "Open up!" I yell.

And right then, the sirens on either side of the door light up, a red so bright it robs me of vision and leaves me unsteady. On the heel of that is the first shriek of the siren.

Followed by the second.

Then the third.

# TWENTY-ONE

The panic of the sirens blasts throughout the island, the roar of the ocean barely audible behind it. There's no place to go. Bile floods my mouth. My knees are shaking. I can head to the backstreets, but everyone will be on lockdown. A cove, a niche hidden into a rock, is our best bet.

That's when I remember: Stormgold is out there, tied to the stables. She'd have been fine against people, but so many creatures? A swarm of bloodthirsty aquabats? She can fight but she can just as easily get hurt. And what if she gets loose and runs into the ocean? No, I have to get to my maristag.

A black cloud leaps into the sky from the thrashing sea and swarms toward the island. The flying amphibious reptiles swoop toward us. Screams tear the thoroughfare.

"Where are you going? Come on!" Dorian shouts. "We have to take cover!"

Hundreds, *thousands*, of aquabats screech overhead. Against the rapidly lightening sky, still soaked in red from the horizon, the aquabats arise like demons. Pocked skin like blood spilled into blackest ink. Wings of muscle membrane, doubling as front limbs, connect to claws at the back. Beneath each stretch of wing is a network of thin, exposed bones—at the front tips of which are shining pincers.

The ground rumbles and I almost fall on my face, but Dorian's arm comes around my waist. "Got you!" We run back to the alleys. The capricorns must be surging toward the thoroughfare, as fast as they can, making the ground rumble as they go. But the aquabats have broken up. They're spreading. Swooping down all across the island, not only near the Terrafort.

Wraith-like bellows from the edges of the water ring loud in the air.

The Renter fishermen!

An aquabat snatches a man by his shoulder. The man struggles, and the aquabat's grip loosens. He falls, flailing and yelping, only for the aquabat to plunge and grab him again, tearing him in half, pincers drenched in red.

Sickness courses through me.

Gunshots echo at our backs. I duck instinctively, almost twisting my ankle. The terrifying sound reverberates in my mind as a reptile-bird flies straight at us, mouth open wide. All I see is the dark abyss down its throat, its four fangs. Every thought, every wish, every hope of mine struggles not to disappear down that void.

I bolt backward, gasping for breath. We have to outrun them. There's no way we can survive a swarm.

Dorian hurtles behind me, his hood torn in half.

Bloodbaths explode all around us. A hurricane of claws and pincers and fangs. People running, aquabats swooping. People dropping dead in puddles of their own blood. A nameless, faceless mass.

Cold dread pounds through me.

We're left on our own here while the Terrafort shut its door.

"Cowards!" I scream in the air.

"Do that later!" Dorian yells over his shoulder.

I see it a second too late—the aquabat dives and sinks its fangs into Dorian's arm. Dorian flings out his staff, but the aquabat has him pinned to the ground. His staff flies into the air and lands at my feet. I grab Dorian's staff and pull out mine, the weight of both coursing strength through me.

The aquabat rises on the heels of its claws and opens its terrible mouth, crying out, and readies for a strike with the sharp pincers at the top of both of its wings.

Dorian snaps to the side and the aquabat smashes its head against his, as I slam both of the staffs into its side. The metal collides with hard bones and the leathery stretch of red-black wings. The aquabat squeals and slumps off Dorian, sprawled on the ground, immediately knocked out by the force of the blow.

Dorian swears and pulls one foot toward himself and sits up on his side. He's heaving hard. He tries to get up and slips back. My pulse is heavy in my ears as I hold out a hand, and he takes it. For a second, the solidity of his warm grip grounds me.

He climbs to his feet, unsteady for a moment, then takes his staff from me. "Damn you. We could have taken shelter somewhere if we ran earlier."

The sky has lightened, the dawn-red receding behind the pale cerise. And nothing has changed. A circle of death surrounds us. The ocean is thrashing loud, the island is nothing but aquabats. How many are there? We run again because we must.

At the far end of the street, a large cloud of aquabats gathers around a capricorn. It slashes at them with its claws as the guard stands atop the back of the giant creature and shoots down the flying reptiles. But more keep coming. More and more.

As if the Panthalassan Ocean demands an end to all humans.

A boy, his face caked in blood, dashes past us. He's carrying a crude knife. He falls to his feet, gasping. I stop to pull him up.

"Thank you," he wheezes, limbs shaking. "So many...so many. My father...he's down at the shore..."

Without another word, he turns and runs again, legs visibly shaking, but pushing on.

"Look out!" Dorian throws his staff like a spear. An aquabat slams to the ground, pierced by the staff. Dorian wrenches out his staff with disgust.

"Let's find shelter." Dorian grabs my hand, and we race toward the nearest exit on the thoroughfare.

When we get to the alley, a bunch of street children spill out, aquabats tearing at them. I let out a harsh cry. An aquabat leaps at me. I jump backward, but what feels like a sharp blade slices through my arm. There's a *rrriiiip* sound and suddenly ice rakes my sides. The wind grows pins and needles. Dorian wrenches an aquabat off me with his hands—the creature is half his height—and sends it splattering to the wall. We look up. Aquabats flood the alley.

Panic wells in me and my throat closes.

Bloodied teeth and claws and endless eyes begin hurtling toward us.

I stand frozen.

"Man the beaches!" comes the cry of a guard, tugging me back. "Push them back!"

Dorian and I exchange a quick glance before we take off at a sprint to the beaches.

Everywhere people are armed with stones and kitchen knives and anything they can grab. Ugly squelching and guttural cries echo over the sea, near the beach. *Where is Stormgold?* I look, as I dash and duck, but there's no sign of my maristag here. If the aquabats get her—or worse, she turns and kills a human—

We reach the boundary held by a group of Renters under the command of a capricorn guard. They're overwhelmed. "Kill these monsters!" he yells at us. Dorian doesn't seem to care he's being yelled at. His gold will not keep anyone safe out here.

We fight and kill our way to the edges of the beach. Dorian smashes his fist against an aquabat, which immediately takes flight. My arm pounds furiously, as if a ton of iron weighs it down, but I slam my staff blindly at the oncoming aquabats. Where did this swarm come from? A raptor in the sea. A swarm on land. We're facing some kind of reckoning.

I turn—just as an aquabat bites my foot. For a second, I can do nothing but stare at the fountain of blood from my punctured foot, then flames of pain sear my bones. I plunge my staff through its skull, then fall to the ground, head cracking against a rock on impact.

Dorian watches me with horror, then immediately turns to stab another aquabat, leaving his side exposed. A pincer plunges through the gap and into the face of the man in front of me, stopping inches from me and splattering me with blood and gore. Terror and revulsion choke me. I hurtle back, palms and soles chafing against the stone, scrabbling for purchase until I'm out of the skirmish.

Panic grabs me by the throat.

My skin is slippery with warm blood.

I can't do this.

All around me. Screams. Claws. Terror. The smell of metal shimmers in the air. This is what made my sister sick. And now I'm going to die. They're going to pile my body up with everyone else and throw us into the sea. I'll never see my sister or my brother or my parents again. They'll never know what happened to me. The aquabats will eat me alive. I'll die, tortured. *Alone.* Lost in the wind and the water. *Forgotten.* I can't hear anything but own heart. Blood drumming in my ears. Rhythmically. An echo in my mind. *Echo. Screams. Silence.* It's too much. *It's too much.*

"Hey," says Dorian, crouching before me. His face is lined with

193

tears of blood. That's when I realize how hard I'm crying. My bleeding hands are wrapped around my knees; my dress torn to shreds.

"You're okay," Dorian is saying over and over again. "You're fine. We'll be fine. We'll beat these bastards back, and we'll be fine. Get up. Come on, Koral, *get up*." Then he's too close. His hands placed firmly on my ears. He tips my face upward. The sounds of the battle dim. He pulls me to his chest. And I stop crying. Around us the world is splintering to pieces, and I *know* I shouldn't trust this boy again. But in this moment, I feel the safest in a long while.

"You're a Hunter," he says, the bass of his voice emanating from his chest. "You fight and you survive."

I nod, still trying not to tremble, and grab my staff. The surge of *wanting* to fight dims the throbbing pain in my hands.

Dorian pulls me up.

The pain in my foot blazes anew and I clench my jaw to contain my scream. But the swarm has only grown. How will we fight this? I look at Dorian. At the cruel viciousness of his face suddenly turning into the will to live. And I know that we have to. I was born with no other choice.

This land has always been quick to show us what fools we are to fancy ourselves a power greater than the unbending leviathans in this vast ocean. We do not matter to this world; we never have. That we survive here is more a testament to stubbornness than dominance.

And I'm nothing if not stubborn.

I slash my staff in arcs. Screaming and groaning with pain but never backing down. We began pushing forward. Toward the sea.

Dorian and I fight, coordinated, keeping one another's backs safe and striking together. The capricorn, its huge tailfin thumping the whole ground, sweeps one horn in the air and aquabats are torn apart. There's a roar of aquabats in the sky. And then, atop the capricorn, the guard's lifeless body jerks and slips off, thudding to the ground.

The giant creature stares at the guard, then howls. It stumbles here, then there, but manages to recall its training. Huge claws come down to the ground in quick successions and serrated horns point forward. The capricorn bounds once, landing miles ahead of us, in the thick of a swarm, scattering them. It opens its giant maw and swallows tens of aquabats at once.

They skitter over its body, trying to distract it, but one lash of its scaly fins and they scatter like grains of sand.

I lift my staff above my head and whirl, sending the closest aquabats flying back. They crash into others and fall to the ground.

I wish all five capricorns could be here. But I can hear clashes off the thoroughfare as well, from all around the island. We have to do our best here, contain this side, and hope the rest come through, too.

A new set of guards bolts down the thoroughfare, armed with guns and staffs tipped with fire. Blue-gray flames crackle loudly and leap into the sky. Aquabats begin fleeing from the fire. The sight of it sends a cheer through the people. Then, halfway toward the top of the Terrafort, an opening reveals itself. Three cannon mouths emerge. They fire at once. And clear half the sky.

"What is that?" I cry.

"State-grade cannons!" Dorian answers from behind me, wheezing as he kicks another aquabat down the cliff. "Installed three months ago!"

A rush of triumph sends me back into the fight recharged.

Someone with a fire-tipped staff darts past me, the blue glow attracting the aquabats toward us.

I slam my staff in an arc, cleanly taking the head off of a giant aquabat. Pausing to draw breath, I turn to the other side. Slam my staff into another. Whirl and strike one more. Suddenly my body is not the body I'm used to, but something stronger. Adrenaline charges through my veins. I rush at an aquabat, shoving it off a man, and arc the staff from the ground to the sky. The aquabat flings like a doll back into the sky then falls down the cliffs into the sea. There's no going back now. The Landers saw me fight in the Drome, the Renters will see me fight now, outside it. They'll remember who it was who fought for them until the end.

A girl cries behind a large stone. Her staff lies broken. "Run to an alcove! Hide!" I say and start clearing a path for her.

A pincer cuts my side open. Fire erupts beneath my skin, and fresh blood weighs the clothes clinging to me. I split the zargunine staff at its center, grab both halves, and thrust them forward. The aquabat slams to the ground. Another round of cannons rattles the island. They're slow but effective.

I turn, heaving, sweat in my eyes, and see the carnage behind me. My fingers begin to slip from the staff. The swarm is dwindling, but so are those fighting back.

"Dorian!" I shout to him, right before an aquabat rams into his back. But he spins and crushes it. He looks up, his breaths heavy, and his face dark with blood.

He looks nothing like Dorian Akayan, the statue of cold marble.

He looks alive. Like he remembers he's made of flesh and blood and bones. His eyes are bright, like the ocean rising high. And I know in that moment that if Dorian Akayan wasn't hostage to the system he was born into, he would be the boy I knew. He'd be himself.

There's a single heartbeat that wonders if he sees me as more than what I am, too. But the thought vanishes before I can make sense of it.

I haul myself to Dorian, leaving a slick trail of blood behind me. We fight together again. Three more. Four. Five. I lose count this time. Dizziness begins claiming me. I have to keep fighting as long as I can, but I can sense myself fading. An extraordinarily large aquabat makes its way toward us. It's easily the size of five grown adults. Dorian and I break formation and come at it from the side.

It screeches so loud that every other reptile-bird in the vicinity turns to us. It swipes its wings at us, and half my hair flies off. If it had touched my skin, I'd be sliced through.

I block the next swipe with my staff. The effort slamming brutally into my bones. And I kick at its ribs. Dorian drives his quarterstaff in from behind and the aquabat cries out. Dorian pushes it off the cliff and into the water. He's immediately pulled into backing another fighter. A guard with blue fire.

I turn away from them, my legs trembling with the effort of staying upright. Even now, I see nothing but my house burning.

My lungs scream. My hands tremble. I can't keep fighting.

The aquabats are regrouping into cloud formation again, the same way they surfaced from the ocean. It changes everything. They suddenly become too big to deal with. The guards shoot bullets and throw fire-staffs. But the cloud keeps rising. And rising.

Until it suddenly dips and charges straight into the ground. Like a damned bullet. The cannons aren't ready. I push my staff into the ground and force myself to stand straight. The moment of stillness forces my body to catch up with the injuries. My foot is still bleeding. I see vivid colors of pain: red and black and white and yellow. My eyes begin closing.

I brace myself for the oncoming surge.

I don't plan to die cowering.

The screech of the aquabats is loud in my ear. Growing and growing and then my entire world is darkened. The pale sky vanishes behind the cloud. I can hear shouts behind me. I can hear the roar of fire.

Then, a large aquabat comes at me from the right. I hold out the staff. Ready to pull it back and slam it down—

My reflexes are gone. I can barely wheeze when the claws of the aquabat grab my shoulder and I flail, my staff crashing to the ground. A scream tears through my throat. The pincers clinch a breath away from my eye as I struggle in its claws. My fingernails scrape the leathery wing, but the claws sink deeper. Pain explodes like supernovae in my body. Gooey warmth slides down my arms, cradled in the crook of my elbow. Red gore spurts into my face, and the aquabat shrieks and loses its grip.

Then I'm falling.

I hit the ground hard into a puddle of my own blood.

The pain is so excruciating that I can think of nothing else.

*I'm on fire.*

I try to crawl out of the way. But my hands are slick. I slip, scraping my chin. The taste of blood fills the back of my throat.

*Try to breathe.*

But my ribs pinch together.

I can't breathe.

A huff of desperate breath blows bubbles in the blood on the ground.

*I can't leave my family…*

The lights behind my eyes go white.

*Not like this…*

Coughing is a wave of pain so strong I want to die.

*No. I have to win, and I have to live.*

Where's Dorian?

*Stupid of you to rely on a boy who tried to kill you…*

An aquabat lands on the street near me. Its black eyes bore into me. It screams, stretching its skin-wings wide, snapping its pincers, and leaps.

*Will being eaten alive hurt?*

One moment the aquabat is in the air, inches away from my face. The next, there's a shadow over me, wind roaring in my ears, and half the aquabat's body is gone. Its torso drops to my feet, cold black blood merging with mine.

I stare through the slits of my eyes.

Stormgold lands on her hindlegs, her front claws tearing a piece of aquabat from her mouth. She turns to face me. Fangs drenched in the aquabat's blood.

A sob escapes me.

Stormgold grabs and swats at the aquabats around me with her claws. Snatching them out of the air. The aquabats circling me begin scattering. A gap opens up. My maristag stands over me. She growls at the aquabats in warning. In response, they skitter loudly, hissing at her.

Stormgold looks me in the eye. Then leans down. I grunt with pain. But I *reach*. I pull the pin from her contraption. She roars, her frillfin flying open, and shoots poison barbs at the aquabats.

The aquabats drop from the sky around me like rain.

# TWENTY-TWO

I jerk awake to bright lights streaming down at me. For a moment all I hear are disjointed screams, feel nothing but absolute terror. I'm on a battlefield, surrounded. My fist tightens on scratchy white fabric stretched over me. I frown and pull at the sheet.

The pungent smell of disinfectant suffuses the air. I lift my head.

A white room comes into focus. More angles. More sharpness. Above my bed, the wall is a large window with double glass screen.

A woman clad in silver and green waits at the foot of my bed. She's smiling.

"Oh, great, you're up." Her voice is neutral, not polite but not antagonistic, either. She's studying me closely, even as she's still smiling. As if I'm a specimen. I return the gaze—she has a strangely thin stature, a *lack* of something. Her heavy-lidded eyes sit on a somehow inhuman face. I don't know much about doctors and nurses; I've never been inside—

"Where am I?" I ask, looking around. The room is so bright, you could stick a grain of sand on a wall, and it'd sorely stand out. I've never seen a place this *clean.*

"At the Hospital, of course," she says.

My heart starts beating so loud I can hear its echoes against the walls.

"How long have I been here? Is everything all right? Where are my parents? My sister?" Dread fills me. Have I missed the Glory Race?

"Your family was informed." She checks the time on the water clock. "You were brought in an hour ago."

"Huh?"

"You should be absolutely fine now, except for mild discomfort in your chest for a few hours." She almost chastises me, "You *did* break three ribs and puncture a lung."

I concentrate on finding a spot of pain. My skin tingles in places, but no part of me hurts. The bruises are gone. I press my face. No scratches.

"How is this possible? You said I've been here only an hour."

"What do you mean?" She sounds like I asked her if the ocean is made of water.

I brush my hand down the center of my chest, tentatively. My ribs were broken. My side was *gored*. An aquabat bit my foot. I'm so sure all of these things happened. I shouldn't be alive right now. Did I make up the whole attack?

Even before that, there was a whole week's worth of trauma on my body.

"I don't understand how I could be okay in an hour." My body is springy and feels strangely *new*.

The hair on my right has been cut short to match the shorn left side.

"Well, we put you through the medshell, of course."

"Medshell?"

Instead of an explanation, all I get is, "The Landmaster made an exception in this case." She continues to smile. Even when she turns

201

to put her board down after taking some notes, that smile is still on her face. It's the strangest thing.

"Why don't you get ready," she gestures toward a neat stack of clothes, "and we'll head over. The Landmaster asked to see you once you were up on your feet."

I notice a mirror hanging across from my bed and take a good look at my face.

Half my tattoo is gone. Just like Emrik's. I touch the remaining black scales, tracing them. Wistfulness pulls my shoulders down. I turn away from my reflection.

The material of the black pants and white shirt is rigid, not really fit for hunting. But anything is better than the tatters of my dress that have been dumped unceremoniously next to the new clothes. I collect the dress, anyway.

The Lander Hospital is a sprawling, hexagonal structure of metal and glass, its center an open space that overlooks the courtyard below. The smell of sharp, undiluted cleaning liquid claws at every corner. Nurses and doctors dressed in silver and green move with machine-like precision throughout the building. The conditioned, sterile hallways are lined with doors and piercing red labels.

Ironically this place feels dead.

We cross a glass door, inside which several full-body medical scanners are kept. Above the door, the label says "Out-of-Service."

"A medshell," says the nurse, noticing my gaze, "is a device invented in the age before the Renaissance, building on the Empyrean Elders' sacred medical knowledge. It is a miracle worker and reliably fixes ninety-five percent of all ailments afflicting a human body."

The Landers always have spent their greatest minds in the medical sector, to the detriment of other things. Whatever social progress we have made all comes to a stop at the Hospital. And it *is* miraculous, but perhaps I'd appreciate it more if it wasn't closed off to the rest of us.

"What happens to the other five percent?"

The nurse only grimaces. At least she dropped her false smile for once.

Even with those odds...if Renters had access to this treatment...

But we don't. I'm a Hunter, and I didn't even know what a medshell was.

If *Liria* undergoes the medshell treatment, would she also be healed in an hour? My head spins. If she could have this opportunity, if *only*.

We're always fed lines about resource limitations and priorities. The official mandate states that we live in a constrained world, that we cannot spread ourselves too thin.

The resources wasted during the Glory Race must drop from the skies.

An elevator outside the Hospital descends three floors down to a bustling street filled with administrative buildings. People with harried looks and hurried steps pass by, muttering to themselves. An armed guard takes over from the nurse and leads me through the row, turning left once, then right, and then straight until everything else falls away and the space turns gloomy, like the loneliness I felt in the Landmaster's Mansion. Or privilege, now that I think about it.

When I arrive at the Landmaster's office, Dorian is already there, standing in front of the Landmaster's desk with his hands locked behind him. He turns to look at me once, his wounds gone as well, then faces forward again.

The office has a ceiling tapering to a point. I feel small, wishing I knew how to act and what to say in this place. How do people talk in this cavernous office without feeling intimidated?

In the strong red lamps on either side of her, the Landmaster's white hair looks like it's dripping blood. She sits behind her large desk on a tall chair carved of wood. The spires behind her chair rise into a sort of crown behind her head. I met the Landmaster before at her public office, not her private one. Only Emrik has been here with Baba. He never mentioned this chair.

I pull my gaze away from the chair and look at the Landmaster. But not in her eyes, the white parts in both also burning a demon-red. I know my limits.

Her thin fingers—they look like *knives*—are interlocked beneath her chin.

"What happened this morning," she says serenely, "is a tragedy. We lost many lives, and every human life lost is a misfortune. Both of you have the island's gratitude."

"Thank you, Landmaster," Dorian and I say in unison.

"I wanted to inform you personally that the Glory Race is still on schedule. The second race will take place in five hours."

It isn't the Landers who will be attending funerals today, after all. I dig my nails into my palms and feel slightly more like myself. I'm lucky to even think like this now that I'm healed. A seed of an idea starts germinating in my mind. If the Landmaster put *me* through the Hospital— our help must have made a difference. The Lander guards, the capricorn handlers—they must have noticed, must have mentioned me.

Could I...ask for something?

"Landmaster Minos?" I say.

She raises one sharp eyebrow. "Yes, Koral?"

I take a moment to steel myself.

"I am sure, Landmaster, that you already know our house and our stables were destroyed."

"Yes, a tragic accident." She's watching me with the intensity of a raptor waiting for a prey to make its move. Neither the end of her sari nor her headcover moves an inch.

"I...I don't believe it was an accident." She doesn't react at all, and that's when I realize that she doesn't care—not unless I give her something to care about. I hope I'm not making a mistake. I take a deep breath and spill, "I believe it was the work of rebels."

Her eyes flash like the sheen of the gilded furniture in her office. On the desk is a small, black paperweight. Obsidian, probably. Dorian shifts next to me, a movement so sudden it must be involuntary. I'd almost forgotten he was there.

"How do you know?" the Landmaster says, too soft. "Can you provide names?"

I swallow. No, I can't. Despite everything, if I take the name of the pharmacist, or even point out the group in that alley, the whole row of shops and the families living there will burn. I can't do that to them. Not after this morning. And what if one of them reveals Crane's name?

Why did I open my mouth at all?

I try another tactic. "A man came to us. I never saw him before, Landmaster, but he warned us. We would have gone to the guards' station before to report it, but he's a stranger. I never saw him before," I repeat.

Landmaster Minos tilts her chin up. Her headcover stays exactly where it is. But I know now that this expression on her face, of absolute authority, is why Aiala Minos has been the Landmaster of Sollonia for the past thirty-five years. That glare of stone is why even on the Council, a bench of shared power, no one will question her.

"Can you describe this man to the sketch artist at the guard station?"

"Yes," I say quickly. Maybe I'll just describe the dead capricorn guard. They can't go after a dead man.

The conversation seems to be over. If the Landmaster dismisses us, that's it. So I barrel on, "Landmaster? May I request something?"

A muscle twitches at the corner of her mouth. "What is it?"

205

"My sister fell into a coma after last night's fire. The medic said if she was at the Hospital, they could figure out what was wrong with her." My voice starts trembling despite my best efforts. The thought is too stark, too painful to even put in words. "Please, Landmaster. Is it possible that she can be admitted? To the Hospital?"

*Don't move. Stand straight and still.*

A strange miracle transpires, then. The Landmaster smiles. "Of course, Koral Hunter. After your services to the island, standing with us against the rebels, this will be our gift to you."

Everything is a little lighter, a little brighter. This is why I'm fighting after all. This is what I'd been waiting for. I touch my hand to my heart and repeat the phrase Emrik and I have grown up memorizing, "We are Hunters, loyal to Sollonia, and to you."

A guard escorts us to the elevator. Dorian hasn't spoken a word so far. I thought we would be past that pretense now.

The street is crowded, although nothing like a Renter backstreet. No grimy walls or stones jutting out in the middle of the roads. The carved stone walls are hidden behind rows of buildings and false circadian day-night lights. It's only when I squint too hard, focusing on that narrow patch visible between two buildings that I can even see the Terrafort's walls.

At the elevator, Dorian steps in first. I frown, but follow, right as he says, "Hey, is that the Landmaster's helper?"

The guard turns, tilting his head to check, and the elevator bars starts dropping.

"Where—? Oh, wait!"

Dorian's palm hovers over the stopping gear. "I'm trying, it's not stopping. Take the next one, we'll wait," he yells as the great cage starts lifting in the face of the guard.

I stare at him, bewildered.

"So." Dorian says calmly. "What do you think you just did?"

He sounds as if I've committed a crime. "My sister is in a coma," I say through gritted teeth. "I don't have the luxury to think about what's right or wrong."

"Do you think you got Liria *help*?"

"Last I heard, your father thinks the Landmaster will bring Landers to ruin because I'm in the race and you seem to agree. Have your thoughts changed?"

He stares at me, his chest rising and falling. "The Landmaster helps no one. She doesn't hand out gifts. Least of all to Renters."

Blood rushes to my cheeks. "I know she's on no one's side. I'm not stupid." How dare he think *he* knows better. This is how I *live*: making the best of every situation. If I got to stand in front of the Landmaster, I wouldn't let that opportunity swim by. Especially when my sister's life is at stake. How can he, a Lander, understand that?

We are about to reach the Grand Bazaar on the entrance floor of the Terrafort. "Forget what you heard from those rebels. If the Landmaster sends for you again, don't say anything. If there's something you truly know about the rebels and their activities, tell *me*."

I raise a brow. "Why would I do that?"

"Because I'm asking you to."

A moment rises in my memory. Me, crying on the ground, and Dorian telling me to *get up*. He could have left me there. If our places were switched, if he was the one having a panic attack and I had the chance to run, leaving behind a rival in the Glory Race, I would have. I'd think of Liria, and I would have.

He didn't.

But does it make up for threatening me?

"I don't have to do anything you say. And don't interfere in my business."

"You don't trust *me*, after everything we lived through? After we literally fought together and saved one another's lives once more? I've saved you so many times, but you trust the Landmaster? She knows how to twist every word spoken in her office. She'll find a way to use your words against you."

"If the way you've acted is called *saving* me, I'd hate to see how you would actually hurt someone," I snap. "You only tried to kill me until *your own life* was literally on the line. Forgive me for not taking you seriously now. What's making you so upset? A Renter getting Lander medicine and treatment?"

He laughs harshly. It isn't a small laugh, but a quiet, frustrated one.

"Why *are* you trying to kill me?" I say, before he gets away with embarrassing me again.

He stops laughing. He takes one step closer, his gaze never straying. "So you are frightened enough to get the *hell* away from this tournament."

That's nowhere near the answer I was expecting. I study Dorian's mask of calm. A nagging feeling says that catching me off-guard *was* his intention. To infuriate me, to say something so ridiculous I can't shake it off. After all, no matter what happens off the track, Dorian Akayan is still my rival. When has that not been true?

"I'm not going *anywhere*. I'm going to stand right here and take that crown from you. You want to know why anger is my only answer? This is why. Negotiations never work for me. So stop trying to do anything for me. You try to kill me one day and call it saving me the next."

"I only tried," he snaps. "My father will *actually* kill you, Koral."

For a moment I stare at him. I know he has no great love for his father. Whatever their relationship, it's as twisted, as thorny as mine. If my father was trying to kill someone—even the thought is revolting.

"Is that why you left? Before?" The thought quietly settles over me, like flakes of ash after a fire. All this time, was the answer so simple? He always hated his father; he was always scared of what might happen if his father found out about us. So much more than me. I had Emrik and Crane. He had no one to assure him.

Did he not believe I could handle this simple truth that perhaps I always knew?

Dorian looks away, his throat bobbing up and down.

I say slowly, carefully, "If my life is in danger still, I deserve to know. I always deserved to know." I can't just disappear. If I disappear now, what will happen to my family? Will the Landmaster keep her word if there are no public stakes for her?

"You're not your father, Dorian, please tell me."

When he looks at me again, he's not the Dorian I saw at the thoroughfare this morning. He's Dorian Akayan, the one on the banners. His gaze is heavy as he says, "You need to go. Now. I don't care where. But get away from my father's reach. Once he has you, nothing will help you. I won't be able to, either."

"Where could I possibly go?" I say quietly, gazing up at him.

He has no answer to that.

A whole wide world out there, and there's no escape. For either of us.

# TWENTY-THREE

The Grand Bazaar is a tumultuous babel of voices.

In the immediate aftermath of the attack—going by the early news, it's the biggest one in five years—most businesses are seeing little to no activity. But the crowds are still here, questions and half-baked answers on their lips, everyone more interested in the details of the tragedy. Collecting facts, or what passes for facts. Body counts. The worse, the better. The more tragic, the more exciting.

I hope this cruel joy at the expense of others means they have finally moved on from my family's devastation. We need a moment of reprieve. At least they were inside the Terrafort, safe.

Dorian still walks beside me. We have reached a silent agreement: there's nothing else to say. After several minutes of this grating at me, I ask, "Don't you have to go home?"

"My stables are up here. I'm going to stay there until it's time for the second race."

"Won't your family want to know if you're okay?"

He only snorts in response.

As we step into the main hall, I immediately spot Crane. She's pacing in circles, chewing her lip, and by the way she's blocking the entrance, she's waiting for me. Before I can distance myself from Dorian, Crane looks up. Her concerned expression evaporates the second she spots him next to me.

"See you at the race," Dorian says.

I can barely muster a reply.

Dorian crosses Crane's path, infuriatingly slowly, their eyes locked for an infinite moment. I used to think they had nothing in common, that it was best to keep them apart. But I was wrong.

They share the same anger. The same misery of existing in their eyes.

The door of the Terrafort is now open again, chilly wind making everyone pull their robes together. It's like walking among corpses, with guards in black and red making sure the dead don't deviate from their paths.

"Is Liria okay? Emrik?" I ask. *And my Stormgold*, I think. I have to find her, but I have to see my family, too.

"Everyone's as they were." Crane waves a hand. "Though Emrik nearly got kicked out for the fuss he created after we got word about you. He wanted to see you immediately."

I swear under my breath. Trust my brother to have no sense of self-preservation.

The second we step onto the terrace of the Agora, Crane says, "What were you doing with *him*?"

"We ran into each other when the attack happened."

"You do something stupid again and it won't be only Emrik saying 'I told you so' this time."

"Crane—"

"Just thought you should know where I stand on this," she says. "Make a mistake twice and it's a habit."

Color rises in my cheeks. The rage, the humiliation, the shame. "I don't want anything to do with him. Everything will go back to normal once this Glory Race ends. Him pretending I don't exist, and us never having to interact again."

The thought leaves a bittersweet aftertaste in my mouth.

"Nothing is going to be normal after this," Crane mutters. "Not if the Ark has any say in it."

I grab her arm and stop her. "Even after you know that they burned our house? That they left us homeless?"

"Those are *not* Sollonia's rebels," she says. "They take their instructions from their faction leader. We can't control everyone. But they'll pay for what they've done. When we get the plans, Bitterbloom will—" She falls quiet, regarding me. There was always a brightness in her eyes when she looked at me, of joy, trust, familiarity. It's not there anymore. "If you help us, we can take these rebels to the Ark leaders. Your insight into…places could make or break this plan for the Ark."

It's unnerving that she always dances around the Ark's secrets with me. Almost as if she knows how close I am—was—to betraying them.

But how can I betray something I don't believe in?

"I'm sorry, I won't help you. I know when I win the Council will dig into my past. I will live under scrutiny for the rest of my life. I won't hand them any reason to strip me of the crown of Champion."

"I never realized that you gave up on everyone," Crane says. "I thought when the time came, you'd be equally willing to uproot the Landers. What has you so scared?"

I start to speak, to argue, to shout again—the frustration of Crane not understanding a word I'm saying is a stab in my gut. If the one person you have always trusted to make sense of the snakes of anxiety knotting in your mind over and over again, suddenly stops even *listening* to you, what do you do?

Instead of another broken argument, what comes out, strangely, is the truth. "No one wants to listen to my reasons. Everything aboveground is a fight to survive. And for some people, yes, it seems the world will right itself if you defy it and break it and rebuild it. Maybe the ones who are truly fighting for change and not destruction, will achieve what they want. Maybe the need to fight burns so strong in their hearts that it's enough for them." I look at my hands. The calluses are gone. So are the scars. Years of labor wiped out in a single, unearned, and seemingly magical hour. "I've seen a woman grow old alone at her doorstep waiting for her son to return. And I've seen miracles that bring back people from the touch of death. It's that simple, Crane, I want a life of wanting nothing for my sister. That's it."

"And what about everyone else? Do others not have sisters? Families?"

"No other Renter would've been denied the antidote to maristag venom that morning, Crane. No other Renter. Now excuse me, I have to go see my family."

Baba and Emrik are sitting outside the shop, leaning against a pillar.

My brother has his hands clasped together, pressed against his mouth, elbows digging on his thighs. When was the last time he ate? My eyes feel heavy, suddenly. All our stock was burned in the house. We have no money, we have no food, we have no clothes save the ones on our backs.

*Three more days. Three more days and I will have a sea of gold laid out for them.*

Emrik notices me first. He blinks as if out of a dream, gets up, and crushes me into a hug. "We heard—we thought—there were guards, and everything was shut down. It was a nightmare—the screaming and all that noise. There were capricorns, we heard? Are you okay? You look—"

His eyebrows furrow as he studies me and the lack of life-threatening wounds that *should* be covering me. He steps closer, one hand on my shoulder, the other on my cheek, over my half-erased tattoo. His fingers are cold, callused, just like mine used to be. The confusion that spills onto his face makes him look like a child. "How—?"

"I'm okay," I say. He meets my eyes. This is not making any sense to him. I take his hand off my shoulder and hold it between mine. *Trust me.*

"Baba, Mama," I say, leaning through the door to call my mother out. "I have news. The Landmaster has agreed to have Liria treated in the Hospital." Elation floods me at finally telling my family this. I can't contain the grin on my face.

That is, until I see no one else joining my relief. Mama is straight-backed, standing on the doorstep of the shop.

Emrik says, "Why?"

"Why what?"

"Why would Landers agree to this?"

"The Landmaster said it's a token of gratitude for how I fought when the aquabats attacked."

Emrik says, "Why were you outside instead of being here? And right now, when we're stretched so thin—"

"ENOUGH." Baba gets up. "Liria will go to the Hospital. You heard the medic," he adds at Emrik's incredulous look. "It will work. Koral did right."

Emrik deflates. It's the first time Baba has ever taken my side. Neither of us are used to it.

Baba sinks to the ground, and Mama takes his hand. They sit close, but they don't look at one another. Still, I know what they're feeling. Because I'm feeling it as well.

A dying hope, come to life.

We decide that Mama will take Liria to the Hospital, while Emrik and Baba stay in the shop and keep it open for patrons to avoid being evicted. It's the only shelter we have right now. After that's settled, I head out to look for my maristag. It takes me an hour to track down Stormgold. I check around the Terrafort, where she came for me, down the thoroughfare, and to the shore. But of course, when I find her, she's resting behind the remnants of our stables, the only familiar place she knows.

She lies half in the shade of the charred roof, and half in the sun. One side of her is heaped with half-eaten aquabat bodies. And I'm reminded, again, not to take Stormgold's nature for granted.

But when she sees me, she raises her head. Watches me serenely.

They call these animals monsters, why? Because they have claws and fangs and look scary? No, they are monsters only because we made them so.

I kneel in front of her, a good distance out of her antlers' reach. "Thank you," I say warmly. "You saved my life." She may not understand my words, or anything I've ever said, but she must understand my trust and gratitude.

Slowly, never breaking our eye contact, she tips her head more, her antlers dipping backward.

I smile, tears of joy pricking my eyes. "Come on, we have a race to win."

# TWENTY-FOUR

This way, please," a handler says. I glance at the posts—barred and empty—and back at him. He's gesturing toward a corner of the Charioteer Hall that looks like a wall. But then I see a small door is cut into it, and a narrow slope goes upward. "To the balcony above," he adds.

This race is not going to be like the others.

The only light along the slope is through the door at our backs. Stormgold bucks and refuses to move until I get down from the chariot and walk ahead of her, unsteadily, checking for distance from her antlers every couple of seconds.

We emerge into a plain hall. To the right, a large balcony over-looks the arena, at perhaps the same height as the first stands. The other charioteers are already assembled on it. As I pull up, I know they're annoyed I'm here, and late, all over again. Did they hear I stole a drop from their ocean of resources? Are they upset they were made to part with something they didn't even need but might have saved my life, and my sister's?

Fortunately, no one is having an easy time up here with their maristags, so at least they keep their mouths shut.

I take my place next to Dorian who, now that we are back in the Drome, ignores me.

The Drome buzzes with excited chatter and frantic new bets, even though most of the Renter seats are empty today. It makes no difference to the true celebrations on the island. My stomach rumbles. Going through the medshell means my body is completely healthy, but the last actual meal I had was at the First Celebration. More than a day ago...

I'll have to figure something out. We can't go without food for three days, especially not when I have to race.

From up here, the Drome looks strangely unreal. Smoother than I *know* it is from having been down there. It doesn't appear sandy, as if the flat side of a blade swept away loose grains and left behind solid, packed ground. This is an odd place to look down at the Drome because we're not up in the actual stands looking at the tracks or looking up at the Landmaster's Tower. It feels like a transitional place that isn't supposed to exist. The not-knowing what's to come is the worst part.

Arlene's maristag slams its antlers into the balustrade, and she cringes. In response, the other maristags begin grunting.

I clench my teeth. Whatever comes now cannot be any worse than the aquabat attack.

The conch shell blows, loud and clear.

Landmaster Minos steps onto her balcony, dressed in a pale-gold sari. Her hands rise.

"Welcome, People of Ophir." A loud cheer rings in my ears. Dorian frowns and shakes his head. "We have all had a somber moment earlier this day. A moment of reflection, a moment of remembering the sacrifices our Empyrean Elders must have made to escape from their torn world only to arrive here. But this, the Glory Race, is a reminder that we will always prevail."

"Always prevail," murmurs Dorian mockingly.

I snort. The way she speaks, it's as if Landers were actually affected. What they hide in what they say is how the Council works. Why should that be any different for the most influential Landmaster of recent times?

"And now, how many of you know that maristags react to a change in the elements? A lot more than last time, I'd say." She pauses as wild laughter rumbles like thunder across the Drome. My heartbeat picks up. The race today will be a reflection of our Opening Ceremony, then. What could it be? Waterfall obstacles?

My question is answered as the conch shell blows. And it's answered brutally.

The sides of the Drome lift open. What I thought were walls, are doors. A groundquake shakes the balcony, thundering through the metal. My chariot shudders. The maristags cry out in unison. And a deluge of glistening blue water floods the Drome floor. I gape, not believing my eyes. Instead of the black-blue waters of the sea, this looks strangely, piercingly cyan under the lights. Gasps and shouts and applause resound in the Drome, blending with the rhythmic roar of the water still flowing in.

The sea ripples on the land.

My head swims, and I sway dangerously close to the chariot floor.

Joining the reflection of the throng on the stands are shadows floating in the water.

"For our second race," booms the Landmaster, "charioteers will battle it out with one another and a sea full of Ophir's deadliest creatures. Don't worry, there are no aquabats," the Drome laughs, "but there will be Murrain eels, gorgon, and one Scythe Crab!" She barely finishes speaking when the Scythe Crab breaks the surface of the water. The giant silver-gray Crab—it's over twenty feet tall—slashes its bladed limbs in the air, before diving back under, splashing the stands and causing a cruel and delighted uproar.

The Drome erupts. Thumping feet. Hoots. Cheers. Thirsty for blood and battle. My fingers tighten into fists on Stormgold's reins to hide my trembling.

"Each charioteer is required to retrieve one of the seven gold coins in the water and finish the event by crossing the finish line. They must complete *at least* one full round of this sea of glory."

Through the applause, the charioteer placed before me chokes on his voice, "Is this a damned joke?" Mateo Lee, I've never talked to him. No one answers him as he continues to curse. "This is supposed to be about trained maristags and chariots. Not wild sea creatures. This wasn't the deal. I'm leaving and," he looks down the row, "if any of you have any common sense, you'll leave, too."

He leaps off the chariot and shouts at the handlers to get his maristag down. Angrily, he strips off his jacket, nearly tearing the sleeves in the process. The last I see him, he vanishes down the slope, still cursing like a Renter fisherman.

The uncomfortable silence left behind is so vast, it masks the irascible noises of the Drome. Stormgold grunts, stepping back from the water splashing over the edge of the balcony floor.

It *is* a poorly timed event.

Dorian watches Mateo leave, then he too murmurs, "This can't be a coincidence." We exchange quiet glances. "There's still time to leave," he says so softly that only I hear him.

"I wasn't the only one out there today. *You* leave."

He doesn't try again.

The Landmaster still has her hands raised high, but she looks at the charioteers now. At me. She smiles, as if benevolently.

But I know.

This is the price of her gift.

And I know this is why I cannot rely on that gift. I must win this tournament. Only gold matters. Only gold will save us.

The giant Scythe Crab rolls in the water, sending sprays all over the balcony and the stands beside us. The crowds continue to be a mix of laughter and mock indignation.

"Are you ready, People of Ophir?" rings the Landmaster.

*I am a Hunter.*

With a groan, the balustrade of the balcony recedes into the ground.

*I have grown up in the sea.*

The conch shell blows a sharp, elongated note.

*I will win this, no matter the odds.*

The charioteers burst forward in a sharp dive. Slick liquid flies at me. When we crash against the first solid blue wave, the cold grips us in searing chains, as if the water was a raging fire. My chariot lurches and the freezing water echoes in my bones.

This water is unnatural. Sticky. My ears throb with pain. The bright blue below the surface is somehow crystal clear. I gasp, crashing through the surface, and right as I'm about to drag in a lungful of air, the poison barbs shoot out from the maristags.

I duck inside my chariot, the water washing out.

A shower of darts thump against the outer surface. One whooshes over the top of my head, narrowly missing, and smacks against the inner edge across from where I'm crouching. I stare at it in disbelief.

My clothes are sodden, the wind rapidly numbing my body. Over the reins, my fingers seem to have locked over in fists. How will I find a tiny *coin* like this?

Head spinning, I pull Stormgold to the surface. My chariot is useless. If I didn't have it, this would be my natural turf, but with a chariot, I'm *bound*.

The others are already scrambling, their gilded chariots above the surface. But it doesn't matter if a chariot is above the surface or only halfway up if their maristag isn't controlled.

Small, harmless fish dart past us. Stormgold lashes out, trying to swallow them. But something bigger is rapidly moving toward us. *The Scythe Crab!* We have to move.

"Go, go!" I yell. The splashes of all the charioteers ring behind me. No one has any idea how the others are doing. The wall of blue rises and dips. The stands seem farther and closer at once.

A hiss echoes in the water, and a charioteer screams.

We have to grab a gold coin now. That's the only way to get out of here. A serpent-like Murrain eel has grabbed hold of Arlene's ankle. She shrieks. The other eels are rapidly converging. It's been five minutes and no charioteer has managed to move past the Landmaster's Tower.

We're still struggling to get our maristags under control.

Stormgold cleanly snaps an eel in half and swallows it. Blood snakes past her jaw, floating toward me. I snap the reins and she bucks. I'm thrown off the chariot, halfway into the water, held back only by the straps.

But then, just as fast, she *races*.

The sheer speed of her keeps my chariot above the surface, almost hovering. We curve away from the Tower and hurtle onto what would have been the tracks in a normal race. The icy water, like shards of glass, cuts at me. There's no hint of a coin so far. They must be spread out around the Drome. But there have to be a few on this side, right?

As I'm trying to squint at the water, trying to look past the surface, a gorgon's dark-green body springs out of the water. Its serpent-like tentacles grab at the edge of my chariot. We're not allowed any weapons—not legally, at least, and I doubt I'd be allowed the leniency afforded to Arlene Bashir—so I don't have my knife with me. I slam at it with my shoe. But it only hisses and grips the metal tighter. Then, one by one, its tentacles grasp the edge. I grip the reins with one hand and with the other, wrench the gorgon off the chariot. It fights me desperately, viciously, but finally lets go and splashes loudly, sending needles of water in my eyes.

I rub at my face. And see a swarm of gorgons leaping through the surface coming straight at me.

*Not again!*

I urge Stormgold to *go go go*. To my left, someone's maristag has lost control. It cuts loose from the chariot and is now fighting the other creatures. If a charioteer gets caught in that...

*Focus.*

*Find a gold coin.*

But the pain of the cold water is dragging me down. If I hadn't walked—*splashed*—into this second race perfectly healthy, I probably would be floating in the water, facedown right now. Behind me, the gorgons are catching up. They move grotesquely fast, their tentacles whipping up a frenzy.

Another chariot zooms past me. Whoever it is immediately goes underwater and as quick, emerges with a *swash*, drenching the first stands to the spectators' delighted squeals. In his hands, gleams a brilliant gold coin.

There are gold coins here. My heart nearly bursts with relief.

And then I see the charioteer: Dorian.

An eel is writhing at the base of his chariot. I start to shout a warning instinctively, but at that moment, the Scythe Crab breaks the surface of the water on the other side. Screams erupt from the charioteers and the spectators alike. The Spine separates me from that Crab, but its bladed limbs flash silver terrifyingly, the sound like a cleaver cutting through air.

I do not want to get in that Kraken's way.

Stormgold starts clashing with another maristag—a deep-red one that belongs to Saran Minagi. He swears at me as if I purposefully broke his dive forward. For a moment Saran and I are dead close, struggling with our maristags. The water slams against my chariot, and it dips halfway beneath the surface. There—to my right, the sheen of gold is unmissable. Just as I reach for it, my foot slips. Water forces its way down my throat, a burning sensation lines my mouth, and I cough and hack. It's Saran who pulls away. But not before smashing against the side of my chariot, nearly sending me tumbling over.

My buckles hold. I slam back in place.

Damn him.

Something moves to my left. I jerk Stormgold away. She listens, but she's rushing around, maddened with water. She probably thinks this is the sea, and she can swim out, but she's going to get her head slammed against the Drome's walls.

"Down!" I shout, releasing the reins a little, nudging her to the bottom of the Drome. She plunges into the water and cold pierces through me. Breathing out air bubbles, I quickly check for any creatures. A gorgon locks eyes with me.

It spins toward me. If it grabs me, I have nothing to fight it with.

I grasp the edge of my chariot and pull it along toward the bottom. A coin shines. So close, so *close*.

The gorgon lashes a tentacle and the coin soars in the water, crashing the surface. I barely push my head out of water when a maristag leaps over my head. Arlene grabs the coin mid-air with a triumphant shout, and I'm left shrieking with frustration.

Fury rises in me fast and hard. I lean down, bearing the weight of the wave thrown against me by Arlene's move. The second the gorgon tries to lock its tentacles around my wrist, I hurl it into the air.

Straight at Arlene.

The gorgon screeches as it shoots forward and lands on Arlene's head.

Arlene screams.

She lets go of her reins, sending her maristag in a sudden tizzy, and yanks at the gorgon.

Stormgold bolts forward, past the other maristag, and as soon as the gold coin flies from Arlene's hand, I'm there.

Closing my fist around it.

I leave the fighting girl and gorgon behind. We're coming up the corner, *finally*, and I won't have to return to the fray once I reach the finish line.

But there's still the Scythe Crab between us and the finish line.

The crowd's going wild.

Large waves of water slam against the walls of the Drome, the smell of animal blood filling the air—a reminder of what this island faced this morning and survived.

This side of the tracks is also crammed with fish and eels. Not deadly, but distracting. It's impossible to get Stormgold to listen as she starts devouring the fishes right there in the Drome.

"You ate a ton of aquabats this morning!" I shout. "You can eat later!"

Immediately, she dives. As if to reprimand me. Water washes over me, and I'm left gasping for breath. The gold coin's ridged edge dig against my palm. I tighten my hold on it. Several seconds of struggle later, I finally manage to pull Stormgold up.

In front of us is the Scythe Crab.

I look behind. Three charioteers—Arlene, Isidore, and Emmanuel. A *new* gold coin shines in Arlene's grip—*damn*, she's good—but the other two are still diving for theirs.

And ahead of us all, Dorian.

He'll reach the Scythe Crab first.

I have to get away from this impending Scramble around the Scythe Crab. If all of us reach it at the same time, one defensive swipe of its bladed limb could *kill* us all.

I lean forward, loosening the reins. Stormgold listens. She lets the distance between the three charioteers behind us grow—but the Scythe Crab, slashing in the air, gets bigger and bigger.

It lashes at Dorian. He dodges it in a flash. The scythes come down in arcs, blocking the underwater tracks. I see it now. The only way through is *under* the blades—skirting skin-close to the Crab.

Dorian tries to deflect and race through, but the blade comes at his maristag. Rhyton shrieks, falls backward, and for a second Dorian is underwater. They immediately pull up but I'm too close to them. Stormgold snaps at Rhyton. Dorian swears.

He gets reckless.

He tries to shoot forward, but the Scythe Crab cuts off his escape. Blood spurts on my face—Dorian's blood. He howls, his maristag echoes his cry, and all the sea creatures around us are drawn to Dorian's bleeding arm. The distraction is all I need to dive down deep and glide right past the Scythe Crab.

We cross the finish line and leap back onto the balcony.

Cheers and screams rend the air inside the Drome. The handlers immediately rush to subdue Stormgold. Right behind me, Dorian is hurtling through red-laced water. As he climbs onto the balcony, water splashes and startles Stormgold again.

As I step away from her, I see a dark shape floating in the water, next to a maristag frothing at the mouth.

A tangled group of gorgons and eels.

Dead.

The scent of green blood, tinged with the thickness of iron, snakes through the water and the air.

"CLEAR THE WATER AND GET THE CRAB OUT!" someone bellows. "Get the charioteers off the tracks!"

The metal gates pull up, draining the water and sucking the creatures back along. But the screams don't stop. If anything, the draining of the tracks reveals the full horror of what's gone wrong: the maristag that broke free is frenzied and facing down the handlers. His forelegs are poised in the rapidly receding water and the froth around his mouth is tinged with green blood. Another touch of green glints between his eyes and along his antlers.

He looks like a raptor.

He looks ready to hunt.

# TWENTY-FIVE

The handlers yell our names, trying to make sure the charioteers are out of harm's way. But one is missing.

I squint at the mass of animals unconscious on tracks. They're all amphibians so being on wet sand won't kill them. But there's chaos. Too much scrambling. Too many people in the Drome shouting in the overwrought air.

These handlers can't control a maristag, not one maddened by the sharp change in the elements. This isn't a regular stable fight or a maristag trying to protect itself, like the one that bit Emrik.

This is the green blood in them, the dark ocean unleashing in their veins.

A savage howl cuts the cries from the stands.

A human howl.

Forgetting protocol, a handler yells, "That's Isidore!"

Isidore is fenced against the Spine by his maristag. What was the idiot *thinking*?

Two handlers run down the slope with zargunine rods.

"No!" I shout, pointing to grunting maristags behind us. "You have got to keep these stags under control!" Fawns are individuals, with their own thinking, their own feelings. But as they grow, their green blood outweighs the land's influence. When afraid, maristags tune in to the hive mind. They soak up the violence of even a single troubled beast in their vicinity.

"Get back, Koral," Dorian's voice is clear. I look down. I'm in a running stance; my instincts kicked in involuntarily.

The giant maristag below lunges at Isidore. In a flash the boy is swung onto large antlers and hurled like a doll. Out of reach.

Four handlers and two Helix Stratis guards come running out of the Charioteer Hall's ground floor. Pathetic.

"Get the manefin!" I shout.

Someone's hand wraps around my arm, holding me back. I try to pry it off, but it holds tight.

The six men form a defensive boundary. A hopelessly frail one against the puffed-up maristag. It's horrifyingly comical. Beyond, Isidore is crawling on his side, trailing dark, fresh blood. Handlers stretch the line between them.

The maristag lashes its tailfin so sharply the men fall back. It sinks its yellow fangs into the arm of one handler and kicks at another. Then it crushes the bitten man. There's a crunch of bones and screams erupt from the stands.

This is no glory.

It's a bloodbath.

My heart surges. I've done this so many times the outcome of this is clear as crystals. I'm trying to scream, to tell them to leave, to save themselves. But words don't leave my mouth.

Dorian swears.

The remaining men haul the line against the mad maristag, pulling it off the dead handler, but one strong toss of its antlers and it's free again. The maristag is on the hunt. It turns slowly, casting long shadows on the Spine, eyeing Isidore.

The men forget precaution and rush for the maristag. They snag a line around its antlers—four tines, jewel-toned. These are the biggest antlers of any animal in the race.

No one is trying to subdue this maristag by its manefin.

I yell again.

They don't hear me.

The men on both ends of the line tug at it from either side. But the maristag is too powerful. Too clever. I can tell the waves of his mind are rising. If Emrik was here, he'd ask me to hide, to run. Even up here, no one is safe. This beast has too much ocean in him.

He digs his clawed arms in the sand and lets go. The captors on the right side of the maristag tumble into one another. Loosened from the line, the maristag lunges.

The men are in a bad place. This maristag will not tire—they will. The gasps of their heavy breathing fill up the tracks. Where's more security? Why are the people in the stands not demanding more? What is *wrong* with all of them?

The maristag snaps backward, pulling the handlers toward him. It slashes a handler from navel to neck, buries its fangs in the entrails, the man is still alive, and screaming like *hell*. Until he stops. The others, terrorized, freeze for a fatal second, after which bodies begin collecting on the ground like tangles of seagrass.

It's a nightmare. This isn't what people root for.

I think of my brother, attacked by the maristag.

Then I leap down the balcony onto the wet sand and run as someone shouts behind me.

I can do this. If I can get the maristag under control the rest of them can get out and take the charioteer. He'll have a fighting chance. Even if it's Isidore Grae, I'm Koral Hunter—if anyone should help, it's me.

"Here!" Someone throws me a line, and I catch it in air.

The maristag senses my presence. Its giant, piercing antlers come down, pointed at me. I throw the line to the right, between the maristag and the Spine. Like I thought, the maristag turns, startled, at the large stone structure looming next to it. The maristag whips around, snorting wildly, which gives me enough time to slide to the left and grab its manefin with one hand by snapping the fins together and an antler branch with the other hand.

In a second, I'm atop the maristag, and a man slams the zargunine to its nostril.

"Enough!" I bellow.

The world falls into shocked silence. There's only gasps and fading screams. The maristag totters backward and sideways for several tense moments, and finally comes to a shuddering stop.

The handlers rush to get the maristag, relieving me. I slide off, pain rocketing through my feet, and stagger backward.

Isidore lies still in the middle of the tracks. Around him, a spreading pool of red. The Helix Stratis guards are speaking into their radios, shaking their heads.

Even from the distance, the tiny black barbs of the maristag are visible on Isidore's leached-white skin. Narrow trails of blood form spider-veins on his face, dripping with little *plunk plunk plunks* into the pool below. Chasing them is the black ooze of maristag venom. His body has deflated, like all his organs and bones have turned to mush inside, leaving only a husk behind. The venom works differently on the dead, when there's no beating heart and fighting brain to overcome. And it's still working, turning Isidore into something that doesn't even resemble a human.

He was only seventeen.

A creeping sensation scrapes in my ear, rust over skin.

It's too much to handle, even for me.

I thought this morning was over. Death had walked away from the island, and I wouldn't have to see someone suffer like this. And for what? For gold and glory.

I glance up at the stands. Hysteria. Cries. The Renter stands are almost empty. It's the Landers grieving now, shocked at the turn of events.

Is Isidore's family here? Does he have siblings? Did they see him die? Powerless and desperate, being up there, while he bled down here?

*Liria is safe, she's getting treatment at the Hospital. My sister is safe.*

The Landmaster returns to her balcony. She raises her hands. A solemn, if reluctant, quiet falls over the Drome.

Nobody moves to cover up Isidore Grae's mutilated body.

He lies there, a spectacle in his death.

The Landmaster speaks. Without thought, I listen. A routine speech of expressing sadness at the loss of a precious human life. She calls Isidore a great charioteer, which he really wasn't. It's the last part of her announcement, the one before she pauses, that has the entire Drome holding its breath.

"Because of this tragedy, no other charioteer will be eliminated this round. We will see them all in the final race of glory."

That leaves me, Dorian, Arlene, Judas, Saran, and Emmanuel.

There will be a final race, of course. A death on the tracks won't stop Ophir's biggest event. The shock of what *just* happened, the pain and sorrow and disbelief, is now contained in a small circle moving down from stand to stand. The Grae family. But everyone else is turned to Landmaster Minos, cheering her on. Discussing whom to bet on next.

This is the glory of the race: blood sport.

It means nothing else. It never has, and it never will.

I'm suddenly cold—colder than I've ever been before. A cruel wind whips at the edges, daggers of ice nipping at my exposed skin.

I flex my fingers, clench and unclench my fists. And I walk away.

Stormgold and the other maristags have been put back on their leads. I look at her, and my eyes snag on the chariot tied to her; it's splintering. My heart sinks.

People watch me as I pass by in the Charioteer Hall. Judas tries to stop me. I pretend not to hear him. My face throbs with pumping blood, heat rising in my brain, but I force my expression to stay flat. My feet carry me down the row of corridors, and I make for one of the empty stalls, where I can lock myself in and breathe.

The buzzing in my head is still loud.

Perhaps that's why I don't hear any noise, and the first open door I reach roots me to the spot. Dorian, his hands pressed to the wall, his head lowered, is heaving and retching. Shivers wrack his body. The back of his shirt is torn from the blade of the Scythe Crab, crusted blood darkening. His eyes are shut tight, but tears spill down his pale face, which glistens with the sticky water from the Drome still.

I can't breathe. Something about Dorian Akayan—the golden boy of Sollonia who smirks down from posters, the one who fought hundreds of aquabats, the one who speaks with a will of iron that could command the sea—breaking down like *this* feels as if the ground beneath the island is shattering.

He gasps. Trembles.

I say nothing.

And quietly back away.

# TWENTY-SIX

We have no stables in the Terrafort, much less a drop of metal to rent one. So I turn from the Terrafort's mouth and head for the beach with Stormgold.

The shore reminds me of nothing but the attack this morning. The dead guard on the capricorn, the little boy who couldn't find his father, and the girl whose fear unraveled her. I hope she found a safe way out.

But that leaves me nowhere to go. Nowhere but the charred remains of my house. Is this what my shelter will be if I don't win? A blackened, burned structure. A taunt.

I tie Stormgold to a large stone sunk halfway in the ground. In the late afternoon light, her scales shimmer magnificently. I kneel beside her, carefully, and reach out. Her scales are rough like sand, but smoother along the edges. For a quiet moment, she lets me run my fingers along her scales. Then she makes a sound like I've never heard from a maristag. A short chirp, twice, like a purr.

She's—*happy*?

The thought overwhelms me, and I grab at the ground to balance myself. Stormgold was always different than other maristags. Maybe it's not only her color that sets her apart. She seems smarter and more attuned to her emotions. She's a miracle.

Even as I'm reeling from this new emotion I've witnessed in a maristag, she makes another *clack* sound. And this one I definitely know. Hunger.

After dragging an aquabat carcass from her morning pile, I step back. The chariot is hopelessly splintered. Today's race wreaked havoc on its old body. I have to fix it, first thing.

Even this one beat of silence sends pain lashing through my veins. Hunger bites at my stomach. The daze is beginning to settle in now that the adrenaline has ebbed. Where can I get some food? I don't have the courage to face Emrik and Baba. I can't see *them* hungry, too.

But I do need food. I have to attend the second race event tonight. Maybe they'll have food there. I could probably smuggle some out in my pockets. Best to wear something with bigger pockets, the jacket Emrik got—

*My clothes are ash.*

The realization is a blow. I need strength for the last race. Just because I finished today's race first means nothing if I don't finish first in the final.

Stormgold rends the flesh of the aquabat. The fist of hunger tightens around my stomach. What if I fish something out of the ocean?

"I thought you might be here."

I turn. Mama stands there, looking small. When was she last outside under open skies? She hasn't handled the stables in years, not since Liria got sick. It was lucky I inherited her intuition, her whispering abilities. She glances at Stormgold, who suddenly stops eating. The maristag's antlers dip forward, and she makes a low grunt.

"Don't come closer, she doesn't know you," I say and get up.

We settle on the sand some distance away. Behind us, the thoroughfare is empty. Most people are gathered nearer the Terrafort, celebrating the aftermath of another race event. And gossiping about death.

"How's Liria?" I ask.

"Baba is with her. She's stable for now; they're waiting for tests."

Mama then pushes a rolled flatbread in my hands. I gape at it. It's not fluffy, exuding fresh warmth, like at the rows of Lander bakeries. It's hard and stale. But it's flatbread, nevertheless. Flatbread is special. Land food always is.

"The Hospital has trash cans on every floor." There's no humiliation, nor sadness in her voice. It's a simple fact.

My voice is stuck in my throat.

How did we come to this?

"Have you eaten?" I ask in a small voice.

"Don't you have to race? You need more energy. There are still two nights to the final race."

She's right, and yet I can't swallow the bite I took knowing that she hasn't eaten in days. "Mama, come on, take some of—"

"No," she says sharply, as if I've offered her poison. I'm left blinking at her.

"I'm sorry," I say, although I'm not sure what I'm apologizing for.

"Let me do something for you."

"You've done plenty for us your whole life."

"I was like Crane once," she says. "When I thought you had to break things to remake them." I stare at my mother, and her soft face, listening to her voice, and yet my mind balks at what she means. My mother, a rebel? One after another, questions spill into my mind. Who was my mother before? We've never really known. Asked. My father's family, at least until a few years ago when our grandmother was alive and his sister's family still lived in Sollonia, was so large that I never looked beyond them.

Her words stir my memory. Laughter. Inside my house. I was small. Happy. It's a fleeting memory, something that feels stolen from someone else's life.

"Twenty years ago, the Freedom's Ark was united under one goal: getting a say in the Council of Ophir as a political force. In those days, it felt like the Ark might at least be legitimized as a program of social reform.

"But so many political clashes... The Landers who didn't want us united, didn't want to extend amnesty to former militants..."

Mama stops talking for a moment. Presses her brow, smoothing the tense lines that have cropped up.

"And the betrayals. Those of us on the ground forced to act against one another. Made scapegoats. Do this, Leela. Do that, Leela. Don't question your superiors, Leela. *Frame your best friend, Leela*. And I was only—I was your age." She looks up, as if suddenly realizing what she's saying makes no sense, not when it's happening to a sixteen-year-old. "I was scared, and I wanted out. So they named *me* a traitor. Said I was working to cause disruption in the Council-Ark union on behalf of a group of rich Landers who didn't want to work with Renters. There was nowhere to go once the rebels turned against me.

"So I ran and I ran, straight to your father. He'd wanted to marry me. And the Hunters' house was the only place where I *could* hide."

"So you married Baba?" I ask with dread.

"So I married your Baba."

"Did he know? Did he protect you willingly?" If nothing else, perhaps *this*, this might redeem—

"No," she sighs. "Not at first."

I raise a brow.

"I got him to convince Minos the rebels were targeting our stables. We were given security. By the time he figured out it wasn't the stables but me they were after, I'd become an intrinsic part of the stables. Minos knew me personally as well. And we had Emrik. Your father, he couldn't..." she sighs.

"The resistance had been cut off. They burrowed in the Warehouse; the old leaders gone. It had always been a wrangle of factions and networks, and without its leaders, it scattered brutally. For years it was nothing but older Arkers who spread far and wide that Leela of Sollonia betrayed the Freedom's Ark. The Hunters used to be revered, but they were now reviled for sheltering me. That's why your aunt and the rest of the family left Sollonia."

She laughs a short, bitter laugh. The wind tugs at her hair, spilling strands across her face. "And everything that has happened after, since I escaped the Arkers and joined the Hunters, all of it culminates to this."

My mother plaintively looks down at the hard bread speckled with grit, a morsel of food fished from the trash of a Lander, in my hands.

She says nothing else.

Stormgold is asleep. I wish I could be a maristag as I crouch next to her, examining the chariot.

An entire side is gone, its edges ridged with splinters. The leather Emrik held it up with is torn, hanging limply. This chariot is not racing again. Which means, *I* am not racing again.

I curse in a shaky voice.

The piece of bread has staved off the worst of my headache, and the whole gallon of water that I drank helped.

But looking at this broken junk now...

I can't believe my luck.

Or, actually, I can. Who else would this happen to?

Stars spark in my vision.

This chariot is beyond salvaging.

What will I do now?

The final race event is in two nights. Where can I get another chariot? The silver chariot from Bitterbloom?

*Did you listen to a word Mama said?*

The memory sends my mind reeling. I want to do something. Go back in time. Somehow stop Mama from joining the Arkers. *Don't trust your leaders*. And perhaps everything would be okay. What if Mama had got out in time? What if Mama never married someone as abusive as my father?

My parents fought, but my mother was always the one who quieted first. She was always the one pacifying everyone else in front of my father. If she left, the rebels would've gotten her. And this life was all she knew. I wondered at her weakness, at her surrender. But she stayed for us, for Liria. She provoked the ghosts of her past for the first time for *me*, standing up to my father.

I hate how tight my throat is, how I will probably cry if I open my mouth.

Who might my mother have been without *her* anger?

What legacy would I carry if not my mother's pain?

The weight of *what-ifs* is heavy on my mind, blurring my vision.

I head down to the shore to clear my head. The rush of water is pleasant now. But I can't help glance around for any stray creature. An aquabat biding its time…

Everything looks okay for now.

The sun's a few hours from sinking, but the sky is reddening already. I take my sandals in my hand and dawdle to the edge of the sea. The tide is far out. I wonder what happened to the raptor. It must have been driven back along with the aquabats.

I, for one, will not miss it.

Dull pain thuds all over my body. But when you've been capturing and training maristags half your life, bruises are the least of your worries.

I rub my face, leaving a trail of sand sticking to the tears on my cheeks.

Death on the tracks is a normal part of the tournament. Always gets the crowd going.

But there's a difference between watching someone get mauled when you're far away in the stands, looking at snail-like figures on the tracks, and when you're just steps away. When you can smell blood and fear, when you can hear screams close. So close.

Could I have saved Isidore if I'd acted faster?

My fingers dig in the sand.

A shiver scuttles down my spine.

When the horizon turns red, a shadow lengthens next to me. I don't immediately turn. He still speaks brazenly. "Have you changed your mind now?"

Dorian stands over me, arms crossed, mouth pressed in a flat line—like he owns the land, and I should be thankful he's letting me stay. The banners around Sollonia did quite a job in capturing this quality in him. So different from when he thinks no one can see him.

"No."

He lowers himself next to me, stretching his legs, and leans back on his hands. His sleeves are pulled halfway up, fabric bunching at the elbows, and his shoulders aren't tensed like always.

I want to ask if he's all right. But back out at the last moment.

He looks at peace, strangely, and I don't want to remind him of this afternoon. The wind ruffles his hair as he turns to stare out at the ocean.

I don't look away.

And it hits me. The difference between other places and here. No one's surveying us. No one's listening in. We're back in time, hiding in the soft light of our secret, free of every chain that binds us.

The effect of this freedom is stronger in him.

"He didn't deserve it," Dorian says. "Those handlers didn't deserve it. Nobody who dies on the tracks deserves it."

"Yet it's going to rile up everyone anew, so I guess it's part of the games."

"If you understand that, you must also know whatever happens in the Drome, on tracks or off, is not in our hands. You could have saved Isidore no more than you will win the Glory Race."

"Stop your preaching," I say, sharper than I intend. A wave reaches my feet. "Why are you here? You..." I pause, searching for words. "You don't enjoy the violence. You've always hated pushing Rhyton, and you said you would never put a harness on him. And you don't exactly need the gold. So what's keeping you in the Glory Race?"

He doesn't answer for several moments.

When he speaks finally, his voice is gentle. "In the ways it matters, after you gave me Rhyton, I became worse." I wince, but he holds on. "I spent all my time analyzing past races. I was obsessed—"

"You weren't—"

"You didn't see it because you didn't want to. It felt good and... peaceful to be alone with you. But the moment I was away..." There's a silent look in his eyes, fixed as they are on me. A—desperation, a yearning. He shakes his head and the look vanishes. "At first, I wanted to be my father, so I had to win at any cost. And then, that need became so strong that I wanted to grow bigger than him. I had to defeat his hold on me. I had to defeat *him*."

He tosses a pebble to the water.

"If you're still trying to be free of him, why are you doing exactly what he wants?"

"Because without that ambition fueling everything inside me, I am nothing but a boy with a broken violin. When I race, I race for who I am. To see what I am capable of. I never thought I'd try to run you over. I never thought someone would *die*—"

"But you didn't," I tell him. "You pulled back. You chose to do that."

"Maybe it was an accident."

"That's not true, Dorian. I know you; I saw you. I saw your eyes. Your father pushed you into this corner where the Glory Race was your only outlet, but you don't have to be like this."

Dorian keeps staring ahead, but the corner of his mouth lifts— with a bitter edge. He looks down, tapping his fingers against the wrist of his hand. The smile falls.

"What you did today...trying to save a Lander..." He gazes at me, as if not quite sure what he's looking at. "I always wondered why Renters care about the Glory Race when they can't participate. Maybe, I reasoned, they liked to see how brave the Landers are."

I raise a brow.

"But I know why now. After this morning. They come down to see if Landers know how brave *Renters* are to live like they do outside the Terrafort."

"Bravery implies there's a choice," I say irritably.

He considers me, then nods.

That he chooses to keep silent annoys me further. I *want* to argue, *want* to rail against the Landers and everything terrible. But I'm forced to stay quiet.

I'm so tired.

And Dorian is chained to the crown. I wish he'd cut away these chains. They're what's keeping him locked inside the marble statue he presents to the world. Without their removal, even if he wants to walk farther, those chains would coil and spring him back to the start.

Whoever that Dorian is, he's not the real one. The real one is here in front of me. Not exactly the one I lost, but at least a shadow of him.

Blood rises to my face. Anger. I think it's anger, the real kind. At the way Solomon threatened him as a child. How he shoved his own son into a wall.

What will Solomon do to Dorian if he doesn't win?

It's wretched disgust that now roils in my stomach.

Not enough for me to put my family aside. But enough to haunt my every step when I win.

Why is this world so strange, so awful? Scavenging for food. Struggling to live. Trying desperately to keep our souls intact. My father and Dorian's father grew up and changed nothing of what turned their hearts into stone. They only made things worse and made sure we suffered as they did. We fight for morsels of power and dignity, just like them. We live through their trauma. We hide ourselves the way they were forced to.

Dorian meets my gaze, unraveling the threads of my thoughts. He covers my fingers with his hand. And holds it there.

As if he understands everything without my saying it. As if he knows. The thought doesn't trouble me. We used to be like this before, too. Talking to him is always strange. Like I can say anything. He wouldn't tell anyone. Just like I don't talk about his secrets to anyone. His eyes have darkened again. What does he see? Does he trace my face like I do his? When did he come so close? His chest rises and falls with a deep breath. He begins saying something but has no chance to finish it.

Pebbles roll down the cliff. Startled, I look up and see two men at the cliff's edge. Watching us. They're dressed in black. Guards? Dorian pulls his hand back like he's been electrocuted. He stands straight, wrenched ruthlessly back into his world.

"Dorian," says one of the men, his tone flat. "Your father wants to see you before the Sanctuary Pilgrimage."

They don't look my way. Like I'm nothing but a stone on the shore.

# TWENTY-SEVEN

It takes over an hour to convince Emrik to come to the event with me. Mama and Baba have already left to see Liria, and he isn't doing anything particularly riveting. "Come on, Emrik," I say. "All charioteers are supposed to bring family. I can't be the only one who's alone."

I make my sad face and that's all; he dusts off his jacket and locks the shop behind us.

Only when we step on the sandbar, does Emrik murmur something about leaving a note for our parents in case they return earlier.

But everything before this moment feels insignificant. This is the path of the Empyrean Elders. Shipwrecked on a strange island, the blistering sun overhead. What was going on in their minds? Were they scared? Hopeful? Even lined with tall lamp holders, fire lighting up the night, this path is a shadow of itself now. How long until it's swallowed? Will the Sanctuary sink? Will our history be lost to time?

The clouds shift and, in the moonlight, the soft golden glow along the sides of the pitch-black Empyrean Sanctuary glints brighter. The sphere building is larger than a capricorn, powerful like the stone of the Terrafort. There's no marvel like it. Emrik and I look at one another and back to the Sanctuary, suspended in the moment, filled with a sense of weightlessness, a sense of awe at what the Empyrean Elders achieved.

We step off the path together.

Already, I am late and have missed charioteer orientation. But I had no clean clothes. I had to wash the ones I was wearing with sand and wait for them to dry. I brush a hand down the sleeve of my white shirt. So different from my real clothes, and yet so recognizable after two races wearing the same colors.

At least they're not filthy.

The entrance is guarded by armed Renters, same as at the Terrafort. But if I thought I was prepared to see the Sanctuary after having been inside the Landmaster's Mansion and the Hospital, I was mistaken.

The unnatural coolness of the interior hits me first. As if I walked into a dream. I step farther in, and the sound and smell of the ocean are snuffed out. Not even the Terrafort makes the ocean this quiet.

"Does the air feel different to you?" Emrik asks, rubbing his thumb and index finger together, as if he could *catch* the air.

I know what he means. "It's definitely got a synthetic quality."

Uniformed guards stand at attention everywhere. Emrik stays close to me, distrust of the guards etched in his frown.

Everything's made of precise lines, teeming with clean mirrored surfaces. It makes the Sanctuary seem full of people in every corner. My footsteps, even the lightest ones, tap loudly against the diamond-black floor. None of this is stone or wood, but it's built of a knowledge so deep it went to sleep with its practitioners. The Sanctuary seems as if one hall of the Landmaster's mansion has stretched itself to be an architectural giant. Grandiose and unique and, perhaps, lonely.

The area open for visitors is a large hall, with a vaulted ceiling supported by twelve pillars. On either side, alcoves are glowing brilliantly with ornamental lanterns set along the walls covered with milky golden-cream glass. Though it is a museum, a construction of the bygone era, it is also sanctimonious, maintained in place of any temples of gods. Its unrepeatable build holds a place that many believe hears your wishes and hopes and can, one by one, grant them.

Near the first alcove, Arlene and Saran are signing a large plaque. Gold filigree webs on the plaque glitter, even from a distance. Whatever it is, judging by the glass it's kept in, it's important. Too shiny to be simply sand blown.

I stop one of the guides. "Hi. I missed the orientation for charioteers. Can you tell me what that is?"

"Sure, Koral." The guide knows my name? But, of course, I *am* a charioteer in the Glory Race. "As charioteers making Pilgrimage, you may sign the visitor's panel, which will be preserved as a source of inspiration for those who will follow in your footsteps."

I fail to see my footsteps as inspirational, but we go toward it once the Landers have moved on. Everyone's been here already, except Dorian. Judas waves from across the hall before turning to what looks like his family. They're talking with Emmanuel and his parents.

No sign of the Akayans. I sign my name in a corner.

"Can you believe we're here?" I say. "Aren't you glad you came?"

Emrik waves a dismissive hand, but his gaze roving over the glass walls decorated with murals says otherwise. The skin on the side of his face is covered in gauze. He adjusts the edges once, wincing. Ocean knows how long it will take for him to heal. I'm glad even for the few hours he can be here and distract himself.

This place, the inside of the Sanctuary, isn't for everyone to see. Renters can't afford the price of the tickets. *We* can't afford to be here. I take in a lungful of cool, satiny air and steady myself.

The murals display a mix of Ophir's history and landscapes that are thought to be recreations of Empyrean Elders' home territory, some colors faded, some new and shiny. Most of them show strange animals on lands full of green grass with no water nearby, some also set scenes of tall structures under a sky bluer than I've ever seen before. Perhaps the sun is calmer in this part of the world, wherever it is.

"Why did the Empyrean Elders ever leave?" I murmur. A place full of plenty, full of land and free air. Now we cling to rocks in a vast ocean under the cruel heat.

"I want to know why they did not do everything in their power to leave *this* island," Emrik says with a twisted mouth. "Monsters in the sea, another in the sky, why stay?"

Nobody else finds this curious. But most of the crowd is made up of guards and servers who have seen this enough times, or charioteers and their families. I mask my face with nonchalance, not wanting to stand out more than I already do.

What if Emrik and I sound ignorant to these people?

Maristags and other ocean creatures may be my expertise, but here, I'm a fish caught in a net flapping uselessly.

At least I have Emrik. But he's jaded, his focus always on the now.

Crane would understand what I'm feeling.

Arlene steps next to me. I try to give her space, walk away, but she says brusquely, "Can I have a minute?" I glance around, checking to make sure she *is* talking to us.

Emrik looks at me, and I nod—what can Arlene do in front of armed guards and other people assembled? He takes off, following the path down to other exhibits.

"My father used to bring me here often," Arlene says. "The last time when I was ten. He was fascinated by the Empyrean Elders, and we used to play a silly game, Ask and Find. We described some random thing from the murals here and the other had to find out where it's drawn. Most of them were little obscure things like a different colored leaf, and I was always losing to him." Her voice turns soft at the memory, the golden glass walls reflect off her black hair, a cloudy-day sun glowing inside her. She straightens her shoulders and meets my eye. "That was the last outing we had. Do you know why?"

She answers herself. "That day a maristag lost control and ran down Sollonia." Unease grows in my stomach, and I know what she's about to say even before she finishes speaking. "I lost my dad because of you Hunters."

Awareness trickles down like a searing ray of sun without the protection of skaya on me, leaving red welts in its wake. Arlene's hatred is no common one.

No one can buy maristags unless they've already kept at least one or have permission from the Council. So once a maristag is gone, what it does is not our responsibility. But Arlene's father died for something we should've prevented—if we had better managed those maristags. Never let them lose control.

A strangled, useless apology is caught in my throat.

I watch her leave, her long curtain of black hair gleaming in the light. She *didn't* outright threaten me, I suppose.

Light shifts in the lines of the alcove next to me.

No, not light. Someone's moved in the shadows across the hall. It isn't someone who is supposed to be there. The movement was furtive. Like a predator spying underwater, waiting for a drop of blood, a hint of weakness. The hair on the back of my neck stands. I turn instantly—and still not fast enough.

Lights go out.

And screams explode.

I crawl on all fours, tentatively, making sure I'm moving toward a flat surface. The floor is even harder than it seemed through the soles of my boots. It pushes against the heels of my palms and my knees and the bones twinge.

Where the hell is Emrik?

Everyone is yelling for their families. I recognize several voices. Arlene, Emmanuel, Judas, Saran. Only Dorian and the Akayans are missing. Did he know something was going to happen?

I chance another glance, calling sharply, "Emrik? Are you here?"

A glass wall shatters somewhere close. I cover my head and continue moving forward. Someone hurtles across me, and I narrowly avoid getting my fingers trampled. Next to me, someone else gives up. They curl on the floor and whimper. In the darkness, it's impossible to tell which way the exit is. All around me, people are scrambling. *Please Emrik, move toward the exit.* I keep scurrying, refusing to stop in one place. My heart beats at the tips of my fingers with every move I make.

And then it hits me. This is where Freedom's Ark is going to carry out its next mission. *This* is the place with a formidable guard unit everywhere.

A shiver almost makes me lose balance.

The guards are yelling in all corners, disjointed in the dark. The hall is suddenly too cramped, too *small.* As if the air is being sucked out. I still move as much as I can. Keep calling for my brother. *Where* did he disappear to?

The second I find Emrik, I'm bolting. But all exits are blocked, including the main entrance. We're trapped in this place. The museum feels like a grave boat.

I keep my gaze down, not letting it past the perimeter of the diamond-shaped tile of the floor. A panic attack inside this closed structure could kill me. I don't know who's ahead of me, or who's behind me. I breathe through my mouth, trying to ground myself, and rub my arms. The chill in the air is suddenly too strong. Only when my breaths start slowing, do I raise my head.

My eyes have adjusted to the dark. The Landers are bunched, family by family. I stand alone in a corner, squinting in the dark, *hoping* I can find Emrik. But I don't see him anywhere. I stare at the diamond pattern on the floor again, concentrating on any noise that might give away what's happening. I can hear a confrontation. It's far away. My head begins to hurt as I try to focus more. Startled, I remember I'm still hungry.

There wasn't even food here.

Now I wish I hadn't come, hadn't brought Emrik.

The rebels were right about one thing. There haven't been any gunshots in the hall. No smoke in the air. The guards are exercising restraint so they don't hurt Landers. Instead, three guards finally enter the hall and command everyone to form a line and follow them.

One says, "We will keep everyone here safe. A curfew will be in effect across the island—"

"Tell us what's going on!"

A chorus of affirmation rings the air.

"My brother—"

But the guard overrides me, "There is an active militant situation on the island. We don't know the full extent yet, but we will get you to an outer chamber. It is best to stay here until an escort is sent for you from the Terrafort."

It is so incongruous to all my experiences of being caught in a clash that I check around first to see if the others really trust these guards.

They do. Dazed, I have no choice but to follow. Muscle memory has me make myself smaller, so I don't bump into anyone. The streets are one thing. A confined, dark space under the watch of an armed gun is completely different.

The Landers are directed to the side of the hall. Just as I reach the door, passing under the flashlight of the guard, one of them grabs my arm. "*You.*"

Behind me, everyone comes to a halt.

"You came here alone?" the guard asks.

"No—my brother's here. I can't find him. We got separated."

"Right. Very convenient for a Renter to come in and get separated at the same moment the lights go out. There's no point lying, we'll find out one way or another," he says.

"Lying—what?"

"Can we move?" comes Judas's voice from the back of the line. The guard lets me go, but not before offering me a glare. And then I realize what he's implying.

That *I* brought someone in.

I need to get Emrik out before they blame this attack on him. I duck out from the yelling guard and go to the back of the queue, nearer the hall.

"Emrik!" I shout. "Come on, we have to go."

A shot echoes inside the Sanctuary, somewhere farther away, and behind me, the Landers scream. Panicked jabbering breaks out in the chamber. And then, the noises grow. Like thunder. But this time they are outside.

The guard up front calls to the Landers, "You will be escorted to the Drome so you can head down to the Terrafort via the Charioteer Hall. Please remain calm and line up."

Arlene takes the hand of an older woman who has the same hair as her. Probably her mother.

As I'm forced to move with the queue, another group of guards crosses down the hall, out of a nearby door, dragging behind them people who are clearly Renters. Their chain-link armbands gleam in the low light. Rebels.

And Emrik.

"Wait," he protests, struggling against the grip. "I wasn't with them. There's some kind of mistake! I'm a Hunter. I'm not a rebel!"

I yell, "No, that's my brother! He came with me!"

The guard leading them stops. "*You* brought him in? Is this a confession? Are you with the rebels, then?"

I take a step back. My own panic mirrors what I see on Emrik's face.

"No, I'm not—" I never even get a chance to bring up the fact that I'm a charioteer. They're quickly shuffled away. I lunge forward, shouting my brother's name. He shrieks, "Run! Get yourself out!"

I'm shoved to the front of the Landers' queue. "The rebels will be dealt with. You stay here, you're coming with us."

"Where are you taking him?" I'm panicking, barely forming words.

"They're all going to the holdings."

If my brother goes to Lander prisons, getting him out might take *months*. They'll hold him for interrogations, they'll torture him. And even if he's innocent—which he *is*—they won't want to admit a mistake.

They'll toss him in the sea.

The thought fuels the fear in me to burning terror.

*Fight*. But the barrel of the gun is in my face. *Fight*. It won't only be me they might shoot at. *FIGHT*. It's my fault that Emrik is even here.

But I can't fight. Not in front of the rows of armed guards, all dressed in the shades of night, red glinting on their shoulder pads. *Wraiths*.

They march the prisoners toward a different exit, leaving me scrambling out after the Landers.

The night outside is not the one we left behind. The freezing wind carries the scent of gunpowder and smoke.

The air smells like it did the night of the Opening Ceremony.

It smells of fear.

Instead of following the Landers toward the Drome, I rush toward the guard station. They have to bring the prisoners up there first. As I move, it's impossible to miss the uproar.

Loudspeakers blare all along the thoroughfare. That only happens during a mandatory hearing. Against the light of the moon, dark shapes of more guards gather outside.

Even in the din, I can hear what the loudspeakers all repeat in a terrifying monotone.

*State emergency. Please take cover. State emergency. Please take cover.*

# TWENTY-EIGHT

Guards in riot gear spill out of the Terrafort. Over their regular black uniforms and visors, they're armed to their eyes in a wave of bulletproof glass and black leather, with shields and batons.

The Sanctuary has vanished. Usually, it'd be visible from the Terrafort. If only a glint. But today, the smoke spiraling through the air obscures it.

I was inside it *just* now, and yet it feels unreal.

I don't know what's happening, but I need to get away from here. I need to get to Emrik.

Yelps and defiant cries ring from the Renter neighborhoods, toward the end of the thoroughfare. I know that area. Tin-roofed Renter neighborhoods, like the Opal Den. That's where most rebels and gamblers, the vulnerable, come from. I stay in the shadows. The sounds are painful, pathetic. Even more guards pour out of the side opening of the Terrafort, the one connecting the thoroughfare to the guard station.

The main entrance to the Terrafort has been shut again.

There's nowhere for me to run but to the shore.

Stormgold is where I left her, next to the stables. She watches the organized chaos with angry eyes. Her reins are still around her, and I'm thanking my past self for letting them stay.

When I approach her, she snaps. I grow still where I stand, my hand held out. Waiting for her to approve. She tilts her head. A few days ago, I'd have backed off. Put my chin down, avoided eye contact, and stepped away. But after what I saw in her this afternoon, I stand my ground.

I have to get her out of the line of fire.

*Finally* Stormgold dips her antlers back.

I get on her back, and she hurtles down the cliff to the shoreline. To a semblance of safety.

A row of guards marches past right above us.

I want to stay under the arches, hidden, but Stormgold stomps anxiously, triggered by the noises on the island. So, instead, I try to distract her. Keep her focused on racing around so she doesn't cry out and bring attention to us.

The shore is foamy today, curling around its edges. The water whirls in a ghostly manner, laced with a storm loading the wind. In the commotion of the aftermath of the second race, it wasn't as obvious. But the month-long tribulations in the ocean are culminating. It rained briefly yesterday. If it rains again tomorrow, during the race, if the maristags sense the salt in the air, everyone will be in danger.

I let Stormgold trot, fingers clutching at the tufts of hair beneath her manefin. Antlers rise high from the top of her head.

The ruckus of the island roars high beyond the cliff, the movement of the guards spreading. If I get caught in their midst, they won't listen.

They'll arrest me as well.

So I keep Stormgold moving. With each of her leaps, I wonder how I'll get Emrik out. How I'll explain where he is to my parents.

If Emrik dies, his blood will be on my hands.

Stormgold breaks into a canter, itching to go faster. We move through the water toward the end of the cliffs, the spray of cold needling at me, before we turn and I dig into her sides.

Her frillfin flare dangerously, but she doesn't release them.

The next instant, she *charges*.

Through the water roaring in sync.

Every scent—sand and sea and smoke and metal—mingles, changing the landscape of the world, rushing through the feral wind. We cut under ancient arches, here before any of the Empyrean Elders stepped onto the Islands of Ophir. I feel Stormgold's scales on my legs, beneath my hands. Dashing this fast, without a saddle, wrings my thigh muscles, but I don't relent.

Stormgold is running.

I'm flying.

I begin to cry.

I think of my brother, chained in a cold cell. The longer he stays there, the less chance I have to ever see him again. They'll torture him. What if they send him off to work at the mines in Kar Atish? They'll pretend that's not what they did and keep us running to the Magistrate, handing out new dates until one day, I'll fall on the street on my way to the court with the petition to get my brother released fluttering uselessly from my grasp.

*No, my mother will never wait for her child to return from the sea.*

Isn't everything I'm doing *for* my family? How can I save Liria but lose Emrik? This cannot be happening. I have to find my brother. He left the safety of the Terrafort for me. I have to bring him home.

The tears are relentless as I imagine the worst.

I need a plan. But I don't know where to start. Baba and Mama are already occupied with Liria. It's up to me to save Emrik.

Only when I've exhausted my tears does the coldness resettle on the edges of my face. A new vigor fills me. I will not give up.

The noises above us seem to have changed. Instead of organized boots, we hear scattered cracks. Short and snappy. Familiar.

I press my hands beside Stormgold's manefin, pulling her back. She grunts, then leaps to the cliffs. We reach the top in mere seconds.

And I understand the sounds I heard: the crackle of blazing fire.

Far across the thoroughfare, flames are licking the air at the edge of a quarter near the Drome. It's a ceremonial tent, the kind that hosts small-scale fairs for children during the Glory Race. A Renter tradition. Several tents collapse one after the other, the toys inside burning like effigies, precious chocolate candies melting, grotesque shadows cast high in the sky.

Stormgold slows down, the surface of her scales reflecting the livid flames.

The entire skyline of Sollonia is engulfed in a wave of fire. As if it isn't ocean we're surrounded by, but flames of red and gold. This isn't like the night of the riots, which was contained in comparison, and there were no guards because Landers were protesting that night.

Tonight, rebels are being rounded up. There's no caution, no second-guessing.

Sky-shattering cries of "*No gods, no Landers*" rise like terrible monsters. Rebels, fighting back. Clashes erupt all around the Terrafort, surging like an ocean wave. I've never seen Freedom's Ark make such a public stand.

Something is changing.

A barred cart hurtles past. In the back, several boys are loaded in, with plenty space to add more. They have black sacks over their faces, their hands are tied together. These are the people who disappear off the streets. The people who everyone says will be released soon. The people you never hear from again.

Like Crane's neighbor, Remide's son.

The cart rumbles like a beast down the thoroughfare, having its fill. Toward the Renter quarters. Maybe it will pick up more people. What if Emrik is with them?

"Emrik!" I shout.

I rush after the cart. Desperately. Each thump of Stormgold's feet shaking the ground.

But then the alleys split up, and the cart disappears. The sounds recede the farther we ride, as if the cart was swallowed by the island. I race through streets of stone. There's a wall straight ahead. I must have reached the edge. If I take a turn now, I'll—

Silver arcs gleam high in the night, a split second's orange flame reflected in the curve.

I freeze.

The Scythe Crab lets out a loud screech.

How did it escape?

Or was it *let* go?

I jerk Stormgold backward. Trying to make no noise.

The Crab is still half a mile away.

But it brings down its blade-limbs, and the ground shudders. *Click, click, click.* It's using the blades to move on the stone. Where are the capricorns? Has anyone been alerted?

In the darkness, I know I'm hidden.

For now.

Terror beats in my mouth.

I keep inching Stormgold backward, away from the beast.

But the Scythe Crab scuttles forward. Each snap of the bladed limbs loud in the night. *Click.* One step. *Click.* The next. *Click.* It edges forward. I never noticed how big its mouth is. The size of those curved, yellow fangs. Easily the length of my arms. They could cut me clean at the center. I'm so small. So insignificant in front of this gigantic creature. Beyond my control, beyond my comprehension.

I'm *nothing*.

Something snags at Stormgold's foot. The sudden tug at the back of my stomach tears a scream from my mouth, splitting the night in half—the night before the scream, and the night after. The Scythe Crab's attention latches straight onto me. Its giant red eyes fixed, burning with *hunger*.

I can only take one sharp breath and then, it's scuttling toward me, blades irascible against the stone.

I spin Stormgold away, darting as fast as I can. *Madness*. I can't escape a Scythe Crab. It's too big, it's too *strong*.

Stormgold viciously lashes her tailfin to the sides, itching to fight, and the snap wakes me up. All the confusion and anxiety messing with my mind vanishes. In the moment, I have never felt clearer. The Scythe Crab hurtles after us. I am prey. It won't let me escape. My panic only pushes me harder. I pin my legs to Stormgold's sides, forcing her to keep moving forward.

The Scythe Crab is getting closer.

I make Stormgold run fast. *Faster*. The ocean lashes out. The fire at the heart of the island rises higher. But if I don't escape this monster—it's all over. For Emrik, for me, for everyone in my family.

I refuse to let this be the end.

*Emrik. Liria. Mama. Baba. Emrik. Liria. Mama. Baba.*

A pillar blocks our way, and Stormgold stops so suddenly that I crash down. The ground slams my shoulders, pain hammering down my spine. I don't let go of the reins, even as they tighten in my fingers, almost stopping the flow of blood in my hands. I force myself up, fists pressed against slick, fanged stone. Stormgold bleats and tries to snatch herself away. A rock catches the edge of my pants, ripping the leg, but I don't stop. Stormgold struggles, shrieks, and I press my foot against the rock and jump on her back. Then we're hurtling down the streets again, dashing from shadow to shadow, until we reach a corner.

It's a long, empty street.

I look back.

The Scythe Crab is upon us.

We rush into the street and quickly duck behind a broken pillar sticking out at an angle from the ground. It's too small, too narrow. But the awning of the structure next to it covers it from the top. I plead with Stormgold, pull her backward into the tiny cave cut into the rock behind the pillar.

"Come on, Stormgold," I hiss.

She finally moves, still struggling against me. We slip around the pillar as the ground rumbles.

Blades clicking and clicking. Nearer and nearer.

*Closer.*

Until they're clanging in my head.

The Scythe Crab waits.

If it swiped one blade at the pillar, the awning would fall, trapping us in darkness. There would be nowhere for us to run. I murmur desperate prayers to the water.

*Thrash, thrash, and call this monster back.*

The earsplitting bang of the blades passes us by.

Relief floods me so sharply that I nearly cry out. I press my bloody palms to my mouth and stifle the sob, the smell of sulfur choking me as Stormgold's sharp fins fill the small cave.

She crouches close to me, and I stay there, hidden inside the cave, breathing in the watery rot. Freezing amid the cold stone as the wind knifes its way in. I grow so numb that everything else goes still and silent, too. There's a strange sense of being out of my body, like I've

260

no substance at all. Nothing matters, except this darkness, this violence, and the creatures of the horrifying ocean that lashes at our door, *waiting* to devour us. I curl into myself, squeezing my eyes shut until the first ray of the sun seeps through a crack in the stone.

The smoke of last night swirls like gray poison in the air.

# TWENTY-NINE

A single candle struggles to light the black walls of Crane's house.

"Emrik is in the central prison," she says. Her palm is wrapped in gauze, proof that she was out last night. I cannot thank the ocean enough that she's safe. After last night, if I had walked in here to an empty house, I don't think I'd have been able to hold on to my own mind. "He's being kept separately from the others. They won't do anything. Not until the end of the Glory Race."

"And if I lose?"

I've forced myself to not even consider the possibility up until now. But I've lost and lost. And what happens when I have no gold to get Emrik out? First, they'll force me back into hunting for them. Then they'll torture him. They'll throw him in the water or in a mine. What if one day I'm hunting, and I find my own brother at the bottom of the sea?

Crane hands me a set of clothes, and some warm water to drink. When was the last time I drank water?

I sit quietly, sipping water. It tastes like nothing. Empty air.

How can I face my family again?

Crane moves quietly around me, as if afraid I'll lash out.

I ask, "What really happened last night? What did…Freedom's Ark do?"

She rubs the back of her neck. Her hair is limp, she has shadows under her eyes. "The Ark wanted to take over the Sanctuary and use it to negotiate with the Council."

I shake my head. The sheer audacity of the rebels to think they could pull this off.

"There were complications," Crane continues, "with the raid. Disagreements in the factions on how to proceed. Your refu—we only knew about the Sanctuary from a couple of Renter servers working there. The group I'm with wanted to back out until we could really map out all of the Sanctuary's interior instead of just the museum—"

I inhale sharply.

"—but the older group wanted to act *now*. They refused to listen, to wait. Guess they were getting antsy about dying. But last night was all wrong. The rebels inside the Sanctuary opened a wrong way and alerted the guards. We had to go fight and create a distraction to get them safely out, but the guards were prepared for a big assault. Now we've lost rebels. Watch them be tortured and give up our secrets. If the Warehouse is exposed…"

"How did you get in so deep?" It doesn't sound like she was only posting pamphlets.

"Everything started small. Little favors for people around the street. I mean, I knew they were some kind of rebels, but there are so many factions even within the Ark, it didn't feel like I was helping actual Arkers. It wasn't one concrete moment, I was just drawn in. One day I was talking to Arkers, next I was working with them. It happened so smoothly that it made sense, Koral."

"You should keep out of there now," I say.

She looks up sharply, and I prepare for her to tell me off, but she nods. "The rebellion is fractured from within. I thought working with my faction would be enough, that we could operate on our own, help our people. But you can't move a drop of water without everyone wanting a damned sea for themselves. We don't even know who the leaders behind this underground movement are. I'm sorry for not seeing it sooner."

She falls quiet, contemplative, before murmuring, "We both ran headlong into different walls."

I study her. My best friend who loves wearing bright colors and seastones, whose glare matches no one else's—sitting here, defeated. Bone-pale. The sun has been pulled from her. All her beliefs, all the rebels' efforts, will be for nothing if the Landmaster sends her armies down.

I didn't miss what she was about to say before, either. That I refused help. If I'd said yes, would yesterday not have imploded in the face of the rebels? I'd know they were planning something in the Sanctuary and wouldn't have taken Emrik.

It's been less than twelve hours since he vanished. Already it feels like an eternity.

But what if I *had* said yes? Perhaps things would still have imploded. Perhaps I would also be behind bars. Then who would finish the Glory Race? Would Liria be allowed to stay at the Hospital?

I haven't even visited my sister yet.

I've made too many mistakes. What I've done, I can't fix. I can't go back in time and pull the maristag off Emrik. If he hadn't stopped me from going in with him, maybe he wouldn't have been caught in that skirmish alone. Nor did I know that the rebels' seething hatred for our family was not my struggle. It was cre- ated by outsiders—a burden put unfairly on my mother—whose need for power made them turn cruel and vengeful. It cost me my sanity, made me keep my head down, and follow after the Landers mindlessly.

Crane glances around the bare hall. What kind of a home is this? A rock hollowed out for someone to lie in until they die.

"Are you tired?" Crane asks. I know what she's truly asking.

"I'm too far on this path now to sit and feel tired." It feels like relief, saying it out loud. To Crane. "I thought I was going to get some gold and that would be it. But look at them all, from the rebels to the Landmaster. What is this if not a fight for power? Everyone trying to control me?"

I think of my mother, who believes all our misfortune is her fault. Why would the rebels turn on my mother? Why would they betray the good of all people and target their own allies, unless they were like Lander elites themselves? The need for control was strong in the rebel leaders' bones, the thirst to share power, not dismantle it. I was right. Those who call themselves leaders of the Freedom's Ark are just another face of the kind of power Landers hold. Nothing else.

"Where do we fit in, Crane? What about people like you and me? It feels like all we do is fight."

Crane, who prefers moving in shadows and working quietly for the rebels—last night against guards in riot gear. Me, who sees nothing beyond my family, fighting against aquabats not seeing if they attacked Renters or Landers.

I know better now, the rules of this game of power were always stacked against people like us. And while we fought one another, they ran things like they wanted. We're made to feel like we're part of them, but only as long as we keep our heads down.

I'll take whatever they give me. I'll use it against them. Pull up my family as I rise with the use of their own gold. And however it happens, Crane and I will change things. For all people.

We have to stop pushing one another down. We have to end this distrust that has grown like a sickness, that keeps us fighting each other, as if this island hasn't proved again and again that our best bet at survival is together.

The Empyrean Elders did not hope for a future to see us shattered like this.

Their memories deserve better.

*We* deserve better.

I arrive back at the Opal Den right as the old woman, Remide, is gingerly moving out of the street. She feels her way, wall to wall, and walks as if on shards of glass. When she stumbles, I reach for her.

She grabs my arms and straightens. She doesn't seem frightened of the maristag behind me.

"Do you want me to take you home?"

"I saw you," she says, gray eyes piercing me. Before I can ask where, she pushes something cold in my hands. A U-shaped metal pin with a seven-petaled flower in the middle. At the back, faded words are engraved amid rust: MAY THE WATER HORSE WATCH OVER YOU.

"When you win," she pats my shoulder, "wear this."

"Okay," I say automatically. What else *can* I do? I don't have the courage to go see my parents again. They're still with Liria. They think Emrik is at the shop, resting where they left him. I won't let them turn into this woman.

I leave Stormgold in Crane's yard once more. She promptly finds a spot, which, judging by the maristag-size dent, is her favorite. Stormgold remembers this yard. I smile at her, once again wondering how much we really know about the creatures of this world that we inhabit.

But for now, I have another issue. I need a new chariot.

# THIRTY

Crane waits for me at the shop. "We'll paint it red," she says, pointing at a can and brush. "And no one will realize it's the First Champion's chariot." The chariot was in perfect condition, maintained as a relic, before it went missing. Plus, it was stolen only to spite the Race Council for not letting Renters in the race. Bitterbloom always keeps her treasures intact.

"I don't think that's going to work," I say, but there's a buoyancy in my voice that I've missed.

It's my best friend that I've missed.

We hurry to the Warehouse, squeezing down narrow alleyways. Even with Crane beside me, the very air feels different here. The emptiness between the Warehouse and the black market sinks in my skin, claws at my throat.

We plunge into darkness. With my first step, I sense the change. Slick heat clings to this cavernous hall, carved into the very edge of the Terrafort's stone, and running the entire back length of it. Ghostly voices fill the air, and yet no one seems to be speaking. Everyone hides their faces behind masks. And the few Lander Arkers, who always used to intrigue me, are missing. As if all of Sollonia's rebels vanished in one night.

"It's only a matter of time before someone spills the secret," Crane whispers.

Decades of secrecy, a semblance of safety, gone overnight.

We move quietly. No one can know who I am. Not only because I'm banned.

"Stop," Crane tightens her hold around my arm. She pulls me into a niche that I hadn't even noticed. A group of Renters walk by, dressed in padded clothes. They're armed. "Some of them are preparing for an all-out assault if the Landers find their way in." We wait until they're gone.

It's foolish to think a scattered, ill-organized rebellion splitting at its seams with various factions will ever emerge successful if there *is* an all-out assault.

The hall narrows halfway from Bitterbloom's shop, then begins to dip into alleys and niches. I've never been this far in. Every shadow feels like eels around my ankles. Every hiss, the arc of a scythe. The constant feeling of grubby fingers reaching out from foundry walls. As the day begins weeping into the night, people are edging out of the black market. We move in small steps against the current, trying not to bump into anyone. Not to give anyone an excuse to look at us twice.

Someone blocks my path, face hidden behind a mask. "The order's come from above," he's whispering hurriedly to his companion. "If we get this done, the Ark will at least have time to regroup on another island."

"Why in the Drome?"

"What happens in the Drome is the Landmaster's will."

I startle, turning on my heels. Crane reaches for me, trying to grasp my hand, but I end up blocking the flow of the people. An angry murmur rises around me. I hastily pull myself back, muttering apologies. There goes any attempt at keeping myself hidden. I can only *hope* people are too upset to recognize who I am.

Even worse, the two have already melded with the dark.

Crane pulls me to a corner. "Have you lost your mind?"

"What's going to happen in the Drome?"

"I don't know, Koral." She sounds miserable and angry at once. She said last night she didn't want to visit here again. Renouncing the rebels is no easy task.

They come for you. They drag you back. They shut you up.

But she's still risking this for me, and it'd be poor repayment if I got us caught.

So I stay quiet as we continue on our way, stumbling in and out of the crowd, but the words of those two don't leave me. What *can* happen in the Drome, where the Landmaster reigns supreme?

By the time the thin snake-like alley ends at what seems like the far side of the Terrafort, I'm out of breath.

I take a moment to pull myself together before I step around the corner. I've never seen the inside of Bitterbloom's quarters. Crane hasn't either. But she did give us directions once, "for emergencies." This is definitely an emergency.

Bitterbloom sits outside the door in a small, square space, washed out by an almost-melted candle.

"Nice office, Bitter," Crane says.

For someone as old as her, her glare when she sees me could cut the ground in half. But that's not what makes my heart hammer. Under the ashen light, she looks like a rotten corpse returned from water. "What are you doing here?"

"Bitter," Crane intervenes. "Come on."

"No, our laws are true laws just as the Landers rules above. There will be no exception once someone is blacklisted." Her hands tighten around her teacup, her blackened fingers sticking to the handle.

"The race is tomorrow," I say, swallowing my fear. "I want that chariot."

"You're not going to win the race, girl." The creases in the folds of her skin get deeper, as if she was cut along those lines. "Heard they took your brother. You should run before they take you, too." The heartache in her voice rings clear.

"I can't leave my brother in their prison. I can't let my sister wake up only to go back to coughing and dying. And I can't let my parents suffer for the faults of others." Bitterbloom looks at me sharply at that. She's old enough to know the many times Freedom's Ark tried to unite. She must have seen firsthand what happened. It occurs to me that she's not angry. She's...afraid.

Of me? *For* me?

"I'm going to win that tournament tomorrow, and I need a chariot. You can have me dragged out, but I'll scream the entire way through. If I can enter the Glory Race and shake the foundations of the Terrafort so that the Landers come pouring out like ants running from water, you can bet I'll shake the foundations of this place as well if you don't help me. I have nothing left to lose, Bitter."

Bitterbloom's face darkens. She doesn't like being threatened, but I'm running out of time.

"I think it's best if you leave."

When I say nothing, she gets up. Probably to yell at me. Instead, she whistles. A couple of people hurry in. Bitterbloom snaps her fingers, and they grab my arms.

Crane cries, "Are you serious right now?"

I jerk myself out of their grip easily, my reflexes much faster than anyone who has grown up inside these alleys. In an instant I'm moving from the mouth of the alley to the back, beyond their reach unless they want to break down Bitterbloom's seat.

I lift the knives I yanked out of their belts and hold them up.

They stare at me like I'm a maristag gone wild. Not breaking eye contact, I say, "I'm not here to fight. There's no other way for me to race tomorrow without that chariot. When I win," I look to Bitterbloom as Crane shakes her head in the corner of my vision, as if she already senses what I'm about to say, "I'll let you have a share of the gold."

Bitterbloom scoffs.

"You've always helped me. I trust you. And I know you truly care for all our people. The kind of gold I'm promising can fix a lot of these lives. You, of all people, *know* the dangers of selfish leaders. You saw what renegades with no proper plans did last night. Take the gold I'm offering. Help me win it."

Then I look at the other two and drop their knives. They clatter to the ground.

Crane and I exchanges glances. I know she, too, is waiting, not daring to breathe.

Finally Bitterbloom says, "You'll need a new base for the chariot. I think some boards in the back will do."

Our shop is too cramped, but I don't want to be seen with the chariot just yet, so instead of heading back to Crane's house, we stay at our cramped shop.

I need to put some thought into this. I've never built a chariot. It just wasn't high on the list of life skills to learn. But I *have* fixed the roof of our stables many times.

There's only enough metal for *one* base. If I mess up the measurements, there are no do-overs. My teeth dig into my lower lip as I gesture to Crane for the saw. Carefully my heart beating in the tip of every finger, I begin cutting the shape of the base.

When I'm certain I have the hang of it, I push a little harder. Pain spikes along my arm. Raw and sharp. It bites and stings. Like a thousand tiny barbs of a maristag.

I welcome it.

Every motion hurts. It's probably what Emrik is feeling right now. It's exactly what Liria must wake up to every day. I push and pull my arm, the knee of my left leg and the sole of my right foot pressed firmly on the stone of the ground and continue sawing the zargunine board that Bitterbloom arranged in exchange for a hundred more gold.

It hurts.

And by the time we're done, by the time the lamps around the Agora terrace outside are switched off, the chariot stands in the center of the shop gleaming in stripes of silver and a brilliant, bright red. My arms throb with pain, but it's only an echo of what I've grown used to. An echo that reminds me with every one of its beats that I have to win the Glory Race tomorrow.

"Go see Liria," Crane says, her voice thick. "Whatever happens tomorrow, take heart tonight."

The Hospital's sharp *whiteness* is still a shock. What will I say to Mama and Baba about Emrik? Has he eaten? Is he sleeping well?

It's not even been a full day.

Emrik and I have gone without seeing one another for more than that. Sometimes looking for more skaya jelly, sometimes for hunting. Sometimes, when the fighting between our parents got too intense, we crashed at Crane's and turned up two days later. Mama and Baba knew we were all right.

They have nothing to suspect today, either.

But what happens if they ask?

I duck under the full-body metal detector, and it pings. Immediately three guards are on me, demanding I put my hands up.

My courage drains. "Please, it's a pin," I force out.

A gun staring in my eyes, I bring out the metal pin the old woman gave me. It shines bright in my face.

I keep it squeezed in my palm all the way up to Liria's room.

Liria lies straight on the bed—the ghastly burns gone—attached to a drip.

Mama is asleep on a chair next to the bed, one hand inches away from Liria, and one curled around her stomach. A scarf is draped around her shoulders. In sleep, too, she looks tense. As if she never really lets go of her reality. As if she has no dreams.

The rise and fall of Liria's chest is even. There's no sign of bluish lips.

When she was younger, I would leave gifts on her bedside table for her to find in the mornings. Pots of color. Shells (always Emrik's finds). Seastones. An unusually shaped leaf. Some mornings, the gifts elicited squeals of delight; others, forgotten because she'd had one of her coughing fits.

She's been here for over a day. Already been through the med-shell once for the burns. Wouldn't it be great for them to wake Liria up before Crowning Ceremony tomorrow? I brush her hair and leave a kiss on her soft forehead.

No point waking either of them. They deserve the rest they can get.

Fingers lingering on the starchy white sheets, I turn. And startle, almost falling backward.

"Careful," Baba says from the door.

Even though I know it's only my father, my shoulders stay strung, fingers refuse to unclench from where they reflexively reached for my knife, which I now remember I left at the shop.

"There was a schedule conflict because of the Glory Race," Baba says, "otherwise they would've prioritized your sister. She should walk out of here in two days." He doesn't look me in the eye, but at Liria.

Mama stirs, but her fingers only tighten on Liria's hand. I rearrange the scarf draped over her shoulders like a shawl, studying every line on my mother's soft face. Three strands of hair lie across her forehead, almost obscured in the darkness of her tattoos.

Withdrawing from her, I say, "I should go, I have a race tomorrow."

I hurry out the door. As it shuts behind me, I hear a ghost of Baba's voice.

It sounds like *good luck*.

# THIRTY-ONE

The last twilight of the 150th Glory Race is bitingly cold and windy. I hope the rain holds off—during the race, it might prove deadly.

I get up from my curled position, clenching my teeth so as not to gasp. My body is stiff and sore from sleeping on the cold floor. Stretching only makes it worse. I barely slept anyway. My thoughts are a jumble of what lies ahead.

Light streams inside the shop, illuminating the gleaming silver chariot. There's no space to move so when I start to squeeze my way around, my gaze lands on a blue pot on the otherwise empty shelf. Inside is a dried strand of sea grass.

*Home.*

A sharp pain spikes in my chest.

It's too early in the day, but this is the last event of the Glory Race for another four years, so everyone's up. Crowds weave in and out, hawkers selling tournament shirts and caps. At the center of the Grand Bazaar, someone wearing a maristag costume is walking on a rope. Already the smell of fried shrimp laces the air.

I keep my hair around my face as I head to Crane's house. The streets are once more *feral*, suddenly no one remembers the curfew, as if no fires have burned this island, and no gunshots rang only two nights ago.

For today, humans remember we're all one on this spit of rock.

Crane has laid out a jacket to wear over my worn clothes—an expensive-looking black one embellished with seastones so perfect they look like jewels.

It's nothing I've ever worn. At least not outside of events I'd be forced to attend as a child. My hunter clothes were always plain. Jackets that Emrik and I shared. That's who I was. Who I am. A Hunter.

My hand grazes the collar of the shirt that was given to me at the Hospital. Even they knew the kind of clothes I wear.

Crane says softly, "You're more than what they want you to be."

I put the jacket on, aware of my heart beating in its cage as I push my arms through the fitted sleeves. I tie my hair and fasten the metal pin that Crane's neighbor gave me.

In the mirror, I see myself, as I am. My mother's daughter.

One way or another, this is coming to an end, in a few hours. The only question is whether I get the honor of a title and glory, or the taste of sand and sea in my mouth.

Crane waits for me in the main hall. "Breakfast?"

I shake my head.

"It's so unlike you."

"What is?"

"Staying quiet and not snapping at me."

I raise my hand and hold it steady. Except it trembles on its own. "I can't rest. I can't go near the maristags like this. They'll rip my head off my shoulders."

"Hey," Crane says. "What's wrong?"

I murmur, "What if everything goes south? What if the Landers

276

band together to take me out first?" I know I've given at least Arlene reason enough. Arlene, who wants to win this to take her revenge for her father.

Crane says, "Do you remember the first time you promised that you would never leave me alone?"

A storm cloud shrieks somewhere far.

Years ago, I said those words to Crane under another stormy sky at the rapidly darkening shores of the sea. I promised her friendship and love and family. I asked her to trust me, despite life teaching her the contrary.

I was a very serious six-year-old.

She takes my hands in hers. "No matter what happens today, I promise I will never leave you."

When I say nothing, Crane adds, "I, more than anyone, know how much you love your family and how you'd do anything for them. Even give up your dreams. I'm here to urge you not to give up."

"This is not a dream. I'm doing this so I can get my sister the treatment she needs."

Crane smirks.

I stare at the stone table next to us, trying not to think of how it felt to ride Stormgold a few nights ago.

"See? You're lying not only to me, but to yourself. The sooner you accept why you're here, the better."

I glare at her.

The unmoving flatness of her expression reminds me of Emrik, of Mama, even of Baba. Crane has always been one of us.

This is who we are: family comes first. Even if we're fighting blood and tooth, we will never turn against one another.

And when I win, I will go back to a home where my sister's life won't depend on the maristags in our stables. To a family that will know a better life.

*Why the Glory Race?*

The answer to Emrik's question is starting to form in my mind. I only wish he was here.

I get up.

Crane says, "Where are you going?"

"I need to get Stormgold to the Drome. I won't risk her on these streets later. Get my chariot there in an hour?"

"Of course."

Even in the older neighborhoods, the air is different. Perhaps not festive, but there's movement where there's always been a stubborn stillness. At the spectators' gates of the Drome, state newsrunners line up, chatting animatedly to each other, comparing reports and gossip. I can hear the throng outside. Before the actual race on the final day, student athletes from the Lander school participate in prep races and celebratory events.

But I don't have time to care. Stormgold is being exceptionally difficult. It takes us fifteen minutes extra to reach the Charioteer Hall. She circles instead of walking straight, snaps and snorts, forcing me to pull my hand back.

I hiss, "What is wrong with you?"

Only Saran is here so far, and he ignores me. But his maristag bares its fangs. Fear crawls under my skin.

Stormgold's antlers are thrown back, like she wants to bolt.

"You're green-blooded, too," I say, trying to steady her. "If they scare you, you give it back to them."

I tentatively reach for her. She shies away. This time, I force myself to let her be. There's plenty of time until the race—no point in pushing her. Anyway, until Crane brings the chariot, I can't do anything.

"Koral."

I recognize Dorian's voice even before I turn in the direction of my name.

He stands halfway down one of the hallways, shadowed behind a pillar, which explains why I didn't notice him when I entered the Hall. His silver crown is tucked in a belt loop on his black pants.

He leans against the pillar and looks Stormgold in the eye. I wouldn't do that to a maristag that wasn't mine even from the distance. "How is she doing?"

"Jumpy," I say flatly. I'm aware of movements behind me in the Hall, and how everyone's running around and can see us if they only look around the pillar. It's probably not wide enough to hide us.

Dorian is oblivious.

He was different at the shores. Mellower, unsure. Startled when his father's guards found him. He always did try to avoid getting us seen, and for good reason, I suppose. Now he doesn't seem to care who sees us.

"Rhyton is upset, too." He glances back at his silver maristag peeking out from one of the stalls.

"Has he been here the whole night?"

"No, of course not," Dorian says, appalled. "I had him brought here earlier. Thought he'd get used to the Drome and be a little less... Anyway, he'll be fine. It's the ocean."

"What?"

"It rained all night. The maristags get worked up—"

"I am a Hunter. I run the stables." He doesn't need to know it *had* slipped my mind to make the connection. And then, I remember. There *aren't* any stables. Not now. Perhaps not ever again, for me.

"I—that's not what—I know. I mean, of course you knew that."

We fall silent.

Handlers check and recheck contraptions. Outside, we can hear the spectators swarming in.

There's a nick on Dorian's right brow-bone, disappearing under his eyebrows. I'm not sure what I'm supposed to say. Looking at him, so close, only reminds me of our last conversation by the beach. What would've happened if his guards hadn't arrived? Would I have met the Dorian I lost once more?

I wish I could talk to Crane. Wish it wasn't *Dorian Akayan* again who has me so confused in the first place.

"I heard about your brother," he says, breaking the quiet between us. "I'm sorry."

"Why didn't *you* come?" I say. "You knew, didn't you? You figured it out."

His eyebrows pull down. "Figured what out?"

"The Ark was going to attack. Now my brother's imprisoned. They think he was one of the conspirators. He'd gone with *me* and if I hadn't gone, if *you* told me you had suspicions, I wouldn't have. You could—"

"Koral, stop," he says, softer this time. "I didn't know." His eyes glitter. *Strange*, I think. His gaze is a slow hum. I cross my arms.

"So, how will you get your brother out?" he asks.

"Once I win, he'll be the Champion's brother. They can't pretend *then* that we were at the Sanctuary for another reason."

Dorian withdraws. "You're not going to win."

He says it nonchalantly, like he's observing that the ground of Sollonia is so black it sucks in every crumb of light, that I merely blink. But he doesn't seem to realize how *final* his words seem to me.

"Everything in the Drome happens with the Landmaster's permission," he says. It stirs something in my memory, a dark night and a fog of voices, but my mind is too addled. "You can fight it, but is it a fight you'll win? And what if you win, what happens then?"

"I rise."

I've caught him by surprise.

"I rise," I continue, "against everyone's wishes. Against everyone who will see me trampled and begging. It's that simple."

He takes a step forward.

By now, the noise inside the Charioteer Hall is deafening.

"All my life, I've lived by my father's code. We represent humanity amid the seas that will devour us, he's always said. One day we'll triumph, and it'll all be ours. He's followed in the footsteps of his forefathers. Ambitious, future oriented. Bitterly ruthless. He's respected everywhere. Feared everywhere. Even if I hate him, that's still what I have to be to continue our family's legacy."

Breathing is too much disturbance between us right now.

"My father took everything I cared about. Broke it, locked it away, tore it to pieces. He is drowned in his own hubris. He would've had you killed if I didn't go back to him. But you..." His breaths grow shallow. "I've tried to do what you did and failed. I've tried to hurt you and failed. I've tried to hate you and failed. You defied everything he built, you challenged him, you did something he never thought possible. You shook the ground on which he stands." Dorian leans toward me and, despite myself, I inhale deeply. I study the contours of his face as he says, "Stay clear of the Scramble. They won't go out of the way for you. Not today. It's the final race. Everyone's here to win."

"Just like you."

"Would you have any respect for me if I lost on purpose?"

"It will be offset by the feeling of triumph."

The pin on my collar clinks together with the button on his as he presses his soft lips to my cheek, heating me up like a match caught fire. "Good luck, Koral of Sollonia."

Despite my thundering pulse, I'm not so conceited as to think Dorian will throw the race away for me. He can't and he *won't*. He wouldn't even have done that before.

There's only one Champion, and it has to be me.

I keep repeating that—forcefully at first, then slowly, to let the idea sink in my skin—until it's finally time.

The roof over the Drome prevents rain from ruining the tracks, but the maristags sense the dampness in the air. They're strained. The Charioteer Hall is filled with more handlers than usual.

The final race is inside the Drome. This time, the preparations are more intense, nerves heightened, terror burning in everyone's blood. Arlene is at the top of the hall, her maristag struggling with the tense green blood in its veins. She doesn't know how to handle it.

If this isn't luck, I don't know what is.

I smile, despite the threat of a downpour, despite knowing that when this race is over, it's possible neither Dorian nor I will ever have anything to do with each other again.

Crane finally drags the chariot on a cart. The sheen of the silver chariot draws every gaze in the Charioteer Hall.

"This thing attracts people like blood attracts raptors," she says. She doesn't sound like she regrets it. Together, we haul it off the cart and fix it to Stormgold's harness.

Judas passes by and, catching my eye, he stops.

"Hey, how's your sister?"

"She's getting treated at the Hospital. I'm so grateful for your help."

"No, of course. I hope she gets better soon." He rubs the back of his neck. "You are a good charioteer. Better than most here." He looks at Arlene once. Then he smiles, "I wish you the best, Koral. See you after."

"Thank you, Judas. You, too."

He takes his leave of me, nods to Crane once, and finds his chariot. It's petty but I'm thrilled that he ignores Arlene.

"What did he do for Liria? Who *is* that?" Crane says.

"Someone who can't mind his business," Dorian answers from the chariot next to us.

The heat in my cheeks reignites.

"The irony," Crane says coldly, but thankfully, chooses to ignore him for now. I know it's only for my sake, to not ruffle things right before the race. Crane will never forgive Dorian, even if I have.

The commotion in the crowd grows. They must have cleared the tracks from the last of the celebrations.

The Landmaster's voice fills up the hall, calling attention. I lean away from the speakers right above my head. Her voice startles the maristags all over again. I shush Stormgold, placing a hand tentatively on her neck.

"You knew you weren't going to stay in the stables alone, didn't you?" I press my cheek against her. The abrasion of her spiky jaw is warm, comforting. "Good girl."

"It's time, Koral," Crane says. Her voice is quieter than usual.

The Landmaster's voice blares across Sollonia. "The 150th Glory Race is an event that will go down in our history. Its power has been challenged in a way it hasn't been for centuries. But our charioteers faced it with valor and honor. Welcome, Heirs of Empyrean, to the 150th Glory Race!"

This shouldn't send jitters through me. But it does. The Landmaster's will is supreme in this Drome. When she speaks, everyone listens. When she smiles, the world cracks open. And if she wanted to, she could unleash fury on Sollonia that none of us could counter.

"For our final race, the charioteers will enter a maze of glass and shadows. A maze that will hide their foes but reveal their own true faces. There will be paths that lead to dead ends, there will be paths that will throw them *out* of the maze and out of the race," the Drome gasps in unison, "and there is only one way out to the ultimate finish line."

The ground beneath my feet rumbles. At first slow, drawn out, but then it *moves*. Stormgold grunts, stepping back. The roar is excruciatingly loud, and then there's silence. Outside, shouts and applause resound in the Drome.

Sounds like we have new tracks to fight over.

"It's a thing of beauty, isn't it?" comes the Landmaster's gleeful announcement. That alone makes my teeth clench. "The winning charioteer must enter the first gateway and complete a full round of the Spine before exiting only through the gate that overlooks the finish line. They'll know it when they see it. Crossing that golden line, first, will be the winner's crowning glory."

Earsplitting roars reverberate beneath our feet. My heart lurches and panic begins seeping into my veins. The floor of the chariot is too close...

*I'm okay. I'm okay. I'm okay.*

"Ready?" says Crane.

I raise my head. *No, I'm not.*

"Liria would have loved to see the race," Crane says. "Now you go win this for her."

I wish so desperately that she was here to see this moment. "For Liria," I say.

The uproar of the spectators is a many-headed snake, inescapable, everywhere. Stormgold shudders. No—she'll throw me off—

Crane holds my wrist, grounding me, saving me from the panic spiking in my blood again. "Don't die."

With that, my best friend steps back. I'm left alone between a wave of green-blooded maristags barely restraining themselves.

The bars rumble open.

And the brilliant lights steal my vision.

# THIRTY-TWO

The race has already started. But all six of us stand stunned at the mouth of what looks like a giant white maze. Its outer walls gleam like crystals flaring under brilliant sunshine. I *know* these can't be real crystals. But the material is luminescent, streaming dazzling light. I tug at the reins. Stormgold moves forward, slowly, as if sensing my uncertainty. I blink several times before my eyes adjust. The chariot trembles beneath me.

Dorian enters through the arch-gate first. Then Arlene, then me. The walls narrow around us. It's a network of alleys. I can't help but grin. There's no roof above us, but beneath us, the ground is a glistening blue-black, like I'm riding above the wide ocean. Yet sand still swirls along Stormgold's feet.

I look around. The walls are real, but the floor is a mirage built of mirrors and lights.

The surprise of it is over before I draw another breath. Inside, as we tentatively start speeding up, the walls become mirrors. As we cross the walls and our shadows fall across glass, it turns frosted. Distorted. Then it cuts off right in front of us, forking in separate directions.

Towering above us are the pillars of the Spine.

The labyrinthine maze is laid around it.

Whoever takes the center fork has the best chance of sticking next to the Spine. The realization hits everyone, at once, that we're truly in the third event now, and the Scramble of Death is about to start.

Up ahead, the spectators are one giant mass, clashing and swaying with the beats of gigantic drums.

I'm between two chariots. The maristag to my left is bright green—Emmanuel's. I lean back, clutching the reins tighter. My knuckles are white and drums pound in my ears. I remember, as we reach a narrow alley, to pull away. I check Stormgold, and she slows.

Two chariots charge past me. And I zoom into the alley, twisting toward the right. The alley shimmers beneath me, light flickering momentarily and revealing the dust of the tracks. I rocket past the walls as they rapidly turn foggy and then clear. The walls block us off, so we can't tell who's coming up around the next bend. Good thing the spectators above have a bird's eye view.

Sweat trickles halfway down my temple. The briny scent of the ocean swoops down on us from all sides, throwing Stormgold off.

I snap at the reins and get her focus back on the race. The ground is slippery, as if it were made of metal.

Today, the Spine weighs under booming drums and huge conch shells. Its brackets are packed with armed guards. Today, they're prepared for war and blood. They loom over us from the center of the maze.

I turn left and almost slam into a glass wall. It rapidly turns dark. I go right. Left. Right again. And left. I'm hurtling, but I can't slow. Someone is zooming past the next alley. This is a giant puzzle. We *have* to be careful, or we'll crash into one another. But that means I have to be faster than the other charioteers.

Screams resound from my left. Scramble has begun in earnest, clouds of dust puff up ahead on my path. I shut my eyes and cough as the sand stings my eyes and all I can do is let my tears wash it all away. Stormgold knows what she's doing—she slides to the right, avoiding collision with another glass wall that I hadn't realized was a dead end.

We come to a sudden stop as the dust swirls in front of us. Outside, the cheers rise. Inside, I can barely hear my fellow charioteers. How will I know if someone manages to cross the line before me? My heart begins to thump. No, I have to get out of here *first*.

My hands are cramped and tired from pulling Stormgold, a fire-like burn in my shoulders.

I can't hold Stormgold back any longer, I have to let her free. I have to trust that she knows what she's doing.

I let go slightly and we hurry forward. The dust clears as suddenly as it appeared. I pass by a charioteer on the ground, sleeves torn, hands skinned and bloody. A retch builds in my throat.

*Please don't be Dorian.*

I lean left to avoid them. The charioteer's maristag is losing control. It slams into a wall, which darkens dangerously. It can't *break*, can it? The maristag flies at me, trying to goad Stormgold into a fight. It's green as seagrass. I press forward even as relief floods me. That wasn't Dorian.

I look back under my arm. *Emmanuel.*

Five of us are racing now. I don't know where Dorian is. Probably far ahead. It's time to push Stormgold. We can't linger anymore.

I hurtle down the alley, following the sounds of a maristag nearby. Shouts erupt again, somewhere close. Stormgold starts to pick up speed. We pass clear wall after clear wall, turning left and right and left again.

Two charioteers are packed tight in the next alley. I know by the way the walls are darkening and clearing, and I hear the sound of multiple maristags. Which direction does this alley open to? If it forks at the end of mine, I'll be in their direct path.

Judas won't try to kill me but what about Arlene and Saran? Getting past them is critical.

A chariot thuds against the wall, and I'm suddenly grateful for the separation between us. The sound of antlers clashing rattles in my ears. We're coming up the end of the alley on my side.

Judas and Arlene barrel into my path. Suddenly we're three chariots in one alley. But their maristags are fighting each other and *themselves*. They snap at the mirrors along the glass walls, turn round and round, chasing their own reflections. I pull back—there's no gap for me to escape.

Over the howling wind, I hear people on the lowest tiers jumping and screaming for blood. It startles me, and I narrowly avoid being caught between Judas and Arlene again.

Judas's maristag unleashes a blood-chilling scream—the kind of noise you don't hear one make unless it's dying. Barely a lap in and already this race is making the previous ones look like a joke.

Frustration builds in me as I'm forced to lag behind Judas and Arlene. But right as that impatience rears, and I consider doing something fatally stupid, a second five-direction fork rushes at us, and I somehow know this is the equivalent of a second round. It widens the tracks for several precious moments. My only chance to get ahead of these two before Dorian and Saran find their ways back into my path. Stormgold bleats anxiously. I won't be able to hold onto her for longer without slicing open my gloves. My hands. I need a breather.

Sweat drips in my eyes. My lungs burn. We splash through a pool of blood.

Stormgold snorts, hurtling too close to Judas and Arlene's chariots. I pull her back and she drives to our right. Straight into a path that's too narrow for most new chariots but perfect for my old one. Maybe I can trick one of the others to follow me.

I make my move.

And we're through.

Stormgold leaves behind the fighting maristags as a large alley opens up again. The floor glimmers brighter here, but the Spine looms farther away. With Arlene and Judas fighting, it's only Saran and Dorian I have to watch out for. I don't remember passing them. Who knows where they are? Their maristags might snap, too.

I increase the gap between myself and Arlene and Judas.

And then, as I turn the corner down a new path, I see Dorian. But Saran emerges out of a path diagonally to my right and blocks my way. I spin wildly, barely able to pull Stormgold back. Saran disappears down an alley to my left. By my calculations, he is going opposite to the Spine. I follow the path where he came from.

But what looked like a straight alley is blocked by a glass wall. I double back and hit a dead end. Then another. Heart hammering, I'm forced back to the big fork.

The drums beat to the rhythm of my heartbeat.

Stormgold cries sharply at their clamor.

I urge her forward.

The speed makes the wind roar in my head, suffocating the sounds from the stands. Overhead, a cloud growls. And far in the ocean, lightning strikes.

Terror fills my mouth.

If it rains hard enough, the maristags will break through stone to reach the ocean. This maze will do us no favors. It's already infuriating the maristags.

None of us will survive.

*Focus*, I tell myself. This is not the time to think about what-ifs. I am here. All I have to remember is the ground beneath me and stay clear of the charioteers around me.

I find another large alley, walled off with what looks like gleaming white minerals. It lets me race at full speed for several seconds

We turn the corner to the thunder of drums and hooves. I can't tell if it's coming from my left or my right—Stormgold is so fast that I don't know if the walls next to me are mineral or glass turned foggy. I bend around a corner. Two handlers are collecting shards of a chariot.

"WATCH OUT!"

The handlers part, leaving me a straight shot.

"Sorry!" I shout as I hurtle past them.

Stormgold hammers over the debris, throwing me off-balance.

I slam to one side. The extra belt Crane strapped on keeps me from going overboard. But my weight pushes at the chariot—

One of the wheels is in air, the ground too close to my face.

Sand flies at my mouth, it's in my ears and eyes.

I'm racing behind my maristag sideways.

The wheel whirls above me, staggeringly fast against the fluorescence of the Drome.

My left hand slips off the reins. I flail for the chariot. The second I find a grip, I push at it with all my strength. The chariot crashes to the ground, rumbling over the flickering black ground dangerously, before steadying again.

A stream of swears escapes me.

It's taken them ages to come get Emmanuel's broken chariot. What happens if someone gets hurt farther inside the maze?

What if I get hurt and no one can find me? What if Dorian—

A chariot emerges out of the alley next to mine. The maristag ignores Stormgold, focused completely on the track. Fierce and fast. I check the distance and then the rider.

"You're here!" I yell with relief.

Dorian has one foot on the top rim of his chariot, his reins shortened.

"Arlene!" he shouts. "She's coming for you!"

Before I can thank him for the warning, he shoots down another alley. The next instant, Saran, *again*, cuts me off. I can either crash into him or slow down. I swear and pull Stormgold back.

A wide square opens up, the alleys converging again at the far end of it.

Tall, angled walls arise everywhere in the square like rows of upright cards. *Strange, how does this stop the charioteers?* The question barely forms in my mind when the card-like wall swivels, coming straight at me. I scream. We careen between the swinging card-walls.

I curse the Landmaster and every single person attached to this Glory Race.

My head pounds. There's someone else beside me now, avoiding the spinning walls. I sneak a glance. Judas hunches close to the front of his chariot, his face scrunched in concentration. He's far from me. He won't hurt me.

But then my eyes catch the rider behind him.

Through the multi-tined monstrous antlers of her maristag, it's Arlene.

I want to win desperately. But if I don't—I want Dorian to win. Not Arlene.

*Please not Arlene.*

She looks straight at me. I need to get away from her.

The fangs of her maristag flash. Her desire for violence has seeped into the beast.

"Let's go!" I scream at Stormgold.

We zigzag our way from wall to wall, forced to double back, slow down, try again a different way. All of us are trapped inside this square of death.

Then I realize: Arlene is on my tail.

Judas inches forward beside me. He swings away from a spinning card-wall. I forget about Arlene and instead race Judas. He may not race ugly, but he's a serious charioteer. His maristag groans as he pushes it harder. We're coming up on the final row of card-walls. *Finally.*

And suddenly, he shouts.

I turn.

The axle of Arlene's wheel is sparking against the wheels of Judas's chariot.

"Get out of my way!" Arlene growls.

Judas's maristag slams into the wall, cutting in front of me.

He manages to pull back and yells at Arlene, "Are you out of your mind? You'll get us all killed!"

Arlene's maristag shoves its antlers against Judas's chariot.

Damn her. I know what she's doing. She's opening up a larger gap between me and Judas.

It's me she's aiming for.

Arlene's maristag is a beast, broad muscles and antlers and teeth as big as my fingers. It sinks those teeth into Judas's maristag. Dark green blood spurts across my face and on Stormgold.

Disgust courses through me. Stormgold shudders, twisting around and facing the wrong way—facing Arlene and her blood lust. I nearly run into a card-wall about to slam at our faces.

She comes straight for me. "You will never get out of this Drome!"

I loosen the reins, yelling for Stormgold to move.

Judas's maristag breaks free—I duck as the harness snaps and flies at me. Stormgold rears back against the monstrous green maristag hurtling at her. She turns around and races forward, and we're through the row of walls.

The straps that connect me to the chariot are torn. I can't reach for them without getting thrown off.

We near the next set of alleys. I have to decide quickly which one to take. I need one closer to the Spine. We choose one, but slam right into glass. My feet slip out from under me. I pull Stormgold back to the square to take her down another alley. But there's a battle going—Arlene and Judas trying to get to the right alley.

Judas tries to pull away. He knows it's me Arlene wants. His chariot is rapidly splintering, his straps fly around his maristag like water snakes. Judas looks at me like he's apologizing for trying to save himself.

That's when the knife in Arlene's hand flies.

And catches Judas between his shoulder blades.

# THIRTY-THREE

The impact of the knife ripples throughout the Drome. A collective loud gasp, and then a hush.

*You are a good charioteer*, he said and wished me luck. The last thing he'll ever say to me. I blink tears out of my eyes, trying to ignore the memory of Judas coming to see me at the Agora. The only Lander who never treated me with disgust. He argued with Liria's doctor, helped him diagnose her illness.

Before I realize what I'm doing, I'm screaming. My throat is raw, my fingers chafe beneath my gloves. I hear nothing; my brain can't process what just happened. I can't focus and if I don't get my mind to work right—

I stifle my scream, let it fade, and block my thoughts.

I look back.

A swarm of dust rises from the spot where Judas's body lies. The Drome's wall splits apart like doors, and three maristags gallop toward the carnage, the riders armed with zargunine quarterstaffs.

Judas's maristag has gone wild as it screams, bleeding and slashing at the walls.

Arlene is caught behind it. Hopefully she never escapes.

Because if she does, she'll come for me.

I shake my head until wind shrieks in my ears again. On its heels is another storm cloud booming. I turn down a path that provides a breather; I'm the only one in this area for the moment.

Dorian and Saran are somewhere else, both focused on themselves.

Arlene may never survive Judas's maristag.

If I catch up now—

The thought charges my blood.

Only four of us are left. The odds of winning are looking up once more.

Through it all, the monstrous drums beat steadily, growing in intensity, rumbling within the ground, the glass walls, and the chariots. Like the ocean taking form and slamming into the islands. By the excitement pouring from the stands, the spectators love the rhythm of death's march across the Drome.

The ground beneath me shimmers, startling Stormgold. She slows, slashing at it with her tailfin like it's water. I force her forward, desperate for her to not get fooled. But it's not her fault. Only in the last race, this Drome was filled with water.

I wonder how much time has gone by. I keep moving forward, putting as much distance between myself and Arlene.

Screams go up on my left. Something's happening in the stands. I crane my neck, but the mineral walls of the maze hide the lower stands from view, as do the drummers and state broadcasters clustered over the Spine.

It's time to stop pulling back. But the moment I head down a new path, I hear chaos.

Maristags and men and carnage.

Judas's maristag has leaped onto the stands. It's climbing higher and higher, scattering the crowd and leaving wails behind him. People are going to die. My heart slams against my ribs.

What if Crane is there? What if Mama and Baba decided to come watch the race?

I lean back and squint through the dust of the Drome at the stands. Helix Stratis guards with stunguns are driving the maristag into a corner.

I can only hope my family's okay.

Stormgold has gotten her stride back and is learning to avoid walls on her own.

"TO YOUR RIGHT!" someone in the stands yells. I swerve to avoid slamming into Arlene who emerges out of the alley parallel to mine.

Dust and rubble begin piling up everywhere in the maze. We must be repeating our routes by now.

Far ahead, through the glass walls, two alleys darken and clear simultaneously.

Dorian and Saran are struggling with a sandstorm rapidly swallowing them up. I'm getting closer, and it's time to follow their leads. Get past them instead of guessing and backtracking.

If only I didn't have to go through an ocean of sand and grit, too.

Right before they disappear, my gaze drops to Saran's wheels. The axles jut out. His wheels are spiked, like in the first race. If he gets even a hand's length closer to Dorian, he can damage the wheels on Dorian's chariot.

We no longer have the advantage of other charioteers busying our enemies.

That's when it hits me.

Arlene is not on the tracks to race anymore.

She only wants revenge.

As if to prove me right, she pulls her maristag toward me the moment we cross into the network of crisscrossing alleys that Dorian and Saran were in, choking with the sandy billows.

"GO!" Stormgold cuts left to avoid a whirring wheel from a broken chariot. The gold is coated with brown. It's Emmanuel's.

We're back in the area we started from.

I spit sand out of my mouth. It sticks everywhere. On my face, in the crevices of chafed skin, inside my clothes. We zoom out into an open square—straight into Arlene's path.

She begins to gain ground. I push Stormgold on, on, on. My hands are blistering on the reins, my ribs ready to snap. We're not far from Dorian and Saran. The thunder of their chariots is close. If I reach them—if I get ahead of them, it'll deter Arlene. She won't hurt them. Saran's and Dorian's fathers would rip her and her family to shreds.

Arlene shouts, "Was this worth it, you Renter freak?"

Her maristag snaps at the back of my chariot, teeth clamping at a shredded strap, its breath crawling on the exposed skin of my leg. Antlers slam hard against the side of my chariot. A breath higher, and they'd have pierced me through. The hair on my neck rises.

Then, bitter water begins pouring from the sky.

The race needs to stop. But there's no indication of anything changing.

"The maristags can't take the rain!" I bellow, hoping a camera picks it up and brings it to the attention of the Landmaster.

Nothing happens. And nothing will.

Like gods of the Empyrean Elders' world, the only source of entertainment for the puppeteers behind the Glory Race is visiting tragedies on human beings.

Arlene is screaming at her maristag.

And before I understand what's happening, her chariot bangs into mine.

My foot slips out from under me, but I catch myself. The past races may have been carried out for the fun of watching the chario-teers fight it out, but they've all taught me their tactics.

We arrive at a fork.

Arlene's hand shoots out as she makes a direct attempt to grab the reins out of my hands. I strike out. Not caring if I hit her chest or her face. "Get away from me! Do you want to die?"

She laughs and I grab the moment to wipe my face on my sleeves.

Outside, rain is slamming down in sheets. Inside, the wet warmth of sand suffuses the air.

Stormgold tosses her head, antlers coming a breath's distance from my chest. I try to get her attention, but we are pressed so close to the walls, sparks erupt from my wheels as we turn the corner. Flames flare for a terrifying, heated moment, startling us both, before vanishing into dust.

But the sound of the fire is so loud half of the Drome gasps. Several feet ahead, Dorian cuts through one alley and into another, and looks right at me. Then immediately swivels to Saran and shouts something.

"Careful!" I yell at him, pressing Stormgold to go right. I glance back, only to see Arlene whipping her maristag into another burst of speed. She's given up pretending. She isn't finding her own path—she's following *me*.

I snap at the reins, my blood boiling, and Stormgold hurtles to the center, giving me a moment's reprieve to catch my breath. Only just, though—Arlene inches forward to my left.

Maybe I can push her into the wall.

Someone cries my name. I don't have time to look.

The path begins tapering, turning right.

I lean back and loosen the reins. Stormgold releases every bit of her power, and we pull away from Arlene, whose maristag is still busy tossing its antlers dangerously at the transparent walls.

Unless Arlene beats her maristag into submission, my immediate problem now is getting past Saran and Dorian.

We bolt past handlers trying to rein in Judas's maristag, who leaped back down to the tracks. Stormgold streaks past. Everything is a blur of wind and noise and drums.

It's then that Arlene catches up again.

She's next to me, hurling curses at me. The walls in this alley are solid, shimmering white, no glass. My gaze is straight ahead—I won't allow her to break my concentration. By the way her voice moves near and far, and the hiss of a whip striking flesh, I know Arlene is having trouble controlling her maristag.

It's an opportunity presented on a platter.

One little shove, and she'll go flying in the air.

I don't have to think. I'm about to move, but the Drome breaks into whoops and shouts again. Something has happened. I squint up at one of the screens on the Spine.

Saran's right behind Dorian's chariot.

He's going for the wheels.

"Dorian!" I yell.

"You can't save him, and he can't save you!" Arlene shouts. A blade glints at her belt. She's fixed herself upright on the chariot. She can let go of the reins without spinning out.

It's against the rules.

So this is their plan: to isolate me and Dorian and take us out one by one. Arlene can break a thousand rules right now. No complaint I make after the race will matter. I won't live long enough to see her reprimanded.

I have to take Arlene out.

I maneuver Stormgold forward. Before the ocean latches onto Stormgold's thoughts, I have to make her listen.

We hurry into the narrowest path I can find.

Arlene follows, hunting me, as I lure her into a trap. The *sssiiiirrr* of sparks explodes on either side of her chariot. I stay right in front of her, making it look like I'm trying to escape her.

Arlene takes the bait. She ignores her heating chariot and keeps on course—on my tail, never wavering.

We move into an alley of glass again. Even though it fogs up, we are the only ones on the track. The glass walls quickly frost and clear. So I can see several lengths away from us, to where Dorian and Saran are locked in what looks like an actual fight. Saran leans over his chariot, arms outstretched. And just as quickly, they turn a corner.

I lower myself in the chariot, stretching the reins. Stormgold understands. The rain beats above and the drums roar. Stormgold sweeps to the side and into an alley wide enough for at least three chariots abreast.

I hope this doesn't go terribly wrong.

Arlene whips her maristag. It scrambles faster toward the wall, coming up next to me.

I snap the reins. Stormgold speeds up.

Arlene does what I expect her to—she tries to cut us off as we reach the fork. Tries to block our way in her haste to throw me off my chariot. She is forced to lean completely to one side, to her right.

"Your family ruined everything! You're dead!" she shrieks, one hand whipping the maristag, the other clenched around the reins. Her eyes stay on me. I need to keep her this way.

"You can't touch me!" I shout, goading her.

She curses. Her attention is focused on me. Trying to aggravate me into retaliating. I hold myself. I won't give the cameras anything, even though I know Arlene can have her maristag impale me and get away with it.

By my calculations, we're turning around the Spine.

Any moment now.

"You will never wi—"

Her words cut in the middle, transforming into a terrible howl. Her chariot crashes into the wall and shatters, sending two wheels spiraling across the incandescent blue grounds.

Arlene is trapped beneath her chariot. She screeches for help. But Stormgold has already sped ahead. I exhale, reminding myself that I had no choice. I had to act.

Her own hubris brought her down.

But knowing that does not shut out her cries or the shrieks of her angry maristag.

The next few seconds are a haze. I have to make quick use of them. Dorian and Saran are still in my line of sight, but beyond a range of glass walls, their own fight has slowed them down.

I hurtle toward them, and for once, it's almost as if my path is being cleared. I hit no dead ends.

Any second I'll be Dorian and Saran's direct path.

It's only us three now.

The finale of the 150th Glory Race has begun.

But while Judas's maristag has finally come under control, Arlene's giant one has gone mad from the crash and the rain.

The rain slams down faster now—enough to be pouring inside the Drome from the gaps on either side of the roof and swelling the air with the thick smell of silt and sea.

The impact of the water is so strong that for a shocking second, the power running the maze glitches, and we're left exposed in the Drome. Groans and cries flare up everywhere, and the maze suddenly shoots up from the ground again.

But now I know how far I am from the finish line. We're at the other end of the Drome. I have to keep moving forward.

I lurch to the side, to avoid collision with Arlene's maristag. Its antlers are pointed down, and mouth pink with bloody froth. I swear. Is that Arlene's blood?

Dorian and Saran split apart at a small fork, finally breaking their fight, and the maristag charges past them, forcing me to go backward in the wrong direction. As I pull Stormgold on a straight path, my eyes lock with Dorian on a parallel path. This time, the glass does not frost. Saran swears loud enough for me to hear as he glances back and realizes that Arlene couldn't take me down.

That he can't overtake Dorian and me, both.

That the two of us together will never let him win.

For several seconds we are leveled with geometric precision on parallel paths. And all three of us in the opposite direction of the finish line. The crowd builds to an uproar. The drums have taken up a new beat, faster, wilder, like they're the ones directing this entire show.

I have to win this race. I have to get the remaining two charioteers to continue fighting. I have to force their hands.

We emerge out of our paths onto a third square.

Steering Stormgold forward, I press toward Saran. He wasn't expecting that. Immediately, I'm several inches ahead of him and he's tucked behind Dorian's chariot.

Making Dorian vulnerable to the spikes on Saran's wheels.

If they keep at it, I have a straight, unobstructed shot ahead of me toward what should be the final network of alleys.

Dorian and Saran's chariots are too close. The bend rams them together and sparks fountain between the two chariots, bright enough to light up the corner of my vision. Dorian roars, his chariot bumping into the air and slamming down hard.

I loosen the reins and Stormgold takes the lead.

My chance to win is here—

Something hard and razor-edged grabs me by the throat and pulls.

I gasp, my right hand involuntarily reaching to release the grip.

The world tilts and I'm staring at the roof. It's a whip. *Saran.* The roughness chafes at my fingers and my hand on the reins goes lax. Stormgold's speed continues to increase.

I choke and cough. Darkness converges in front of my eyes, stars popping loud.

I can't lose my hold on the burning reins, or I'll fly off my chariot. If the whip doesn't crush my throat first.

Something twists in my lower back, and I'm screaming.

Gasping, I reach for the whip and, instead of trying to get it off me, tug. It catches Saran by surprise. He's pulled off-balance. He loosens his grip on the reins, which instructs his maristag to go forward and *strike* ahead—only to crash straight into debris on the tracks.

The maristag's harness breaks.

The chariot overturns. Saran spins in the air before hurtling down the tracks for several lengths.

One of the wheels from Saran's chariot gyrates right into the side of Dorian's chariot, taking half a wheel off. His maristag shrieks. It's a sudden, haunting sound that will howl in my nightmares. Dorian's chariot slams to the ground and drags against the track, screeching and clamoring as its bolts start coming loose. Swarms of sand and dust obscure everything.

Stormgold whirls.

The square tapers to alleys again. They're thinner than any others so far. I can't—

*We're too fast.*

I lose control.

The chariot swings to one side, springing above the shattered remains of Arlene's chariot and bits from Dorian's collapsing one— and it hits me that we're being *led* through repeating paths, still competing in laps.

My face bounces against the ground, hammers banging my skull.

My cheek is skinned, the sting of sand nearly blinding. Then I'm tossed like a ball to the ground.

The impact with the ground is an explosion in my head, all my senses momentarily snuffing out, and I'm floating in the dark.

Hard thuds rumble on the tracks.

I wrench my eyes open. My broken chariot soars above my head and crashes to the ground, shattering to crumbs. I hear wheels—one wheel—nearing me.

"Get up, Koral!" Dorian's voice charges past on the path parallel to mine.

The hard ground beneath is still reminiscent of a brilliant black ocean. It flickers so close to my eyes; the burning sensation feels like I haven't closed my eyes in a year. Blood is rushing out my nose, pooling at the back of my throat. I want to curl into my side, contain the pain exploding in my ribs. But there's no time. Did I make it through the alley? But I'm still inside—

Who am I kidding?

*I lost. I'm dead, it's over.*

And that's when the spikes of a maristag's muzzle nudge me. Over the shouts and rumblings, I pull my gaze down. The small act sends ripples of ache behind my eyes.

Stormgold looks at me as she did the day I entered the stables, like she was waiting for me.

In my haze, the entire Drome fades away. The fluorescence is bright behind Stormgold, walls reflecting the distorted spectators as the rain fiercely drums on the roof, and she's here, kneeling in front of me.

I roll on my side with her help, blood dripping from my nose and mouth. There's a mirrored wall facing me.

And looking back is not a girl born to bleed red on the sand, but one with the furious black sea in her veins.

My hand catches Stormgold's antlers. She doesn't whimper.

Over her shoulder, through the glass walls—Dorian is not even halfway ahead, owing to his splintered chariot, which drags him down, and the rain wreaking havoc on his maristag.

But Stormgold is here. Steady. In control.

My fingers lace tightly in Stormgold's manefin, and I press my knee down, hauling myself up. This is senseless. What purpose will this serve? I can't finish the race like this. No one has ever ridden a maristag in this Drome, no one except—

The First Champion. The prisoner who refused to die trampled on these tracks. The one whose chariot I've finally destroyed. But it wasn't *his* to begin with, was it? It was *gifted* to him, when he was forced to give up his defiance, to change his narrative.

*You'll win, Koral. I know it.*

Liria's voice from weeks ago becomes tangible, the air whispering it in my ears. Her memory is a shot of thunder in my veins. My fumbling feet find their place on either side of Stormgold as she stands straight.

There are no reins in my hand.

But I've ridden the maristag beneath me.

I see myself in the distorted mirror wall. I know why I'm here. Why I chose the Glory Race.

*Because I want to win.*

In this Drome, I've become someone else. It was the only way I had to prove to the world that I wasn't here to vanish without a trace.

I pull my legs slightly up, and lean low until my breath is on Stormgold's skin. The muscles in my thighs scream, like they did at the beach, but my body fits against Stormgold's with ease. Dorian is struggling with the chariot—but if he crosses out of the maze, he'll win.

I pin my legs on Stormgold's sides. "My star—go!"

Stormgold barrels with everything she has. She's powerful under my hands, her body solid and muscled, built for this. Without the burden of a chariot, she finds her stride in less than a second, shooting straight like a burning star.

We zigzag through the alleys, the walls crystallizing around us. We shoot forward, not letting even the dead ends dishearten us. I know I'm moving in the right direction.

I started from the bottom rung, working hard all my life, and I'm here with my maristag, having fought for every scrap. They will not take this from me.

I ride through the Drome mirroring the First Champion. Screaming at the entire world. I will not die.

*I will survive, I will survive, I will survive.*

Every second brings Dorian closer until we're a hand away from him. Our speeds are steady. I'm ready to ask Stormgold for more.

The finish line is blinking now, just beyond a set of three alleys, only one of which will lead us out. A furious gold, desperate to turn green. It stands for everything I want in this moment: honor, glory, wealth. All of which will change the lives of my mother, my sister, my brother. And me.

Winds of water kiss my skin.

I chase it with everything I have.

Even as I near him, Dorian swoops past through one of the alleys.

Dread fills me. What if he's chosen the right one? What if he gets there first?

At the end of everything, he has been my only real contender.

It is Dorian, son of Solomon Akayan, whom I need to beat now.

He's powerful, and he knows his tricks. He's put his weight to the side, balancing the chariot and helping his maristag as much as he can. And Rhyton trusts Dorian as much as Stormgold trusts me.

He can cruise to a win.

My fingers at the sides of Stormgold's manefin tighten, asking her for more. I trust my instincts and take the alley running parallel to the right of him.

I meet Dorian's eyes as I pass him for the barest of seconds. His lips are split and there's blood on his arms through shredded sleeves. He only gets time to glance incredulously at the maristag beneath me. But his expression is wild, like he might start laughing.

Then I'm past him, and the Drome's gone, and I'm soaring.

The golden line burns green.

# THIRTY-FOUR

The moment I bring Stormgold to a stop, I tumble off her, gasping, the iron taste of blood swelling in my throat. I don't care. My legs tremble as the sensation of flying slows. The race is over.

I crossed first.

I won.

I am the Champion.

The Drome has gone anarchic; screams and cheers cut through the roar of rain still beating down on the roof, powder bombs blow and swirl everywhere.

Handlers rush in from every side, reaching for Stormgold.

"Stay away," I warn them.

Then I hang onto Stormgold's neck. Blood and tears mix and drip down my face, but I bury myself against her, fingers broken, my entire body shaking. And she lets me. A maristag that doesn't care for one wrong touch lets me stay clinging to her. My legs are on fire, and I'm crying and crying and crying.

A scraping noise of metal against the ground makes me look up.

The entire Drome is covered in fluttering banners bearing the sigil of the Glory Race, drowning in shrieks and tumult. And from the maze, Dorian appears, stumbling alongside his maristag, holding himself up against gravity.

His hands unsteadily try to pull the harness off Rhyton.

Handlers with staffs surround them and push him back. He lets them. One bleeding hand wrapped around his middle, he staggers toward me. "You did it," he says, words fumbling, eyes rimmed with blood and wonder. "You actually finished it."

But he's not looking at me. His gaze is turned upward—where the Landmaster stands, in her finery, a silver figure of wax, gleaming as the world she looks over rejoices with fanaticism.

Before I answer him, the gates open and for a wild moment, I'm anticipating maristags.

But it's Solomon Akayan.

He marches so fast he'd probably run if the entire island wasn't gathered above our heads, waiting to see this—the real final lap of the 150th Glory Race—unfold.

"This is what we spent eight years on, boy?" Solomon shouts.

I try to look away, but Solomon is so loud he may as well be broadcasting on every screen. The Race Rep and the state helpers catch up, along with the Landmaster's officers.

Abruptly, Solomon stops. Instead, he points to me. His face is red, jaw hard. "This girl cheated!"

The accusation was coming as sure as I know I have won fair and square.

"I crossed the line first," I address the Race Rep.

"On bareback!" Solomon roars. "This is a chariot race."

"That is a fair point, Koral of Sollonia," the Renter state helper says. He's not saying it with venom or like he wants it to be true, but merely giving me an opening to speak.

"If the Glory Race was started in honor of the First Champion, then nothing that has happened here counts as unfair." I put my chin up, blood still dripping down my face.

Solomon snaps, "The fair winner of this race is Dorian."

"I conceded, Father," Dorian says. Every set of eyes in the vicinity trains on him. Blood trickles down the sides of his face and the rawness of my own cheek stings warmly.

Do I even have skin on my cheek right now?

He repeats, "I conceded. The path I was on was a dead end. I had to double back and return to get out. Koral had already finished the race. I was only bringing my maristag back." He glances at the maze. At the mouth of it, his crown lies, gleaming alone. "You can argue the use of chariots but seeing that no other charioteer has crossed the line, Koral of Sollonia is the rightful winner of the 150th Glory Race."

A stunned silence follows his speech.

The Renter state helper says, "Well, that settles it. If a fellow charioteer vouches for a win, who are we to argue?" He gestures for me to proceed inside the Charioteer Hall. Solomon's voice stops us. But it's not me he's yelling at.

"This is where you destroy everything, do you realize that, you stupid boy?"

Hatred burns in me.

"Come back here!" Solomon bellows and Dorian halts. "You think the Landmaster up in that balcony is on your side?" he screams, spit flying. The Race Rep shuffles nervously while the Renter state helper's mouth is pressed. The officers collectively straighten their weapons. "This is what we wanted to prevent from day one when this girl decided to sabotage everything!"

Nobody speaks, even the spectators' noise has slowed. People jostle toward the bottom stand, trying to listen to what's going on now.

And then, something both miraculous and horrible happens.

"Oh, shut your damned mouth, Solomon Akayan," Crane shouts, stepping out of the Charioteer Hall. She stops next to Dorian, who looks white. He glances at me in alarm, then at my friend. "What are you—"

"Stay out of this," Crane says sharply. "And you," she turns to Solomon, "if Dorian lost, he did so with honor. He gave it everything. More than anyone can say about you, flying into a rage like a half-mad aquabat. Have you no dignity at all?"

The world stills in this moment. It stretches for far too long.

"It's time for you to leave, sir," says an officer. He raises a brow, chin up, one hand on his gun. We all know what that means: they don't care who Solomon is, because the orders came from the Landmaster.

Solomon looks at Dorian, who pulls up a corner of his lip. It's clear he's made a choice, too.

But when he leaves, I feel like the tide has pulled back only to slam into the entire land soon.

Crane faces me. "You look like you're half in your graveboat. Let's get you out of here." She puts an arm around me. I hiss with pain. Her apology is the last thing I hear before my legs finally give out and I collapse.

I wake up in the familiar white room of the Lander Hospital.

I wonder if they tried to stop me from getting in because I had a metal pin on my collar.

A clear liquid drips into the tube attached to my forearm. My cheeks are warm but smooth. Nothing hurts. Of course. I can't step inside the Landmaster's box dragging half my body across the floor.

Because I won.

I find myself whispering feverish thanks to the ocean.

"You're up," the nurse's voice floats over my head. Again with the creepy smile. "Congratulations!"

Well, that confirms I really *did* win.

"Can I see my parents?" I say, trying to sit up. "They're here in the Hospital."

"Oh, sweetie, you'll have time later. We have to get you ready for the Crowning Ceremony." Despite the enthusiasm in her words, her smile's intensity remains unchanging. She quickly checks my vitals and then steps out as I dress—a new set of black pants and white shirt. My clothes almost feel like a joke at this point.

Right outside my room, two armed officers wait for me. The entire way from the Hospital through the Terrafort tunnels up to the Charioteer Hall is empty. Everyone is ready for the Crowning Ceremony either inside the Drome or already celebrating in the thoroughfare.

Right as the officers begin climbing the stairs, someone shrieks down the hallway.

"I can't believe it! It's the Champion!"

I recognize Crane's voice, I recognize her face—behind the elaborate makeup—as she jogs toward me. Yet she acts like she's never seen me before in her life. "I can't believe I caught you right before the Ceremony. This is so exciting!"

"Please get back—" an officer says.

But Crane continues the stream of compliments. Bewildered, I'm about to tell her to stop when I realize why the officers have simply not threatened her with their stunguns: she's dressed in white and gold, face gilded with paint. And that's what she appears to them, a Lander fan of the Glory Race.

"Just one hug," she squeals, "and then you can take her!"

Before either of the officers say anything, Crane crushes me in a rib-crunching embrace, and whispers in my hair, "We need to talk."

I drop my voice as well. "What's wrong?"

"Arkers were rescued during the Race. Emrik got out, too. He's hiding at my place, but we can't stay here for long now."

Dread makes my blood run cold, making it hard to hold on to one thought. Emrik escaped—he's safe.

But is he?

Am I?

Crane releases me, beaming with faked excitement.

"Good luck!" she adds for the effect as the officers finally get between her and me and direct me upstairs to the Charioteer Hall.

# THIRTY-FIVE

Minutes later, I'm back inside the Charioteer Hall for the start of the Crowning Ceremony. My heart is still racing from Crane's words. The chatter from outside swirls in my mind together with thoughts of my brother, hurt. *Get a damn grip.* But the more I try to pull myself together, the more I seem to hear strange voices.

I absolutely *cannot* have a panic attack right now.

I need to clear my head.

Stormgold is draped with a white and gold sash. I grab onto the fabric, the satiny touch grounding me. *Think of the ocean, the strength of the waves, flonners hopping, gray sand.* Beneath the sash, the scales of the maristag press firm against my palm. Her antlers shimmer with green iridescence, catching at the lamps' shine.

*Think of the hunt.*

That, finally, sinks every other thought down. I take a deep breath and stand straighter.

Near the gates, Dorian waits with his maristag, too. As the runner-up, he'll be felicitated before my Crowning. Dressed in simple black shirtsleeves, a silver crown hanging at his belt, he looks exactly like he did before the race.

When he sees me, his shoulders drop. He looks apologetic. For his father's behavior? This can't be easy on him—despite everything, I still don't know if I can let go of Baba.

I don't understand what exists between me and Dorian. If the uncertain warmth I feel for Dorian is only sympathy borne out of shared hurts. Or if the root I buried deep has sprouted again, taking the place of all the anger I was holding onto.

I can't tell if it's a flower or a fungus.

He's asked to step out in the Drome for the Ceremony. After him, they come for Stormgold. Instead of following my maristag, I'm ushered up to the Landmaster's Tower. The Crowning Ceremony takes place in the box above—which, of course, makes my newly healed knees woozy.

But I keep walking. The Landmaster's officers, probably embarrassed, pretend I'm not about to keel over.

Even if I was sent a pair of familiar clothes, the fabric is clingy and uncomfortable. And ridiculously heavy. Hunting in this outfit would be a nightmare. I slog through a hallway decked with photos of past Champions.

How will I hunt maristags this way?

And then I remember. I won't be hunting anymore. Will the name be passed on to a new family? Generations of Hunters will suddenly have new members. All because Emrik and I let go of one maristag.

Music from the Drome suffuses the air. I'm getting close. The air in my lungs is turning into rocks.

My escorting officers and I step around a corner and at the end of the hallway, the bright lights of the Drome filter through the balcony box, dazzling me. I squint and turn—to a photo of Solomon from his Crowning Ceremony. I quickly look away to the other side and

315

catch a glimpse of myself in the silver surface of a pillar. There's no marked change in me, except hollow cheeks that sit awkwardly over my rounded chin. My hair lies straight, obscuring the remaining half of my tattoo. I resist the urge to tie it up like I usually do. My hands are too clammy.

Once the Landmaster gets word of my arrival, she opens the Crowning Ceremony. After a small speech about the Glory Race coming to a close, the guard at the gate gestures toward the box. "Koral Hunter, Landmaster Minos is ready for you."

It hits me like a punch that I'm about to be crowned Champion of the Glory Race.

Every step forward is a step away from my old life. The unease in my stomach clamors for attention. But I can't pay mind to it right now. I step over the threshold. Bright lights wash over me.

"Welcome, Koral of Sollonia, Champion of the 150th Glory Race," the Landmaster says. She's wearing a mic in the collar of her glittering silver-blue sari, a speck in her otherwise impeccable attire. Her raspy, authoritative voice is amplified across the Drome.

I breathe deeply and step forward. At the balcony, I'm greeted with hundreds of tiny mirrors studded on the balustrade, reflecting the fluorescence back at the Drome and resembling glittering stars. The sight is so beautiful that I stop, dazed, before remembering the many spectators trained on me. I hurriedly step up, only to meet the white-lined blue eyes of Landmaster Minos.

The corners of her lips lift slightly. As if she knows a secret. As if she can't wait for the entertainment of her lifetime to start.

"It is a great privilege and honor to hold this glorious Crown to your head, a tradition passed down from Champion to Champion." She pauses and I shiver at the words. Traditional is not exactly the description associated with me. "Koral of Sollonia, take your Crown."

She gestures behind her, where a second door identical to the first one opens in another hallway.

Champion Sonnys steps inside, unsmiling. He holds up a velvet cushion. On it sits the gleaming silver and gold Crown, cut exquisitely, set with hundreds of small glittering jewels. This Crown is a legacy, a gift from the Empyrean Elders. And for the next four years, it's mine.

"Repeat after me," the former Champion says. "I, Koral of Sollonia, do swear in the name of the Empyrean Elders that I will uphold the glory of the Crown and keep obedience to the Council of Ophir as established by law—"

"I, Koral of Sollonia, do—"

Screams break out in the Drome.

A dark banner unfurls amid the white ones, concealing a quarter of the spectators. The colors fuzz together. I squint, trying to see what's happening—until I catch the Landmaster focused on the screen in the corner of the box.

My heart stops.

The banner is lined with silver chain-links with one bold phrase in the center.

FREEDOM'S ARK.

A masked group holds the banner up.

They're chanting something, its echo squeezing into every crevice of the island: *Koral of Sollonia. Koral of Sollonia. Koral of Sollonia.*

Furtive movements ripple through the stands—guards are on their way.

The start of my time as Champion is going to be marked with blood and arrests.

Someone roars close, "Protect the Landmaster!" Then, "She's still in the box! Get her!"

My hands are shackled before I can gasp. I didn't even see the

Helix Stratis guards step in the box. Stunned, I stare from the handcuffs to the guards swarming the hallway outside. A wall of blue-maroon uniforms surrounds me. The ground beneath me tilts.

On the screen, I see Stormgold slash her tailfin anxiously. She snaps and bares her fangs. And that act of aggression has handlers slamming zargunine staffs at her.

My voice finally explodes, "No! What are you doing? Landmaster Minos—what's happening?" I try to kick myself free and the guards immediately pull me back from the Landmaster.

Minos straightens her undisturbed headcover, dusts her clean silver-blue sari off, and takes a cautious step back from me, as if from a wild maristag.

"Koral of Sollonia," she booms over the chaos of the Drome. "You were given the chance of a lifetime, but you choose to betray the trust of Ophir and bring rebels into our homes. You let them in our Empyrean Sanctuary and helped them steal from us, and seeing as your brother was rescued while you distracted us all with the Glory Race, it is obvious now, you are here on their behest. You are not fit for the glory of our world."

*Run! Get yourself out!*

I hear Emrik screaming in my head, the last thing he said before he was arrested. I should've listened to him. Now it's too late.

The Landers have finally snatched the last line from me.

I am Icarus.

# THIRTY-SIX

Sollonia's conch shells don't reach so far underground.

I have no way of knowing if hours have passed or days. The dark on Sollonia is supposed to be safe, it's supposed to be our salvation, but not for me. For me, it's a prison. In the dark, the Landmaster's face takes shape so strongly I could touch her if I reached out. Her white hair gleams bright like the sun, but the jewel on her staff reminds me of blood, frozen solid like ice.

*Pity*, she surveys me and says.

I agree. So I don't cry.

I think of my family and dread transforms my heart into a ball of lead. They were in the Hospital. What will happen to them? Will I ever see them again? I wish I'd have told them about Emrik. Perhaps *they* could have run.

But how could they, with Liria unconscious?

Please let them escape this unscathed. Let them forget me and live.

*All of this is for me*, Dorian said.

For me, it's this cell, far beneath the ground. Away from the

Drome. I swallow my frustration for the hundredth time. If they've hurt Stormgold—if—

I slam my fists down on the solid, cold floor.

"I hope the ocean breaks into your homes!"

My voice echoes and dies in the silence. After a while, I hum. If only to keep my wits. But soon, it's too much effort. The cold settles inside my lungs. There's nothing to protect myself with. I press against the wall. My feet, curled beneath me, stick to the chilled floor.

I move. Sharp pain courses through my bones. I try not to move.

"You shouldn't have let the maristag escape," Emrik says.

"You shouldn't have ignored me while you had the chance," Crane says.

"You shouldn't have fought with the rebels," Baba says.

The worst comes from Mama, as she grips Liria's hand. "We needed you. You ruined everything."

"No," I whisper in the darkness, reaching out, but my family is only a lie told by the dark.

The footsteps finally come. Maybe they're not real. I'm hallucinating. Maybe—

Light flares from the open door, and in this dark it seems the stars have come down, a cosmic fire to cleanse everything. A spike in the ache that's eating my brain from the inside. I want to reach into my skull, pull out what's hurting, throw it away. *Please, take the light elsewhere.*

"I am disappointed, Koral of Sollonia," says the familiar, hateful voice of the Landmaster. Her clean, sharp clothes feel as out of place as if I, and not a Lander boy, wore the silver crown.

Etiquette demands I rise. Bow. I only stare at her from the floor.

"I did warn you that ambition in this world can only be served by the rules of this world."

The story of Icarus and his miscalculated wings.

"Your brother will be found soon, as will your sister."

I look up so fast I hear a *whoosh*.

"What about my sister? What did you do? My family had no hand in this. You *know* this, Landmaster."

"Do not speak out of turn, girl. As for your family, thank *you* for delivering them right into our custody. If they hadn't been in the Hospital, arresting them could have been ugly. We will deal with them, of course. And I promise you, the minute we find your brother and sister, they will meet the same fate."

My heart beats so fast it *burns*. She truly doesn't have Liria? Could Emrik and Crane have gotten her out? It's too much to hope. The sudden surge of emotion stabs me in the eyes. I hold on to this faraway beam of hope.

"Rebels run around like dust in air. Then they get buried." She waves a hand and the lights behind her—lamps—cast huge shadows in the claustrophobic cell. "I wanted you to be better than you are, Koral of Sollonia. I wanted to see how much you would listen. If only you'd listened."

"I did listen," I whisper angrily. "I'd have done anything. I'd have kept my head down, I'd have—"

"You could not even follow the simplest directives, Hunter. You say a lot of things, but they rarely translate into actions. Pity," she says, in the same voice I imagined.

The dress she sent for me at First Celebration. It was a test. To see if I'd do as she asked. I didn't.

"Had you only listened, Koral, things would be different. Had you only stayed in your place, you would have lived a life far better than your own."

I *almost* resist from scoffing. "So will this Glory Race have no Champion?"

"We both know there was only one Champion for this Glory Race from the start. Dorian Akayan has been raised to be Champion since he was a child. You could never take that from him, no matter what you both shared once."

My hands clap over my mouth, almost involuntarily. I stare at Minos. Of all the puzzles falling into place, realizing that the Landmaster had a hand in crushing Dorian and me, is the one that rocks the ground beneath me.

"Did you spy on us? Did we threaten you so much?"

"You amuse me, Koral."

"You did," I rasp. "And what did you say to him now? Did you tell him you'd let me live if he joins you?"

She watches me dispassionately, and that is all the confirmation I need. Solomon Akayan threatened to kill me. But Dorian was the one who warned me against trusting the Landmaster. How could he believe her *now*?

He may not have wanted me dead, but he was always going to betray me. He did it before, he did it again.

Hurt me and call it saving.

"I'm not fond of stagnation, Koral. But I am aware of what happens when you shake a small world. This is not a world that can be shaken. Dorian will continue as he would have before." She takes a deep breath. "He's a Lander who knows that violins aren't what will save us. Only knowing our limits, knowing what we can expend."

"Was it truly Freedom's Ark, Landmaster? In the Drome?"

"Freedom's Ark," she says, tasting the words. "I suppose freedom means different things to different people. If you mean those who understand when the tide is against them and bend to the greater will, then yes."

The factions. The splits in the Freedom's Ark. They were right there in the Drome, talking about the Landmaster's will. Ark leaders scapegoated rebels once before, and my mother was driven out then. Now, a faction joins hands with the Landmaster and decides it's my turn.

"You wanted me to win," I say, shoulders slumping. "You did this."

Every Renter bolstered will be crushed. No one will challenge them again. They'll knock back the Renters who managed to push forward. They'll use me as an example of what happens when you challenge the gods—for it's true, the gods we left behind only made space for these new vengeful ones. We will live and die aboveground forever.

The realization is the last shove off a cliff.

It isn't only my family I brought to ruin—it's an entire people.

I raise my gaze back to her. There is a long, dead silence in which Landmaster Minos watches me. She looks strangely insubstantial as she says, "I did this for all of us."

Then, she leaves.

I press my palms against my mouth to contain the sob trying to break free and my arm digs the pin on my collar against my skin. The metal pin. It's such a ridiculous thing, I rub a finger on the engraved back. Even without light, I remember the words enough to see them.

MAY THE WATER HORSE WATCH OVER YOU.

I'll take it. If there's power in any world, anything who's listening, I beg them to watch over my family. My parents, and Emrik and Liria, wherever they are.

I believe the gods of the Empyrean Elders now. I believe powers existed that could bring famine and plague and earthquakes and smite people with nothing more than one word. Perhaps they wrote this tragedy, too.

Of a girl too angry, too willful, and too ambitious for her own good.

~

The Helix Stratis guards come for me. I don't resist as they pull me up, still handcuffed. My tongue is stone dry. The remaining dregs of my rage vanished in the dark and the cold. Even slight glimmers of light from beyond the corner don't make any difference.

I squint, we're in a narrow hallway lined with cells.

Looking at it is exhausting.

I let myself be dragged, unable to even *cry*.

Only when the faint noise of the crowd begins snaking in my ears, I look up.

They're taking me into the Drome—the clock dripping seconds above the gates of the Charioteer Hall displays the same hour a race would be starting.

One last entertainment from the Renter charioteer.

My hands brush against the metal pin—a mother's blessing—on the torn collar of my ragged clothes.

Landers dominate the seats; Renter areas are empty. There's no sign of my family. Above, the Landmaster presides over us all. Next to her—Dorian. They look like two sides of Ophir, a bright washed day, and a deep dark night.

Dorian had warned me the Landmaster chooses the Champion. His own silver crown has been replaced by the Champion's Crown, glinting in the shimmering fluorescence.

He doesn't meet my eyes.

"Coward," I murmur, not taking my gaze off him.

The crowd curses me. How fickle are these beings. The dread at not knowing my fate in the darkness had coursed through my veins, but I see now that nothing I could do for these monsters would change things.

The realization is liberating. I straighten my shoulders.

If they strangle me now, I will not beg.

"Welcome, Heirs of Empyrean." The Landmaster's cold voice rings across the Drome. The cheers that follow are deafening. Bloodthirsty raptors. Tonight Landers are the only ones in the Drome. The way they've always wanted.

"When we spoke for this Renter girl, when we opened our hearts for her," I struggle not to laugh, "we did not know the treachery she carried in her veins. We gave kindness only to be repaid with mockery and blood—the blood of our people. But I thank Koral of Sollonia, for she reminded us of our untarnished power. From this day forth, we will never be fooled again."

Savage screams and applause follow her ridiculous speech. The command for my blood is about to come. Every muscle and sinew in me tenses. If they want entertainment, I will give it to them. They've already taken everything from me, why should I hold back now?

"We start at the root of this problem, at the rot that grew while we gave them a place to live. Emrik Hunter and his sister, Liria of Sollonia, are hereby declared fugitives. Anyone who comes forward with information about them will be rewarded with a thousand gold."

Chaotic cheers break out in the Drome.

The Landmaster cuts them short with a new command, "Bring them in."

A gate under the Landmaster's Tower groans open. The Tower is so huge that the gate feels comically small. Then two figures, their heads covered with black cloth sacks, are brought in. Their hands are tied behind their backs. The frailty of their gait—the blood on their clothes. The Helix Stratis guards drag them both in front of the Spine.

*Go to them,* I tell myself. But the rattle of the handcuff is too loud. The slight movement scrapes the wounds on my wrists, and I grow still where I'm standing, grinding my teeth, swallowing the hiss of pain.

They are sent to their knees. That's when something deep inside me begins to understand.

My voice is caught in my throat. But I'm screaming. I know I am. And when the black sacks lift from their heads—my *parents*—I am thrashing against the grip of the guards who materialize out of air to restrain me.

But I keep fighting, kicking like *hell*. I can think of nothing else, until something hard slams against the back of my head and I crash forward. The impact gushes the air out of my lungs. Strong hands pin me to the ground.

I struggle to raise my head, pushing against the sand sticking to the wounds on my face, the pain too sharp.

"We will grant you one last chance. Know this: any loss of human life on the Islands of Ophir is a loss for us all. Tell us, Koral of Sollonia, where the leaders of the Freedom's Ark hide. Tell us where we can find them and bring them to justice. Tell us this, and we will send you to live out the rest of your life in Kar Atish's mines."

I stare at her, bewildered. Is she being real right now? Maybe she is, maybe even the Arkers who work for her refuse to betray everyone. Maybe they only wanted revenge against the Hunters. I don't know what the truth is. I don't know if knowing would matter. I can only muster every drop of strength in me, and shout, my voice breaking, sand in my teeth, "I don't know!"

The Landmaster raises one elegant, cruel hand. A Helix Stratis guard beside Mama and Baba draws out his quarterstaff.

"No," I struggle against my captors, writhing and screaming. "No! I swear, I don't know. I don't know!"

"Who sent you here to disturb our Glory Race?" Her voice is laced with pretense.

"I came here only for the tournament! Let my parents go, they never wanted me to race!"

"We have let our laws and our land be disrespected for too long. Long enough for us to see our Sanctuary violated, our history played with." She pauses as a round of affirming jeers ring the Drome. "No longer."

Her hand drops to her side.

I kick and shout. I swear vengeance.

My mother's head is lowered. She has nothing to say to me, I know the things she carried in her heart. But my father's eyes find me.

*This is how it ends*, I think, numb. The persistent hatred between my father and me, the relationship we once had, lost to the quarter-staffs being lowered now.

The glint of metal flashes, and my parents drop to the ground.

A blinding pain, like a staff plunged through me, tears at the center of my body. It's too much—it's unbearable. I can't see. My vision blackens and whitens. I'm screaming but I hear nothing. And despite it all, the stream of blood finds it way toward me, thickening with sand and spiderwebbing around itself. I wrench myself back.

My parents' blood.

*This is not real, this is not real, this is not real.*

I will do anything, *anything*—

"Speak, girl, will you reveal your conspirators?"

"Do it," I rasp. Angrily. Desperately. "End this."

For a vast moment, an unnatural silence fills the Drome. Nothing exists but my shamelessly beating heart. Tears spill down my face, uncontrollably, and I murmur the faint words of the final ritual for my parents.

*May the Water Horse watch over you,*
*May you sail the ocean of stars,*
*May you find the home of elders,*
*May the end begin once more.*

The Landmaster booms, "Koral of Sollonia, for corroding our sacred Glory Race, for colluding with the militant movement Freedom's Ark, you are hereby sentenced to die..."

I close my eyes. The terror pounding through me tries to drag me to the ground. But I picture my loved ones: Liria's soft giggles, Emrik's annoying scoffs, Crane's lack of respect for every rule ever made.

I think of my parents. I might get to see them soon.

"...by the jaws of Ophir."

A sadistic cheer goes up in the Drome at her words. Any air still in my lungs whooshes out. No, no—she can't mean—

The metal gates on the sides of the Drome groan open. At first, only a set of giant white-brown horns swish outside.

Then the capricorn emerges.

# THIRTY-SEVEN

**Y**ou said you'd let her go!" Dorian roars, voice amplified through the Landmaster's mic. I look up, his hands are clamped on the balcony, staring at me with the raw horror of what he's done. *Good.* Let him see what his bargaining has bought him: nothing.

We were on the same path, once more, and he chose to walk backward, once more. In some sad way, this heartbroken song is familiar like my own skin.

*Goodbye, Dorian.*

Beside him, Landmaster Aiala Minos stands tall, unbothered that her Crowned Champion is shouting at her to stop this horror. The gleam surrounding her, as if her lifeblood being energized, is inhuman.

*No,* I think, *it is exactly human.*

The violence in this world doesn't belong to the sea creatures. It belongs to us. To what we brought with ourselves.

The capricorn screeches so loud the air shivers. If the Drome wasn't made of marble, it would have blown apart. The light gleams on its scales as the half-goat, half-fish creature moves onto the tracks. Sniffing. Upset.

Its gaze lands first on the bloodied bodies of my parents. It traces the stream of blood—and finds me. There's an infinite moment in which it opens its maw, before the thunderous roar deafens me. The capricorn slams its tailfin down hard. A splinter in the ground travels toward me.

*Run*, I tell myself.

The capricorn launches itself at me. I duck under it, sliding to the other side. The reek of its breath washes over me. I slam at the door of the Charioteer Hall. "LET ME OUT!"

The shadow on me grows, and I hurtle away. A second later, three claws scratch the metal gates out, leaving jagged gaps. Above me in the stands are screams of cruel delight, provoking the capricorn.

The creature rises, claws in the air, balanced with its tail. Its horns almost reach the roof of the Drome.

I try to run but a giant horn slams sideways into me. Luckily, I catch the edge and grab at it. The capricorn yelps, shaking its head dizzily to throw me off. I'm flung in the air. It lunges toward me, maw wide open, but I smash into the stretch of its scaly back.

The scales provide my fingers good grip. I begin crawling my way upward. Until the capricorn starts shifting, body undulating rapidly. My hand slips. The capricorn slams its claws down on the ground, and this time I go flailing toward the top of the Spine. The stone sends an agonizing spasm through me as I cling to the edge, dangling off the crest of a pillar.

The capricorn and I are now at eye level. It charges, horns pointed at me.

I dart forward, until the top falls off abruptly and the pillars in the middle stand disconnected. I look back once, fear pulsing in my body, and leap off, jumping from pillar to pillar, putting as much distance between me and the capricorn as possible. The waves of pain turn my legs to ribbons. Twice I almost fall. But sheer terror of becoming capricorn food pushes me.

The capricorn slashes at the pillars. A fracture crumbles the stone. I tumble off the last pillar, grabbing at the debris, and fall back on the ground.

All around me stones rain.

That frightens the Landers at last. They cannot both control the capricorn and have me killed.

Maybe I can outlast until the capricorn is forced to be subdued. I dash toward the Landmaster's Tower. But before I reach it, the door of the Charioteer Hall opens.

An absolutely frenzied Stormgold is thrown out.

Stormgold cries blood—a sound I've never heard from her. She thrashes against unseen claws. I swear. Those are marks of a zargunine quarterstaff around her neck. They've angered her—*maddened* her.

The capricorn slams at her, and she darts out of the way. The green shine outlining her scales is larger, pulsing cosmically with her heartbeat.

She tosses her head and looks up. Straight at me.

A ghoulish growl emerges from her throat. Terror beats in my bones. Two of them. How can I run? *Where* can I run? The maristag is *fast*, the capricorn is *giant*. I'm dead—

I don't even have time to contemplate my coming death as Stormgold rushes at me, unseeing, like she would devour me whole.

My mind is locked, my body frozen.

"It's me!" I scream over the renewed jeers howling for my blood. My heart thunders with the might of a seastorm. "For the ocean's sake, it's me! Clear your head and see me!"

But she's still thrashing against the effects of the zargunine. She probably doesn't remember me at all...

There's only thing left for me to do.

I turn—and I bolt.

The back gates of the Drome! I have to get to them. But Stormgold's screech gets louder in my ears. And the capricorn swings toward the other side of the Spine, amid the stones and dust, faster than ever. It'll block my way out.

Sand flies in my mouth, gashing my lips and tongue. I keep running from the wildness of Ophir, manifest in these two creatures.

Pain lances in my limbs.

The spiked shadow of the maristag I love begins catching up to me. Still I run. My heart is about to burst. I run. My legs tremble. And I run.

"It's me!" This time, only a sputter and gasp come out.

Darkness pools in my vision as my body strains. Stars burst in my vision, my heart wheezes, begging me to give up.

I fall flat on my face and go tumbling several feet over. Whatever life is still in me almost snuffs, but the blood gushing in my veins makes me think of Emrik and Liria. I roll over on my stomach and lift my head. Blood pounds in my fingers, the weight on them is too much.

The capricorn now rushes straight for me.

At my back, Stormgold bounds, her eyes gleaming and the green of her antlers pulsing maddeningly.

There's nowhere to run anymore.

It's over.

I push myself to make a final, quiet stand, and close my eyes.

*Mama. Baba. Emrik. Liria.*

Cold acceptance washes over me, my body suddenly lighter than ever. I try to remember our pre-funeral prayer. Only broken verses come to me. I murmur, "With strength may you cross the final sea, with hope may you find the next shore."

The world splits into *before*, and *after*, ash and grit filling my mouth to the beat of my pounding heart.

The Moon Fest is only a month away. I wish I could've taken Liria to it.

The capricorn bellows, getting bigger, its mouth open to swallow me whole.

Mama's dress was beautiful. I wish I'd seen her in it.

Behind me, Stormgold's ringing stomps grow louder. And louder. I hope she gets me first. She pulled me out of an abyss. She made me want to live. This is what I ultimately gave her: madness brought on by zargunine.

Wind roars in my ears, an ocean thrashes in my rib cage.

*Keep Liria safe, Emrik. I entrust her to you. And I hope you learn to live with the grief and despair that is to come.*

*Mama, wait for me—*

Stormgold leaps above my head. For a wild second, she's suspended in the air. Then she smashes down on the capricorn. An antler slashes at the capricorn's mouth. Black blood sprays me. I stumble back, shocked.

Stormgold pounces atop the capricorn, her claws drawn. The two are locked in a fierce battle. The capricorn lunges and turns. But its bulky frame is no match for Stormgold's speed. She swipes her antlers at its white belly, streaming rivers of blood. The capricorn backs up, surprised, and turns over.

I gasp.

Stormgold rockets back at me, and I fear she means to charge at *me* now and that I should have used the distraction to run, but she's slowing. She slams to a stop, inches away from me. Her claws drenched in black blood, her eyes gleaming red beneath the white, and her antlers a brilliant green. She looks like a creature of Ophir.

One second of her antlers rising away, one second of her

permission, and I'm on her back. The soft hair beneath her manefin fills my hands, a feeble shot of adrenaline.

The capricorn struggles to get itself straightened, shrieking as it does. By the time it manages to pull its tail from under itself, Stormgold shoots forward.

Shouts fill the Drome. Every Lander drowns in such arrogance, they never could've imagined a maristag rescuing a human. If the animals had only ever shown *them* claws and fangs, how could it ever befriend one of us?

I wanted to rise but the chains with which the Landmaster strangles us were never going to let me. Some day, someone will bring the people screaming in this Drome down with their own hubris. Even if it's not me, the thought alone comforts me in this pandemonium. This old world will come to an end, the seeds of a new world will shoot out of this monument's broken ground; those they call monsters will be born and made.

The capricorn roars.

At the far back, doors are thrown open. Riders flood out holding stunguns and quarterstaffs.

This time, they are coming for both of us.

We're close to the other side of the Drome. A wooden door separates us from the courtyard where I waited before registration.

Wind rushes from all sides, almost wrenching me off Stormgold, but we streak ahead. The door never stood a chance against a maristag's green blood roaring with full strength.

I shove off a piece of wood dragging behind us. Then we're under open sky.

If I thought riding Stormgold in the Drome was freedom, I had sorely mistaken the true meaning of that feeling. This is what freedom means. We bound across Sollonia, not caring for the shocked faces, or the incredulous shouts.

No one can match us; no one can stop us.

A vigorous, unchained cry escapes me—and Stormgold joins it. We scream our glorious song, leaving behind the world, and even as streets give way to sand and sand gives way to rocks and rocks give way to ocean, I don't ask her to stop. I will not give up this freedom for anything.

Not even the unknown.

# CREATURES OF SOLLONIA

**AQUABATS:** Amphibious reptiles that can fly short distances. Their "wings" are muscle membranes that are supported by a network of bones. The ends of these membranes are claws that act as limbs, and they also have pincers at the front. All in all, they are vicious and bloodthirsty creatures that are very hard to control. Their name comes from rumors of similar creatures called "bats" deep beneath the ground, although no one has ever seen one for themselves.

**CAPRICORN:** One of the biggest creatures known to mankind on Ophir. These scaled creatures resemble mountainous goats along the upper half of their bodies, and fish along the lower. They have giant corkscrew horns. Their front limbs are clawed, and their tail fins, a hundred meters wide on average, also acts as their hind limbs. Along the sides of their bodies, capricorns have stretches of skin that they can enlarge and use to balance in strong winds. These creatures usually keep to themselves but are ferocious fighters.

**FAKWES:** A diamond-shaped soft-shelled creature that lives in caves beneath sea shores. They rarely venture out of their shells outside of water, but when they do, they emerge with six slender limbs with retractable claws, and two horns just above their eye sockets. Even though they appear demonic, these creatures are not very aggressive. But they are defensive and when threatened, a fawkes will release a black tarry substance that catches fire on contact with air.

**FLONNER:** Small reptiles that live in lagoons and backwaters. They have flat limbs to paddle in water with, and a hard shell for a body into which they can retract wholly, save for their long fuzzy ears which are used to distinguish a flonner shell from a rock. Although harmless and friendly, they are very protective of their young and if threatened, a parent can throw its whole body at an enemy hard enough to break bones.

**GORGON:** A spherical scaly creature with dark-green blood. It has tentacles with sticky pads that it uses to wrap around victims and impart deadly shocks.

**MARISTAG:** One of the strongest, fastest creatures in the world. They are lithesome and scaled. These creatures are bipedal with shorter forelimbs and powerful hindlimbs. Their rudder-like tails are body-length and help them to swim across the seas. Their claws have retractable webbed skin, and their eyes have a white film over the pupils. Around their necks they have retractable frillfin, which also hold venomous barbs that they can shoot out with enormous speed at considerable distances. Their antlers are multi-tined, which they use to fight and display dominance as the proud creature that they are.

**MURRAIN EEL:** A serpent-like aquatic creature that has slippery skin. It lives in large colonies entangled into one another for life. If one creature gets sick and dies, the whole colony will die with it. When separated from its colony, a murrain eel can enlarge the skin around its neck to appear bigger to its enemies.

**RAPTOR:** These are very aggressive aquatic creatures known for the sharp tusks around their snouts. They are small and have an octagonal body, with four tiny feet.

**SCYTHE CRAB:** A giant decapod crustacean. They are usually silver or copper in coloring and their shells are shiny. They are extremely fast on land, and faster still in water. Unlike their smaller brethren, they have razor-sharp blades in the shape of scythes as one set of their limbs that they can use to both attack and move.

# ACKNOWLEDGMENTS

Every time I buy a new book, I first flip back to read the acknowledgments. It makes me so happy to see these connections and relationships that make the person whose words I'm about to read. Which is probably why I'm both delighted and *scared to death* about writing the acknowledgments (?!) for my first book.

To Rena Rossner, for her absolute faith in this book. Rena, we went on sub in the height of the pandemic in 2020, and your belief that we *will* sell it kept me afloat in that horrible time. Thank you for your steadfastness.

To Annie Berger, thank you for your enthusiasm for this book. From the first time we spoke, it was just so *exciting* to have you on this story, I couldn't be luckier. To Annette Pollert-Morgan, thank you for the grace and brilliance with which you took care of this story. I'm so grateful for your guidance.

To Jenny Lopez, Cassie Gutman, Neha P, Kelsey Fenske, Michelle Mayhall, and everyone else who worked so hard to bring this book to life so beautifully—thank you so much. To Liz Dresner, Natalie C. Sousa, and Sasha Vinogradova for the cover of my *dreams*. From the moment I saw that first concept to the final art, I have been in awe and cried approximately a thousand times. To Travis Hasenour for being a magician and turning my did-a-3-year-old-draw-this sketch into the beautiful map.

To Valerie Pierce and to the entire publicity and marketing team, thank you for all the tireless work you've put in getting my book out there. To publicity wizard Madison Nankervis, who always answers my absolutely nonsensical one-line emails promptly and patiently—thank you. I cannot emphasize what your enthusiastic support has meant to me and how much of my sanity I owe to you during this whole process. To the library and educators team, especially to Emily Luedloff—I think it was fate that I landed at Sourcebooks, don't you? Thank you for your friendship and kindness, especially during these past couple of years.

To the indomitable Dominique Raccah, I couldn't ask for a better publisher.

Thank you to my parents, who bought me all the storybooks and folklore even when they wanted me to finish my homework first. Thank you, Papa, for being my constant support, for taking care of us after Mummy, and providing the best life I could possibly imagine. And most of all, thank you for the patience with which you let me go after my dreams even though you were worried. Thank you for everything.

To Mini—you have always hyped me up even when we were fighting like cats constantly. I have no words to convey how much I love you. You're my best friend, and I will buy you all the art tablets you want.

Thank you to my Dadaji, without whom I would not be where I am. He was a man of integrity, and honoring him is my life's dream. Thank you to my Dadi, a storyteller in her own right, who has regaled so many of our family stories to me over the years, making them all feel so tantalizingly real, thanks to her brilliant skill of painting pictures with words, and to my two Buas for the many, *many* bedtime stories during the desert summer days. It was there my love of stories began, and I can never repay what you all gave me. To my Chacha—I don't know a bigger *Dracula* stan, you're a rockstar. Thank you also to the extended Madhukar family for their blessings.

Thank you to Brenda Drake, Pintip Dunn, and the entire erstwhile Pitchwars committee—without this mentorship, I wouldn't have found my next step. To my mentor, Rebecca Schaeffer—Rebecca, I have said this countless times over the years, but I'll say it again: you saw that spark in the absolutely dreadful mess of a draft and helped me make it right. Without you, this book wouldn't exist.

To my Fork family—guys, where would I be without you? Thank you for the laughs and the constant validation and your friendship. I'm so happy that I have you all in my corner and wish I could name all of you like Whitney did in that speech.

To the #22Debuts—to go through this journey with some of the kindest souls I've met as a baby writer in this industry is a privilege. I'm so excited for all of us.

To Michelle Wong and Megan Scott, for your unending enthusiasm for this book.

To my Wildcats—my very first friends in this industry. To Chelsea Beam, thank you for your patience with my hyperactive thinking and being the best anime rec'er. To Crystal Seitz—Sansa supporters for life!—for your unfailing compassion. I can't wait to see your career soar. To Rosie Brown, for the absolutely bonkers memes; maybe also for all the helpful knowledge you're so kindly passing onto me. To Swati Teerdhala, for paving the way and being so incredibly smart and disciplined; you're an inspiration every day.

To Janella Angeles, for teaching me so much about writing, and for your absolute trust in my talent. Thank you for being so kind to a wide-eyed writer. To Shveta Thakrar, for always being so welcoming and sweet. To Emily XR Pan and Nova Ren Suma, for the excellent opportunity that was Foreshadow. It gave me the confidence I so desperately needed to continue in this industry. You two have my eternal gratitude. And to Melissa Albert for choosing my weird little story.

Thank you to VS Holmes, Sofia Fionda, and Maggie Fisher—critique partners for my earlier work. Your encouragement kept me going when I had no idea about any of this.

To Aimal Farooq, Aishwarya Tandon, Ayesha Mubasshar, Bidisha Das, Elyse Eisenberg, Hayley Mallary, Kelly Tse, Marcella W, Maryam Khan, Meg McGorry, Niyla Farook, Sairaa, Sharon Sibyl Gatt, and Zermeen—thank you to all of you for your support. It means the world to me.

To some of my oldest friends—Yasmin, Nikita, Akshita—thank you for your incredible tolerance of my absurd penchant for going AWOL. I'm literally so lucky you guys are still here.

To Onaiza—okay, Mom Friend, thank you for being you. Having you in my life makes it so, so much better. No one is doing it like you. To Samriddhi—we've known each other since we were five-year-olds, thank you for being my friend when I was an awkward, bad-haircut-having kindergartner.

To Uday—I am so glad to call you a friend and brother.

Thank you to the Booktokkers, Bookstagrammers, Booktubers, and Bloggers for hyping this book all the way through.

And lastly, to you, for picking up this book and helping me realize a dream, decades in the making.

# ABOUT THE AUTHOR

Tanvi Berwah is a South Asian writer who grew up wanting to touch the stars and reach back in time. She graduated from the University of Delhi with a bachelor's and master's in literature of English, and always found ways to fit *The Lord of the Rings* and *Game of Thrones* in her academic life. A history and space enthusiast, she would've loved to be an astronomer, had her lack of mathematical skills allowed it. Find her at tanviberwah.com.